Dogism Saga

Dogism Saga

Dogism Saga

Mark Anthony

www.urbanbooks.net

Urban Books, LLC
97 N18th Street
Wyandanch, NY 11798

ISBN 13: 978-1-62286-915-2
ISBN 10: 1-62286-915-X

First Trade Paperback Printing August 2015
Printed in the United States of America

10 9 8 7 6 5 4 3 2 1

Distributed by Kensington Publishing Corp.
Submit Orders to:
Customer Service
400 Hahn Road
Westminster, MD 21157-4627
Phone: 1-800-733-3000
Fax: 1-800-659-2436

Dogism Saga

Dedication

This book is dedicated
to my mother, Dorothy.

Look, Ma, I did it again!

Chapter One

I once heard a brilliant saying. It went something to the effect of, "A successful person will always put himself in a position to take advantage of an opportunity when it presents itself. Not only will the successful person put himself in a position to take advantage of an opportunity, but when that chance presents itself, he will be the first one, if not the only one to spot it. After he has spotted it, he will pounce on it with the vigor of a hungry, ferocious lion, allowing nothing to let that opportunity slip away."

As I drove down Pennsylvania Avenue in Brooklyn, I suddenly realized that a golden opportunity was presenting itself. It was in the form of one of the most beautiful females on whom I'd ever laid eyes. The ironic thing was that this catch was one I'd let slip away in the past.

As she drove in her black convertible, I made sure to ride right alongside of her. *What's her name?* I agonized, trying to remember from where I knew her.

When the light turned red, I had time to recollect my thoughts. After sitting through torture for a minute and a half, it hit me like a brick. "She's that beautician."

The light turned green. I thought, *Lance, don't let this opportunity pass you by.*

It must have been fate that brought us to yet another red light. After we stopped, I stared at the captivating woman. I gazed with the most lustful, awe-filled expression I could muster. I wanted her to know I was looking. If she returned the favor and glanced my way, I wasn't gonna be a punk and quickly turn my head.

She must have felt my passionate stare because she finally did look at me. Unfortunately, she didn't look for very long because the light turned green again. But she'd turned long enough to smile as she nodded her head to the music on Hot 97 FM. Her convertible top was down—she knew she was fine. The look I gave her was the start of an affair. Although I didn't even know her name, in my heart, I'd just committed adultery once again.

Again, it must have been fate that allowed us to continue to travel in the same direction. It was the same fate that caused the light to again turn red. I thought, *I got a smile out of her at the last light, now seize the moment, Lance. Don't let it pass you by.*

I had to do something quick 'cause this traffic-light affair was bound to end soon. So again I lustfully stared. She knew I was clocking her, but she kept her eyes fixed straight ahead as she continued to nod to the music.

Wave to her, Lance, I intently urged myself. *Wave.*

I could sense the light was about to change, so, very lightly, but hard enough for it to give off a sound, I tapped on my horn. She still didn't look my way, so I ambitiously blew two more times a little harder.

Yes, yes, yes. I was mad excited because she'd finally looked my way. Being as cool as I could, with my bald-head glistening in the sunlight and with my shades on, I lifted my hand and said very softly, "Hello."

This time I got no smile. She just stepped on the accelerator and my ego all at the same time. But yo, I was a hungry lion, and I wasn't gonna let this sly fox get away.

"Come on, just don't turn," I earnestly hoped. "Please let me get one more red light, please."

Fortunately for me, as fate would have it, four blocks later the light did turn red again. I moved in for the kill. Without any hesitation, I pulled up alongside her in my white Lexus GS300. Right away I tapped on the horn three times. She looked. I quickly motioned with my index finger for her to pull to the curb, like I was a cop instructing a speeding driver to pull over. She smiled, but she shook her head no.

Feeling rejected, I put my hands together as if I was begging or praying, and I mouthed the word, *Please.* She again smiled and shook her head to say no.

Man! The light was turning green. Not only that, Pennsylvania Avenue was running out, and we were both about to reach the Belt Parkway, which was my point of destination and probably hers as well. I didn't want to enter the parkway's jungle because then my fox would surely escape the grasp of my claws.

As the light changed, she took off. I, too, hit my accelerator. I managed to stay neck and neck with her car as if I was in the Indy 500. Feeling a sense of urgency, I vivaciously tapped on my horn to get her attention, which, thank God, I finally did.

Seeming kind of annoyed, she lifted her hands, arms, and shoulders as if to ask what I wanted.

"Pull over. I have to ask you something," I said as I motioned toward the curb. I waited for her reaction. She gave me a look as if she was gonna suck her teeth and keep going.

Fortunately, her right blinker came on.

"Yes!" I wanted to piss in my pants I was so happy.

After signaling to pull over, she sped up to pass me. Finally, I'd lured her in. I pulled right behind her, put my car in park, and turned on my hazards. Feeling like a state trooper, I got out of my car as if I was preparing to ask for her driver's license and registration. The navy blue tank top I had on revealed my dark, chiseled physique.

"How you doin'?" I asked as I approached the driver's door of her car.

She answered with a hello, then she added, "I had to pull over or you might have caused an accident. What's wrong with you?"

"Nah, I had realized that I knew you, and I wanted to see if you remember me."

She looked at me as if to say, "You better have a better line than that."

As I looked at her, I felt star struck and perplexed. I thought quickly and said, "Nah, but for real though, I wanted to know if you could cut my son's hair."

"How do you know I do hair?" she asked.

The ice was broken as I reiterated, "I told you I know you."

"From where?" she asked.

"You work in International Hair Designs on Franklin Avenue, right?"

She slowly looked me up and down, trying to figure out who the hell I was. Then she answered, "Yes, I work there."

"See," I said as I smiled, "I told you I knew you. And you probably thought I was trying to kick game to you or something."

She looked at me, confounded. Slowly shaking her head while smiling at the same time, she asked, "So you almost killed yourself trying to run me down, just so you could ask me if I can cut your son's hair?"

"Word. See, I'm not satisfied with the barber I'm taking him to now. You know like most barbers, mine doesn't clean his clippers and all that. And I'm sayin', you know what kind of diseases you can get from dirty clippers."

She looked at me and nodded, but she didn't say anything. I was simply in adoration because I was speaking to someone so beautiful. I don't know from where on earth I'd pulled that haircut story, but it was a start.

As I attempted to protract the conversation I said, "Besides, I figure a female beautician probably isn't cutting sweaty men's heads all day, so her clippers should be a'ight, you know what I'm sayin'?"

She answered with a laugh, "Wait. First of all, what's your name?"

"Oh, my name is Lance," I answered. "Excuse me for being rude."

"Hi, Lance. I'm Toni, but you probably already knew that. . . ."

"Maybe," I responded with a smile.

"Lance, you don't even know if I'm any good or not."

Instantly my hormones went daft with thoughts of good sex. I thought, *Baby, I would bet money that your stuff is good.* Holding my hormones at bay, I responded, "If your work is as beautiful as you look, then there won't be a problem."

"Oh, stop," she jokingly said as she batted her hand at me. "You're making me blush."

Inside, my hormones were cheering insanely loud, as I said to myself, *Yes, Lance. Yes, you are the man.*

"Here," she said, "let me give you my card."

With her seemingly soft hands and her butterscotch complexion, she reached toward her dashboard area and handed me a shiny black card with gold lettering. As I took the card, I couldn't help but notice the gorgeous airbrush design on her freshly French-manicured fingernails.

She advised me, "On certain days it's mad busy in the shop, so just call me or page me before you come in, and I'll let you know how long a wait you'll have."

"A'ight, that'll work," I said.

As I went to take her business card, I made a conscious effort to reach for it with my left hand. The reason being, my wedding band was on that hand. I wanted to make sure that the gold and diamonds blinded Toni. I didn't see any rings on her beautiful hands, which let me know that she'd definitely taken note of the fact that I was married. If there's one thing that I've learned in my five years of marriage, it's that a wedding band on a man's hand can be spotted from one hundred yards away. Maybe because it's such a rarity, especially among young, good-looking cats like myself.

Her seeing the ring accomplished a couple of things. It put some doubt into her mind that maybe I wasn't just some sexy nigga trying to kick it to her. I needed that doubt because unless she had no class at all and if she didn't fall for that haircut game, she would've immediately written me off.

Toni appeared to be a high-maintenance female, and most of them ain't trying to give no play to some guy they meet on the street, especially one who pulls them over in his car. They might give a guy their phone number or they'll take his number, but in their head it's a whole different ballgame. They'll be like, "This player probably has all types of women. I ain't trying to mess with him 'cause I ain't gonna be another notch on his belt. Besides, he looks too good anyway. He probably thinks it's all about him."

At this stage, I didn't need negative thoughts like that flowing through Toni's head. My ring played a big part in killing that negativity, and it left open the opportunity to push the right buttons later.

As I prepared to walk back to my car and put an end to this traffic-light affair, I said to Toni, *"Conduit avec precaucion,"* which in Haitian Creole means, "Drive with caution."

Taken aback, she responded, *"Vous Haitienne?"* Which means, "Are you Haitian?"

Walking away, I said, "No, but I know that you are."

Those were the last words I spoke to her as I got in my ride and drove off. Inside my heart I knew that she would be thinking about me, especially after I'd freaked her mind with her native language. I must admit that I "reached" when I spoke those words of broken French. See, I have a thing about Haitian women. To me, they are all off the chain! I've dated many Haitian women, and I just learned to pick up on the language. I'm not fluent in it, but I figured that I should at least make the effort to vaguely know the language of such fine sistas.

Her card said Toni St. Louis, which was a tip-off that she was Haitian. Last names like St. Louis, or as she would pronounce it "St. Looie," and names like Joseph and Pierre are instant giveaways to a Haitian descent. Hey, I reached, but it worked.

On the ride back to my house I fantasized about Toni. I wondered what it would be like speaking to her on the phone. I pondered what her feet looked like. My heart rate was slightly accelerated as I felt happier than a kid on Christmas morning.

After the twenty-minute ride to my crib was complete, I had to switch gears. I had to take off the mack attire and don the husband outfit.

"Hey, baby," I said to my wife, Nicole, as I walked in the back door.

"Hi, honey."

"Nicole," I said, "I've been thinking about you all day. I couldn't wait to get home to see you."

As a smile appeared across Nicole's face, she replied, "Really, baby?"

"Yeah," I answered, "now come here and give me some sugar, you sexy thang."

After taking off my shoes, I made my way to the living room to catch the last fifteen minutes of *Oprah*. My wife sat next to me.

"So, Lance, how was your day?"

"It was a'ight. You know, same ol' same ol'."

"Lance—"

Before my wife could ask me anything else, I interrupted her by diverting her train of thought. "Nicole, where's LL?" LL, which is short for Little Lance, is our son.

"He's here somewhere. He's probably watching cartoons or whatever."

"LL," I screamed out to my son.

A minute later he came running and jumped on my lap while simultaneously slapping me five.

"What's up, little man?" I asked.

"Nothing. I was watching *Barney*."

My son is the most adorable kid you would ever want to meet. He's the spitting image of his daddy. I just hope when it comes to the gene that controls infidelity that his is not a clone of his father's. I was feeling a little guilty, so I played with my son for the remainder of the evening. I didn't really want to look my wife in the eyes for the rest of the day. Not that I'd cheated on her or anything, it's just that for today I belonged to Toni. Actually my wife would have had a hard time stimulating me. She looks good and all—a banging body—but this evening I wanted to be mentally stimulated by Toni and no one else, not even Scarlet, the exotic looking Brazilian stripper who'd been my mistress during my entire marriage.

While we were eating dinner, my wife caught me daydreaming.

"Baby, what are you thinking about?" she asked.

Startled like a little kid caught with his hand in the cookie jar, I quickly responded, "Huh? Oh, nothing. I ain't thinking about anything, just something that happened at work today."

"Oh, tell me what happened. Was it funny?" she inquired.

"Nah. It was nothing," I said as I, like a boxer, tried to back my way out of a corner. I'd just gotten caught out there thinking about Toni. I quickly excused myself from the table as I sought out a solitary environment.

Later that night when the lights were out and my wife and I lay in the bed, we cuddled and pillow-talked. I was hoping she would go to sleep so I could reminisce about the traffic-light affair I'd had with Toni. Unfortunately my wife had other plans in store for me. Nicole's period had ended a day ago. Usually she's in the mood right after her "friend" departs, and tonight she was holding true to form.

Nicole began to kiss on me and caress my chest. Uninterested, I played my role as husband. I was praying that Nicole wasn't physically in the mood for an all-star performance because I wasn't in the frame of mind to deliver one. No foreplay, no massages, and all that—if she wanted it, she had better get me aroused, hop on, and do her thing so I could go to sleep. Hopefully she'd climax before I did, but if not, I could have cared less.

Chapter Two

More than a week had passed since I'd pulled Toni over in her car. She was out of my sight, but she was always on my mind. I must have looked at her business card a hundred times. I had the beauty shop's phone number and Toni's pager number engraved in my memory. Just about every day I wrestled with myself to keep from calling Toni.

Saturday finally rolled around, and I had an excuse to go to Toni's shop. Although LL was not in dire need of a haircut, I decided to take him to the shop anyway. Like always, LL objected to getting his hair cut. However, after a little coaxing and a McDonald's Happy Meal, we found ourselves in the jam-packed beauty salon.

I immediately searched for Toni. After I spotted her working at her chair, I calmly walked over to her. "Remember me?" I asked.

Toni was in the process of doing someone's hair, so she looked into the wall mirror she was facing. She paused and thought for a second, then turned around with a curious smile and said, "Yeah, I remember you."

There was another pause of silence. Then I asked, "Do you have a lot of customers?"

"Well, it's Saturday, so it's always packed in here . . ."

"I brought my son with me to get his haircut. Do you—"

"Oh, that's right. Is this your son? Oh, he's so cute. Hey, cutie. What's your name?" Toni asked while reaching to pinch LL's cheeks.

In a shy voice my son answered by saying, "LL."

"Oh, he is so adorable. Didn't I give you my card? Why didn't you call before you stopped by?"

"Actually, I wasn't gonna come today. It was a spur-of-the-moment-type thing."

"Lance, right?"

"Yeah."

"Well, Lance, you can wait if you want, but I'm mad busy. I should be able to squeeze LL in about an hour and a half. Is that all right?"

"That's cool. We'll just chill. I might get a manicure to kill time, I don't know."

LL and I took a seat in the waiting chairs, and I contemplated whether I should get a manicure. As I sat, I couldn't help but stare at Toni. She had on a pair of navy blue spandex pants and a white T-shirt that was tied into a knot. With her belly button exposed, I noticed that Toni had what looked liked a red rose tattooed near her navel, and she also had another large, exotic tattoo that was located at the base of her back right near the crack of her butt.

I damn well knew that I shouldn't have used my son as an excuse to go to see Toni, but hey. I was there, and there really wasn't a regretful bone in my body that would have made me leave. As I sat with LL, I constantly kept staring at Toni. I don't know why I did it to myself. I mean, I'm married and all, yet there I was on a Saturday afternoon checking out a beautician.

I always told myself and believed that nothing would happen as far as me literally cheating, and so far in my marriage it hadn't, except of course for the five-year thing that I've had on the side with Scarlet del Rio. But to me the Scarlet thing shouldn't really count against me because for one, I had gotten involved with her before I was actually married—even if I met her on the night of my bachelor party, it was still before I had said, "I do."

Although nothing was ever officially confirmed by the two of us, we acted as if we were a couple, especially from her end. I mean, many people will say I'm naïve to believe that Scarlet had not been with any other man sexually except for me during the past five years. But I know what I know, and I know that Scarlet, despite being a stripper, had been very loyal and faithful to me during the time we were involved, despite the fact that my marriage was and continued to be a very limiting factor for both Scarlet and myself.

Early on in my relationship with Scarlet, I realized what had caused her to be so drawn to me. See, number one, she is crazy. And number two she is a got-damn psycho-bitch. The stalker type. Scarlet really had all kinds of emotional issues, self-esteem issues, and all kinds of drama in her life. I think from the time I met her, something told her that I was genuinely a good guy with good intentions who represented safety, security, and emotional support, which she was desperately craving and searching for in a man.

Scarlet definitely had her issues, but she was like a female version of me when it came to sex—a literal freak and fiend who was willing to sex me at the drop of a hat without all of that unnecessary foreplay. I was willing to overlook a lot of her crazy stunts and her emotional issues. The sex was beyond good, and she kept her body tight. Her waist-to-ass ratio was always in proper proportion, plus, she looked good as hell, and deep down she was really a good person at heart. Really, she was.

Scarlet was like my dual wife. In the hood she would be known as wifey. Every man, married or single, whether he is willing to admit it or not, has someone other than his wife or his girlfriend who he would consider to be wifey. Wifey is the one he calls when things aren't going right at home. She has his back, no matter what. She's down to do whatever, whenever, and wherever. Wifey is the one who knows about the real wife or the real girlfriend and doesn't flip out about it. In fact, wifey remains faithful to him even though he's tied down. Wifey puts it on him like no other woman.

But it just gets harder and harder to stay faithful, especially when I keep feeding my lust hormones with women like Toni. I mean, there I was trying to distance myself from Scarlet and permanently end things between us. I'd been doing a good job at that for the past three months, yet I still let myself entertain and act on the thoughts of being with yet another woman.

Toni caught me gazing at her, and she kind of down-played it by waving to LL. Yeah, I was busted, but any man in his right mind would be staring at Toni. Man, everything about her was turning me on.

It's like every move she made was erotic, even if it was just her reaching for a pair of scissors.

"You're not getting your nails done?" Toni asked.

"Nah, I think I'ma just chill."

"Why not? I think that's cool when men take good care of their hands. It says a lot about them."

The girl who was sitting in Toni's chair getting her hair done, abruptly objected to Toni's statement.

"Any man with manicured nails is about one of two things. Either he's gay, or he's all into himself, which means he ain't nothing but a good-smelling, pretty dog."

Another beautician responded, "That's right, girlfriend."

Toni took the floor as she said, "That's not true. Just because y'all dealt with the wrong brothas in the past, that doesn't mean that a good man can't treat himself to a manicure."

This conversation was about to erupt into a full-fledged debate. Therefore, I decided to get up and just get the manicure. As I walked over to the nail technician, I gave Toni a high-five for sticking up for the brothas. "You go, girl," I jokingly said as I walked past her.

The other beautician sucked her teeth, and sounding as ghetto as ever, she said, "Whateva! Men ain't nothing but dogs."

LL was still in his seat, and after seeing my hands in two bowls of warm water, he asked, "Daddy, what you doin'?"

"I'm getting my nails done."

"*Ill,* that's for girls. *Ill,*" LL remarked as he frowned.

With half of the shop amused and laughing at my son, the comedian, I felt mad embarrassed. It was cool, though, because the laughter also made me feel very relaxed in the ambiance of Toni.

After about thirty minutes of getting my nails cleaned, pulled, pricked, and tucked, I sat back down next to my son.

"Daddy, let me see."

I showed LL my hands, and he replied, "Your nails ain't all that."

Those who were in close proximity burst out into laughter as LL was slowly melting the hearts of every woman in the place. The boisterous beautician, whom I later found out was named Shaniqua, egged LL on.

"Good men don't get their nails done, right?" she asked LL.

"Nope," LL replied as he shook his head.

"See, even little shorty knows what time it is. I'm telling y'all, if you want a good man, you better find a brotha with some rough, ashy, jacked-up, mechanic-type hands."

"And, Shaniqua, what is your man's name again?" Toni asked.

Shaniqua rudely snapped back, "I don't have a man."

"Oh, yeah, that's what I thought. Anyway . . . um . . . Lance, don't even listen to Shaniqua. She's just going through something."

I laughingly replied, "Nah, I ain't sweating the small stuff. I'm sayin', I'm a secure brotha. You kna'imean?"

I want to believe that I'm secure, but in actuality I'm the most insecure man on this planet. It seems that all I do is done so that I can receive positive attention from females. All the time I spend in the gym working out and all those protein shakes that I drink, is definitely not for me alone. Sad to say, but it's not even just for my wife's pleasure when we're in the privacy of our bedroom.

What I wear, how I smell, how I'm groomed, the car I drive, and how much I bench press is all done for particular moments, moments when there is nothing but nice-looking women around and I'm able to make good eye contact with them.

See, women are not as blunt as men in terms of making the first move. Sistas are sly with their game. Excluding the women who are just out there whoring around, most women have game slicker than Luster's Pink Lotion on a Jheri curl. But with women, I've learned that it's all in the eyes. That's why I am all about eye contact.

After I sat back down, I continually tried to look into Toni's eyes to see what kind of vibe I would get. I stared in a way as to not make her feel uncomfortable, but at the same time, I wanted our eyes to lock.

Toni kept busy as did the other beauticians. As Toni worked, the salon became increasingly crowded. I'd always heard good things from females about this salon. I was beginning to see first hand what all the hype was about. It was often frequented by female stars such as Lil' Kim, Mary J. Blige, and Faith Evans to name a few. The salon is also a spa, and it's very spacious and elaborate. It's decorated with dazzling mirrors, leather couches, a nice big-screen television, and a surround-sound stereo system.

There was a buzz that filled the air as women canvassed the parquet floors. In that buzz I was able to decipher some outrageous conversations. I wish that I had brought a recorder to tape some of the things being said. Some of the conversations and gossip were fit for a trash talk show. Other conversations actually taught me a thing or two. You had your "inspirational speakers," and of course you had your "Amen" and "You go girl" conversations.

The women involved in those, "You go girl," slapping-each-other-five conversations made me think they were auditioning for a part on *Girlfriends*. Like most women, these sistas had no mercy when it came to the way they were talking bad about men. Brothas who were not there to defend themselves were being labeled everything from dogs to cheap to no good in bed.

To me, that kind of talk gets sickening after a while. Throughout my life, I've learned something about women who participate in those slapping-each-other-five conversations: their memory is way too short. Most of those women are constantly complaining about being dogged, hurt, or disappointed by men in the same way. To me, you would think they would remember the warning signs and realize when they are dealing with a dog. But no, they always con themselves into thinking this one or that one is *different*. And when this one or that one turns out to be the same as the rest, women turn around and label all men as no good.

Whether or not men are the problem, one fact remains about the "Amen/You go girl" women. These women are always dishonest with themselves because usually right from jump street they see the warning signs of a dog, yet they con themselves and say, "But he's different."

To me, the "You go girl" conversations are nothing but a big justification party. Women need to start owning up and accepting a big chunk of the responsibility as to why many relationships have no substance.

During the many conversations that were going on, I managed to finally lock eyes with Toni for about three seconds. After that time, I felt as though I was a crack fiend who'd had his hit for the day. I was convinced that Toni's eyes hadn't just caught mine in a passing glance. Rather, she wanted to look my way. Her look let me know what she thought about me. In those three seconds, she told me that she liked dark-skinned guys. Her eyes told me that she thought I had it going on.

Before long, it was time for LL to get in the chair and get his hair cut.

"LL, can I cut your hair now?" Toni asked.

LL didn't respond.

"Come on, LL. Don't show out in here. Let Toni cut your hair," I admonished.

As LL made his way to the chair, I remarked to Toni, "That was fast. It didn't even feel like we were in here for an hour."

Toni responded, "Well, I figured while my other customer is under the dryer I'd take care of LL. I mean she's gonna be under there for about a half hour. Plus, my other appointment called and said she was gonna be late."

As Toni adjusted a cape around LL's neck, she asked, "So, LL, how old are you?"

LL kept silent, but he managed to put four of his fingers into the air.

Toni responded in an alto tone as she said, "Wow, four years old. You're a big guy."

LL smiled. Toni was making him feel very comfortable.

"So, LL, how would you like your hair cut?"

"I want it like my daddy."

"Lance, he is sooo adorable," Toni said while smiling in my direction.

Toni quietly asked me if it was all right for her to actually cut his hair the way mine was since I have a Michael Jordan–style baldhead. Unbeknownst to Toni, I seductively made my way closer to her and said, "Yeah, it's no problem."

I was standing as close to Toni as I possibly could. The smell of her Gucci Rush perfume was like an aphrodisiac. As I pointed out to Toni the sensitive areas of LL's head, I contemplated just pulling her close to me and giving her a kiss. Fortunately I had enough self-control to not do that, but my heart rate was definitely accelerated, so I decided to stand back a little.

LL was very calm in the chair. He's not like most kids who cry, kick, and scream when they get their hair cut. As I stood next to Toni and watched her work, she advised me that I could take a seat if I wanted.

I responded, "That's okay. I like being close to beautiful women."

After I said that, Toni looked at me. She didn't smile or respond. I was wondering if I had just blown my cover. I had to change the subject quick.

"So, Toni, how long have you been doing hair?"

"Oh, for years, but I really got serious about it when I turned eighteen."

"That's good. And you're how old?"

"I'm twenty-four. Why?"

"No reason. I was just asking, you know, being that you said you started seriously doing hair at eighteen."

"Yeah, I really just do this during my breaks. I'm in graduate school at Howard University."

"Oh, word. That's kinda fly, an ambitious, intelligent, and talented woman."

Toni smiled.

Whew, I thought. *Back on track.*

LL was just about finished. It didn't take long to shave his little head. Toni asked if it was all right if she put alcohol on his head to prevent any infections or bumps. I nodded in agreement. As Toni sprayed the alcohol onto LL's head, he squinted in pain for about ten seconds. She then sprayed hair spray onto his scalp and applied powder to his neck.

To make LL feel good she said, "Now let me see my little man . . . Um, um, um, you gonna have all the little girls going crazy over you now."

LL replied, "The girlies are already sweatin' me."

The other females in the shop fell out in laughter.

"Oh, he is too much," Toni said while laughing. She reached for a bowl of candy and gave LL a Blow Pop and a pack of Now & Laters.

"Thank you," LL said.

"You're welcome, sweetie."

I asked Toni how much I owed her. She informed me that they charged seven dollars for children's haircuts.

As I reached into my pocket, I advised Toni that I would be bringing LL back in about two weeks. Then I nonchalantly handed her thirty dollars. After cordially telling her to take care, I took LL by the hand and prepared to leave. As we were walking out, LL stopped at a wall mirror to verify that his haircut was tight. With LL having no objections, we continued on our way out the shop and headed toward my car.

LL and I were about to start the car and pull off when I heard Toni yell my name before she ran over to the car.

"Lance, you know his haircut was only seven dollars, right?"

"Yeah, I know. I gave the rest as a tip."

Toni asked, "Are you sure?"

"I wouldn't have given it to you if I didn't want you to have it."

Toni was quiet for a second, then she looked at me and said, "Thank you. So, you're gonna be back, right?"

"Definitely."

Toni offered me her million-dollar smile as she reached into the passenger window and pinched LL on his cheek. I started up the car but didn't pull off until Toni had vanished out of my sight. As I drove off, I was feeling good. My calculated moves were working. The radio in my car was blaring, and I had a Kool-Aid grin on my mug. I was happy because I was envisioning all the possibilities between Toni and myself.

Chapter Three

My wife thought LL looked cute, but she had objections to me letting him get a baldhead. Her reasoning was that if we allowed his hair to be cut too short at such a young age then there stood the possibility of his hair remaining short in the future. I simply told Nicole that LL wanted a baldie and that her theory was not a proven medical fact, just some old wives' tale.

Fortunately for me, my wife didn't put up much of an argument. She isn't the argumentative type, and neither am I. I would have to say that's one of the reasons why we've remained together for so long. However, that isn't the only reason our marriage is healthy. My wife and I are both God-fearing Christians. Yeah, I know I don't come across like the God-fearing type, but in my own way, I really am. My wife and I attend church service every week, but by far, we are not just Sunday Christians; we are quite active in the ministry. We often lead Bible studies, we open our house for Christian fellowships, and we regularly pray together.

I might not look like the religious type, but I know the Bible from cover to cover. Yet the struggles that I have with lusting over women seem to keep me entrapped. My wife and I can talk about anything. I often tell her about my struggles, but my insecurities keep me from being totally honest. I'll tell Nicole about women who might have come on to me at work, or I might tell her about a past girlfriend who called the house to say hello, but never deep details or dark secrets, such as my affair with Scarlet. See, I'll tell my wife insignificant things because I know that she's a very secure person—actually, she's too trusting. Then again, if according to God, a man and a woman become one at marriage, I guess she is only doing what is natural by trusting me.

By me only telling Nicole part of the real deal, subconsciously I feel as though I'm confessing to her all of my shortcomings. But half truths are what have done man in since the time of Adam and Eve. I would never tell my wife about the many times I've sneaked and watched porno movies or that I've found myself gazing at the dirty pictures in the X-rated magazines at the local candy store. Not to mention the few times that I've found myself placing dollar bills into the garter of some naked, big-butt, hips-gyrating female at the booty bar.

One thing I'm certainly not proud of is the fact that I have a unique ability to hide my dirty deeds from everyone. Yet even though I'm not proud of that unique ability to be a double person, there is something I can guarantee and take to the bank right now and throw away the bank book because it is never gonna come out. In fact it will probably go to the grave with me, and that is all the dirt that Scarlet and I have rolled around in. Rest assured that I will never spill the beans to Nicole as far as Scarlet is concerned. Besides, now that I'm ending things with Scarlet, there really would be no future reason to bring it up to Nicole.

What is funny is the relationship my wife and I have makes us the envy of many. We have financial stability, a house, two cars, a healthy child, we're young, educated, good-looking, and the list goes on. As for me in particular, I'm viewed as the most positive black man aside from men like Michael Jordan and Jesse Jackson.

It's scary, because although no one knows about the dirt I do, it's as though I'm leading a double life. The thing is, I don't always consciously realize the possible consequences of my split life. I just find myself doing things that I've been conditioned to do from the past. Not that that's an excuse, but hey, I don't ever want to be viewed as just a little better than Satan.

Well, like every week, Sunday rolled around, and I found myself in the front row of the church pews. I was singing songs, praising God, praying, and really doing it up, yet I still was thinking about Toni. She wasn't the only female who crossed my mind. I also found myself looking at the bodies of some of the sistas in the congregation—that, too, was becoming commonplace for me. It's mad wild 'cause the sexual thoughts just pop up out of nowhere.

Fortunately, despite my sexual fantasies, I also had a chance or two to pay close attention to the sermon, and I was very convicted by what was being said. But just how long would that conviction last?

After service was over, I did like I usually do, and sought out visitors of the church and made them feel welcome. I thanked them for coming and encouraged them to come again. I extended to them the opportunity to study the Bible and told them I was there to answer any biblical questions they might have. If one didn't know better, one would have thought that I was a pastor in training. Yeah, I had the charm and charisma of Denzel Washington, but the guilt of being a Christian-slash-sinner was becoming very draining. I always wonder how long I'll be able to keep this up. I know that eventually I'm gonna either have to repent or just give in to my desires, 'cause I can't keep playing both sides of the fence.

That evening after Sunday dinner was over, Nicole, LL, and I were in the living room. LL innocently asked me if Toni could cut his hair from now on. His question sparked some curiosity in Nicole.

"Lance, you switched barbers?" my wife asked.

"Yeah," I nonchalantly replied.

"I like the way Toni cuts my hair," LL joyfully inserted.

My wife replied, "LL sure is crazy about this *Toni.*"

"That's just because he got free candy when he went. Baby, I forgot to tell you that I decided to try a new barber. A guy on the job got some type of infection on his scalp from dirty clippers, and he was using the same barber that we've been taking LL to."

"Really?" Nicole inquired.

Knowing that I was lying through my teeth, I jazzed up the lie by adding, "Yeah, these ghetto barbers don't take good care of their blades."

Then LL totally blew up my spot when he smiled and devilishly said that he thought that Toni was pretty.

"LL, what are you talking about? Wait a minute. Toni is a female?" Nicole asked.

Trying to downplay it, I simply said, "Yeah, women know how to give men hair cuts. You didn't know that?"

"I know that, I just didn't know they had a woman working in the barber shop. I guess that unisex name threw me off."

I replied, "Oh, Toni doesn't work in the barber shop. She works in a beauty salon."

"Oh, where at?"

"In Brooklyn," I answered.

"Brooklyn? You went all the way out to Brooklyn for LL to get his hair cut?"

I had no idea where this line of questioning was going, so I was trying to think of an evasive statement. Fortunately, LL spoke up.

"Yeah, and Daddy got his nails done like a girl," he said.

My wife smilingly asked, "Honey, you got your nails done?"

That was my out. I had to divert Nicole's attention because I knew she was gonna ask who Toni was and from where I knew her. I didn't want to be forced to lie again.

"Yeah, I got my nails done. And you didn't even notice," I jokingly said. "Baby, I'm trying to make this marriage thing work, but if you can't even notice when I go out of my way for you and get my nails done, well I don't know . . ."

As my wife playfully slapped me, she gestured for my hands so she could examine them. Without warning, I took her hands and pulled her close to me and gave her a real passionate kiss. Although LL was in the room, it didn't matter because we were always lovey-dovey around him. After the kiss my wife smiled at me. We both knew what time it was. I left the room, and my wife proceeded to take LL to his room to prepare him for bed.

Later that night Nicole and I made love for about a half hour. Throughout the whole sexual encounter, passion was bouncing off the walls. I was hoping LL didn't hear us or the bed constantly squeaking.

When we were done, I felt great because not once during sex did I think about Toni or any other woman for that matter. Nicole was the only person on my mind that night. We had a stimulating conversation as we cuddled in the dark and kissed each other until we fell asleep.

Chapter Four

My wife, who has a master's degree in forensic psychology, works for the New York City Department of Probation. Basically, she is the boss for about fifteen probation officers. She has a very stressful job—it's like she's constantly taking on all of the stress that the probation officers feel. Plus, she has to deal with obnoxious judges, lawyers, and district attorneys. Despite the stress, Nicole loves her job, but if it were up to me, I would have her stay home with our son. Unfortunately, she sees her career as a very high priority in her life.

I work as a service technician for Con Edison. I started the job as a co-op when I was in high school, and I stayed on and became a full-time employee after graduation. Basically, I respond to all types of gas and/or electrical emergencies as well as regular service calls. The blue-collar job is definitely not a glamorous one, but it pays extremely well, and with the benefits, I would be a fool to leave for something else.

I received my bachelor's degree in business by going to college at night. The company paid for the whole thing, so it was like I went to college for free. In the future I might look to move into management, but right now I'm more than happy with the position that I have. It's like I'm my own boss. I'm out in the field driving around all day by myself, except for the days that I ride with a partner. The beauty of the job is the freedom it affords me while I work. Unfortunately though, the job can also get me into trouble. I say that because every day I go into houses with gorgeous women and the temptation to flirt is always there. I also have to deal with seeing nice-looking ladies when I drive around on the street. The battle that I have with preventing myself from approaching many of these females is enormous. I would be lying if I said that I have never succumbed to my hormones while on the job.

As a matter of fact, after searching the database in my brain, I realized that it was on the job that I first encountered Toni. A couple of weeks ago I'd received a service call for "no hot water" at International Hair Designs. When I responded to the beauty salon, I walked into the midst of chaos. There were about seven women who were mad as hell because they had to get their hair washed in ice-cold water. I was like some sort of savior when I walked into that shop. I quickly put everyone at ease, and I explained to them that it was probably just the pilot light that was out and needed to be lit.

Being that the spring was in full swing and the summer was right around the corner, it meant that it was time for me to show off my body. I accomplished that by cutting the sleeves of my uniform very high, about to the top of my triceps. That way whenever I carry my tool box, the weight of the box naturally made my muscles flex.

I'd noticed Toni as I made my way to the dark basement to examine the water heater. She really hadn't paid me any mind, but I was whipped from the moment that I walked past her and saw her. As for the other females who were in the shop, I heard them whispering and making remarks about how I looked. They were saying things like, "Girllll!" and "Um, um, um!"

The comments were flattering, but I really didn't sweat it because I was zoning off on Toni. She had a real exotic look. What struck me the most was her butterscotch complexion, her nice eyes, and her hair. I immediately noticed that her hair was the type that doesn't even need a perm in order for it to be straight. It looked as though if she were to wet it, it would be wavy. Her body was slamming from head to toe. She wasn't like *bam, bam, boom*. She didn't have one of those ghetto butts with a one-to-two waist-to-butt ratio or a chest like Dolly Parton, but she was very well proportioned and had more curves than an hourglass. I would say that Toni's measurements were about 34-25-40.

When I left the shop that day, all I could think about was Toni. The first thing I did when I had reached home was call my man Steve to let him know about my day.

Steve and I have been tight for years. In fact, he was the best man at my wedding, the man responsible for throwing me the wildest bachelor party on record. The bachelor party where I'd met and sexed Scarlet. The cool thing about Steve is that I can tell him anything. He knows that I'm trying to be sincere in my Christianity, yet he doesn't trip if I join him on a visit to the booty bar. He understands what it's like to be a man. It's bugged because sometimes he says that I should have never gotten married, and then sometimes he'll say that I am the stupidest man in the world for even looking at another woman.

I feel mad at ease around Steve because when I'm around him I don't have to put on a front. I mean the majority of my other friends, who unlike Steve are from the church, don't keep it real, which forces me to put up a front whenever I'm around them. If I ever mentioned to a church member that I looked at another woman, they would be ready to crucify me. But on the inside, I know that 95 percent of the men in my church if not a 100 percent of them have the same lust and sex problems that I do. It's just one of those things that no one talks about.

It's like masturbation. If you had one hundred men in a room and asked those who masturbate to raise their hand, I would be surprised if five men responded. What would happen is you would get one hundred men who, in an attempt to hide their embarrassment or insecurity, would start laughing and looking around at one another. Very few, if any, would dare to raise their hand. Yet, if you took an anonymous survey of the same one hundred men and asked them the same question, where absolutely no one would know the results, I bet you 95 percent of married and single men who responded to the survey would indicate they masturbate.

I know I'm not alone in my struggles, because what on earth could these men be masturbating about? It has to be the women around them they are lusting over. Some of the men in the church keep it real but not enough. So that's why I'm always hanging out with Steve. My wife encourages me to hang out with men in the church, but I don't. I feel like it's work just hanging out with people who don't keep it real. Then again, I guess that I'm just as afraid to keep it real with them. After all, it's not like my struggles are a good thing.

After I left Toni's shop the first time I met her, I called Steve and told him that I was coming by his crib to kick it with him. The moment I got to Steve's house, I flooded him with excitement.

"Yo, Steve, it's over, kid. It is over. I'm telling you, I think it's over."

Steve curiously questioned, "Man, what's up? Whatchu talking about? Get at me, dog."

"Steve, I saw the baddest female ever. Hands down the baddest. I mean slammin' from head to toe."

Steve nonchalantly downplayed my excitement as he responded. "Yeah, and?" while looking at me as if to say he'd seen this routine before. "What else is new? Lance, you tell me that ish on the regular, and I keep telling you it don't matter how good a woman looks because there's always someone else out there who will top her. It's a bottomless pit. There ain't no end to the madness."

"Steve, but yo, I don't know. I had a job in this beauty parlor today, and I'm telling you, there was this female, man, she was straight bananas! Yo, she had that fly Brazilian look that I like, you know? Her look was different than Scarlet's, but man . . . Her hair was slammin', her complexion, her shape, her eyes . . ." I paused, then I devilishly laughed as I added, "Yo, I know that her toes have to be the bomb. I'm sayin', as good as she looks, her toes must be all that. Steve, you know I'm a foot man, no doubt."

Steve sarcastically replied, "So let me guess. You're coming to me with your sob story about how you don't know how it's gonna last between you and Nicole. And you feel mad guilty about creeping because you're a Christian and all that ish, yet you're ready to turn this new ho into your housewife."

"Steve, yo, like I said when I first walked in the door, I really think that this time it's over between me and Nicole. I love her and the whole nine, but I can't keep putting myself through this."

"Through what, nigga?"

"Through what?"

"Yeah, through what? First of all, did you get the digits from this new chick?"

"Nah, but—"

"Did you even kick it to her?"

"Nah, see you—"

"Lance, tell me that this chick was at least flirtin' with a brotha."

"Nah, yo, let me explain."

"Lance, you never seen this chick before today, you didn't kick it to her, you got no phone number, and she wasn't even giving you any rhythm. What I'm trying hard to understand is why the hell are you ready to leave your wife? I hope it ain't over this chick. Wait, hol' up, tell me you at least know her name."

When Steve got no reply from me, he burst into uncontrollable belly-ache laughter. Watching him come to tears in laughter, I, too, had to give in to the humor of the situation. After almost regaining his composure, Steve laughingly said, "See, that's exactly why that marriage thing ain't for a nigga. Lance, you got a dime-piece wife, yet you ready to leave her for someone who you never even spoke to. Lance, you still getting skinz at home. I can understand the married men who have reluctantly become recycled virgins. I can see them wanting to creep or bounce, but you . . . *Ha, ha, ha, ha, ha* . . . Yo." Steve continued his laughter.

"Steve, you keep laughing. I bet you you'll be in my shoes one day when you get married. Watch."

Steve tried to keep a straight face, but he could not. He started laughing again as he said, "There ain't no way in hell I'm gonna be in your shoes. Why the hell am I gonna get married if I'm gonna cheat? I can do that by staying single. Plus, I'm not the churchgoing type or anything like that, but if there's one thing I've learned from Jesus, it's to stay away from that marriage thing. I mean think about it, if marriage was all of that then why didn't Jesus do it? Because he was smart enough to know that niggas need to avoid that marriage thing like the plague."

"Whateva, kid. Just mark my words. I'm gonna bag that chick, and when you see how she looks, that's all that will be necessary. I won't have to say a word 'cause the joke will be on you."

Although Steve took my feelings for Toni as a joke, I became determined to prove him wrong. As a matter of fact, I was determined to keep Steve in the dark about Toni until I was at least up to bat with her. I didn't even tell him about the roadside encounter I had with her and that had been like two weeks ago.

Chapter Five

When the start of the work week rolled around, I realized that I had to refocus and take care of the home front. I started the week by waking up early and surprising Nicole with breakfast in bed. I carried a tray that held a plate of scrambled eggs, French toast, and a small glass of orange juice. When I woke Nicole up, she was truly surprised.

"Ohhh, thank you, baby. You are so sweet."

My wife proceeded to sit up properly in the bed, and as she reached for the tray, she simultaneously closed her eyes and puckered up in a request for a kiss. I purposely caused my lips to miss hers, and instead I planted a kiss on her cheek. Then I jokingly informed, "The breath, baby. The breath is kickin'. Let's keep it real. It's like five in the morning, and you haven't seen a toothbrush."

With that, we both started laughing. Nicole snapped back at me, "Yeah, that's why you still got eye boogers caked in your left eye."

Again we burst into laughter. I playfully tapped Nicole on the head with my pillow before making my way to the kitchen to grab my breakfast tray so I could join her in eating. When I made it back to the room I said grace and we began to eat.

"Lance, I love when you surprise me like this."

"I know. That's why I did it. There's gonna be a lot more surprises like this, so be prepared."

As we ate and talked, I realized that marriage was made for moments like the present one. I constantly needed to remind myself of such. As we ate, we discussed the highlights of the passionate sexual encounter we had engaged in about eight hours ago. We said how much we loved each other and how we wished we could spend the whole day in bed. But we knew that Mondays were never fun, and we were actually spending too much time in bed as it was. If Nicole didn't catch the 6:59 train she would definitely be late for work. We put the trays out of the way, and rolled around in the bed and hugged for a couple of more minutes. Then Nicole went to take her shower and to get dressed.

As Nicole got ready to leave, I woke LL up so he could see his mother off to work. As was the case every morning, after LL kissed his mom good-bye, he asked for a bowl of Fruity Pebbles and proceeded to make his way to his usual location, which was in front of the television to watch cartoons. With Nicole out of the house, it seemed as if the morning was flying by. I got LL dressed and I, too, got dressed. Before I knew it, it was time to drive LL to the day care center. LL and I had a ball every day during our ten-minute ride. I enjoyed our morning rides because LL and I would always converse. Our conversations allowed me to teach LL so much about life and answer all of his poignant questions.

We made it to the day care center, and I signed LL in for the day. LL's teacher was married, and although she was about ten years older than me, she had it going on. I was always thoughtful enough to let her know it. His teacher would always smile and laugh whenever I flirted with her. She also would warn me that she was gonna tell Nicole, but I knew she was just playing. See, the way I figured it, my flirting was definitely healthy for both of us in the sense that the attention that LL's teacher got from me had to be flattering being that I'm a younger man and all. She is probably very much in love with her husband, so I knew that nothing would come of my flirtatious ways. For me, it was healthy because it allowed me a good way to keep my game sharp. I was never rude or obnoxious to LL's teacher, so to me it was always a harmless and playful thing.

After I dropped LL off, I attempted to make my way to my car so I could head to work. Notice that I said I *attempted* to make my way to my car. When I walked out of the day care center, I noticed Scarlet del Rio leaning against the driver's side of my car. She had her butt pressed up against the glass, and her arms were folded in a defiant, confrontational manner.

She was the last person I expected to see. Even though my heart dropped to my stomach when I saw her, I calmly prepared myself to walk across the street to my car and confront Scarlet. But I knew I had to play things cool in order to diffuse any possible violence on Scarlet's part.

"Well, isn't this a pleasant surprise?" I said as I leaned and kissed Scarlet on her right cheek as she continued to stand with her arms folded across her chest, displaying all kinds of attitude.

"Lance, don't come at me like that," Scarlet barked.

Oh, boy, here we go, I thought.

"Come at you like what?" I asked.

"Like everything is cool between us, you all kissing me on my cheek and talking about 'isn't this a pleasant surprise?' yet your ass don't know how to call nobody."

As Scarlet began to raise her voice I didn't want her causing a scene because I didn't know who was around, and the last thing I needed was someone at LL's day care center calling Nicole and telling her about the huge confrontation that her husband and some beautiful, voluptuous Brazilian woman had in front of the building.

"Scarlet, go to the other side of my car and get in so that we can talk," I said as I pressed the button on the remote to my car's alarm.

"I don't feel like sitting in your car. Why can't we talk out here in the open?"

"Because, Scarlet, you're causing a scene. Now either get in the car or I'm outta here. I don't need this."

"Oh, you don't need this? And I suppose you think I do need this. I don't need this either, and I don't deserve to be treated the way you've been treating me."

As I brushed Scarlet out of the way in order to attempt to open the driver's door of my car, she started flippin' out. She began screaming and started attacking me like she'd lost her mind.

"Don't you put your hands on me. Who the hell do you think you are?" Scarlet yelled as she started throwing a series of right hooks to my head. She wasn't exactly a small woman who couldn't hold her own in a street fight. She was a heavy-handed momma who was originally from Harlem and could practically hit like a dude. So needless to say, I was feeling every punch she threw, not to mention her accuracy was right on point as each blow landed flush in my face, head, and neck.

"Scarlet, get in the car," I screamed. "Are you crazy or something?"

"Lance, you're gonna talk to me, and you damn sure are gonna apologize for putting your hands on me."

Although I knew that I had not put my hands on her, I had merely bumped into or brushed her body as I attempted to open my car door, I simply wanted to put water on this fire ASAP because people had begun to take notice of the two of us.

"Okay. Okay. I'm sorry for putting my hands on you. Now please calm down. We can talk, but let's just do it like civilized people. So please, just go to the other side of the car and get in, and we'll talk about whatever it is that you want to talk about."

Scarlet was breathing a little heavy from the anger that had built up inside of her. She didn't respond verbally to me; she simply pulled down the tight, skimpy, short-sleeve shirt that she was wearing, which had managed to ride up a bit and expose her stomach. The shirt actually looked like it could fit my twelve-year-old cousin, but that was beside the point.

As Scarlet got into my car, she made a point to slam the door as hard as she could. "Come on, Scarlet. It doesn't take all of that," I said in a raised voice.

"Lance, you are so wrong. How could you be so cold? It's like I might as well have fallen off the face of the earth because you just completely cut me off, and I don't think that's fair because I haven't even done anything to you. I'm always leaving messages on your cell phone and paging you, and you never return any of my calls. Lance, I don't deserve to be treated like that."

"Baby, first of all, calm down. Both of us need to just calm the hell down. I mean, it's way too early in the morning for all of this. Like I said when I first saw you, it is a pleasant surprise to see you, but what isn't pleasant is all of the yelling and screaming and punching. Don't you know that you don't hit like the average woman?" I asked in a joking manner as I took hold of Scarlet's hand and gently pulled her closer toward me.

As we hugged, the smell of her Donna Karan perfume turned me on like crazy. "See, doesn't this feel good?" I asked.

"Lance, of course it feels good. And that's why I'm so hurt. I don't get to touch you, kiss you, feel you, talk to you, and you seem like you don't even wanna give me none anymore."

I moved my mouth close to Scarlet's, and after our lips were perfectly aligned, I began tonguing her down. She was acting like an animal that had been caged up for weeks and was ready to go on a sexual rampage.

As I kissed her, I managed to slip my hand in her pants and get her even more turned on. I didn't know where things would lead, so I wanted to quickly move from in front of LL's day care center. Even though I had dark tinted windows, I still didn't want to take a chance of freaking Scarlet right in front of the day care center.

"Baby, I want you so bad," Scarlet moaned.

"I want you too," I replied, "but we just can't do it right here in front of the building."

So as Scarlet sat up in her seat and adjusted her pants, I started up the car and drove around the block. Before I could find a real good secluded spot to park, Scarlet had unzipped my pants, had my privates in her mouth, and was getting busy.

See, I had genuinely wanted to sit and talk things over with Scarlet, but apparently she had other plans, and I wasn't about to interrupt her. I simply sat back, closed my eyes, and enjoyed every minute of the early-morning surprise blow job.

When she was done, swallowing and all, and asked me if I enjoyed it, she wiped her mouth, looked at me, and said, "Lance, don't just shut me out of your life like that."

Now what was I supposed to say? I didn't really want her feeling like a cheap two-dollar ho, and I didn't even feel that she was. I had strong feelings for her—I mean she was still wifey—but I just had to stop seeing her and being with her. Five years was way too long, and I had to hold my ground.

But like an idiot I replied, "Scarlet, I'm not gonna shut you out, and you know that."

"You promise?"

"Yeah, I promise."

Scarlet attempted to move closer in order to start kissing me again, but I wasn't trying to have that. She had just gone down on me, and I didn't wanna be tasting all of *that*, even if it was mine.

"Baby, I gotta bounce. I'm gonna be late for work," I quickly blurted out in order to avoid her tongue landing in my mouth.

"Lance, forget that job. I keep telling you that I make enough money to support us. You don't even have to be busting your ass every day the way you do. Just play your cards right with me."

"Yeah, I know. That offer always sounds tempting, but . . . I don't know. . . . See, Scarlet, why do you do this to me? I gotta hurry up, but I promise you that we'll speak. I'm gonna call you, and we'll hook up. I promise. But you just have to promise me that you're not gonna be popping up and flippin' out on me like you did today. That's what scares me about you. I mean how do I know that you're not gonna do that when Nicole's around?"

"Lance, you know that I wouldn't do that to you. I mean I accept the fact that you're with Nicole. She's number one to you, and I know that. But I damn sure am gonna be number two, you better believe that. As long as I don't see you with some other chick, you don't have to worry about me. Just keep me happy and satisfied."

My head instantly began spinning from Scarlet's twisted logic. "Okay, Scarlet, I hear you. But trust me, there is no other number two, a'ight?"

"Okay. I trust you, but I'm just putting you on notice. I know you gotta hurry up and go to work, so just drive me to my car around the block."

I quickly circled the block and made it to Scarlet's pimped-out black Mercedes Benz S600.

As she got out of my car, she kissed me on the lips and said, "I better hear from you."

"You will. Don't worry," I said as I watched her walk to her car with her 36-24-48 measurements. "Damn! Look at that,"

I said to myself as I shook my head and lustfully stared at Scarlet's body.

I quickly gathered myself and rushed off to work. I knew I would have to think of something in order to get Scarlet del Rio completely out of my life. *But then again*, I thought, *I could really be a ho and stay with Scarlet and Nicole and still try to bag Toni all at the same time.*

I knew it would take a lot of hard work, but I didn't have too many other options. Otherwise Scarlet was bound to throw all kinds of monkey wrenches into the whole program that I had planned for Toni. My head was spinning from the pressure, so I told myself to just keep Scarlet completely blocked out of my mind until I could think of a good enough plan.

"Yeah, Lance. Just forget what you just told Scarlet. Keep things the way they've been for the past three months. Don't call her, don't see her or anything. Just block her out."

I tried to take my mind completely off Scarlet as I wondered if there was any plausible excuse that I could muster up to see Toni later on during the day. I drove myself crazy trying to think of something. Finally I realized that it was Monday, and in New York City, most beauty salons are closed. As I continued to drive to work, I thought that during the day, while I was on my route, I would drive past the beauty parlor just to make sure that the shop was definitely closed.

By the time one o'clock in the afternoon pulled in, I decided to make good on my promise. I drove past the shop, and everything held true to form. The shop indeed was closed. Inside, I kind of felt real empty. It was like I had built up all this excitement and anticipation of possibly seeing Toni, but with the shop closed, I felt like a deflated balloon. For the remainder of the workday, I had the most dejected feelings running throughout my body. I couldn't even concentrate fully on my work. I felt like a crackhead who needed a hit in the worst way. I kept telling myself, "Just call her." I wanted to at least speak to her, but I really had nothing to say. It wasn't like she was a friend of the family or whateva. If I called her, I didn't wanna call her with no mack of the year player lines. I simply decided to scratch that idea.

Enough was enough. I had to convince myself to stop sweating this Toni chick. I had to get the thought of her out of my head. It was almost three in the afternoon, and I still hadn't taken my lunch break, so I decided to pull into a McDonald's drive-thru. As I spoke my order into the menu board, I realized that the female who was taking my order sounded very sexy. I was wondering how she looked. I told myself, "I bet you one hundred dollars that when I pull around to pick up my food that she will be the most busted-looking female you ever wanted to see." I loved placing bets like that with myself just to test my McUgly/McSlammin' Theory.

The theory states that any female who takes your order at the drive-thru and sounds sexy is almost guaranteed to be ugly. But if she sounds regular or even if her voice sounds a little masculine, then it's highly probable that she will be slammin'. So after placing my order, I pulled around to the pick-up window. Man was my theory wrong. The girl who came to the window was definitely off the meter. Although she looked as if she was barely old enough to have her working papers, she still was a cutie.

She was a young Spanish chick with crazy long hair. She was even able to fill out those stiff but loose polyester pants that are part of the McDonald's uniform. When she reached for the money, I held on to it so she would have to tug it when she grabbed for it. After she realized that I wasn't going to let go of the money, she looked at me and repeated the price.

"Yeah, I know how much it is," I replied. "I just wanted to look at you a little longer. You don't mind, do you?"

She didn't respond. She just smiled and took the money.

When she came back with my food and the change, I noticed that her name tag read Carmen.

"So, Carmen, how old are you?" I asked.

"Sixteen," she replied with another smile.

"Would your man mind if you gave me your number and I took you out?"

"I don't know."

"Listen, my name is Lance. Carmen, I was thinking, why don't you just give me your number and I'll call you. I mean, I don't wanna hold up the line or get you in trouble."

Carmen quickly wrote down her number and gave it to me. As I drove off, she instructed me to take care. I put her number on the dashboard of the work van that I was driving like I've done with literally hundreds of phone numbers in the past. I knew I wasn't gonna call her. I mean, I'm not one to rob the cradle or anything. She was a little cutie, so I'd just make sure I stopped back at that McDonald's and I'd go inside next time to take a better look at her body. If the body was whack then I could still gas her for some free food or something.

I knew that sixteen years old was way too young for me. For some reason I would always bug out with myself and think stupid thoughts about young girls like Carmen. I just hoped my thoughts wouldn't get me locked up one day.

Well, at least Toni was out of my mind. My lunch break was over, and as for my cupcake job, I only had to sit around and do nothing for another twenty minutes, and after that I would be on my way home. I decided to pass the time by digging into the pile of my X-rated *Black Tail* magazines. I gazed at the magazines and got my heart racing a little, then I was ready to bounce. The remainder of the day passed with no unusual occurrences, except for Scarlet blowing up my pager and my cell phone like some deranged nut job. She left like twenty messages for me, and I didn't return one of her calls. I knew that would really just piss her off but hey, what could a brotha do?

Finally, evening time rolled around, and I could have won an Oscar for the way I romanced my wife. As I romanced Nicole I was feeling like a little kid on the day before his birthday. I couldn't wait to go to sleep and wake up the next morning and open my present. I just hoped that Santa would bring me Toni in some form or the other. Toni was the last person I thought about after my wife and I said our prayers and lay waiting to fall asleep.

Chapter Six

Tuesday was upon me, and I was as vibrant as an aerobic instructor. I was ready to conquer the world. Even my wife, before she departed for work, had commented on what a good mood I was in. I guess I was subconsciously excited about the prospect of seeing or speaking to Toni.

Unfortunately, as the day played itself out, I still had no plausible excuse to go see Toni or to call her for that matter. I thought that at least if I went by her shop while I was working, I could play it off like I was just in the neighborhood and had dropped by to say what's up.

But that was how I would approach going to see someone like Carmen or any average female for that matter. I had to pull out all the stops with Toni. I decided to go ahead with something I had been contemplating for the past two days. I called up 1-800-FLOWERS and had them send Toni two dozen roses. I told the operator that I wanted the card inside the flowers to read:

> *Dear Toni,*
> *Just the thought of you brightens my day. So I hope that the smile on your face from being surprised will brighten your day.*
>
> *With love,*
> *From Your Secret Admirer*

I didn't care what the cost of the flowers was. All I knew was that I really felt good about having them sent. In my mind, I was convinced that Toni deserved the flowers. It made me feel good just knowing that I would be making someone else feel good. Women melt from things like flowers and love letters. I think they melt due to the fact that someone took time out just to make them feel special. Hopefully Toni would be melting over my anonymous gesture.

I have to admit that later on that night as my wife, Steve, LL, and I watched the NBA playoff games, I felt a little guilty about having sent Toni the flowers, but I blocked out the guilt and went on like everything was normal. I was cheering my team on. I had my Heinekens and a full tray of Buffalo wings, so in actuality everything was quite normal. I was giving LL and Steve high-fives and kissing my wife whenever a critical shot was made. The beer was giving me a little buzz, and coupled with the elation of having surprised Toni, it made it easy for me to block out the guilt.

Earlier that same evening, I had caught Steve up on all of the latest details between Toni and myself. I told him how I was planning on calling her the next day and seeing if she'd received the flowers. Steve's response, well, he simply shook his head and laughed at me. Again, I warned him he wouldn't be laughing when he saw Toni.

Nicole, who is very comfortable around Steve, had on some tight shorts and a T-shirt, just your regular relaxing type of gear. When she got up and went to answer the phone, Steve tapped me, and while pointing to Nicole, he asked why I would cheat on "that." Having no reasonable response, I smiled and said, "Yo, kid, I'm just sayin'."

It's mad ill because it's like men have this impenetrable code of silence when it comes to cheating. Like, I could have just told Steve that I'd had sex with Toni an hour ago. Yet he would be able to look Nicole in the face as calm as ever, kiss her on the cheek, and comment on how great her food is and the whole nine. Similar to what he has been doing. See, like any other guy, Steve knows how to play the game. If roles were reversed, I would play the game the same exact way. Men never took a class on this stuff, and we don't even have to discuss how to do it. But we had to have learned it somewhere 'cause it just oozes out of us too damn smooth. I would bet that LL was subconsciously learning how to play the game by just being around us, and we didn't even know it.

When Wednesday showed up, I couldn't wait to call Toni. I'd been wondering if she'd actually received the flowers. I was starting to lose my mind. I was thinking thoughts like, *What if she chose not to come in to work on Tuesday? What if she thinks the secret admirer is some other punk who's sweating her?* All kinds of thoughts were rambling through my mind.

When I work, I carry my cell phone with me, and that day was no different. I decided to wait until around eleven o'clock in the morning to call Toni. I figured I would catch her before she was real busy with customers. I felt a little nervous about calling her, but those jitters were normal. I would say most men are a little nervous when they make that first call to a female who has got it going on. I had no idea what I was gonna say or how I was gonna say it, but that usually works better for me. I knew I had to just come at her as myself so she would at least sense the sincerity.

I dialed the shop's number, and it rang twice. Before someone picked up, I quickly pressed the END button on my cell phone. I decided to page Toni and put in my cell number for her to call me back. My reasoning was, by having Toni call me it would help break the ice a bit. So after I paged her, I simply went about my business as usual. I didn't want to be sitting around with sweaty palms and all that. I did, however, keep an eye on my watch and noticed that it was only ten minutes later when my cell phone rang.

I answered on the first ring, but I tried not to sound too eager as I said, "Hello."

"Hi. Did somebody page Toni?"

I was screaming inside. Toni had actually called me back. She sounded sweeter than ever. "Yeah, how you doin', Toni? This is Lance."

"Oh, Lance what's up, boo?"

Boo? Ah, man. That was all I needed to hear, I reasoned to myself. If I never spoke to Toni again it would have been a'ight 'cause she called a nigga "boo." Yo, plus she knew right off the bat who I was.

I decided to get right to the point and not beat around the bush. So I donned my mack voice and replied, "Nothing much. I was just calling to see how you were doing, and I wanted to know if you liked the flowers that I sent you."

There was a quick moment of silence followed by a child-ish-sounding laughter of embarrassment.

"Lance, you sent those flowers? When I found out they weren't from who I originally thought they were from, I was trippin' the whole day, trying to figure out who sent them. Yes, of course I liked them. That was so sweet, but—"

Before Toni could mess up the flow and throw acid all over my program, I interrupted her by mackishly playing down the situation. "What were you gonna say? Listen, before you say anything, I just wanna say that I'm glad you liked the flowers. I also wanna ask if it's okay if I drop by your job tonight and pick you up. After I pick you up, why don't me and you go to Junior's restaurant?"

Toni chuckled and said, "Lance, whoa, slow down. Slow down . . . I heard of being straightforward, but man . . . Lance, like I was saying, the flowers were very nice and thoughtful, but I can't go out to eat with you."

"Why not? All I wanna do is take you to get some cheesecake. That's it. No strings attached. A'ight? We can eat cheesecake and talk about a few things."

"Talk about a few things like what?"

"Things."

There was another brief pause, then I heard a sigh, followed by short laughter.

"Oh my God, Lance . . . All right, I'll go get some cheesecake with you."

Yes, yes, yes, yes, yes! I screamed in my head.

Toni then pessimistically added, "Lance, I don't even really know you. I mean—"

I quickly interrupted, "Toni, like I said, no strings attached. I just wanna talk to you about a few things."

"But Lance, by the time I get off I'll look too through. You don't even wanna know how busted I'll look by the time I leave here. Plus, I ain't even dressed to go out."

I responded, "Toni, don't worry about how you'll look. See, you making this more than it is. We just gonna eat some cheesecake. You don't have to be dressed for that, right?"

"Yeah, okay . . . Lance, I gotta go. It's getting hectic in here."

I joyfully said, "Oh, no problem. So what time does the shop close?"

Toni replied, "I'll be leaving here around eight."

"Eight o'clock is good. I'll pick you up from the shop."

"Lance, why don't I just meet you in the lobby of Junior's, at let's say . . . eight-thirty? It doesn't make sense for me to leave my car here and then afterward have you drive me back to the shop to pick it up."

"That's true. Okay, so I'll see you at eight-thirty. You know where it's at, right?"

"Yeah, on Flatbush Avenue, downtown."

"Okay, so I'll see you later."

"Okay. Bye."

After that conversation, I had to check to see if my pants were still dry.

"I knew it," I confirmed to myself. I knew I could bag that. I knew it. Ever since I looked into Toni's eyes at the shop that day, I knew I had it locked. Yeah, if I was some busted nigga who had nothing going on, Toni would never have accepted my offer. But she saw the face, the Lexus, the muscles, and the baldhead, and that's why she accepted. This date had been confirmed ever since the day I pulled her over on Pennsylvania Avenue. I tried to calm down and concentrate on the rest of the day, but it was extremely difficult.

About fifteen minutes after having confirmed the date with Toni, I called my older sista, Tiffany, to make arrangements for her to pick up LL from the day care center. Tiffany had no problem with doing me the favor. In fact, she often looked out and picked LL up for me when I would work overtime or something. When I was done speaking to my sista, I immediately called Nicole.

"Hi, baby."

My wife, sounding very excited and surprised, said, "Lance! Hi, honey. What's up? I'm glad to hear from you."

"I just had to hear your voice, so I decided to call you."

"Really?"

"Yeah. You know how much I love you, right?" Nicole responded with a laugh, and I added, "What? You think I don't love you or something?"

Nicole giggled then she replied, "Nah, I know you love me."

"Okay, just making sure. I have to stay on top of those kinda things, you kna'imean?"

After telling me that I was crazy, Nicole laughed. I interrupted her by saying, "Oh, yeah . . . Listen, baby, I wanted to let you know that Tiffany is gonna pick up LL, so can you pick him up from her house when you get off?"

"Why? What happened?"

"Well, my supervisor just asked me if I could work until about ten tonight."

"Until ten? Lance, tell him you can't do it. Did you forget about Wednesday night Bible class at the church?"

"I knew it. Man, I knew I had something to do. Man, I already told him I would work late. See we had this big gas main that broke, and we have to restore about eight hundred homes that have no gas."

My wife, sounding disappointed, said, "Well, if you already told him you would, and being that it's an emergency, I guess you have to work. So I'll see you around eleven, right?"

"Yeah, that sounds good. Oh, Nicole, don't worry about dinner 'cause I'll just eat Chinese food or whateva."

"Okay, but Lance, you know we've already spoken about your work hours interfering with other things. I don't mean to be nagging you, but you can't keep putting your job before God."

"I know, baby, but I really can't help it tonight, a'ight? We'll talk about this later, okay? I love you."

"Okay. I love you too. Bye."

It's not easy, but lying comes so natural to me. It's to the point that when I lie it doesn't even feel like I'm doing it. It's especially hard when it comes to lying to Nicole. But like always, I just mentally block out the wrong that I do. As for missing Bible class so I can creep with another woman, I definitely felt horrible. But I block out the feelings of guilt of leading my wife to think that I'm husband of the year, when actually I'm using my skills to diss her. I mean I don't let those feelings sit in my conscious mind, 'cause if I did, there would be no way I could carry out my devilish actions. Yet the dark side of me wants to go ahead with the evil deeds. It's that dark

side that rises out of my subconscious and plays itself out
consciously. But the guilt and all that, I always quickly force it
back to my subconscious so I won't drive myself insane.

When work was over, I rushed home. I was excited like
crazy. I blasted the basement stereo as I showered and
changed clothes. I knew that I had to be in and out of the
house quickly so that I wouldn't get busted by my wife or
anyone who might see my wife later on in the evening. Before
I left the house I called the dispatching office at Con Edison
and informed them that if my wife called they were to call me
on my cell phone and let me know, but by no means were they
to tell her that I had already left for home. In reality I knew
that if Nicole needed me that she would just beep me or call
me on the cell, but I still had to cover all my bases.

Before I knew it, it was a little past seven, and I was already
parked and waiting near Junior's. It's so ill, but as was the
case with any given day, as I sat in the car, I found myself
thinking some sick sexual thoughts. I would say that I easily
think about sex, sometimes six times or more every hour of
the day every day. I'll fantasize about a woman I saw during
the course of the day, a sexual encounter I had when I was
seventeen, the topless dancer I saw—it didn't matter. Sex of
some sort was always on my mind.

Being that I had some time to kill, I decided to try to reach
Scarlet, so I called her at her house. When she picked up, I
stated, "See, I kept my promise. I told you that I was gonna
call you, and I did."

"Lance?"

"Yeah, this is Lance. Oh, you done forgot my voice that
quick, or are you confusing me with some other cat?"

"No, I didn't forget your voice. It's just that I only paged you
and called you like two days ago and now you wanna return
my call?"

"Scarlet, you know that if I ever don't return your call it's
because I'm with Nicole. You know that."

"Oh, so you're saying that you've been with Nicole for
forty-eight hours straight?"

"Got damn, Scarlet. Damn. Why do you always come at me
with so much drama? It's like lately every time I speak to you

or see you, you come at me with some rage and drama. And you expect me to wanna eagerly gravitate to that?"

"Lance, listen. Don't even go there. Because it is not about me, and you know that. You are an expert at spinning the situation and making it seem like I'm always the one to blame. But how the hell do you think I'm supposed to feel? You didn't have no problem with me going down on you the other day. Did you? Of course you didn't. I guess that wasn't no 'rage and drama' at that moment because you was getting something out of it. Then you got the nerve to not even return my calls. You tell me, how the hell am I supposed to feel? Tell me because maybe I got this whole thing twisted."

Well, she did have a point. I mean, I guess that was foul. Considering she had serviced me quite lovely that morning, I could have at least called her during the day or even the next day so she wouldn't feel so cheap and whorish. At the same time Scarlet was forgetting that I had told her we had to stop seeing each other. *Why couldn't she just get that through her head?* She must have had some short-term memory loss because I had never asked her to go down on me.

In a very calming tone, I replied, "Scarlet, see you're getting things twisted. I never asked you to go down on me. You took that upon yourself to do that, and plus—"

Scarlet immediately and rudely interrupted me. "What? Oh my God! Lance, I can't believe you would even say something like that. You were the one who was reclined back and enjoying it. Why the hell didn't you tell me to stop?"

"Come on, you know that no man in his right mind would tell a woman to stop in the middle of some head unless it wasn't good."

"Lance, you know what? That just proves that you think it's all about you. You really are only thinking about yourself and looking out for yourself, so I guess I should just do me and not even worry about you."

Finally, I thought. Scarlet was finally getting it.

"Scarlet, see it might come across that way, but deep down you know it isn't even like that."

"Lance, I don't know what to think, but I guess that deep down you don't even know what you want. I know this has nothing to do with Nicole. Lance, I know and you know that you can't ever be faithful to her, so why are you even fooling yourself? Lance, just admit it. This is all about you getting with somebody else. You think that I'm stupid? Yeah, when everything was new and exciting and I was the hottest stripper in New York, you had no problem being with me, right? But now that the whole fantasy is wearing off you feel like it's time for something new, and you figure that you'll just dump me and move on to the next best thing."

"Scarlet, that is so far from the truth, and you know it. Because if it was about wearing you out and moving on to the next best thing then tell me how did I stick around for five years? I could have easily moved on much sooner. Why can't you just respect my wishes and know that the best thing to do is to give me some space—permanent space—and we'll just see how things turn out?"

"Lance, I've told you this time and time again, and I'll tell you again. I'm not gonna be your third option, and I know that that's all this whole 'space' thing is about. Now I'm gonna end this conversation by telling you this: You better start spending more time with me. And be very clear on this: When I find out who this other chick is, Lance, it's gonna be on. Let me find out. I'm telling you, Lance, you better handle your business because the moment that I suspect some sloppiness, I'm gonna be right there all up in your ass."

With that Scarlet hung up the phone on me.

Man, I needed that type of drama like I needed a hole in my head. I knew I couldn't be sloppy. There was no room for even one false move. I knew that for my sake, and for Nicole's, and *especially* for Toni's sake, because up until now Toni was mad innocent and totally oblivious to all of my ways. The last thing I needed was for Scarlet to find out about Toni and roll up on her or something. Believe me, Scarlet would have no problem rolling on Toni.

Although I had to keep Scarlet in cut-off status, I knew that I had to use the only weapon against her that I had. And that weapon was between my legs. Yeah, in my mind, Scarlet was history, and she would remain history. But so she wouldn't cause World War III, I knew I would have to keep Scarlet satisfied with some good sex. Spending quality time with her was really not an option, because after all, there are only twenty-four hours in a day, and I was determined to get things jumped off with Toni, which was sure to occupy a lot of my time. But for the sake of peace, I would have to make time to break Scarlet off some pipe here and there.

When eight o'clock came, I decided to make my way inside Junior's. I went to the bar and ordered a rum and Coke. The drink helped me relax. While I sipped on it, I contemplated taking off my wedding band, but I knew that Toni already knew what time it was. Besides, I ain't even trying to play no "I'm single and available" crap because that requires too much work. I'ma keep the marriage thing real with her.

Being that it was a Wednesday night, the restaurant wasn't that busy. The waitresses weren't all that either, but that didn't matter, 'cause I knew my girl would have it going on. I must admit that for a moment I started to get paranoid. I was thinking, *What if Toni stands me up?* She didn't seem like a no-class lady, but on a first date I knew to expect anything. Deep down, I doubted that she would stand me up. Besides, if she was gonna do that, I knew she would have had the decency to call me on the cellular. Again feeling paranoid, I thought, *What if she's erased my number from her pager and has no way of reaching me?* I looked at my watch and noticed that it was seventeen past eight. My phone hadn't rang, so I thought it was safe to assume that Toni was on her way.

I finished my drink, and I just parlayed. I had on a pair of black jeans with a beige, short-sleeve, tight-fitted shirt, and some casual shoes that looked like ankle boots. I didn't want to be too dressy being that Toni was gonna be coming with her work gear on.

Well at least work gear was what I thought Toni would be wearing. As I made my way from the bar to the restaurant's lobby, I saw Toni looking as good as ever. She had on black high heels with stockings, and she had on the bomb dress. It was some kind of slinky material that clung close to her body. Her outfit almost caused my mouth to have to be scraped from the floor. After having picked up my fallen jaw, I walked over to Toni and hugged her.

We both were smiling as we greeted each other.

"Look at youuu. . . . You certainly look very lovely. Now what was all of that, 'I'm gonna look through and I won't even be dressed to go out.' Yeah, y'all sistas are all the same. Always tryin'a make a brotha look bad." The ice was crazy broken. I always seem to make women feel very comfortable around me.

Toni smiled and responded by blushingly saying, "I know, I know, but I just can't go out looking busted, so I went home real quick and changed."

"Um-hmm. That's cool. I'll let you slide this time. I mean I definitely ain't mad at that dress."

Toni laughed. "Lance, I'm sorry I'm late. Were you waiting long? There was so much traffic on Atlantic Avenue. That's what took me so long to get here. If I hadn't gone home to change I would have been here on time."

"Oh, nah, don't sweat that. I was chillin'. Do you want a drink before they seat us?"

Toni decided it would be best for us to just order drinks once we were seated. The restaurant isn't the classiest of places, but it's one of those good first date locations. The ambiance is mad cool, with nice music in the background. It's a'ight.

When we were seated, I said, "Now, Toni, you look very gorgeous, and I know you had a long day at work, so I hope you don't tell me that all you want is cheesecake. I mean it's a'ight if that's all you want, but I'ma keep it real and let you know that I'm starving."

Toni laughed and waved her hand at me in a sista-girlfriend kinda way. "First of all, that cheesecake thing came out of your mouth. A sista definitely ain't shy, so you better believe I'm gonna order some real food, and we can have cheesecake for dessert."

We both laughed, and I said, "Yeah, a'ight, there's definitely nothing wrong with a sista with an appetite."

As we both studied the menu, I found out that Junior's was one of Toni's favorite places to eat. I'd been to Junior's on a number of occasions, but I never actually ate the food—I would always order their world-famous cheesecake. When the waiter came to take our order, we decided to get Buffalo wings as an appetizer. For the main course, Toni ordered shrimp parmesan with linguine. I decided to go the traditional route with pork chops and rice. Although it was way too early to order dessert, we decided to get it out of the way. We both ordered small cheesecakes. As far as drinks went, I ordered a Long Island Iced Tea, and Toni requested a strawberry daiquiri.

When we were done ordering, Toni shot right at me.

"Okay, Mr. Lance, so why did you send me the flowers?" she said while smiling.

I smiled as I explained, "I just wanted to do something nice for you. I like making people feel good."

"Oh, so you go around sending everyone flowers?"

"Nah, I'm not saying that. I mean, I do that for people I feel are special."

Toni laughed and asked, "Oh, so you feel that I'm special. Why, because of the way I do hair?"

I tried not to smile or laugh. I wanted to get things on a more serious note. After all, I had no idea as to how long this opportunity would last or if I would get another chance like this again.

"Toni, I'll be honest. I really don't know you at all, but I do know that you seem like a very unique person, and what I'm sayin' is, I feel as if something special could happen between us."

By this time the waiter had come back with our drinks and Buffalo wings. Toni offered me her beautiful smile, sipped her drink, and then she proclaimed, "You know what, Lance? If I was younger I would be falling head over heels for you. I mean, you're a very attractive man, and you seem like you have a lot going for yourself, but I'm not as naïve as I used to be."

I had a feeling where Toni was going with this, but I played dumb. I took a sip of my drink and I looked right into her eyes as I commented, "I don't understand what you're saying."

Toni replied, "Well, let me not jump to any conclusions. What I mean is that I think you have a lot of game."

Sounding astonished, I asked, "Why do you think that?"

Toni reached over the table and grabbed my left hand. Her hands felt as soft as cotton candy. While playing with my wedding band, Toni asked, "Lance, is this a wedding ring?"

Without hesitation, I confidently replied, "Yeah."

Toni let out a quick chuckle, and she asked, "So you're married?"

Again I confidently replied, "Been married for five years."

I guess Toni wasn't expecting my confident answers. Sounding confused, she questioned, "So, Lance, what are you doing here with me?"

"See, Toni, I'm here because of questions like the one you just asked me."

Toni responded, "Come again? You lost me."

At that moment, the waiter came with the main course. We both adjusted our seats and place settings to make ourselves a bit more comfortable. After commenting on how good everything looked, we began to eat. I continued with my explanation. I was trying to cause Toni to have sympathetic feelings for me.

"Toni, what I'm saying is that it gets frustrating being married because everyone expects you to conform to some set of rules or what have you. As soon as you go out of bounds, they want to crucify you. Take tonight for example. What's wrong with me taking you out to eat? I mean it's not like anything sexual is gonna happen. Can't a married man go out to eat with a female?"

After chewing her food, Toni responded, "See, first of all, does your wife know that you're here?"

"That doesn't matter," I replied.

"Yes, it does matter. Second of all, do you find me attractive?"

"Toni, there isn't a man alive who wouldn't find you attractive."

Toni continued, "Okay, so your wife doesn't know you're having dinner with someone you find attractive. That right there is a problem. Let's not mention that I happen to find you attractive. See, you're right, it's not a crime for us to be here eating, but Lance, why play with fire? You're an intelligent man. You know exactly what can come about when two attractive people of the opposite sex go out to eat. Especially when the married person's spouse has no idea he's where he is, doing what he's doing. Plus, you even said that you feel something special could happen between us or something like that."

I knew that I had to switch subjects, so I did. "Well, Toni, let me ask you, are you in a relationship?"

"Yes. As a matter of fact, I am. But it's a long-distance relationship, and you know how those go. I mean, I'm trying to make it work, but he's all the way in Las Vegas. We met in grad school, but he's finished with school, so he won't be coming back for the fall semester."

I could have made a stupid comment by asking her, why, if she was in a relationship, was she with me, but I didn't want to go that route. I iterated, "Well, long-distance relationships can work if you want them to."

"Yeah, I know that, but Lance, he's similar to you. He's young, has a lot going for himself, and I have to be realistic. I mean, I know he's probably with some ho right now dropping the same bull that most men run. I look at it like this: I'm not tied down to anyone, and I don't have to live as if I am."

"See, Toni, you just hit my situation right on the head. I mean I always feel like I locked myself down at too young an age. I didn't get all of the game out of my system before I committed to marriage. When I got married, I really loved my wife. Matter of fact, I still love her. But at the time, I wasn't ready for marriage. I thought I was, but I just wasn't. Plus, she got pregnant and all. You know how that goes."

"Lance, I understand what you're sayin', but you made a commitment, so honor it. I think that when it all boils down to it, it's just about self-control."

I cut a piece of my pork chop, and I said, "Yeah, that's true. See, Toni, this is all I want from you. I just want a friend. You can help me out with my feelings."

By now the drinks were getting to both of our heads; we were both feeling a little nice. Toni laughed and said, "Okay, I'll be your friend. But you've probably got a million other 'friends.'"

"Nah, that's not my style."

Toni stated, "Lance, when you left the shop with your son, the women in that place were going crazy. They were ready to take off their panties and throw them at you for you to autograph. I know you probably get women going crazy over you wherever you go."

I was feeling like the man, but I downplayed the comment. Acting better than Denzel Washington, I looked Toni in her eyes. I shook my head and frowned as I explained, "Nah, Toni, honestly I'm not about that. I'm not out here trying to get off with every woman I see. By no means am I an angel—I mean, I know I have things about me that I have to deal with, but I'm not a dog. I'm past that dog stage of chasing women or catching them when they throw themselves at me. See, you're stereotyping me, and if anything, I think that I, and many other men, are just misunderstood."

We were both just about finished eating our food. I requested the bill from the waiter, and I asked him to put Toni's cheesecake in a box because she wasn't gonna finish it but she wanted to take it home.

The bill came to fifty-three dollars, so I handed the waiter sixty dollars, leaving him a seven-dollar tip. It was now about half past nine. As we made our way out of the restaurant, my ego felt crazy good because I had this trophy walking by my side and mad brothas were clocking her.

Toni had parked a couple of blocks away from the restaurant. So being a gentleman, I walked her to her car. We talked as we walked. Toni defended the comment that I made about her stereotyping me. I, on the other hand, was trying to be as charming as possible. When we got to her car, I asked if she'd enjoyed herself. She informed me that she had.

"So, Toni, can we be friends? That's all I want."

Seeing right through my game, she smiled and said, "Yes, we can be friends, but Lance you better . . ."

Toni stopped in the middle of her sentence. I begged for her to continue.

"I better what?"

"Nothing. Nothing, Lance," Toni said as she, being as classy as ever, reached to shake my hand. I placed my right hand into her right one, and she said, "Thank you for everything, Lance. Get home safe, okay?"

Feeling cocksure, I asked, "Toni, can I have a hug good night?"

My heart started to race. Not in a nervous way—it was racing in anticipation. Kind of like when you're just about to have sex for the first time with someone. Toni held open her arms, which meant that she had accepted my proposition. Toni is about five foot six inches tall, but the heels she had on brought her to about five foot ten inches. Me being six-three meant that when we hugged, her face was planted just above my chest. I hugged her firmly so that she could get an idea of how hard my body was, but not too tight as to hurt her. Toni's long, wavy hair, which was let out, came down to about her shoulder blades.

While hugging her, I simultaneously stroked her hair a couple of times with my right hand. While still hugging her, I cautioned, "You make sure you get home safe too. A'ight?"

Toni replied, "Okay," and she prepared to step into her car.

Trying to show as much chivalry as possible, I closed Toni's driver's door for her. She waved good-bye, and I walked off and headed toward my own car. I felt like doing cartwheels or jumping and kicking my heels together. I was ecstatic. I blasted a slow-jam tape as I drove home in my Lexus. Everything went great. I couldn't have asked for anything more. Inside I knew that Toni was mine if I pushed a few more buttons. However, I would be walking on thin ice being that I'm married and all. One false move, and I could ruin everything. I was excited, but I was also kind of scared. See, it wasn't even Toni's intentions to have me falling head over heels, yet I knew I would sell my soul for her.

As I approached my Colonial home, which was located in a beautiful middle-class section of Queens called Cambria Heights, I noticed that the kitchen and bedroom lights were on. I didn't want my wife to see me because I looked too clean to be coming home from nearly a double shift of hard work. Plus, I still had Toni's beautiful scent on my clothes. I definitely was not going to activate the automatic garage opener because that would make too much noise, and I would be busted. I parked in front of the house, and I sneaked around to the seldom used side door. My heart was palpitating 'cause I had no idea if my wife was looking out of the window watching my every move, nor did I know which part of the house she was in.

I opened the side door and headed straight for the smaller bathroom, which was located near the kitchen.

When I safely reached the bathroom, I yelled real loud, "Hi, honey. What's up, LL? I'm home."

Then I locked myself in the bathroom and immediately began to run water in the sink. I could hear Nicole's footsteps coming from upstairs. I sat on the toilet bowl even though I didn't have to use it. My wife reached for the bathroom door and tried to twist the knob but it was locked.

"Lance, open the door."

Speaking over the running water, I replied, "Baby, you know I don't like you watching me when I'm using the bathroom. I had to go real bad, I've been holding it since about eight o'clock."

Nikki responded, "Lance, how long have we been married? You know I don't care how you look when you use the bath-room. I miss you. I haven't seen you all day."

"A'ight, baby, I'll be out in a minute. I'm sayin', I'm not doing a number one. I'm doing a number two."

Nicole, whom I often called Nikki, sucked her teeth and responded, "Just hurry up."

I immediately stripped naked and turned on the shower. I took probably the quickest shower on record, dried off, and walked upstairs to my wife. When I saw her, she didn't look like she was in a good mood. I immediately became suspicious. What if somebody saw me at Junior's? What if Scarlet had called the crib or done something sick and twisted in order to raise Nicole's suspicions? What if this? What if that?

"What's wrong, baby?"

Nikki quickly and bluntly said, "Nothing."

I walked out of the bedroom and went to check on LL, but he was already fast asleep. I went throughout the house and turned out all of the lights. When I came back upstairs, I tried to make conversation.

Sounding very anticipating, I asked, "So, baby, how was Bible class? What did y'all learn?"

My wife looked at me and rolled her eyes.

"Nicole, what's wrong?" I asked.

"Lance, how are you gonna just walk in the house and not even greet me? I haven't seen you all day. At least come and kiss me when you walk in."

"Honey, I'm sorry. Really, like I said, I just had to go real bad. It was one of those hard number twos."

I know my wife very well, and I knew that at that present moment, all she wanted was for me to shower her with affection to prove that I was really sorry, so that's exactly what I did. I rubbed her body and kissed her all over.

"Come on, baby. At least give me a smile. I said I was sorry. Please . . ."

Nikki just looked at me and acted as if she was pouting. I knew that she wasn't really mad, so I began to tickle her. "Come on, let me see a smile," I said as I vigorously tickled her. Nicole finally gave in and started laughing. "Yeah, see I got you laughing now," I said as I continued to tickle her. "You gonna tell me what Bible class was about, or do I have to keep tickling you?"

My wife couldn't take it anymore, and she yelled while laughing, "Okay, okay, stop. I'll tell you."

I stopped tickling her, and she kept laughing. She finally calmed down and explained that the class was about a passage in first Corinthians that explains how it's wrong for there to be divisions in the church, and that there should be no favoritism at all, just one church united in doctrine and way of life.

"That sounds like it was a deep class," I exclaimed.

Nicole affirmed that it indeed had been a deep class, then she added, "See, Lance, that's why you can't miss the classes. How are you gonna grow spiritually if you're not around for the lessons?"

Feeling very convicted and knowing that my wife was telling the truth, I put up no argument. "Honey, you're absolutely right, and I have no excuses. All I can say is that it won't happen again."

Nicole added, "That's what I wanted to talk to you about tonight."

While Nicole was speaking, I turned off the lights, and we lay in the bed talking in the dark.

"Lance, we have a good marriage, but I want it to be perfect. I feel that if we both are truly committed to the same spiritual things then we won't have any problems at all in our marriage. What I'm saying is that I can sense that in the past month or so you've just been going through the motions spiritually, and if there's something wrong or something that you're holding back, then you should tell me, or at least speak to one of the older brothers in the congregation."

I responded, "Nah, baby, I'm okay. It's just that I haven't been as focused as I should be. It's all a matter of having the right perspective, and lately I've been concentrating on things other than God. I can't blame it on the nice weather that we've been having or on my job, nothing like that. It's just me. I have to refocus, and I promise you I will."

My wife explained that she didn't want it to seem like she was making a big deal out of nothing—she just wanted us to be on the same page. I told her that I understood exactly from where she was coming, and I thanked her for caring about me in that way.

Nicole then switched subjects and asked, "So was it good?"

I immediately got suspicious. Nervously I asked, "What? Was what good? What are you talking about?"

Nikki replied, "Your number two."

Realizing that Nicole was joking, I replied, "Oh! You silly fool." I grabbed my pillow and playfully smacked Nicole in the head as I said, "Don't worry about what I do on the throne."

We both began laughing. When we were done horsing around, we hugged and kissed, and we said our prayers for the night. When the two of us were done praying together, I continued to silently pray on my own. I prayed real long and earnestly then I just stared into space. I knew that my preoccupation with Toni was affecting my whole inner being. It was bound to start manifesting itself in other areas of my life. I thought about being honest and telling my wife how I really felt about Toni. I also thought about talking to a neutral person, someone other than Steve, as to how I was feeling on the inside. Someone like the pastor of my church, 'cause unlike Steve I knew that the pastor would hold me account-able for my actions.

The reason that I felt like spilling the beans to someone was because Toni was bringing up feelings in me that literally scared me. It was more than infatuation, and it was totally different than what I ever got from being around Scarlet. I was scared because deep down inside I knew that the emotions that Toni was causing me to have were the type that would make me seriously contemplate getting a divorce and starting over with Toni. Scarlet or no other woman had ever made me seriously consider that. With Scarlet, and anyone else for that matter, I always knew that it was really nothing more than serious lust and infatuation.

I lay in thought for nearly a half hour, and I came to the conclusion that it was way too early to start confessing, because when I truly observed everything, I realized I hadn't done anything wrong. I mean, for all I knew, there stood a good chance that nothing at all would jump off in terms of Toni and myself. With that in mind, my thoughts switched to how good Toni had looked that evening. I thought about the fact that she actually told me that she was attracted to me. I was so happy. Again, I managed to block out everything my wife and I had just spoken about. I blocked out my religious convictions and just envisioned the possibilities between Toni and myself.

I looked over at Nicole, and I noticed she was sound asleep. I wasn't really horny or in dire need for sex, but the thought of masturbating came into my head. I contemplated doing it, then I changed my mind and just lay there. I could have awakened Nicole for some sex, but like I said, I wasn't really feeling horny.

After about five minutes of not being able to doze off, I found myself gently removing the covers from on top of me. I quietly snuck out of the bed, praying that the box spring wouldn't squeak. At that point the last thing I wanted to do was awaken Nicole. After I'd made it out of the bed, I softly walked to the bathroom. I pulled down my pajama bottoms and sat on the toilet.

It must have been that demon that has been inside of me since I was twelve years old that conned me to do it. He sprang to life and caused me to close my eyes and make love in a ménage-a-trois with Toni and my sista-in-law as I masturbated.

Chapter Seven

During my twenty-seven short years on this planet, I've learned that women are one big ball of emotions. Not that they break down and cry at every sad moment, nothing like that. Rather, what I've learned is that the way to a woman's heart is through her emotions. In a relationship, women need to know that men care about them. They need to hold hands. They need to receive the flowers, the cards, the letters, and the romantic dinners. Women, more than anything, need conversation before they can truly *connect* with a man. Men are completely the opposite. What drives men are all of the physical things.

See, I knew in order for me to really bag Toni, I would have to put my physical needs aside and concentrate on her emotional being. The evening after our dinner date I decided to page Toni. It was very late, probably close to eleven-thirty, but I had to speak with her in order to start developing that emotional bond. The reason I had waited so late in the day was because I wanted Toni to wonder whether or not I was gonna call her. If in fact she had been wondering about my phone call, it would only have caused her to be filled with anticipation. Hopefully when she heard from me, that antici- pation would turn to excitement.

Being that I didn't know Toni's home telephone number I couldn't just call her at her crib. Also I didn't want to page her and have her call me back at my house. After all, my wife was sleeping, and how would it look if she were to answer the phone and hear Toni's voice on the other end? While Nicole was sleeping, I snuck downstairs to the basement of our house. I decided to page Toni from the basement and have her call me back on my cell phone. The basement is the area of the house we use when we want to entertain a large number of guests. Ours is hooked. We have the big-screen television, the bar, the Jacuzzi, the pool table and all of those material toys.

Anyway, I was hoping that Toni hadn't fallen asleep or gone out for the night. Fortunately, when I paged her, she returned my call right away. My cell phone rang, and I quickly answered. Cautious, as to not speak very loud, I kept my voice kinda low, which actually made me sound Barry Whiteish.

I answered the phone by asking, "How you doing, Toni?"

Toni, sounding as if she was half asleep, responded, "Lance?"

"Yeah, this is Lance. Were you sleeping? I was calling to check up on you."

Toni quietly laughed, and she replied, "No, I wasn't actually sleep. I was watching old re-runs of *VIBE* show, but I was just about to fall asleep."

"Can you talk?" I asked.

"Yeah, I can talk."

Then I asked, "So, did you make it home all right yesterday?"

Toni now seemed to be a bit more alert as she replied, "Yeah, I had no problems. I'm a big girl. I can take care of myself."

I laughed as I asked her if she had eaten her Junior's cheesecake. She informed me that she'd tried to eat just one slice of the cake and save the rest for another day but she couldn't. Shamefully she admitted that she became addicted to the Junior's cheesecake and had eaten the whole thing in one sitting.

"Lance, that cheesecake was calling my name. I tried to put it down, but I couldn't. I was like a dopefiend or something. I felt so bad, but I just kept eating and eating. It was like I would close the box and attempt to put it back in the refrigerator, but I just couldn't. It was so sad. . . . I definitely gotta get my ass to the gym this week."

"So what?" I exclaimed. "It's not like you're fat or anything. You can splurge every now and then."

Toni agreed, "Yeah, that's true. . . . So Lance, where are you at? Why did you get in touch with me so late?"

"I'm at home."

Toni asked, "Where's your wife? And, by the way, did you tell her about our little date last night?"

I purposely wanted to avoid Toni's first question, but I was willing to bounce around her second one with a politician-like answer.

"Well, let's just say that indirectly my wife had an idea of where I was at."

I could feel that Toni was smiling as she asked, "What does that mean?"

"Don't worry about that." There was a brief silence, then I asked, "So are you happy to be hearing from me?"

"Yes, actually I am happy to hear from you. But had you really cared whether I'd made it home safely you would have called earlier."

I knew Toni wasn't serious, so I just laughed and explained to her that I had been busy. "So Toni, is it all right for me to call you at home?"

Toni laughed and replied, "Lance, you're married."

"Come on, Toni."

"Lance, I'm serious. I see we have to have a serious talk because I can see where things might be heading."

"So let me have your number, and we can have our serious talk over the phone."

Toni, seeming as if she must have been smiling while at the same time shaking her head, asked, "Do you have a pen?"

"Yeah, hold on and let me grab one. . . ."

Toni gave me the number, and I copied it down. Then I instructed her to get a pen as I gave her my pager number. I tried to give her my cell number, but she told me that she already had it in her pager's memory. Then for some stupid reason, I told Toni to take down my home number. I guess I was trying too hard to falsely convince her that I only wanted to be her friend.

"You're giving me your home number? Lance, what about your wife? What is she gonna think?"

"Toni, why are you sweating it? My wife will be cool with it."

Toni asked, "What's your wife's name again?"

"Her name is Nicole."

"Oh, so you mean that if I call with my soft-sounding voice that your wife wouldn't flip? Imagine me saying, 'Hi, Nicole, this is Toni. I'm a friend of Lance. Can I speak to him?'"

I laughed and explained, "Toni, you can call whenever you want. I wouldn't have given you the number if it wasn't a'ight."

Toni, sounding confused and unsure, said, "Okay, if that's what you say."

Switching subjects, I asked, "So you watching that old-ass show, so who did they have on?"

Toni told me that it was an old episode where Patti Labelle had performed. Just like everyone else had been accustomed to doing back in the days, Toni explained to me that she had been switching back and forth, watching both Keenan Ivory Wayans' show on the re-run channel TV Land and *VIBE* on TV One. She was irate over the fact that the two shows aired at the same time. Toni also mentioned that Michael Jordan had been on Keenan's show.

"You know, you kinda look like Michael Jordan," Toni remarked.

I laughed as I said, "If I had a dollar for every time I heard that, I would be a millionaire."

Toni explained, "No really, you do look like him."

I responded, "Yeah, and if it's not Michael Jordan, people tell me that I look like Malik Yoba. All it is is that people see me, a dark skin brother with a bald-head, and automatically I look like some baldheaded superstar. Soon people will be telling me I look like R. Kelly."

Toni began to laugh, "That's not true. It's not just because you have a baldie. I don't think you look like no R. Kelly or Malik Yoba, but you do look like Mike. And Mike still has it going on."

Just craving to have my ego massaged, I asked, "So then you must think that I got it going on too."

"Lance, I already told you that I think you're cute, but you're married and I ain't trying to be nobody's jump-off."

I didn't want to go back in that marriage direction. My mission was accomplished. I had my conversation with Toni. Subconsciously I could tell that Toni was being drawn to me. I wanted to end the conversation so as not to spoil anything.

"A'ight, Toni, I'ma bounce. But listen, I'll probably be bringing LL by the shop in a week or so."

"No problem, sweetie. Just call me and let me know. So yeah, I'ma hang up too and get some sleep. All right, so good night."

I pressed END on my cell phone and just sat there. I couldn't believe that I had balls enough to give Toni my home number. I wasn't too worried because I didn't think that Toni would actually ever call me at my rest stop. Plus, I knew that Nicole wasn't the type to yell and scream and get ghetto if another female were to call. I just couldn't believe I had let myself get to the point where I would stoop low enough to freely give out the home digits. In the back of my mind I was thinking how I wanted to sex Toni in the worst way. I knew that it could be a reality, but I would just have to wait on it.

Until that time of glory came, I would just have to get off on the times that Toni told me that she thought I was cute, or when she called me boo or sweetie. I could always reminisce about the hug she gave me after we ate dinner, or the way her hands felt when they touched mine. As I turned out the lights and proceeded to walk upstairs, I wondered when the need for phone calls to Toni would wear off. When would the thoughts of her hugging me not be enough?

My heart began to race as I pondered kissing Toni. I thought, *I bet her tongue feels like a water fountain*. I couldn't wait to make love to her. I wondered how soft her thighs would feel. I fantasized about performing oral sex on Toni the first time I got the chance. Usually a female would have to wait for that privilege. That is reserved for only the elite. Toni was elite material, and I knew her cat was clean and disease free, so it wouldn't be a problem. I smiled like a pervert just thinking about the possibilities between Toni and me. The last thought I had before I laid down next to my wife was of Toni in a red thong and no bra preparing to make love to me.

As soon as I lay down, my wife turned over and hugged me. Nicole had unknowingly, but tragically interrupted the fantasy I was experiencing with Toni. Since my dream had come to an end, I willingly kissed my wife, and I began to caress her body. Just thinking about Toni had turned me on to the point that I was ready to have sex. I woke my wife and asked her if she wanted some.

Sounding very tired and despondent, she asked, "Now?"

Seeming as though I was some sort of freak, I responded with a desperate plea, as I said, "Yeah. Now."

I kissed my wife on the forehead and tried to set things in motion, but Nicole wasn't having it. "Nicole. A'ight? Wake up."

"No, baby," she said, pushing my hand away from her crotch. "In the morning."

After being rejected, I was irate. My blood pressure was raised to its boiling point. Had I been a cartoon character, you would have seen steam flowing from my skull. I didn't know what to do with all that pent-up energy. My hormones were going wild, and all I wanted to do was have an orgasm. I thought about going to the living room and popping in one of my porno tapes that I had hidden in my closet. I even considered sneaking downstairs and calling Scarlet to see if she would be willing to sneak into my basement and hit me off. Then I thought about just masturbating right next to my wife and putting sperm on her butt so she could know how much of a freak and a fiend I really was.

I just lay there vexed like crazy. I thought about praying to take the temptation away, but what good was that gonna do? After all, I wasn't even in the right frame of mind to pray.

Chapter Eight

Before I knew it, the month of May was just about over. I took LL into the shop for a haircut so he would be freshly dipped for the Memorial Day cookout my wife and I had planned. It's so funny because now I felt much more comfortable being in the shop with Toni as opposed to the first time. To me the whole atmosphere felt more relaxed and loose.

Toni seemed to be excited because I was around. Unlike the first time I had visited the beauty salon, Toni was very talkative around LL and me. She even picked up LL and paraded around the shop with him. It was kind of like she was showing him off as if he were her own son. She and LL had conversations ranging from what he'd been learning in day care to his favorite toys. Toni actually took time away from her customers to sit down and talk to LL, which is what made the situation seem odd but sincere. LL had game like his daddy, and he managed to slip in that his fifth birthday was in two weeks. Toni melted and promised to buy him whatever it was he wanted.

With Toni looking as sexy as a Soul Train dancer, I felt like a proud peacock who was basking in the sun. I sat back and just clocked Toni's beauty. I knew that in a matter of time I could claim her if I wanted to. And believe me, I wanted to.

As I sat and received another manicure, I noticed that Toni had on some slip-on sandals. They were the type that had a very slight heel to them. All of her toes were exposed, and there was a thong between her big toe. You could tell Toni was into cosmetology because even her toes had an air-brushed design. I couldn't wait to suck on them.

For the first time, I noticed a little ghettoness in Toni.

Toni began commenting on how addictive the Junior's cheesecakes are. She made certain to mention to another beautician that she and I had gone to Junior's the other night. She also seemed to need my confirmation on a lot of petty things. She would project her voice in the direction of where I was getting my manicure and ask, "Right, Lance?" or "Lance, am I lying?"

When I was done with my nails, Toni summoned me and wanted to see how my manicure looked. To my surprise she wasn't happy with the way it had turned out. She made sure to let the nail technician know it. I tried to let Toni know that it was all right, but she again, with her fetching ghettoness, was like, "Nah, it looks a'ight, but your nails are still a little suspect."

After rinsing the head of one of her customers, Toni grabbed me by the hand and sat me at an empty manicure table. She quickly went to work on my cuticles. When she was done buffing and plucking and stroking, I had to admit that my nails did actually look better. I just felt funny that Toni had kind of played the other technician in front of everybody. There wasn't any confrontation or anything, but Toni just embarrassingly voiced her opinion on the other technician's skills, which she felt weren't up to par.

Honestly, I just thought that Toni's actions were a ploy to let people know she was thinking about claiming me and that no one else had better have the same idea. I have to say that her actions definitely made me feel good. See, I knew that she didn't consciously realize what she was doing. Still, something was driving her to act the way she was.

By the time LL was finished with his haircut, it was around two o'clock in the afternoon. Once again I gave Toni a very unselfish tip. Toni took it upon herself to walk us to my car. While we were walking I asked, "So Toni, what are you doing for Memorial Day?"

Toni looked at me curiously and asked, "When is Memorial Day again?"

I responded, "I guess you ain't doing nothing, 'cause it's two days away—on Monday."

Toni laughed and said, "Oh, man. I was supposed to go on a boat ride but I forgot about it and didn't RSVP, so I don't even think I'll be going. Why did you ask?"

I answered, "Well, I'm having like a barbecue-slash-party at my house. You can come if you want."

Toni smiled and looked at me as if to request some more assurance.

"Toni, there's no problem. You can come."

I reached into my glove compartment and retrieved a piece of paper. On it, I wrote down my address as well as the directions to my house. I also wrote the time everything began, then I handed it to Toni.

Toni looked everything over.

"So you'll be there, right?" I asked.

Toni nodded, and said, "Yeah, I'll be there," then she pinched LL on his cheek, which was full of candy. "Cutie, can I have a good-bye kiss?"

I was playful but extremely jealous because Toni was requesting a kiss from LL and not from me. LL smiled as he planted the stickiest kiss on Toni's cheek. Toni then stepped away from the car and waved good-bye. As she walked off, I noticed that her butt was actually rounder than I had previously thought. I guess it looked that way because of the satin-looking white pants she had on.

One day, I thought. *One day.*

When I reached home, I realized my wife and I had to go to Costco so we could purchase the food for Memorial Day. Being that the Nets and Sixers were playing game seven of the eastern conference finals, the very last thing I wanted to do was to go food shopping. However, I didn't put up a fight. I just did what was responsible.

The next day I found myself in a familiar location—church— and as always, the sermon was very uplifting and at the same time convicting. The pastor was preaching about what good is faith if it is not backed up by deeds. He said many interesting things. For example, he asked everyone in attendance to raise their hands if they believed in God. As you would have guessed, everyone in the place proudly raised their hands. Then he asked everyone who believed in Jesus to raise their hands. Again everyone in attendance raised their hands.

After doing that little demonstration, he informed everyone that they now had something in common with Satan. People began looking at one another as they began feeling a bit uncomfortable. The pastor knew exactly what he was doing because now that he had everyone's attention, he told them, "That's good that you say you believe in God and the Son of God, but I'm going to tell everybody in this building something: Satan also believes in God. Yes, Satan believes in Jesus Christ. As a matter of fact, I would dare to say that Satan's belief in God is probably stronger than the belief that some of you sitting here today profess to have."

The pastor, who now had everyone riled up, went on to explain that there is a big difference in saying that one believes *in* God as opposed to *believing* God. I paused, and I began to think about what he was saying. After pondering for a few seconds, I realized how deep his statement was. The pastor asked us to turn to John 3:16, which is a very famous verse.

The pastor went on, "Now let me ask each one of you something. When it's all said and done, when Jesus returns, do you think that Satan will have eternal life? Or do you think Satan is going to perish?"

After asking the rhetorical question, he went on to explain John 3:16, which states that whoever believes in Jesus shall not perish but rather they will have eternal life. "Whoever believes!" He reiterated, "Satan believes so is he going to have eternal life or not?"

Of course, after having asked a radical question like that, everyone began to snicker and laugh because they were feeling uncomfortable. Then the pastor explained that people can be easily deceived into thinking that all it takes is a belief in God and you will be saved, but he warned that we can't take scriptures out of context. If we do, we are only setting ourselves up for a rude awakening in the end.

The pastor shouted, "God is not a liar. He has already condemned Satan. Satan will have eternal life, but it will be an eternity spent in hell. If you read your Bible and tie in other scriptures, you know the answer to whether or not Satan's belief in God alone is enough to grant him a quality eternal life. Obviously John 3:16 isn't talking about just *any* kind of belief in Jesus. It's talking about a belief that causes one to have settled attitudes about how they are now going to live a new life for Christ, due to the fact that they believe in the son of God." That belief, he explained, will be shown by the things you do.

The pastor, who had stopped shouting, was now calmly explaining that, the answers to the questions that deal specifically with areas in our everyday life will show the type of belief in Christ that one really has. He explained that anyone can profess a belief in Christ, just as Satan professes a belief in Christ. Yet as Satan is hell-bent on deceiving people and doing evil, we must not be like Satan and profess a belief in Christ while we continue to get drunk, while we continue to commit adultery, or for that matter, while some of us continue to procrastinate and have never been baptized.

Later that evening, my wife and I talked at length about what we had learned from the sermon. I was the first to admit that I was one who claimed to believe in God, but I wasn't truly willing to let Him be Lord of my life, in the sense that I wasn't willing to give up certain things that I craved. I admitted to Nicole that I did want eternal life. I also admitted that because of the evil things that I continued to allow myself to do, I wasn't sure if I'd actually make it to Heaven.

I didn't fully explain to my wife what I meant by "evil things," but obviously if I really loved and believed God, I wouldn't willfully lust the way I do. I wouldn't be so ready to commit adultery. If I truly believed Christ, then I would listen to His warnings that He gives me via the Bible. Especially when He warns and says that the people who do things to please their sinful desires will not inherit the kingdom of heaven, rather they only have a fearful expectation of the fires of hell.

Chapter Nine

Monday arrived, and Memorial Day was upon us. Our party, which had started at about five in the afternoon, had been underway for about two hours. There were many people who showed up to get their eat and drink on. The party was shaping up to be a nice event. Throughout the whole day, I had been wondering when and if Toni would actually show up. Deep down inside I knew that she would, but I was wondering how I was going to react in her presence.

I also was praying that Scarlet wouldn't pop up and make a surprise visit. See, I knew that Scarlet was the stalker type, so knowing her, she was probably camped out in her ride right down the block from my house with a pair of binoculars and a baseball bat, ready to attack. Believe me, the last thing I needed was for her to see me with any woman she didn't recognize because she probably wouldn't hesitate to disrespect Nicole and march her big round butt into my party with a Louisville Slugger and cause a confrontational scene. Hopefully she had to strip at a party somewhere. Being that it was Memorial Day and all, that was more than likely the case, so I figured I shouldn't get too anxious about any Scarlet drama unfolding.

My wife and I had debated over whether there should be any liquor at the party. Actually Nicole objected to it. She figured people didn't need liquor in order to have a good time, and she didn't want someone to get drunk and spoil everything. My wife also argued that many brothas and sistas from the church were going to be there, and it wouldn't look right for us to have a "worldly" party.

I went against my wife's objections. Although, summer didn't officially begin for another three weeks, I still felt that Memorial Day marked the beginning of the mood that the summertime brings. So how on earth were we going to have a party with a summer feel to it, yet have no liquor? I went out and purchased so many Heinekens that I had to place them inside of two garbage cans that were filled with ice.

The party was being held simultaneously in our backyard as well as in our basement. I took some of the liquor from the bar in the basement and placed it on one of the picnic tables that was in the backyard. I left the rest of the liquor in the basement so people would have open access to the drinks regardless of where they were.

Although Nicole was disappointed in my decision, she didn't let it stop her from having a good time. As a matter of fact, Nicole was the life of the party. She made sure there were no wallflowers. By the time 8:00 p.m. rolled around, people were filled with liquor, and everyone was partying out on the makeshift dance floor. The music was bangin'. I was hoping that none of the neighbors would get annoyed by the noise and call the cops.

We had huge blue and red flood lights in the backyard so everyone could see what they were doing. Way more people showed up than I expected. I didn't even know many of the faces that were at the party. When I walked to the front yard of my house I noticed that the block was filled with dou-ble-parked cars. I also noticed what looked like Toni walking up to the house. She didn't recognize me as she and a friend made their way to the backyard.

With Toni and her friend unknowing, I followed right behind them with a drink in my hand. When they reached the backyard, the deejay was blasting the old school smash Bad Boy Entertainment record, "Mo Money, Mo Problems." That's when I made my move and let Toni know that she was definitely in the right place. I walked right in front of Toni and started dancing with her. I began yelling, "Ah, yeah! Ah, yeah!" while happily raising both of my hands in the air, being careful not to spill my drink on her.

Toni began smiling and slowly bopping her head and mov-ing her body, trying to get in rhythm with me, then she held open her arms for a hug. I was still dancing and throwing my hands up in the air, so she just grabbed me and hugged me, nothing seductive or anything, just a hello kind of hug. Then she introduced me to her friend whose name was Kim.

Kim was a'ight, but she didn't really rank in the looks department. She was a four-drink kind of chick, which means that I would have to have at least four drinks before I would kick it to her.

While being introduced to Kim, I noticed my wife looking at me. I didn't want to act suspicious, so I just kept dancing with Toni. Trying to talk over the music while still dancing, I asked, "What took you so long?"

Toni explained that she and Kim had stopped at another barbecue before they came to my house.

As the deejay switched up the record and threw on another old Bad Boy smash hit, "The Benjamins," I playfully told Toni, "Y'all are so whack. Y'all should have come here first. Which party has it going on more? This one or the one you just left?"

Toni smiled and yelled into my ear, "Your party, of course. Y'all got it going on and the music is tight."

I stepped away from Toni and pointed her in the direction of where the food and drinks were. I told Toni that I would be all over the place, but I instructed them both to still have a good time.

I mingled and tried to talk to everyone to make sure that everybody was having a good time. I made sure to stay clear of my wife so she wouldn't ask me who Toni was. Before I knew it, Steve came up to me panting like a horse and emphatically asking, "Yo, Lance, who is that?" He was pointing in Toni's direction.

Bobbing my head to the music, I just held out my fist for a pound. Steve tapped my fist with his as I proclaimed, "Yeah, nigga. What? Am I the man or what? I told you all of that laughing was gonna come back and bite you in the ass."

Steve asked, "That's the chick?"

"Word is bond," I replied.

Steve put his hand out for a pound while simultaneously grabbing me and giving me a ghetto hug. He informed me that I was officially the man, which was something I already knew, but I didn't mind hearing it again. "Yo, you are the man, Lance. That chick is off the chain. She even looks better than

Scarlet. I mean the trunk isn't as big as Scarlet's, but man, she is bangin'," Steve commented.

I mackishly smiled and walked off.

Fortunately, as the night went on, no one got to the point where they were sloppy drunk. As the deejay threw on reggae music, I searched out my wife, and I began dancing real close to her.

Nikki immediately asked, "Lance, who was that woman I saw you dancing with earlier?"

I knew exactly who she was talking about, but I played dumb. "I don't know, baby. I mean I been dancing with a lot of people."

Nikki seemed a bit peeved. She then made it clear as to who she was talking about, as she explained, "I'm talking about that exotic-looking woman with the tight sarong skirt and the long hair, the one who was hugging all over you. Lance, don't play dumb. I know just about everybody here except for her, so who is she?"

"Oh, you mean Toni?" I said while trying to put water on the fire.

Nikki sarcastically mocked me and replied, "'Oh, you mean *Toni*?' Yeah, I mean Toni. Who is she?"

Nonchalantly I replied, "I told you about her. She's the lady who cuts LL's hair."

Nikki sucked her teeth and warned me to watch how I was dancing with her. I thought, *Ah, man, this is not what I need.* I wanted to make sure I squashed any friction right from jump street, so when I was out of my wife's sight I found Toni.

"You still enjoying yourself?" I asked.

"No doubt," Toni replied. "Some of my sorors are here."

"Oh, yeah? What sorority are you in?"

Toni explained that she was a Delta.

"You?" I questioned. "You look more like an AKA," I said as I playfully did the annoying AKA call. *"Skeeeee Weeeee!"*

Toni rolled her eyes and said, "Whateva."

Then I popped the question—or should I say I instructed Toni on what she would be doing next. "Toni, come meet my wife."

"Lance, I don't wanna meet your wife. Not now."

"Come on. Don't trip, 'cause it ain't nothing. She already told me she wanted to meet you."

Toni was hesitant, but she went along with me.

As we searched for Nikki, I felt as if I was bringing my fiancée home to meet my mother for the first time. I decided to check the basement. On the way, I stopped and introduced Toni to many of the guests. I also managed to introduce Toni to Steve, who was gawking at her like a dog in heat. With everyone she met, Toni gave her million-dollar smile and extended her right hand for a handshake as she would say, "Hello, nice to meet you."

So that Steve wouldn't totally jack up my flow, after introducing him to Toni I sent him to go and find Toni's friend Kim. I instructed him to keep her company as Toni and I continued searching for Nicole.

Finally, I spotted my wife, and I yelled for her. "Honey, come here."

Being that the music was also blasting in the basement, my wife didn't hear me, so Toni and I walked over to her.

"Nicole, I wanted to introduce you to Toni."

My wife's back was toward Toni and me. When she turned around, I noticed that she had a jar of barbecue sauce in her hand. I think I had kinda caught her by surprise.

"Oh," she said as she quickly looked Toni up and down, but not in a way to make her feel uncomfortable. My wife didn't say anything. I guess she was just trying to check Toni's steelo.

I was about to butt in and break the uncomfortable silence, but Toni used her charming ways and spared me the chore. Toni's gold-and-diamond bracelet slid from her wrist to about halfway down her hand as she extended her hand to Nicole for a handshake.

"Hi, I'm Toni. Nice to meet you, Nicole."

I didn't know what to expect from my wife, but she wasn't a bit out of character as she smiled and said, "Oh, so you're the one my son has been going crazy over."

Feeling very uncomfortable and not knowing what to say, like a dummy, I said, "Yeah, honey, Toni is the one who has been cutting LL's hair."

My wife paused, and she gave me a look that said, *No, duh.* Then she replied, "Yeah, Lance, I know that." To my surprise Nicole complemented Toni for doing such a good job with LL's hair. She also asked her if she was enjoying the party.

Maybe it was just in my head, but I felt that there was so much tension in the air that I could cut it with a knife.

Then, being as polite as possible, my wife excused herself from the introduction as she explained that she couldn't talk long because she had to check on the grill. She departed by telling Toni it was nice meeting her.

Toni responded, "Likewise."

After Nicole walked off, Toni seemed a bit surprised as she remarked, "Lance, your wife is very pretty."

"Yeah, I know," I replied.

I didn't want to make more of the situation than was necessary. I mean there probably was no tension or friction at all. Maybe it was just my guilt that I was feeling. Then I thought about it. I realized that I really had no reason at all for feeling guilty. I hadn't done anything with Toni.

As the night went on, everyone continued to have a good time. Although I was enjoying myself, I didn't appreciate being separated from Toni for the majority of the night. Hours seemed to be flying by, and before I knew it, it was getting pretty late. Unfortunately, most of our guests, including myself, had to go to work the next morning. I didn't want the party to end, but I knew I had to start winding things down at around one in the morning. I went to speak to the deejay, and I instructed him to go low key on the music so people would get the hint to leave. I advised him to start playing more R&B as opposed to the party jams with which he had been lacing everyone.

After speaking to the deejay, I noticed that Steve seemed to be really clicking with Kim. The two of them were hemmed up in a cozy corner of the backyard. Being that Kim was still there, I knew that Toni had to be around somewhere. I wanted to go look for her, but I also wanted to make sure to speak to as many of the people from the church as possible. I guess it was obvious to them that I had been acting totally different from the way I act when I'm in church. My actions made it evident that I wasn't trying to be warm with them at all. But at that juncture in the party, I definitely wasn't going to try and repent for the way I'd behaved. I just wanted to show my face to them and politic.

After politickin' and making my final rounds in the back-yard, I realized that Toni had to be in the basement 'cause I hadn't seen her outside. I headed straight there to scoop her up. When I reached the basement I instantly became insanely vexed. I saw Toni standing near the bar smiling and talking to some cat I didn't know. I had plans to march right up to Toni and snatch her up by the arm and ask her who the hell was she talking to and why her smile was so sparkling and wide. I began thinking, *What if the kid slipped a mickey in Toni's drink? What if he is an old boyfriend?* I wasn't trying to hear thoughts like that. I psyched myself to just walk up to the cat Toni was talking to and just punch him dead in his grill.

I couldn't believe how angry I was. It's not like I have a short fuse or anything like that. I just felt like I was a dog who'd stepped away from his food for a hot second and here was some other dog putting his mouth in my bowl.

Immediately, I stormed toward Toni, but then I stopped in my tracks. I didn't get any closer to Toni 'cause I knew I was about to do something I would probably regret later. After pausing, I realized that it would not have been wise at all to cause any kind of an altercation. Believe me, if I were to snuff this cat, it would have caused a major scene. I thought against resorting to violence because I had no idea who the cat was. For all I knew, the guy could have been Toni's cousin or what have you. Then I would've really played myself like a roach. Imagine me carrying on and all, only to find out that the guy really wasn't trying to kick game to Toni.

I yelled Toni's name from a distance. She looked up and spotted me. After putting her drink on the bar, she looked as if she told the guy she would be right back. Toni walked over to where I was standing. I had to remember to remain calm as I spoke quietly but with a sternness in my voice I asked, "Yo, who the hell is that nigga?"

Toni seemed shocked by the tone of my voice. She frowned and replied, *"Ill."*

I knew I had to quickly put my jealousy aside, so I smiled, trying to play it off, and said, "Ah, I got you. You thought I was trippin', right?"

Toni seemed unsure as to whether I was serious. She explained that the guy was a Q-Dog she'd known since her undergraduate days at Hampton University. She went on to explain how the Q-Dogs are the brothers to the Deltas. I played along like I was interested, but I really wasn't impressed at all by all the fraternity and sorority garbage. I'd been tired of hearing about that fraternity crap since I was nineteen years old.

I remarked, "Toni, you're making me jealous."

Toni, who seemed a bit open from the alcohol, laughed and hugged me as she seductively said, "Baby, you know I'm all yours, so why you trippin'?"

With the snap of a finger, my jealous rage had worn off and was replaced by a Kool-Aid smile. That hug turned me on something crazy. I knew I had to be very careful because I had no idea where my wife was or who was watching me. I quickly surveyed the basement, which was starting to empty out. I couldn't locate my wife, so I kept Toni close and gently caressed her back. In the worst way I wanted to take Toni upstairs to the guest room and try to get some. I had no idea if she would be with it, but I definitely was gonna try.

I took Toni by the hand and tried to persuade her as I said, "Come on, Toni. Let me show you the rest of my crib."

Toni seemed as if she was about to hesitate, but she didn't put up a fight as she followed right behind me. That corny, punk-ass Q-Dog nigga who was still at the bar waiting for Toni to return looked at the two of us and just stared as he picked his face up from off the floor. I figured that Toni probably hadn't objected to me taking her on a tour of the house for a couple of reasons.

See, she had been given my home number, plus she'd met my wife, she liked my kid, and she enjoyed my company. All of that had to make her feel very comfortable with an uncomfortable situation.

In a ploy to make it to the guest room as soon as possible, I hastily showed Toni the first floor, which included the living room, dining room, kitchen, and den. Toni nodded and commented how nice the furniture was and how spacious all the rooms were. I wondered if she was thinking thoughts similar to mine. I thought about how all of my material toys, such as my laced-out crib, could very easily become Toni's if she played the right cards.

We finally made it upstairs away from everyone. This is where I wanted to be so I could attempt to make my move. I continued with the tour as I showed Toni the bathroom and the master bedroom. Toni commented that she loved the satin sheets that were on my king-sized bed.

Like a pervert I said, "Yeah, I like satin too. It feels good when you make love on satin sheets."

Toni smiled and playfully punched me, but she didn't respond. We continued on the tour, and we next came upon my son's room. His door was closed, so I slowly opened it and peeked in. To my surprise LL was sound asleep. I didn't understand how he could sleep through all of the noise. He must have been drained from all of the dancing he had been doing. When he's on the dance floor, he swears he's P. Diddy. As I showed Toni LL's room, she remarked how peaceful LL looked as he slept. "Yeah, that's my dog," I replied as I closed the door to his room.

Our next destination was the guest bedroom. I continued to hold Toni's hand as we walked into the room. Jokingly, I told her that the guest room was where I often slept when I was in trouble with my wife. Acting very cautious, as if she was antic-ipating something, Toni didn't respond to my last comment. She just nodded. Then I softly closed the door and stood with my back against it. I lustfully stared at Toni, and I made sure not to say a word. I took Toni by both of her hands and guided her to me. After pulling her close to me I hugged her, closed my eyes, and attempted to kiss her. Toni resisted, and she quickly pushed away from me.

In a loud whisper, Toni asked, "Lance, what are you doing?"

I held Toni so that she couldn't walk away from me. I was careful not to hold her in such a way that would suggest I was trying to rape her or something.

"Come on, baby, just one kiss," I pleaded.

Toni, sounding a bit nervous, asked, "Lance, are you crazy? I can't be kissing you in your house with your wife downstairs."

I didn't reply. I just pulled Toni closer to me and began to kiss her. Magically, her reluctance disappeared. I could tell she wanted to get into a real deep kiss, but at the same time she showed signs of apprehension, which was probably why the kiss didn't last for as long as I'd wanted it to. Nor did it lead to where I wanted it to. We did manage to kiss for about thirty seconds, and I was aroused throughout the whole time. The kiss felt far better than I thought it would when I'd often fantasized about it. Toni's mouth was sweeter than a cherry Blow-Pop.

Toni backed away from me. She seemed as if she was breathing a little heavy as she said, "Lance, we can't be doing this."

Like I said, I understood Toni's apprehension, but I was more than ready and willing to lay Toni on the guest bed and take things to the next level. I was still blocking the door, and Toni demanded that I move out of the way so she could exit. Swiftly coming back to reality, I complied and moved out of Toni's way. She aptly walked out of the room. I wanted to run behind her, but I just let her go.

After she left the room, I slid down the wall of the hallway, which was just outside the guest room. I sat with my butt on the floor, and I let my knees rest near my chin. I thought about what I had just done. I knew that once again I had crossed that line that I'd promised myself and my wife I would never cross. To justify the wrong that I'd just done, I abruptly convinced myself that it wasn't me who had tried to kiss Toni. Rather it was all of the alcohol that I had been drinking that led me to do it. I sat for a few minutes, but I knew that I had to get back to the party and see the remaining guests off. I also knew that I would be up until about four in the morning with Nicole cleaning up, so I had to get a move on things.

Chapter Ten

More than a week had passed since I kissed Toni. During that time, the shame of what I'd done seemed to intensify with each passing day. Having known what I did, I was getting tired of looking my wife in the face and having her see me as a do-right man. I didn't want to feel depressed, but I couldn't help it. The guilt was no joke.

I didn't feel comfortable expressing to anyone how I was being eaten up inside. I could have spoken to Steve, but all he would have given me was more head-shaking laughter. With the way I was feeling, I really was in no mood to be laughed at. I hadn't spoken to Toni in the past week. In fact, I hadn't spoken to her since the party. That, too, was also ripping a tear into my heart so big that I found myself in the booty bar three times within the past week. When I was in the bar watching the sexy women take off their clothes, it was like all of my worries would leave me. I wanted to pay the biggest butt dancer two hundred and fifty dollars to go to a hotel with me. Yet, I didn't want any sex from her. All I wanted was for her to sit with no clothes on and listen to my problems.

I actually propositioned a couple of dancers with my offer, but sadly I had no takers. The dancers explained to me that they made way more than two-fifty a night, so if I wanted some takers, I would definitely have to up my price. They also didn't believe that I wanted to go to a hotel "just to talk." They assumed that once we got there, my plans would change. That certainly could not have been further from the truth. I simply settled for inexpensive lap dances. It was funny because as soon as I would leave the strip clubs, my depression would return. When I would reach home I would continue to combat the depression with masturbation.

During the week, Scarlet acted as a good outlet for me to release some of my depression. I called her and purposely patched up some of the comments that I had made to her. I was so stupid because I knew that I was only leading her on even further. Plus, I knew that I was only setting my life up for more drama. Things were starting to get a little bit thicker with Toni, so I should have definitely stayed away from Scarlet, but I just couldn't. I mean, regardless if I was trying to break up with her and distance myself from her, I still felt like I needed her during that week.

Yeah, even with my trips to the booty bar, my depression, and with masturbating almost every day during the past week, I somehow found the time to have sex with Scarlet like four times. The sex wasn't that psycho, love-hate type. It was much more ghetto-passionate. Scarlet and I had finally been able to sit and talk like sane human beings. I guess that was because there was no talk of me leaving her.

Scarlet had been working real hard on this big project in order to get her Web site, www.braziliancoochie.com, fully completed and ready to launch. Since I have always had a thing for business, I was able to give her some very helpful insight on how to effectively market her Web site and totally capitalize on the hardcore Internet porn industry. Being that the two of us were able to connect on the whole Web site project, it sort of helped to distract us from all of the drama we had been going through as of late. I knew Scarlet needed me, and I definitely felt like I needed her, but I would be a fool if I tried to juggle three women, God, and a son. Although I didn't remind Scarlet of my decision to split from her, I knew that after the week was over, I would have to revert to my disappearing act and continue to distance myself from her.

On Monday evening my wife finally confronted me about my gloomy mood.

"Lance, what's up with you? I know something is bothering you—I mean, you haven't lifted weights this whole week, you're not eating as much. Something is bothering you."

"Nothing's wrong, Nikki. I'm okay."

"You sure?"

"Yeah, I'm sure."

I wanted to talk because I knew that just talking about anything would help my comatose state of mind. I just didn't want to be specific as to what was bothering me, therefore I remained silent.

Fortunately, my wife was persistent as she looked at me with compassion and replied, "Talk to me, baby. What's on your mind?"

Reluctantly, I decided to give in and I explained, "Well, I don't want to be making a big deal out of anything, but do you remember last week when you saw me dancing with Toni?"

"Yes, I remember. Why?"

I started to spill the beans right there, but all week long I couldn't even bring myself to think about how my wife would react if I told her I'd kissed Toni. So now I certainly didn't want to witness her reaction first hand. I took my train of thought onto another track. "Well, were you jealous?" I asked. "I mean was it all right for me to be with Toni?"

"Lance, you know that I trust you. I mean, I wouldn't even think twice about leaving you in the room with my sista if she were half naked."

I liked the thought of that suggestion. I was gonna joke and ask my wife if we could actually test out that experiment, but I had to remain serious as I interjected, "Well, it just seemed to me that you were a little peeved at me. I just don't want you to be thinking that I would be flirting with some woman right in our own house. I love you too much for that. I know you know all this, but I want us to always be able to speak about anything that is bothering us, no matter how insignificant it may seem."

Nikki added, "Lance, you mean to tell me that you were feeling down because you thought that I was jealous of you dancing with another woman?"

I lied as I simply replied, "I guess so, yeah."

Nikki defensively replied, "Well, like I've always told you, I trust you, Lance. I didn't have a problem with you dancing with Toni. It's just that she's a beautiful woman, and I had no idea who she was. See, I trust you, but these women out here are trifling. People say that men are dogs, but women are just as bad."

"Oh, so you didn't have a problem with Toni?" I asked.

Nicole explained, "No, I did not, nor do I have any reason to have a problem with Toni. All it was was that I didn't know her, that's all. After you introduced me to her, I had no problems with her. I mean from what I saw, she seems to be a nice lady."

I replied, "A'ight, just making sure that we're always on the same page."

Nicole added, "By the way, Lance, why don't you invite Toni to church? You should find out if she's saved. Because honestly, that's the way I'm learning to look at people, in more spiritual terms."

It was like magic. By just talking, I was able to slowly but surely slip out of my depressive coma. I knew that my wife was the most beautiful human being in terms of qualities and character that I had ever met. Here I was messing with Toni right under her nose, and she was asking me whether the chick was born again. I felt a bit contrite when she asked me about Toni's spiritual condition, which was something I really hadn't pondered. I definitely wanted to dodge the question about whether Toni was saved. There was no way in the world that I was gonna invite my mistress to church. If I were to do that, I might as well have applied for membership as one of Satan's demons.

In response to my wife's question, I stated, "Well, I don't know if she's saved or not. I mean I don't know her that well."

My wife shot back, "Well, if you felt you knew her well enough to invite her to the party, you could have just as easily invited her to church. Lance, you have to start learning to be more evangelistic."

I readily responded, "Evangelistic? I'm not trying to look like no Jehovah's Witness."

My wife shook her head. "Don't worry about how you're gonna look. It's not about trying to look like somebody. You should be reaching out to lost people, trying to tell them the gospel. Forget about the Jehovah's Witnesses. In the Bible, Jesus tells us to be evangelistic."

For good reasons, I didn't respond to my wife. I mean, I didn't feel like debating religion. Man, I was trying to get over the depression that was caused by my doggish mentality, and my wife was lecturing me on becoming the next Billy Graham or Creflo Dollar. At that point, I really didn't need to be reminded of my weak Christian faith.

Although I didn't care for the religious twist that the conversation had taken, the quick discussion with my wife did manage to cheer me up a great deal. After all, it appeared to me as if Nicole was giving me the green light to be with Toni. I mean, she did say that she wasn't jealous of the relationship I had with Toni. My wife is even openly secure with the fact that Toni is a gorgeous woman. So to me, it was like Nikki had okayed the attention that I'd given Toni at the party. Man, I felt so stupid. All week long I'd been having suicidal thoughts, and as soon as I talked to my wife about the situation, I found out that she's secure with the whole ordeal.

"Nicole, you know what I was just thinking?"

"No. What were you thinking?"

I answered, "I was thinking . . . Nah, actually I should say that I was admiring you because I know the loyalty that you show me is genuine. It's authentic. Nothing or no one can compare to you, Nicole. To me, it's like that's one of the reasons why I love you so much. Come here. Give me a hug."

As my wife beamed, I hugged her tight. I wasn't just dropping her some line of BS. I meant every word that came out of my mouth as I exclaimed, "Baby, I'm so glad that you're not an insecure woman." My wife and I began to kiss each other very deeply as I jokingly asked, "Wanna go make a baby?"

Nikki giggled and grabbed me by the hand and led me upstairs where we made love on our green satin sheets.

Chapter Eleven

Wednesday night, on our way home from Bible class, my wife and I stopped at Carvel's to get some ice cream for LL. He is mad cute, but I am convinced that he is the clumsiest kid I have ever seen. Not once, but twice, after purchasing our ice cream and in the process of leaving the store, LL managed to drop his ice cream cone, sprinkles and all, splat right on the floor. I warned him that I was gonna buy him one more cone and he had better not drop it or he wouldn't be getting another one.

I didn't want to hold the cone for him because I wanted him to learn independence. It was a scary ordeal watching him perform a Houdini act of licking the cone while walking to the car all in one shot. Fortunately for LL, it wasn't three strikes and you're out. He made it to the car with the ice cream running all over his right arm, but he was happier than a pig in slop.

As we drove home, my pager, which was on vibrate, went off. When we came to a red light I looked at it, and it had 911 displayed along with a phone number that I didn't recognize. As I reached for my cellular phone, I thought that it was probably Steve giving me an update on the NBA championship game. He was probably at some chick's house, sitting pretty like a fat cat. I knew that all he wanted to do was rub in my face the fact that I was missing the game because I had to go to Bible class. Although I didn't want to hear any of Steve's sarcasm, when we came to a red light I quickly dialed the number. After two rings, I heard a female's voice on the other end.

"Hello, Lance? Can you talk? This is Toni."

I had to not show my excitement to my wife. I was cool and collected as I said, "Yo, what's up? Listen . . . um . . . actually I'm driving right now. I'll call you back when I get home, a'ight?"

Toni replied, "Okay, but make sure you call me."

"Yeah, a'ight, no doubt," I replied.

Yo, I put the cell phone down and I really thought I was about to have an orgasm in my pants. Toni actually called me before I called her. Either she was calling me to tell me she was upset with me, or the kiss got her hooked. Even though I hadn't spoken to her since the party, which was about a week and a half ago, I doubted that she was upset. If she was, she wouldn't have called at all.

"Lance, who was that?" my wife asked.

"Oh, that was Steve. He was calling to give me an update on the game," I replied.

When we reached home, we entered the house like one big happy family. I was starving and couldn't wait to eat. In addition to being hungry, I also knew that eating would help take my mind off the fact that Toni was waiting for my phone call. As my wife and I ate, we talked about the lesson we had learned in Bible study class. I was into our conversation, but at the same time, I was also chomping down my food so I could get away from the table as soon as possible.

When I was done eating, I was easily able to jet from my wife. I used the excuse that I had to take LL up to his room to put him to bed. After I'd done that, I made my way to the solace of the basement where I knew I would be able to get my talk on with Toni. But of course, this had to be one of those nights that my wife wanted to stay up and talk. I was pissed off because I couldn't wait for her to go to bed and leave me the hell alone.

Nicole, who was smiling, came down the basement stairs and said, "Guess what, honey?"

Unaware what my wife had up her sleeve, I nonchalantly asked, "What's up?"

Sounding very excited my wife replied, "Well, I thought about how I don't spend enough time with you watching sports, so I'ma stay up with you tonight and watch the rest of the game. I've been thinking, and you're right, me watching the games is the only way I'm ever gonna learn to really get into it on the same level that you're into it."

Damn! Damn! Damn! Damn! I thought, wanting to scream. After all the invitations in the past my wife had not accepted, why did she have to choose this particular game to wanna watch? *Why? Damn!* Now I knew I would have to sit and explain to her every little detail about the game. Explaining sports to Nicole is something I have longed to do. I want us to be husband-and-wife basketball fanatics. Had it been any other night, I would have fallen in love with her enthusiastic suggestion. It was just that I had to call Toni as soon as possible.

Luckily for me, when I turned on the game, I realized that it was nearing the end of the third quarter, which meant that I only had about thirty minutes or so before it would be over. My wife was in true student form. The only thing she needed to do was whip out a pad and a pencil in order to take down notes. She began right away with the damn questions. I hated doing it, because I knew I would probably turn her off from basketball forever, but I burst my wife's bubble right away.

As soon as she started with the questions, I interrupted her and said, "Baby, see, let me explain. . . . You can't be asking questions now. The game is too close. I have to concentrate or else my team is gonna lose. This is an important game, a'ight?"

Sounding like a sweet, innocent kid, my wife asked, "Well, how am I ever gonna learn if I don't ask questions?"

Trying to brush her off, I said, "Shhh, be quiet."

After seeing my team make a crucial mistake, I barked at Nicole, "See. Because you were talking, my team just made a costly mistake."

My wife sucked her teeth in disappointed rejection.

I explained, "Baby, don't take it personal. That's just how it is. This is a big game."

I could tell Nicole was mad. Whenever she's mad, she becomes as cold as ice. She won't touch a nigga, she won't speak to a nigga or anything. Nicole was definitely mad as she sat there for ten minutes, faking like she was interested. But as soon as a commercial came on, she abruptly removed herself from the couch. Without saying a word to me, she walked upstairs.

As she walked out of the room, I thought, *Well, it's about got-damn time.* I knew she wanted me to chase after her and say sorry and all that garbage, but not tonight. I couldn't wait for her to leave.

My wife had been upstairs for only five minutes, but I felt that was long enough. I quickly rushed and called Toni. Her phone rang about five times, then her answering machine came on. Feeling disappointed, I left a message as I said, "What's up, honey? It's Lance. Just returning your call. Sorry it took so long for me to get back to you, but . . . um . . . just call me when you get in. A'ight?"

Realizing that Toni wasn't home, I decided to take a chance and try the number from earlier that was in my pager. I dialed it, and it rang a couple of times. Toni picked up. Fortunately, I didn't have to worry about my wife overhearing me because I had the sound from the game drowning out what I was saying. When I began to speak, I was trying to be as apologetic as possible. "Toni, I'm sorry. Listen, I was dead wrong for trying to kiss you. I mean I respect you more than that. It's just that I had too much to drink that night. You understand, right?"

My heart nervously pounded as I waited for Toni to respond.

Toni replied, "Lance, listen. First of all, I accept your apology. I wasn't exactly upset with you, per se. It's like . . . well . . . it's just like I've been telling you. We need to sit down and talk about what's been going on."

Just knowing that I wasn't on the hook for my actions led me to want to thank Toni. I thanked her as if she had just saved me from a raging river that was about to take me under. "Toni, whatever you say. The sooner we talk, the better. What's up with tomorrow?"

Toni replied, "Tomorrow is fine."

I really didn't know what to say, so I asked the common question. "So how have you been? How's Kim?"

"I've been all right. I was wondering when you were gonna call me or if you were ever gonna call me at all. . . . As for Kim, she's chillin'. Matter of fact she told me to tell you that she had a good time at your party."

"Oh, word, that's good. What about you? Did you enjoy yourself?"

I could tell Toni was trying to sound very serious, but I knew she was just as happy to be hearing my voice as I was to be hearing hers. I made sure not to address her comment about me not having called her. I could sense Toni was smiling as she said, "Yeah, you know I enjoyed myself."

I replied, "Good. That's real good."

Toni was starting to lose that serious tone of voice that she had when we began our conversation. She added, "Lance, baby, it is hot as hell in my house."

I asked, "Are you in your crib? I just called you and left a message on your machine."

Toni replied, "Nah, I'm on my cell piece."

I laughed and playfully responded, "Check you out. Sounding all ghetto. 'Nah I'm on my cell piece . . .' What do you know about a cell piece?"

Toni laughed as she explained, "Nah, but for real, I'm just driving around with my convertible top down. I'm trying to cool off before I go to sleep. It's just too hot in my house."

"Well, what's up with the AC?"

Toni explained that was the problem. The AC wasn't working.

I advised, "Listen, if you want, we can talk at your house tomorrow, and I'll fix your AC for you while I'm there."

Toni didn't believe I was for real, and she responded, "Yeah, right."

"I'm serious. Do you have central air, or do you have separate air conditioners in each window?"

Toni replied, "Yeah, we have central air but nothing is coming out of the vents."

"I'll take care of you. I'll hook things up," I assured her.

Shortly after that our conversation ended, I made my way upstairs where I found my wife greasing her scalp and rolling her hair.

Nikki rudely exclaimed, "Lance, if you didn't want me around while you were watching your game, all you had to do was tell me."

I purposely ignored Nikki. In my mind I felt like telling her to shut the hell up. She knew where she could go for all I cared. Nikki glared at me while she continued to sit on the bed fixing her hair. I don't think that she was upset, but I know that by me ignoring her it didn't help to diffuse the situation. I stripped naked and made my way to the shower. Just to irk Nicole, I made sure to leave my clothes in a ragged pile right where I'd stepped out of them. As I walked out of the bedroom and headed toward the bathroom, my frustrated wife yelled, "Lance, pick up your clothes and stop being lazy. I'm tired of picking up after you."

That was the reaction I wanted. I mean, if I had to be frustrated because I couldn't stay on the phone and kick it with Toni, I was gonna do my best to make sure my wife was just as frustrated.

I stopped dead in my tracks and yelled back, "What did you say?"

Nicole screamed, "I said pick up your clothes."

I reiterated, "Nah, nah! Before that. Did you say you're tired of me?" I knew that wasn't what Nicole said. I was just trying to create an atmosphere of drama. I continued, "Nicole, I know you didn't say you were tired of me. Matter of fact, I don't give a damn, 'cause I'm tired of you too, bitch."

After saying that I stormed into the bathroom and slammed the door so hard that the entire house shook. Nicole became enraged, and she bolted to the bathroom door and demanded that I unlock it.

"Lance, open this door right now! Lance . . . Lance . . . Lance, you're gonna apologize for cursing at me. Open this door."

I knew my wife had truly blown her top. She sounded madder than I'd ever heard her sound and for good reason I guess. I mean, that was the first time in my life I had ever cursed at her. Although she was highly upset, I made matters much worse by running the water in the shower. That move on my part sent a signal that I was ignoring her. However, it only caused her dramatic screams to get louder and louder.

After being in the shower for two minutes, I no longer heard her yells. I guess she'd worn herself thin from them. It's wild because before I purposely started the confrontation. I wasn't the least bit upset at first, but although I knew this whole argument had no basis or substance, I was really starting to get upset. After all, I ran the show in my house. Nicole was way out of line when she'd raised her voice to me.

I continued to wash my body, and I became angrier by the minute. All I knew was that when I was done showering, Nicole had better slow her roll. I thought, *If she keeps nagging me she's gonna get smacked before the night is over. Word.*

I stepped out of the shower and dried off. I continued to prep my mind for battle. I stopped moving around for a moment so I could listen closely to what it was that I thought I'd heard. *Yup, I was right.* I heard my son crying in the background. His tears didn't help the atmosphere, as I thought, *What did Nicole do to him?*

I wrapped a towel around my waist and violently ripped open the bathroom door.

Heading in the direction of LL's room, I yelled, "LL! LL, where are you? Why are you crying like you've lost your mind?"

When I made it to the entrance of his room, I saw my son sitting up in his bed being consoled by his mother. "Nicole, what did you do to him?" I rudely asked.

Nicole barked back, "What did I do? The question is what the hell is wrong with you?"

I screamed, "Nicole, let me explain something to you. I wear the pants in this house, and you better start respecting me."

As we raised our voices at each other, LL tried to mediate the situation. "Stop," he cried as he hugged Nicole as hard as he could. "Mommy, stop. Stop, Daddy."

All it took was the sound of LL's voice to snap me out of what felt like a hypnotized and psychotic state. I pulled my son from Nicole's arms and hugged him.

As his precious tears rolled down my bare chest, I caressed his back and assured him that everything was okay. I knew he was crying because he had never seen the two people he trusts and loves the most go at it like cats and dogs.

It was at that point I realized how stupid my actions had been. I'd made LL feel that same hopelessness that I used to as a child when I would witness my father verbally and physically abusing my mom.

Nicole kissed LL and reassured him that everything was gonna be all right. Sensing that the battle was over, LL began to calm down. Nicole made her way out of the room, but before she left she gave me a stare of death and said, "I hope you know why he's scared and crying like he is."

Nicole made her way to our bedroom, but I decided to stay with my son. I put him on the bed and placed him under his Superman sheets. LL didn't ask any questions, and he looked so peaceful as he began to fall asleep. I kissed him on his cheek and turned out the lamp in his room. His night light was on, and I just couldn't get myself to leave his room. I pulled one of his little chairs from the corner of his bedroom and sat and watched him as he looked so serene in his sleep.

Many thoughts came into my head as I watched my son. I was hoping some of the serenity of the room would wear off on me. I knew I wasn't gonna sleep in the same bed with my wife. I probably would stay in LL's room and sleep. As I stared at LL, I began to talk to God. With all that I had in my soul, I prayed that LL wouldn't grow up to see women as objects that feed and satisfy his lustful cravings. I hoped to myself that LL wouldn't even have the problem of lust like I do. I knew he would grow up to enjoy sex as just about every human being does, but hopefully he wouldn't let the need for it to dominate his every thought like his father.

Tears were on the verge of welling up in my eyes due to the sad fact that just the other day I was feeling deeply depressed because I had kissed another woman. In fact, on Monday, and all of last week, I didn't even know if my depression was a result of the fact that I loved my wife and I knew I'd done wrong, or if it was because I had an uncontrollable desire to be with other women.

I definitely didn't want that depressive state of mind to creep back up on me. Sadly enough, I knew it probably would return if I again chose to let days pass without speaking to Toni, and Scarlet for that matter. Deep down, I knew that if I wanted to save my marriage and my soul, then I would have to muster up the willpower to fully avoid all contact with Toni. Yet, like a drug addict, I knew that it was the rushes I received from Toni and Scarlet that were making me feel sane. So how was I gonna just put an end to the cravings of the cocaine-like rushes that were causing a war to be waged in my mind and producing all kinds of irrational actions on my part?

Chapter Twelve

When morning rolled around, I woke LL up and got him dressed and ready for the day care center. My wife was already awake and dressed. She hadn't cooked any breakfast, and being that she was ready to walk out the door, I doubted that she had any plans on preparing any. I knew she was still upset from the previous night, but I couldn't believe that she was gonna just walk out of the house without speaking to me.

Nicole didn't even acknowledge me when she saw me. I said good morning to her, but she was as cold as ice and didn't return my greeting. She whisked past me and searched out LL's whereabouts. She found him at his usual location, in front of the TV. Nicole kneeled down to LL's eye level and said, "Mommy is leaving for work now, but you be good today and don't give your teachers a hard time, okay?"

LL who was deep into his cartoons didn't really look my wife in the face as he answered, "Okay."

Nicole added, "Now give Mommy some suga."

LL finally looked in my wife's direction as he wrapped his arms around Nicole's neck and gave her a kiss on the cheek. Nicole, who looked like a stunning woman of corporate America in her skirt suit, again walked past me without acknowledging my presence. Only this time she kinda bumped me as she brushed by me.

"Good morning to you, too, Nicole," I said.

Nicole gave no reply, and she headed straight out the door. I slipped on my slippers and ran out the house after her. When I caught up to her, I grabbed her by the arm and said, "All right, Nicole. I'm sorry."

Nicole didn't look me in the face, but as she tried to twist loose from my grip she replied, "Hmm, uh, okay."

I hated grabbing Nicole in the manner in which I did, but what else was I to do to let her know that I was really sorry?

"See Nicole, I said I was sorry and you're not even acknowledging my apology. That's not right."

Nicole responded, "Lance, can you let go of my arm? You're gonna make me miss my train."

As I gave in to her demand, I lifted both of my palms face up and said, "Fine. But don't say I didn't try to apologize."

I got no reply from Nicole. She prepared to unlock her car door, and I didn't want to give up, so I tried to play on her feelings by adding, "See, we shouldn't have even gone to sleep last night if we were angry with each other. Honey, I don't want us to go to work still upset. I mean what if something happens to you today and I never see you again? I wouldn't be able to live with myself knowing you didn't forgive me. Or what if something happens to me?"

Nicole finally looked in my direction, but she still didn't say a word. She started up her car and drove off to the train station. I was left standing there like a lamenting fool.

One thing that I wasn't going to do was let this whole argument thing keep my mind bogged down with worry all day long. I'm the master at mind games and mental abuse, so I knew exactly what game Nicole was trying to play.

The remainder of my day flowed on as usual. I thought about Toni and wondered how things would go when I saw her later on in the day. I had a gut feeling that Toni would want to discuss things like how wrong she feels for wanting to be with me. I also knew that I would kick some garbage as to how I really care for her and how I will do whatever I have to in order to prove it to her. Yeah, it didn't take a rocket scientist to know what we would talk about. I just hoped that I would be able to get over with my game.

As my work day whisked by, I decided to go back to the McDonald's where I had met the young girl Carmen to see if she was working. On my lunch break, although I wasn't hungry, I headed straight for a Big Mac. When I reached McDonald's I decided not to go to the drive-thru because I wanted to go inside and get a better visual of Carmen. After I ordered my Big Mac and Sprite, I asked the cashier if Carmen was around. To my disappointment I was told that she wasn't scheduled to come in until 5:00 p.m. I simply advised the cashier to tell Carmen that Lance had stopped by to see her. As I walked out of the restaurant and got back into my truck, I convinced myself that I would in fact give Carmen a call sometime in the near future. While eating my food, I was thinking of how much easier it would be to deal with a much younger and innocent chick like Carmen. It would be a piece of cake.

The Big Mac filled me up. I wanted to relax for about five more minutes so the food could digest, but I remembered that I also wanted to send Nicole some flowers. Actually, I didn't want to spend the money on flowers, but I was like hey, I haven't surprised my wife like that in a while and plus, it would be a good way to get back in good with her. My break was ending soon, so I quickly called 1-800-FLOWERS and placed my order.

I knew that I had to have the card read something spiritual. A scriptural passage would definitely brighten my wife's mood, and it would let her think that maybe I was trying to be more focused on God. I knew which passage I wanted to accompany the flowers, but I wasn't exactly a walking Bible so I didn't have the passage memorized. I told the operator from 1-800-FLOWERS that I would have to call her right back.

I had left my cell phone at home, so I hustled from the pay phone that I was using and went back to my work truck. I knew that somewhere in my truck, amid all of the filthy pornographic books, that I had a pocket Bible laying around. I found it and turned to the "love chapter" of 1 Corinthians: 13 which reads:

> Love is patient, love is kind. It does not envy, it does not boast, it is not proud. It is not rude, it is not self-seeking, it is not easily angered, it keeps no record of wrongs. Love does not delight in evil but rejoices with the truth. It always protects, always trusts, always hopes, always perseveres. Love never fails.

After reading that passage I hurried and closed the Bible, and I ran back to the pay phone and put in my order. When I was done placing the order, in my head I was like, Yeah. See I knew that after my wife read the card, along with the smell of fresh roses, that I would be in like Flynn. That scripture said exactly what I wanted to say, but only much better than I could have ever said it. What I really needed to do was memorize more verses and have them ready and at my disposal for times when I want to kick some serious game to my wife. Man, if I ever started spitting out Bible verses, Nicole would be all over me.

It couldn't have been more than fifteen minutes from the time I was done ordering the flowers for my wife when my pager went off. I recognized the number right away. It belonged to International Hair Designs. Without delay I became ecstatic. Unfortunately, I was in the middle of a job. I was in the process of conducting a gas leak investigation, but I felt the urge to neglect my duties and find the nearest pay phone. Fortunately, I was sane enough as to not risk a gas explosion just to satisfy my insatiable urges.

The gas leak investigation was taking much longer than usual. After twenty more minutes passed, my pager went off again. Once more, International Hair Designs' phone number was in my pager but this time it also had 911. I became intensely impatient. I rushed through the paperwork that went along with the gas leak investigation, and I made a somewhat confident conclusion that the gas leak was confined and not an imminent and dangerous threat. As quickly as I could, I made my way to a pay phone and called Toni.

After the owner of the shop picked up and relayed the phone to Toni, I heard Toni say, "Well, it's about time."

I replied, "Yo, I'm sorry. I was in the middle of a job when you paged me, and I couldn't get to a phone right away."

Toni informed, "Yeah, I called your cell phone but no one picked up."

"Oh, nah, I left the house this morning and forgot to bring it with me," I explained.

Toni, in her sweet, soft-sounding voice, replied, "That's all right, as long as you're okay. Listen, so am I still gonna see you today?"

"Of course," I answered. Knowing that I had to be home this evening in order to put in brownie points with Nicole, I added, "Toni, it would really help if I could see you when I get off work, say around five."

Toni responded, "Yeah, five o'clock is cool. I'll just leave the shop early. Plus, it's slow today, so that'll give me another excuse to leave."

After a brief pause I was like, "A'ight, so I'll see you at five, at your crib, right?"

Toni replied, "Yeah. You still gonna see if you can fix the AC for me, right?"

"Yeah, that's not a problem."

Toni tried ending the call, but I reminded her that she had never told me where she lives.

She began laughing, "Oh, I'm sorry. I didn't even realize that."

I have to admit that I felt like I'd been to Toni's house before. I know she forgot to give me her address because she, too, was probably feeling mad comfortable with me as if she'd known me for years. After letting Toni know that I had a pen, she gave me her address, 99-01 Chevy Chase Road.

"You live in Jamaica Estates?" I asked, sounding kind of surprised.

Toni answered, "Yeah." Then she started giving me directions on how to get there.

Being that I work for Con Edison, I was forced to know just about every street in Brooklyn, as well as every street in Queens. I interrupted Toni, "You don't have to give me directions. I know how to get there."

"Oh, okay, so I'll see you there. Just ring the bottom bell," Toni instructed.

When work ended I sped to the day care center and retrieved LL. After picking him up, I dropped him at Tiffany's house and asked her if she could watch him for about an hour or so. I explained that I had to run by someone's house to fix their air conditioning. As usual, my sista had no problem with watching him.

I would have preferred to have gone home, taken a shower, and changed before I went by Toni's, but being married didn't afford me that luxury. Like me, my sista also lives in Cambria Heights, so I was only about ten minutes away from Jamaica Estates. I was actually surprised to be going there. That would have been one of the last neighborhoods that I would have guessed that Toni lived in. See, Jamaica Estates is a very high-class wealthy neighborhood. Not only that, but it's a predominantly white and Jewish area. Many dignitaries like politicians, lawyers, and CEOs live in the Estates. The most famous resident is probably Fred Trump, Donald Trump's father.

As I weaved my way through the curved, tree-lined streets, I marveled at the mansions and the manicured lawns. It was nearing five o'clock, so I was right on time. I made my way onto Chevy Chase Road, and I looked for Toni's address. I came upon a very immaculate-looking white brick house with huge pillars that reminded me of the white house in Washington, D.C. The lawn had statues and water fountains and the whole look just looked like new money. Being that the day was bright and sunny, it only added to the beauty of the house. I was sure that this was the right crib because I saw Toni's convertible parked in the circular driveway.

Since I had on my blue-collar attire, I felt a bit insecure. But I wasn't sweating it 'cause I knew that I had dough. Maybe not enough to live in Jamaica Estates, but my bank account held mad weight. I parked my car along the curb, got out, and after carefully surveying the grounds, I made my way to the front door. As I got closer, I was feeling nervous. I felt as though I was going to pick up my prom date or something. When I reached the door I gathered myself, took a deep breath, exhaled, and rang the bottom bell.

After waiting for a minute or so, Toni, who had come from the rear of the house, snuck up behind me, jumped up and grabbed me in a headlock. Being that she caught me off guard, I lost my balance and fell on my butt, yet Toni still had me in the headlock.

Toni began asking, "Yeah, what's up now? What's up, punk?"

I couldn't help but laugh as I tried to pull her arms from around my neck. The scene was cute because Toni was squeezing with all her strength, and she really thought she was doing something.

"Yeah, you're too weak to break loose, right?" Toni asked, trying to sound as if she was in a schoolyard scuffle.

Still laughing but sounding as if I was being strangled, I said, "You got it. You got it."

Toni squeezed tighter as she demanded to know, "You give? Hah? You give?"

I was still laughing as I managed to say, "Yeah, I give. I give. . . ."

Then Toni loosened her grip and pushed me in my head. I lay on the ground looking up at the sun while laughing. Toni, too, was laughing.

"Toni, you crazy," I exclaimed as I picked myself up from off the ground.

When I got up, I became instantly aroused. I noticed that Toni had on some tight Daisy Duke shorts, slippers, a tank top, and she also had her jet-black sumptuous hair pulled back. I made sure not to make any lewd comments about Toni's shorts. Toni stared at me and smiled. She was breathing a little hard as she asked, "So what's up, Mista Lance?"

I licked my lips like LL Cool J, smiled, and while squinting from the bright sunlight, I said, "Nothing. Same ol' same ol'. But yo, I am digging this crib."

Toni asked a stupid question, but I guess it was rhetorical, "Oh, so you like it?"

"No doubt," I replied.

Toni took me on a tour of the house. She started by showing me around the outside, which had all of the extras, like a tennis court and in-ground swimming pool. We talked as we walked, and Toni explained that her father was a surgeon and that her mother was a very successful real estate broker.

As we made our way inside, I viewed the plush marble floors and the very expensive furniture. Seeing how Toni was living on a whole other level material wise, I felt like I had played myself by trying to impress her when I'd showed her around my house. Compared to Toni's crib, my house, as nice as it is, was like comparing a Hyundai to a Mercedes.

One thing I quickly noticed was that Toni was not joking when she said it was hot in her house. I was only in there for about two minutes, and I was already beginning to sweat. I cut Toni off as she was explaining to me who was in the pictures that were on her mantel in the living room.

"Toni, you wasn't lying. It is beaming up in this piece."

Toni replied, "You see how I'm dressed, right? I told you it was hot up in here."

I wanted to let her know that she didn't have to keep her clothes on just because I was there. But again, I didn't want to mess things up with a coarse joke.

"Toni, where's the thermostat?"

"What's that?"

"Come on now. You mean you don't know what a thermostat is?"

Toni, seeming as if she was in a very good mood due to my presence, looked confused as she said, "I don't."

I looked at her and didn't say anything. Toni continued to look at me dumbfounded, then suddenly her confusion disappeared as if she had received a revelation. "Oh! You mean that square thing that controls the heat?"

I couldn't help but laugh as I shook my head and said, "You are just like a woman. Yeah, where is the square thing that controls the heat?"

Toni laughed, and as she directed me to the "square thing," she explained she wasn't into "technical stuff." When we walked up to the thermostat, I instantly diagnosed the problem to Toni's air-conditioning woes. Toni looked at me and asked if I also needed to see that "short, round thing" that was in the backyard.

"No, Toni, I don't need to see the *compressor*," I sarcastically said. "I think I already know what's wrong."

"Well, excuse me, *Mr. Con Edison*," Toni exclaimed. Then she shot back like she'd just received her second revelation. "Con Edison. Wait a minute, you work for Con Edison?"

I replied, "Nah. I just like wearing the Con Edison uniform."

"Shut up, Lance," Toni said as she slapped me on the arm. "No, but for real, I knew it. That's where I know you from. Didn't you come into the shop one day while you were working?"

I smiled because I knew exactly to which day Toni was referring. "Yeah, I was there. That was me."

Toni had her mouth wide open as she laughed and said, "I knew I wasn't trippin'. I was trying like crazy to figure out how come you looked so familiar. And you! Oh my God! That day you pulled up to me on Pennsylvania Avenue, talking about, 'I know you.'"

I laughed as I said, "Don't front. You know I was smooth wit' mine that day. My game was tight."

Toni shook her head, and she was about to say something else, but she stopped in the middle of her sentence when she felt a whiff of cool air. She paused and looked at me with a confused expression as she said, "I know that's not cool air that I feel."

Feeling like the chief and master of my trade, I simply blew air on my fingernails and made like I was buffing them on my shirt.

"Lance, you mean to tell me that I've been suffering in this house in this ghetto heat for days, and you come over here and fix it that quick?"

"Yeah, there was nothing wrong with the AC," I explained.

"What do you mean? 'Cause my father is gonna wanna know exactly why it wasn't working. I think he has some repair company coming to look at it."

I went on, "I won't even attempt to explain what I did, 'cause I know it will be too technical for you to understand, but just tell your pops that someone must have accidentally moved the switch from AC and had it on the heat setting. He can call and cancel whoever he had coming to fix it because it's already fixed. I personally guarantee that y'all won't have anymore problems."

Toni looked at me and said, "Well, excuse me."

I felt good because I guessed that with my handy skills I had impressed Toni. If she only knew how easy what I had just done was. I mean it was just a matter of moving a switch.

"Oh my God, it's already starting to feel good in here. Thank you, Lance," Toni added.

Toni's tanned-looking and toned body was driving me crazy. It seemed as though we were the only two people in the house, so I asked for a hug. Toni put up no argument, and she gave me one. I didn't let her pull away as I looked her in her eyes and asked, "So you ready to talk or what?"

Toni looked up at me with her puppy-dog eyes and nodded. She was pressed very close against my body. She was feeling and smelling as sweet as ever, so sweet that I was beginning to wonder if she could feel something poking her. I knew that no matter what happened that day, Toni and I were definitely gonna talk. Regardless of whether what we talked about would prove to be positive or not, I realized now was the perfect time to attempt to kiss her. So without asking for permission I just closed my eyes and allowed my lips and tongue to find Toni's soft lips. As my tongue touched hers, it felt like a wafer was just melting on my tongue.

Not only didn't Toni object, but she was actually getting into it. She began caressing the back of my head as we kissed. She also caused her face to turn into the kiss a couple of times to make it more passionate. Toni finally pulled away from me. She didn't look directly at me as she shook her head and looked toward the floor. There was silence of passionate disbelief. It was broken when Toni said, "Lance, come on. We definitely have to talk right now."

Toni grabbed me by the hand and led me to her apartment, which was sectioned off from the main quarters of the house. She had a separate entrance that led to a door in the backyard.

We reached her apartment, which looked as if it could have been in an IKEA catalog with the way it was decorated. But I was sure that the furniture probably came from a more upscale furniture store like Ethan Allen. Toni sat me at a chair in front of the kitchen countertop. She prepared iced tea for the two of us, then she got right to the point.

"Lance, what is going on between us? I mean, you're married and all, and here I am kissing you."

I had no clue as to what I was gonna actually say, but I knew I had to be as convincing as a con artist. I was still coming off the high I had received from the kiss. I felt like plastering one of those nervous smiles on my face, but I wanted Toni to know I was serious and I wasn't just taking this serious talk time as a joke. I didn't want to be distracted by Toni's face, her body, or anything, so I looked to the floor as I began to speak to her.

I began by slowly shaking my head and saying, "See, Toni, it's like this. I'm not saying that I have the worst marriage in the world, nor am I saying that I don't love my wife. What I am saying—or should I say, how I feel—is, I feel like I have to be real with myself, and if not I'll drive myself insane."

Toni, who was standing up, said, "I'm trying to understand you, but—"

I interrupted her and said, "Okay, I'll try to explain myself better. Toni, there is something in me that just knows that things are not gonna work out between my wife and myself. You don't know how frustrated I feel inside my heart. I feel like I am constantly living two lives just to make things work between us. My marriage is going on five years, and I have felt like this since six months into it. I just can't keep this up, and that's why I know there is nothing wrong with me being with you."

I knew I was jacking things up. I wasn't being convincing enough. I also realized that if I wanted to sound confident, then I would have to feel and act that way. From that point on, I sat straight up and began to look into Toni's eyes. Thoughts of my wife were creeping into my mind, but I swatted them away like an irritating fly.

Toni responded, "Lance, I think I know what you're trying to say, but like I told you at Junior's, you still made a commitment to your wife, and you should try to honor it."

I butted in, "Toni that's just it. I have been trying, and it's not gonna work."

Toni asked, "So how is being with me gonna change things?"

"Being with you, Toni, is gonna change everything because I know that if things work between me and you, then that proves that my marriage was destined to end. Toni, why else would I even be pursuing you if things looked mad bright for the future between me and Nicole?"

Trying to pull out all the punches, I continued. "Toni, I don't want you to think that I'm a dog or anything like that. Don't think that at all, because if I was a dog, I would have cheated on Nicole a long time ago. I've been faithful for all this time. I was doing what you suggested, in that I was trying my hardest to honor my commitment, but, Toni, think about it, why should marriage, day in and day out feel like such a laborious chore? Marriage shouldn't be like that. It's not fair."

I think I was beginning to get through to Toni as she shook her head and explained, "Lance, since I've met you, I've been breaking all kinds of rules I said I would never break. Rules, that if I were to see another woman breaking, I would label her as a skeezer or a chickenhead. Lance, I really do think I understand where you're coming from, but I don't see how things can work between me and you."

Yes, I thought. I knew I had Toni steered in the direction I wanted her to go. I just had to continue to bait her. Sounding like Keith Sweat, I came off like I was begging or pleading as I went on. "Toni, I know I don't have all of the answers. I don't know exactly how this is gonna work between me and you, but I know that with every absolute ounce of my being I want things to work. Toni, listen to me, 'cause I'm not trying to run game on you. I'm too old for that. I promise you that I'll do everything I have to do in order to make this work."

At that point Toni sat down. I knew I was causing her to consider crossing a line she thought she could never cross. Toni remained quiet. I knew I had said enough, and I didn't want to interrupt her. I thought about saying something stupid in reference to Toni's man out in Las Vegas, but that would definitely have been a major error. I wondered what she was thinking about, so I asked her.

Toni informed me, "I'm just thinking, you know, about your wife and stuff like that."

That was the last thing I needed Toni to be thinking about, so I had to come up with some serious game very quick. "Toni, you ever been on a scary roller coaster?" I asked.

Toni replied, "Yes."

Just as I was gonna expand on my game, I felt my pager going off. It was on vibrate, so Toni didn't have a clue that I had been paged. I discretely looked down and checked the number, and it was Nicole. I paid it no attention, and I went on. "Toni, I asked you that question because I see the wheels turning in your head. You're thinking about every scenario. You're thinking about how are we gonna speak on the phone.

You're asking yourself when are we gonna have the time to go out. You're thinking about, what if Nicole and I end up getting a divorce."

I took Toni by the hand to reassure her, as I said, "Toni, I have had those same thoughts for five years, but I've finally been able to honestly answer a lot of my own thoughts and questions. Toni, think of that scary roller coaster, or bungee jumping, or skydiving. You know it's scary, you know the dangers, but deep down inside you still want to experience it. Toni, the thing that stops people from experiencing the joys of the ride is the fact that they stand in front of the roller coaster and they think. They don't have to say anything. All they have to do is just think. Then before you know it they back out and say, 'Nah, nah. It's too scary. I'm not getting on.' See, Toni, when people do that, they rob themselves of experiencing the things that deep down inside they want to experience."

After saying that, I was like, "Damn!" I mean, I was even shocked as to having pulled that game out of my hat. I wanted Toni to think about what I had just said and at the same time I didn't want to keep rambling on to give her the impression that I was gassing her. So after having said all of that, I asked Toni if I could use her phone. As she went to her bedroom to retrieve her cordless phone I realized that it was already a little past six o'clock. When Toni came back with the phone I called my wife.

I didn't want Toni to know who I was talking to so when Nicole answered the phone, I asked that common question, "Yo, you paged me?"

Nicole, who finally sounded like she was in a better mood said, "Yeah, I paged you, baby."

"What's up?" I replied.

"Thank you for the flowers."

"You're welcome," I nonchalantly replied.

Nicole went on to say that she was sorry for not speaking to me that morning. She added that she knew that I was also sorry for what had happened last night. Then she asked about my and LL's whereabouts. Toni was still standing right next to me, and I didn't want to lie. I played things off by saying, "Oh. I had to fix my friend's air conditioner, so I went there right after work, but LL is at Tiffany's."

Nicole asked, "When will you be home?"

"Oh, in like a half," I replied.

Nicole who wanted to verify my response asked, "You mean a half an hour?"

"Yeah."

"Okay, so I'll see you later."

I hung up the phone and placed it down on the counter. Of course Toni asked me who I had been speaking to. I knew that she didn't know who my sista was, so I simply lied and told her that I had been speaking to my sista. Knowing that I had to leave soon, I immediately asked Toni if she understood what I had been trying to get across to her.

She still lacked a little confidence, but she told me that she did indeed understand what I was trying to say. I wanted to remove all of Toni's insecurities and leave her house knowing that a relationship had been officially fostered from this point on.

"Toni, you want things to work between me and you. I know you do, because if you didn't you wouldn't have suggested that we talk about things. I'm trying to get an understanding between us. I have to leave, so I'll get straight to the point. From now on I don't want you overly thinking about things, a'ight?"

Toni shyly nodded in agreement.

I added, "I ain't trying to back you into a corner or tie you down, but I want us to establish a relationship."

Toni shook her head and smiled, as if to say she still had some things to think about.

I smiled, too, as I said, "See, there you go again, thinking. Stop thinking. Don't think about anything except for the fact that I'm gonna do my part in trying to make things work between me and you. Toni, all I want is for you to tell me that from this point forward you'll do your part in helping me make this work."

Toni still was smiling as she walked from out of the kitchen and into her living room. I followed after her, and I hugged her from behind. I asked again, "You're gonna try, right?"

Toni didn't respond.

I had to jet, and I asked her to walk me to my car, which she did. We walked to my car without saying a word to each other. When we reached the Lexus I got in and sat behind the steering wheel. Toni was standing right beside the driver's window, which was rolled down. I started up the car, looked at Toni, and asked her again, "You're gonna try, right?"

Toni nodded to show me her agreement, then she bent over and gave me a peck on the lips. After the kiss, we both seductively looked at each other. Toni stood back and waved as I pulled off. I was in a slammin' mood for the remainder of the night.

My wife and I made up. I managed to explain to Nicole that the reason I was upset and had snapped at her was because I bet a lot of money on the game and I lost. That was a total lie but my wife, after reprimanding me for gambling, told me that she understood.

So with things good on the home front and things John Blazin' between me and Toni, I was on cloud nine. I knew that I had a great dilemma to solve: Which of my two faces was I gonna wear around my wife? I knew that the face of evil was way too painful. All it caused was arguments, stress, and anxiety, but the face of good required tedious, hypocritical work. See, I didn't have the gall to do like some men do, in terms of just walking away from my wife and kid. I didn't even have the guts to get a divorce. Internally I knew that I cared way too much to just walk away from things or to get a divorce. Actually, there is no way that it would have even been about a divorce, because my family is still the most important thing to me on this planet.

It was more about feeling satisfied. I realized that just like prior to Toni, when I needed both Scarlet and Nicole in order to maintain my sanity, that I would now need both Toni and Nicole in order to maintain my current sanity. I was willing to put in the hard work. Just as Toni had made a vow to make the relationship work between us, I also made a vow to myself that from this point on I was gonna be the best Christian family man who ever walked the face of the earth. At the same time, I was gonna blow Toni away and be the best lover since Casanova.

Chapter Thirteen

Nicole and I had worked out a system that is designed to combat boredom in our marriage. We looked at many older couples such as our parents and tried to figure out why they weren't as happy as they appeared to be in their youthful wedding pictures. Our brainstorming produced many hypotheses. But one major conclusion that we came to was the fact that many couples had stopped dating each other after marriage.

For Nicole and me, either Friday or Saturday was always set aside for just the two of us. On one of those days we would do things that led us to continue wanting to spend the rest of our lives together. Whenever we would go out on dates, we would make sure that we kept things spontaneous. One week we would go to a comedy club. The next week we would go out to Yankee Stadium or to a restaurant—you name it, we did it. Lately I noticed that we had both been letting other things take a higher priority over our marriage.

Nicole, who always has great intentions, was becoming very one tracked. Her every thought was church, church, church. Believe me, as the husband, I know that I have to be on a higher spiritual page than she is, but I can't see how that's genuinely gonna happen. I mean, I'm gonna put forth a hypocritical effort to make it happen, however, with Nicole's church-church-church mentality, she was causing me to resent the fellowship of the congregants.

See, what happened between Scarlet and me, that really shouldn't count against me. I mean, yeah, I'll admit that I'm doing wrong in the sense that I'm creeping with Toni, but Nicole is no better because she is establishing a relationship with a mistress of her own, the church.

For example, my supervisor had asked me a week in advance to work late on Friday, but I still knew that I would be home by ten o'clock that evening. I really wanted my wife and me to go out and do something. It had been a couple of months since we'd truly dated. Unfortunately, Nicole turned down my request to take her to a late-night movie. She informed me that the church was having a special Friday evening service, and she had already made plans to attend and she had arranged for a babysitter for LL. Nicole explained to me that the service wouldn't end until midnight, at which time, she knew she would be exhausted and only looking forward to bed. Her suggestion to me was that I either stay home or use the night as a night out with the fellas.

Yeah, a'ight, I thought.

On my way home from work that evening, I knew that I definitely wasn't trying to go home and go to sleep. Man, it was Friday night, and I wanted to unwind from a week of work and stress. I contacted Steve and some of the other fellas to see what they were getting themselves into. Most of my friends were split down the middle. Half of them were just chillin' for the night, while the other half were planning on going out to a club. It had been a while since I'd been to a club, and I thought about joining them, but tonight wasn't really a club night for me. I wasn't feeling real mackish. I wasn't in the mood for dancing, and I didn't feel like spending dough or buying drinks for some ho.

Yeah, I didn't feel like kicking it to females tonight, and that was the main reason that I would not have gone to a club, so I was like 'forget the club thing.' Scarlet was supposed to be stripping, or as she would put it, "dancing" at this club in Harlem, so I thought about surprising her by going to the club and checking her out then maybe chillin' with her afterward.

Although I was trying to avoid it, subconsciously I knew I hadn't exhausted all of my options for the night. I still had the opportunity to call Toni to see if she wanted to take my wife's place and join me in seeing a movie. While still on my way home from work, I called Toni on my cell to see what plans she had for the night. It felt sooo good to hear her voice, one that gets lively and excited because she is speaking to me. Yeah, and it feels extremely exemplary when Toni starts telling me that she missed me.

"So what's up? What are you doing tonight?" I asked.

Toni explained that since it was a Friday, the shop had been extremely busy. She told me she had just walked in the house after a thirteen-hour day in the salon.

"Oh, so that means your pockets are full of dead presidents and you're gonna take me out tonight, right?" I asked.

Toni laughed as she said, "Yeah, baby, I'll take you out. My treat. Where do you wanna go?"

"Well, I was thinking about seeing a movie, especially being that it's so late and all."

Toni responded, "Well, you know what? Actually I'm exhausted from today, and I have to be back at the shop at seven in the morning, so I was gonna just come home and get in the bed."

Sounding kind of disappointed because I had a feeling that Toni was trying to reject my offer, I replied, "Oh, so you trying to front on me?"

Toni laughed and said, "No, no. Of course not. I was just thinking, being that I'm tired and all, why don't you rent a movie and come over here, and we can just hang out?"

Toni definitely wasn't gonna get any objections from me. I informed her that I would be at her place within the next forty-five minutes.

"What about *Training Day*? Have you ever seen that?" I asked.

"*Training Day,* with Denzel, right?" Toni asked.

"Yeah."

Toni added, "Nah, I never saw that. Yeah, so rent that."

"A'ight, so I'll see you later."

I knew that I didn't have to stop at the video store because I had purchased *Training Day* for Nicole. She liked the movie so much that I bought it for her. I simply had to rush home, get showered and dressed, and I could jet over to Toni's. The Toni rushes I got were already starting to kick in. It was the same rush I used to get back in the day when I knew I was gonna see my wife, who was my girlfriend at the time.

I dug deep into my romantic repertoire to see what I could come up with to complement the movie. In no way, shape, or form did I want Toni to be bored while she was with me. Being that I was still in Brooklyn, I decided to drop by the Canarsie Pier, a spot along Jamaica Bay just off the Belt Parkway. It consisted of restaurants and boats and all of the things that any bustling pier would have.

At the pier you could also purchase all kinds of seafood. I am no cook, but the dishes that I do know how to make usually come out slammin'. I perfected my ability to cook certain dishes simply because I wanted to impress women. My plan that night was no different. I wanted to impress Toni, so I purchased three live lobsters. I knew that Toni liked seafood because she had ordered shrimp when we went to Junior's. I couldn't wait to surprise her.

After having showered, I trimmed my goatee and my mustache to make sure my grill was on point. My attire was very casual—Air Jordans, baggy jeans, and a short-sleeve button-down rayon shirt. Before I left my house, I grabbed the movie and I also retrieved the Old Bay seasoning for the lobsters. Just to cover my tracks, I left a note telling Nicole that I had gone out and that I would be back home around two or three in the morning.

I hopped in my car, and before I knew it I was at Toni's place. When Toni answered the door she looked as if she had just come out of the shower. She had a towel on her head, and she had on this sexy, short silk robe. After hugging each other, Toni invited me in, and she explained that she had in fact just come out of the shower. She told me to have a seat in her living room while she excused herself to go change. At that point, all kinds of sexual thoughts were running through my head. The natural high I was on began to elevate.

Then all of a sudden, both my cell phone and my pager started vibrating almost simultaneously.

It was Scarlet.

Oh, damn, I thought. *Not now.*

Being that Toni was out of the room, I decided to just quickly answer my cell phone and tell Scarlet that I would call her back. I knew that was a real dangerous move because I was taking a chance Toni might overhear me talking on the phone then later question me as to who it was that I had been speaking to. I also didn't want Scarlet blowing up my cell phone and pager throughout the night. So like I said, I decided to answer the cell, but I knew I would have to take control of the conversation and make it quick.

I answered my cell phone, and I immediately started talking in a way that would not allow for any small talk, "Yo, what's up, Scarlet? Listen, let me call you back in about an hour, okay?"

"Nah, that's not okay," Scarlet rudely shot back, which sort of caught me off guard. "You're gonna speak to me right now and explain to me what the hell you're doing in Jamaica Estates."

At that point my heart started pounding so fast and hard that I thought Toni was gonna hear it in the other room. I immediately started looking under the couch, underneath the table, and inside one of the closets in Toni's apartment to see if Scarlet was staked out in the joint with a butcher knife or something.

"Jamaica Estates?" I replied, trying to sound ignorant as to what Scarlet was saying.

"Yeah, nigga. Don't play stupid. That is exactly what I asked you. Jamaica-Got-Damn-Estates. On Chevy Chase Road. Whose house are you at?"

At that point I felt like screaming out loud, "Damn! Damn! Damn!" as if I was the character Florida Evans from that famous episode of the TV Show *Good Times* after her husband, James' funeral. Instead I just slightly whispered to myself, "Ahhhhhhhhh, damn." What could I say? I was just gritting my teeth out of both fear and frustration. I wish I could have just jumped through that cell phone and strangled Scarlet.

I walked to a very remote part of Toni's apartment, and I began talking in a very low, stern voice. "Scarlet del Rio, you listen to me. I don't know what you are up to or where you're calling me from or what the deal is, but I'm gonna say this one time, and I'm not gonna be arguing with you here on the phone. I decided to go out with the fellas tonight, but I had to make a quick stop and drop off something for Steve. I didn't even know that this was Jamaica Estates. All I had was an address."

"Lance, don't give me that."

"What do you mean don't give you that?" In my mind I was panicking like crazy because I knew that Toni would be coming out of her room at any second.

"Who is the seafood for, Lance? Oh, let me guess. Steve called you at work and asked you to stop in Canarsie and get some seafood, and instead of dropping it off at his house, you decide to go home and get all dipped out and then drop off the seafood before y'all go out, right? Is that it? You must really think I'm a stupid Brazilian bitch or something."

I knew Scarlet was heated because her accent started to come out as she spoke.

Scarlet was truly pulling my card. Now I was scared because I knew that Scarlet must have been following me, and I didn't want her ringing Toni's doorbell or anything ghetto like that. So like my years of experience had taught me, I knew that when the evidence is strongly stacked against you, it means that it is probably a good time to cop a serious plea-bargain deal. Copping a plea is basically admitting that you are guilty, and when you do that, it's like saying that you're at least not trying to insult the prosecuting party's intelligence. In this case, Scarlet was the prosecutor, the judge, the jury, and she would have had no problem being the executioner.

"A'ight, listen," I angrily and nervously whispered. "Scarlet I'm not going out with the fellas. I lied about that. See, I'm admitting that. I just can't explain to you right now what I'm doing because you wouldn't understand."

"I wouldn't understand what? That you're screwing some rich white lady? Only rich white folks live in Jamaica Estates. So, Lance, what don't I understand about that?"

Since my plea-bargaining strategy wasn't working, I only had one final option, and that was to throw myself on the mercy of the court and beg for leniency.

"Scarlet, I am not with no white woman. But please just listen to me. Please, I know exactly what you're thinking. You're thinking that I'm with someone else and that someone else is gonna take your spot. Baby, that is just not true, and I'll prove it. See, I'm about to say something that I have never, ever said before, and I'm not just saying this because I want you to believe me, but tomorrow, if you give me the chance,

I'll explain everything to you face-to-face as far as what it is that I'm doing here in Jamaica Estates. If after I explain and prove to you the legitimate reason why I was here, you still don't believe me, then I tell you what, you can take every sex video that you and I have ever made, you can take any picture that we have ever taken together, you can take all the letters and cards that I have ever given you, along with all of the gifts and whatever, and you can personally hand deliver them to Nicole."

Scarlet was silent as she thought about what I had just said.

"Scarlet, you know how fiercely adamant I've always been in terms of keeping you a secret from Nicole, so if I'm telling you that I'm willing to break that veil in order to have your trust, that should be telling you something, *baby*." I made sure to stress the word *baby*.

I don't know from where on earth I was getting all of that loose-lip pimp game. I knew it was damn sure risky pimp game that I was loosely throwing around. Everyone knows it's loose lips that sink ships, but I had Toni right where I wanted her, and I was willing to risk and do or say just about anything and to go to any lengths I had to in order to avoid fouling things up with her.

Fortunately, I had somewhat broken through to Scarlet as she angrily and reluctantly replied, "Whoooo . . . uuuughhhh. I can't stand you, Lance. You better thank God that I'm in a rush. I'm dancing at this new club in Harlem for the first time tonight, and I don't wanna stand up the promoter. Otherwise I would sit my Brazilian ass right here on Chevy Chase Road and wait to see which house you come out of."

Man, I didn't even know that Scarlet was actually camped outside. That's just how gangsta and gully she was with hers.

"Scarlet, remember what I said, a'ight?"

"Lance, you are getting real sloppy with yours. Remember what I told you. If I can't be your number one, then I'm damn sure gonna be your number two."

"Scarlet, I gotta go, a'ight," I very nervously whispered in a rushed tone.

"Oh, you're rushing me off the phone? Matter of fact, I do have a few minutes. . . . I tell you what, if you ain't with no other woman then bring yo' black ass outside right now and come sit in my car for a few minutes. I'm parked right next to your car."

As Scarlet was calling my bluff, out of pure disgust I blew air into the phone, and I simply told Scarlet that I had to go. I hung up the phone, and I quickly made it back to where I had been sitting in Toni's apartment. Before I could sit back down, Scarlet was again blowing up my phone, but this time I didn't dare to answer.

As my heart pounded, I remember thinking that there was no way I was gonna be able to relax with Toni. I was too worried that Scarlet was gonna start ringing doorbells in the neighborhood in an attempt to find me or something.

I knew that I had to relax and just deal with the drama that came along with being a rolling stone. If I was able to safely make it through the next ten minutes without Scarlet doing a drive-by shooting on Toni's crib then I figured I would at least be cool for the night.

As Toni was still in her room changing—and thank God she had taken longer than I expected—she yelled out to me, "So did you have a problem getting the movie?"

I yelled back, "Nah, I got it."

Before I knew it, Toni had come out of her room wearing a T-shirt, sweatpants, and those thick socks that bunch up around the ankles. She was also in the process of brushing her hair as she sat down next to me. Toni smiled at me and asked "So, Lance, how was your day?"

Not wanting to mention the drama that could quite possibly unfold if Scarlet were to figure out which house Toni lived in and rang the bell, I responded, "My day was cool. I didn't think it would turn out as good as it has, you know being that I'm with you and everything." Then I went on to tell her that I had a surprise for her.

Toni inched closer to me in excitement. "Really? What is it?"

Totally forgetting that Scarlet was camped outside, I added, "It's outside. Wait right here. I'll go get it."

While I got up to make my way outside, Toni turned the TV on. She then pulled her hair back and placed a silk scrunchy around it to hold it in place as she relaxed on the couch and expressed her love of surprises.

After first tiptoeing up to a huge oak tree that was located near Toni's driveway and hiding behind it, I poked my head out from behind the tree to see if the coast was clear. Feeling like I was playing hide and go seek or some type of game like that, I nervously made it to my Lexus. With my heart pounding a mile a minute, I scanned the entire block, looking for Scarlet. Fortunately, she wasn't anywhere in sight. But knowing her, she was probably in a tree with a pair of night-vision binoculars along with a gun and a red scope with a targeted dot pointed at my head waiting to pull the trigger. I knew that going outside was crazy and bold on my part, but I also figured that even if I had bumped into Scarlet, it would have made me come across in a much more credible manner to her.

Luckily for me, I was able to safely retrieve the lobsters, which were loaded in the trunk of my car inside of a box of ice. The lobsters were still very much alive and moving. I carried the box back to Toni's apartment, and I checked over my shoulder one last time to make sure that Scarlet was not in sight, which thank God, she wasn't. Before I walked back into Toni's living room I told her to close her eyes. Toni was smiling from ear to ear. As I approached her, I instructed her to stand up and to make sure that she kept her eyes closed. When I got directly in front of her, I quietly opened the box, and I raised lobsters to her chin.

Toni, who couldn't see a thing, began to laugh, and she asked, "Lance, what are you doing?"

I replied, "Nothing. Just relax, and keep your eyes closed."

Toni continued to smile and giggle while I remained silent for about ten seconds. Then I said, "A'ight, you can open your eyes now."

Toni opened her eyes. She saw the lobsters and instantly let out a scream as she bolted for cover. When she was out of harm's way she put a hand across her chest. Breathing heavy and sounding fearful, she asked, "Lance, what is that?"

After witnessing her reaction, I fell to the couch in belly-ache laughter. Still terrified, Toni asked again, "Lance, what's in that box?"

Still laughing, I got up from the couch and walked in Toni's direction in an attempt to show her what was inside the box. As I got closer, she ran and demanded that I stay away. Finally, my laughter was beginning to come to an end, and I explained, "It's just lobsters, baby."

Toni gave me an untrusting look. So to prove it, I held the box down and tilted it in her direction. Toni proceeded with caution. She inched closer and closer to the box and attempted to look in. I thought about screaming and scaring her one last time, but I decided that enough was enough. I didn't want her to think that I was childish or anything. When Toni was close enough to confirm that it was in fact lobsters, she let out a sigh of relief and began laughing. She punched me on the arm and asked if I was trying to give her a heart attack.

"Just trying to have a little fun," I advised.

Toni informed me that she loved lobster, but she had no idea in the world how to properly cook them. While walking toward the kitchen I confidently informed her, "Well, I didn't expect for you to cook them. I was planning on cooking for you. If it's okay with you."

"Uh-oh, look out now," Toni jokingly replied. "There is definitely nothing wrong with a man who can cook."

I instructed Toni, "Give me the largest and deepest pot that you have."

As Toni searched for a pot, I explained to her that cooking lobster was as easy as boiling an egg. Toni, who seemed to be delighted by the whole idea, informed me she had to run up to her parents' to get a big pot, being that all of hers were of average size. While Toni went to locate the pot, I made myself very familiar with her kitchen. To make things look good, I put on an apron I saw hanging from the side of her range. I also placed a big wooden spoon on the table along with cooking gloves. I searched inside of her refrigerator to see if she had the necessary ingredients to make a salad.

As Toni returned to the kitchen with the pot, she asked, "Is this big enough?"

I reached and took it from her hand while letting her know that it indeed was big enough. Toni laughed and said, "Oh-oh, look at Lance, got his apron on and all dip out like you know what you're doing. I'm afraid of you. Let me find out you really know how to cook!"

"Just have a seat and watch. I'll show you how to be a chef," I replied.

Toni pulled out a chair from her kitchen table. She sat in the chair with her legs curled underneath her butt and her forearms on the glass kitchen table. As Toni sat with her hands folded, she smiled with excited anticipation.

I began to demonstrate my skills as I said, "A'ight, the first thing you do is fill the pot up with water. That, of course, is assuming that the pot is clean, 'cause if it isn't, the first thing you would do is clean the pot. I'm assuming y'all don't have no roaches or anything, do y'all?"

Toni laughed while shaking her head no. By now she had her right elbow on the table and her right palm was cupped underneath her chin. Toni kinda spoke through her teeth as she assured me, "No, we don't have any roaches. You sure got nerve."

"Just checking, baby. Just checking," I said. I then went on to explain the process. "Okay, after you fill the pot with water, you add your seasoning. Then you bring the water to a boil, then you place the lobsters in it, and that's it."

Toni, seeming to be a little baffled, asked, "That's it?"

"Yeah, that's it," I replied.

"So how do you know when the lobsters are ready?" Toni questioned.

"Oh. Well, let me backtrack a bit. I forgot to tell you that you have to put the lobsters into the water while they're still alive."

Toni frowned and remarked how cruel it was to scorch the poor lobsters to death. I gave no weight to her feelings as I told her, "Don't worry about that. Better them than you, right? But to answer your question, you'll know that they're ready when you see their shells turn bright red. After that you can then take them out of the pot, dry them off, and put butter on them. Once the butter is on them, you can place them in the broiler for a while."

"Does putting the butter on them add flavor or something?" Toni asked.

"Nah, it just makes the shell easier to crack," I said.

During the time I was explaining all of this to Toni, I had the fire under the pot, and the water was at its boiling point. Toni cringed as I dropped the lobsters into the water.

"Lance, that's so mean. Oh, look at the poor things. You can tell that they're in pain 'cause they're moving around so crazy," Toni commented.

Again I brushed Toni's remarks aside as I replied, "They'll be a'ight. Besides, you won't even be thinking about how they're feeling when you're eating them."

Lobster doesn't take that long to cook, so while they were boiling, I began to prepare the salad. Toni expressed that I seemed like I was comfortable and I knew my way around the kitchen very well. Trying to big myself up, I gloated as I sliced the tomatoes, "Yeah, cooking ain't all that. If I put my mind to it, there isn't anything that I can't do. I'm multitalented."

Toni was smiling. She became inquisitive and wanted to know more about my "multitalents." I informed her that some of my talents couldn't be spoken about due to their explicit contents. Toni didn't seem too amused by the nature of my comment. I quickly recovered by adding that I also knew how to do hair.

Toni became instantly amused, as she said, "Yeah, right. What do you mean, you know how to do hair?"

"I'm sayin'. I can do wraps, doobies, and all that," I confidently proclaimed. "Matter of fact, I'll even take care of your split ends."

Toni began laughing, then she looked at me with her head slightly tilted and asked, "Can you really do wraps?"

"Yeah. Wraps are easy. All you need is some setting lotion, a brush, a comb, and a hair dryer, and you're good to go." As I cracked a smile, I advised Toni not to sleep on my skills. Toni demanded proof, and I assured her that I would prove it to her, just as long as she was willing to be my guinea pig.

I was just about done with the salad so I asked Toni where we would be eating. She suggested that we go in the living room so we could watch the movie while we ate. After looking in the pot, I noticed that the lobsters were almost done.

"See, Toni, come here a minute." As Toni walked toward the stove, I added, "This is what I was talking about when I said they'll turn bright red. They should be ready to go into the broiler in about two more minutes."

Toni got two plates and two trays, then she asked what I would like to drink. Being that I wanted the evening to be as romantic as possible, I asked her if she had any wine. Unfortunately, she didn't.

"You ever drank Alizé?" Toni asked.

"Whaaat?" I cheerfully replied. "That's my drink. Why, you got some?"

To my excitement, Toni did indeed have a whole bottle of Alizé. Before long we were in front of the television watching the movie and eating. We were having a good time. Toni admitted that she wasn't very experienced at eating lobster. I watched her make a mess, but I coached her as to how to properly eat it.

I told her, "Yeah, it will be mad messy if you don't know how to eat it. But when you do it right, you'll be able to enjoy it better."

Toni did get the hang of it rather quickly. While she was eating, she told me that she had no idea that lobster was so easy to cook and that she would definitely be treating herself to them more regularly. While we ate, we really weren't paying attention to the movie. We began talking about ourselves.

"Lance, you know what? I don't even know your last name. Knowing a person's last name is important, you know. I can't be getting all close to you and not knowing the simple things like that."

I informed her that my last name is Thomas.

Then from out of the blue, Toni asked me how I knew she was Haitian when we'd first met. I went on to explain that it was because of her last name. After sipping on her Alizé, she agreed that her last name was a very popular Haitian name. Toni informed me that she was born in Haiti, and she didn't move to the United States until she was five years old. The delay was because her father was in medical school in this country, and he wanted to finish school before he sent for his immediate family members who were still in Haiti. Toni also told me that her mother was Dominican.

"Oh, so that's why you know how to do hair," I replied.

"What does that have to do with anything?" Toni questioned.

"You know that Dominican women are famous for knowing how to do hair very well," I said.

Toni was surprised and explained that she really hadn't heard of that stereotype. I simply told her to ask the other beauticians in her shop, and they would confirm it. Then I playfully teased Toni about certain Haitian stereotypes. It was good that she wasn't very sensitive. Toni seemed more than willing to joke with me as I asked her about Haitian voodoo and things like that.

Before I knew it, Toni and I were finished with the lobsters, and we began to feed each other salad. Toni was in a playful mood. With the fork she was using to feed me, she caused it to miss my mouth, which caused salad dressing to get on my face. Of course I didn't mind the joke, as I, too, began to put salad dressing on her face. Toni's playful mood ignited a flame in the back of my head.

See, when I initially came over to her crib, I had no intentions of going any further than kissing Toni. But being that she was so happy, I began to wonder if, in fact, I could fulfill my dream and hit it tonight. I knew that the Alizé would be a big help, so I made sure that we both drank as much as possible.

Toni continued to put salad dressing on my face. Out of nowhere, I informed her that if she was gonna keep doing that then she would have to lick it off. To my surprise and without hesitation, Toni pressed her body up against mine, and she ran her tongue from the area near my lips, all the way to my ear, which she stopped and began to kiss.

Chills ran through my body, and I became instantly aroused. I knew that I couldn't overreact, so I kept my hormones at bay. Toni stopped kissing my ear, and she just looked at me. I was desperately trying to translate her look into words. I was wondering if I should make my move and try to hit it then or what.

The obvious thing to do was to kiss her, so I proceeded to do just that. It wasn't a very deep kiss—it was to test the waters. This time after we kissed, Toni broke some of the ice with a smile. She then stood up from the couch we were sitting on and walked toward her bedroom. The voice inside of me was going bananas. In my mind I knew that the present atmosphere, combined with Toni's mood, was exactly what I had been pursuing ever since I first laid eyes on her. My heart began racing because I had a good feeling about what could possibly take place.

I was hoping that Toni would return from her room with a skimpy outfit or a garter belt and high heels. That would have definitely more than fulfilled every fantasy I'd ever craved. To my disappointment Toni returned from the bedroom and asked, "Lance, how late are you staying?"

I instantly got nervous. Here I was, thinking I was about to get mine off, and Toni was wondering how she could get me to leave.

"Well, what time is it now?" I asked.

"It's a quarter to one," Toni replied.

Sounding very dejected, I replied, "I guess I can bounce now. I mean I know you have to get up in the morning and all."

Toni interjected, "Oh, no. I wasn't trying to give you a hint to leave. I'm just saying I hope you don't think I'm doing those dishes."

Inside I was like, *Whew*. I let out a laugh of relief as I said, "Come on, I'm sayin'. I cooked you the bomb seafood meal, and you're gonna make me do the dishes too?"

In actuality, I knew that Toni could have cared less about the dishes. I told myself that she definitely wanted me, and I had to make my move as soon as possible to put it on her.

Toni went on, "I don't care how late you stay, but all I know is that those dishes better be done before you leave."

"Okay, mama," I playfully said. I added "Toni, come over here so we can finish watching this movie. I promise when it's over, I'll do the dishes for you."

I realized that the reason Toni had gone to her bedroom was to retrieve a bottle of nail polish remover and some cotton balls. She came back near the couch and sat on the floor, letting her back rest against the sofa as she sat between my legs. She took off her socks, exposing her sexy feet. She applied nail polish remover to a cotton ball and began to take off the toenail polish.

I took a sip of my Alizé and I commented, "Toni, you have the sexiest toes I have ever seen."

Toni blushed with embarrassment, as she laughed. Then she questioned, "Well, what about you? How are your toes?"

"My feet are a'ight, but that's not important 'cause I'm not a female," I informed.

"Oh no, that is not true," Toni emphatically remarked. "I know I do hair and nails, but one thing I can't stand is some jacked-up feet on a man or woman. Oh my God! *Ill!* That just makes my flesh crawl."

As Toni continued to discuss other pet peeves, I started to massage her shoulders and her neck. I was sure to be subtle about the way I did it. After about two minutes or so, Toni stopped talking and began expressing how good the massage was feeling. She moaned and let me know that she hadn't had a good massage in a very long time.

"That's not good," I replied. "You work too hard. Your muscles need to be cared for."

Before long Toni had disregarded removing the nail polish from her toenails, and she was totally into the massage. With her eyes closed, she tilted her head upward toward the ceiling and seductively told me that she could get used to treatment like that. I was feeling like a Don. I laughed and informed her that she deserved treatment like that.

When one has been married for as long as I've been, one learns what pleases a woman. All women are similar, and although I hadn't dated other women in a while per se, I knew that I was making all the right moves. My marriage taught me how to be a great masseuse, and boy, were those skills ever coming in handy.

I requested that Toni get some baby oil so I could give her a hand massage. She was very hip to the idea. In fact, she was very eager because she had never had one. As Toni went to her bedroom to get the baby oil, I was going wild on the inside.

See Toni, like most women, didn't know how erogenous the hands are. Again, from being married, I've also learned all the right places to touch a woman. I was thinking to myself how Toni had no idea how good she was about to feel.

When she returned with the baby oil, she turned off the television because we both were not into the movie at all. Instead, Toni turned on her CD player and began playing a slow jams mix CD. When she was done adjusting the CD player, I asked her to join me on the couch where I started to massage her hands. As my slippery hands delved into every nook and cranny of hers, she began to voice her appreciation.

"Lance, this feels so gooood," Toni remarked.

I replied, "I'm surprised that you've never had a hand massage before, especially since you do nails and all."

Again Toni closed her eyes and enjoyed the experience as she said, "Yeah, I didn't know what I was missing."

I continued to massage Toni's hands for about five more minutes. It was getting late, and I knew that I had her where I wanted her. As I leaned Toni back onto the couch, she smiled and puppy-doggishly asked what I was doing.

"You'll see," I devilishly answered. So after laying Toni on her back, I reached for her legs, which I lifted onto the couch. The laugh Toni gave let me know that I could continue with what I had planned. With Toni's entire body on the couch, I quickly rubbed some more baby oil into the palms of my hands. After they were nice and slick, I took Toni's left foot and began to massage it.

"You ever had a foot massage?" I asked.

Toni, who looked as if she was in heaven, didn't say a word. She just kept her eyes closed and shook her head. I couldn't believe guys weren't smooth enough to never have given Toni a hand or foot massage.

After a couple of minutes of massaging her left foot, I took her right one and repeated my technique. Toni then lifted my ego by remarking that I had it going on. I made sure that I put my all into the massage, and I could tell that I was working wonders.

Needless to say, one thing was leading to another, and all I know is that Toni smartly asked if I had a condom. I was glad she asked, because I knew that my dumb ass was ready to run up in her raw. I confirmed that I did indeed have a condom, and before I could blink, I was taking my sinful ways full scale into the next level.

I can't front. My wife was on my mind at that very moment. Regretfully, I hadn't thought about Nicole up until that point. It's sad, but there was no way in the world that I wasn't going to finish what I had started on Toni's couch.

When it was over, I was utterly speechless. For about twenty seconds, I had experienced that feeling I'd been searching and fiendin' for. Believe me, I couldn't remember "it" ever feeling any better. After that feeling had subsided, I realized I had never felt lower or dirtier in all my life. While Toni and I were both still breathing hard, I was wondering what thoughts were running through her mind. We lay cuddled on the couch. Toni's back was pressed against my stomach, and for some reason she remained as silent as a mouse.

Something needed to be said, but no one spoke for close to ten minutes. I then kissed Toni on the cheek. In my mind I was like, I had better hurry up and get home to my wife, but at the same time I wanted to spend the night with Toni. In no way did I want her to feel cheap, so I simply laid there with her and thought about my adulterous ways. Before long, we were both knocked out on the couch.

Chapter Fourteen

I was fortunate that I managed to wake up when I did. It was ten minutes to four in the morning. I had been sleeping real good. When I awoke, I wasn't exactly sure where I was. When it finally hit me that I was still next to Toni, I was like "oh my God!" I couldn't believe I had let myself fall asleep. Instinctively my panicked state of mind almost caused me to make a beeline for the door, but I didn't want to wake Toni in my haste. Although I was feeling shook, I didn't want that to come across to her.

Being as quiet as possible, I eased away from the couch and made my way to my pager, which was on the kitchen table. My worst fears were confirmed when I realized Nicole had beeped me five times in a row. My dumb behind had the pager on vibrate. I had fallen asleep butt naked, so there was no way I could have known the pager had been going off. No way was I gonna allow myself to get even more rattled than I already was. I was gonna have to be a man and just go home and face my wife. Deep down, I knew that I would have no problem lying my way out of explaining my whereabouts for the night.

As I put on my shirt and prepared to leave, I made sure that I got every last drop out of what had been a very satisfactory evening. Toni was still on the couch asleep and naked. I stood there just gazing at every inch of her body. I was regretting like crazy that I had no camera. I analyzed Toni from head to toe, and I couldn't come up with one flaw. Not one. She was more than I had imagined she would be, and she looked better than a porno star. By watching her, I was starting to get very aroused. The thought of waking her up and trying to get some more ran through my mind. I also was two seconds from masturbating right there on the spot when Toni woke up.

She was a bit out of it, so she didn't bust me looking at her. At that point I was almost done getting dressed. While walking over to Toni, I zipped up my pants, and when I reached her I sat next to her and kissed her on the forehead. In a whisper, I said to her, "Toni, it's getting late so I'm gonna leave. A'ight?"

Toni didn't respond with words—she just nodded as she began to fully sit up and gather herself.

As I stood and prepared to make my way to the door, I voiced those famous words: "I'll call you."

Toni still remained silent. I couldn't understand why she had become so nonverbal. I didn't wanna leave without her saying something, so I returned from the door and moved toward Toni's direction. When I reached her, I sat back down on the couch and gave her a nice warm, reassuring hug. As I held her close to me, I blocked out how good her velvet-soft skin was feeling, and asked, "You okay?"

Toni finally opened her mouth, but she didn't look me in the face as she said in a tired-sounding voice, "Yeah, I'm okay."

I gave her one last peck on the lips, and I departed. Yeah, I thought about telling her that I loved her, but that would have been lying. Besides, there was no reason for me to make such a statement.

By the time I actually walked out of Toni's crib and made my way to my car, it was four in the morning, so it was still dark outside. When I got to my car I noticed that a little note was on my driver's side window. It actually was a little yellow Post-it that was stuck right in the center of my window and it read:

Lance, it is 3:30 in the morning, and you are still here. I should have smashed all of your windows, but your tire was a better option for now. I cannot believe you.

The note did not have a signature or an identifying name at the bottom of it, but as soon as I looked at my front tire, I knew that only Scarlet could pull off such an act as actually slashing a nigga's tire at three-thirty in the got-damn morning. *Man!*

I needed that as much as I needed a hole in my head. Fortunately for me, Scarlet had only slashed one. Being that I had twenty-inch tires and some chrome rims, changing the

tire was not that simple, especially considering that I didn't
have the special key to unlock my rims. My only option was
to drive home with a flat. I knew that I was probably gonna
damage my four-thousand-dollar set of rims, but I really
didn't have many options.

Anyway, I slowly chugged home in a very controlled
manner. Scarlet had gotten me real good. I began to wonder
if she had actually sat on Toni's block for the entire night. I
wasn't sure, and to be honest, I was more worried about what
other trail of destruction, if any, Scarlet had left behind. My
blood pressure instantly shot up as I became shook like crazy,
wondering if Scarlet was gonna go a step further than simply
calling my bluff by actually blowing my cover with Nicole.

My heart was racing, and I was nervous as hell. I mean, here
I was after having just had the best sex of my life with one of
the finest chicks on the planet, and I couldn't even savor the
moment. Instead, I was chug-a-luggin' home at like five miles
an hour, scared like I don't know what. Who needed this type
of stress? On one hand, I had some psycho-stripper-mistress
ready to blow my brains out if she could get a clear shot at me,
and in addition to that I had to try to come up with an excuse
for Nicole as to why I, as a married man, was coming in the
house at damn near four-thirty in the morning.

This was definitely not how things were supposed to be
playing themselves out. I am the first to admit I can't handle
drama and pressure, which is why I try so hard to be smooth
with my game. But this was one bumpy road I was seriously
contemplating getting off as soon as possible. The only thing
that was making me consider staying the course was Toni.
Especially now since I knew that the sex with Toni was off the
meat rack.

I realized, though, that if I was serious about pulling off
this balancing act of being with both my wife and Toni, then
I couldn't allow myself to get all worked up, worried, or bent
out of shape over the evil I'd just done. All of the minor set-
backs, such as dealing with a slashed tire and trying to pacify
a good-looking, full-bodied bangin' stalker like Scarlet del Rio
came with the territory of being a dog.

When I pulled up to the front of my crib, the house was in total darkness. While unlocking the door, I felt as if I was an intruder or something. For some reason it was like every step I took was magnified. Although I was trying to creep as quiet as a cat burglar, I still heard every crack and every squeak on the floor as I walked. I thought about jumping straight into the shower, but I really didn't want to wash Toni's scent from off my body, not just yet anyway. Like a little teenager I couldn't stop sniffing my fingers simply because they had Toni's dried-up juices on them.

After reaching my bedroom, I switched the lamp on very dimly. I was trying to be as silent as possible, but Nicole woke up. She immediately asked, "Honey, are you all right? You had me worried sick. Where were you?"

Again, I didn't allow myself to get rattled. Her line of questioning was only par for the infidelity course. There was no reason to have fear because I knew all it really is is False Expectations Appearing Real. My expectation of Scarlet having called Nicole was more than likely false, so in an effort to downplay things I sat on the bed and reached over and kissed Nicole on the lips. I was giving off the brightest mood that I could muster up as I responded, "Ah man, baby you wouldn't believe me if I told you what I've been through tonight. I got your pages, but I couldn't call you back 'cause I didn't have my phone in my possession at the time. And I definitely had no time to stop at a pay phone."

As my wife lay in our king-sized bed, she curiously asked, "Well, what happened?"

I answered back, "Me and some of the guys from work went to this comedy club in Manhattan, and guess what happened?"

Nicole began to sit up as she nervously asked, "What? Did somebody get hurt or something?"

I responded, "Oh, nah, nothing like that. See, we all drove in this guy name Mike's car, 'cause his is not that flashy, and we didn't wanna get harassed by the cops. But when we came out of the club we couldn't find Mike's car."

"Oh, Lance, don't tell me somebody stole his car," Nicole sadly and genuinely asked.

I answered, "Well, that's what we originally thought, but we found out that his car had gotten towed. We thought that we were parked in a legit parking spot, but you know how it is in the city with those million and one confusing parking signs. And get this, they charged him two hundred dollars to get his car back. Yo, this city is a criminal empire, charging people that kind of money, and I mean we weren't even parked illegally. They had this stupid sign that was on top of like a million other signs that read 'NIGHT REGULATION,' that's it. It just said NIGHT REGULATION, and it had a picture of a moon on it. The cop told us that whenever we see that sign it means that they have the right to tow a car on any night that they choose. Can you believe that? That ain't nothing but straight-up extortion. But there was nothing that we could do, though. There was no way that the impound yard was gonna give us that car without us first paying the cash. They didn't even take credit cards or ATM cards, just cash. We all chipped in and helped Mike out, but it took us almost three hours to get his car back."

Nicole expressed what a shame it was that the car had gotten towed. Since she was feeling compassionate, I decided to drop another bomb on her, so before making my way to the bathroom and hopping in the shower, I added, "Oh, yeah! And Nicole, things got a little bit worse."

"What do you mean?"

"After all of the towing and getting the money together to get the car out of the impound, we finally make it back to Queens, and I get in my car and start it up and pull off, and all of a sudden I here this crazy wobbling sound. I get out of the car, and my tire is flat. Can you believe that? It's like when it rains it pours. And I'm not talking about a slow-leak-type of flat. I'm talking about a serious major flat, a time to buy a new tire type of flat."

"Lance, you're kiddin' me."

"Nah, I'm straight-up serious. I didn't have the key to unlock my rims. I mean, if I did, I would have at least put the donut on until I got home, so I practically drove home on the rim and probably ruined it. That's just more money that I gotta now kick out."

"Why didn't you just call me to come get you?"

"'Cause I figured that you and LL would be sleeping, and then after dealing with aggravation all night long it's like I just wanted to get home as quick as I could. So even if I had called you, I wouldn't have felt like waiting for you to come pick me up . . . But anyway, I just wanna take a shower, and I'll deal with getting the tire fixed tomorrow," I said as I made it to the bathroom and began running the water for my shower.

You see how easy that was, I told myself. *I need to change my name to Lance B. Smooth,* I devilishly thought as I prepared to step into the shower.

I hated to be washing Toni's body oils off, but hey, I knew that I had to distract any subversive thoughts from Nicole's mind, and what better way to do that than becoming one with her by making love to her?

Lovemaking was exactly what my wife and I did when I was done showering. While we made love, all I kept envisioning was Toni's naked, baby-oiled body lying on her couch. I guess it was that thought that allowed me to perform so well with Nicole. Yeah, when we were done making love, I'll admit I felt like a dog. But, I felt like a very happy and satisfied dog. One who had more than his fill for the day and was now ready to go to sleep.

Chapter Fifteen

A little more than a week had passed since the sexual encounter that Toni and I had. My wife didn't suspect a thing, mainly because I had been on point spiritually. Nicole had seen an increase in my motivation to read the Bible and attend Bible class. But see, one thing that I've learned is that when you overcompensate in a particular area, there is bound to be another area that is being neglected. In my case, over the last week or so, Toni had been that area that was getting neglected.

If I were a true dog, I could have been like, "to hell with Toni." After all, I had already hit it, and I'm married. So I didn't actually have to kick it with Toni anymore. I could have very easily moved on to pursuing Carmen, the young girl who worked at McDonald's, or some other piece of meat. It's just that I wanted to continue to hang around Toni. I knew the sex was good, and that definitely played a big part as to why I wanted to hang around and continue to please her. But the main reason I couldn't see myself bouncing on Toni just yet was because I didn't have that sense of closure.

I didn't feel as though Toni and I had exhausted all of the possibilities that stood to exist between the two of us, and it's bugged because I always initially feel that way whenever I get involved with a female, only with me that initial feeling seems to never wear off. That's probably why I yearn to stay in touch with old female flings from as long ago as my early teenage years. Those past girlfriends can be married, and my mind still manages to come up with "what if" possibilities. The only female that I feel like I have ever had a sense of closure with is Nicole.

That's also probably the reason that I've allowed Scarlet to hang around for so long. But even with her, I've never felt as if there was a sense of closure, like we still had so much more to explore and conquer. Scarlet has always caused a chemistry inside of me that constantly makes me feel like I have to hit it one last time. The problem is, one last time has turned out to be five years of countless sex episodes with her.

During the week, Scarlet had been causing all kinds of turmoil, but I quickly began to realize that she was just hungry for my attention, and she wouldn't really go as far as blowing my cover. For example, she has been constantly calling the house and hanging up, real childish type stuff that happens with high school teenagers. It's as if she wants me to be constantly on guard, but if she was really serious, she would have spoken to Nicole by now, and I knew that. But regardless, she was a loose cannon, and I had to make sure that I didn't scorn her in any way because any woman who feels scorned is capable of some serious destruction.

I did, however, manage to worm my way out of that thick situation that had ensued when Scarlet had apparently followed me to Jamaica Estates on the night I first had sex with Toni.

I made sure to simply not just call Scarlet the first thing in the morning of which I'd found my tire slashed. Rather, I made it my business to go visit her. When I made it to her crib, I knew the attention was gonna squarely rest on me, so I had to try to deflect some of it in order to decrease the tension that was sure to be in the air.

When I saw Scarlet, my first words were, "Now Scarlet, just explain one thing to me: Why were you going for my jugular vein by slashing my tire, especially when I had told you that I would explain everything to you?"

"Lance, the way I look at it, there is really nothing to explain. I know that whoever you was wit' that y'all ended up having sex that night. I went all the way out to Harlem. Matter of fact, it was past Harlem, practically in Yonkers, and I performed my show and came back to Queens, and your car was still there. So how do you expect me to not do something? Apparently you were trying to play me, and you were being straight-up blunt and rude about it. I'm sayin', out of respect you could have at least got up and moved your car and parked it somewhere else to try and give the appearance that you had left. You had to know I would double back and check out your sloppy, lyin'-ass story."

"Scarlet, I thought we had an agreement. You were supposed to at least hear me out, so why would I think you would double back on me and do something as low and gully as slashing a nigga's tire?"

"Okay, Lance, I'm sorry for slashing your tire. Now let me hear your tired explanation," Scarlet said with some mouth-twisting attitude.

"A'ight. Baby, listen, I was with a chick. I did try to get some. I mean—"

"Lance, you know what? You really are disgusting. I should just spit in your face right now."

"Scarlet, just let me finish. She was just a girl I knew from high school, and the only reason I was there was because I was just trying to gas her into doing a threesome with me and you."

"What? A threesome?"

"Yeah, you know, a *ménage à trois*."

"Lance!"

"Scarlet, how many times have I told you that I wanted to do that? So why would you even flip?"

"Why would I flip? Because it's always about you, Lance. It's always about what you want. Yeah, you've told me about your little threesome idea before, but how many times have I told you that I don't do that? Lance, you know how many girls come on to me at these strip clubs because I'm always telling you about that. And whenever I tell you about those stories, I always make it a point to tell you and assure you that I don't swing like that, and you know I don't get down like that."

"Yeah but see, Scarlet, those women who come on to you are into that lesbian thing, which is cool with me, don't get me wrong, but I'm not asking you to necessarily be down with the lesbian thing, I'm just sayin'—"

Scarlet interrupted me and added, "Yeah, you're just saying that you want two women at the same time and that you would be willing to take them any way you can get them. You'd be happy if they both just pulled their pants down and bent over and let you do your thing. Lance, I know exactly where you're coming from, and like I already said, and I've been saying it all along, it's always about what you want."

"Baby, that's not true, 'cause if it were true, then I wouldn't even want you to participate in the threesome. I mean, of course, I would want you to enjoy it and get something out of it. Can't you see that I'm at least being straight up with you?"

"Lance, what's this chick's name?"

"Why do you need to know that?"

"What's her name?"

"Tina. Her name is Tina," I barked.

"Okay, let me break it down for you. Lance, you wanna get into Tina's pants, which you probably already did, but to pacify me you're trying to suck me into your little fantasy. I'm not stupid. This is all about you, and that's it."

"Would you stop saying that? First of all nothing happened between me and *Tina*. She wasn't with the idea, and I was just trying to convince her."

"Lance, that is a bunch of BS. You mean to tell me that you haven't spoken to this chick or seen her since high school, and out of the blue you decide to buy some seafood, get all dipped out before going to see her, and when you do see her all y'all do is talk about a threesome until the wee hours of the morning? It just doesn't add up. Lance, it is always about what you want."

"See, I never said that I hadn't spoken to her since high school."

"Lance, you know what? Just forget about it. I ain't got time for games."

"What do you mean 'just forget about it?'" I asked in an attempt to keep this ridiculous argument going. See, I wanted to keep it going in order to distract attention from really having to explain who "Tina" was.

"I mean forget about it. Because you know what? This is how I know and can prove that you are full of it. If you really wanna do a threesome, then why won't you try to convince Nicole to do it? Matter of fact, I tell you what. If Nicole agrees to it, then I'll be with it."

"Now Scarlet, you know good and well that I ain't asking Nicole to do that."

"Why not?"

"Because she's my wife."

"Yeah, and?"

"And I know that she wouldn't go there," I shot back as I started to sense myself really getting vexed.

"So your wife wouldn't go there, and you would not try to get her to go there, yet you would want me to go that route? How the hell am I supposed to interpret that, Lance?"

Throwing my hands up in the air, I said, "Scarlet, you should be a lawyer or a doctor because you are an expert at spinning things around and taking things where it is so irrelevant."

"Irrelevant? No, no, no, I don't think so. My point is very relevant. Or maybe I need to spell it out for you. Lance, if you want me to do sexual things your wife wouldn't do, then basically you are calling me your ho."

"See, now why are you even going there, Scarlet? I ain't even call you no ho or nothing like that, and I never have viewed you like that. But like I said, you're a good spin doctor."

"Lance, you noticed that I haven't attempted to hit you or smack you or anything like that, right?"

"Yeah, so?"

"I realized something when I slashed your tire. See, I was gonna slash all four of them, but then I was like 'what the heck am I doing?' It was like something all of a sudden clicked off in my brain, and I was like, 'Scarlet del Rio, are you crazy or something? If Lance can't be faithful to his wife then how the hell can you expect him to be faithful to you?' Yeah, I finally realized it, Lance. I realized that you are a dog, and I don't need to be playing myself the way I do. I mean, why am I slashing your tires and hitting you and screaming and all of that when I can have just about any man I want?"

"Scarlet, come on with that. You know what you got in me. You know that no other man who looks as good as I do could treat you and sex you the way I do. You know that."

"See, that is exactly what I mean. There you go again thinking that it's all about you. You know what? I used to like that cockiness in you because I took it as confidence, and I'll admit it, most men are intimidated by me, so you have an edge in that area, but believe me and trust me, Lance, there are much finer-looking men than you out there who sex a *whole lot better* than you do and who have a whole lot more going for themselves than you do. Lance, you know what? You're not worth all of the drama."

"What drama, baby?" I said as I attempted to move closer to Scarlet and show her some affection.

"Lance, please don't touch me."

"Oh, so now you're gonna act all cold and standoffish?"

"Lance, you know, you were right when you said that we need to end things. I mean, why am I holding on to you and stringing myself along like I have no other options? You're the one who is frustrated, married, oversexed, and has a kid and not many options. I'm young, sexy, I got money, and I can do whatever."

"Scarlet, that was low," I commented, and I truly did mean it because Scarlet was taking big stabs at my ego.

"I don't care if it's low because it's the truth."

"Okay, let's just back up a minute. This all started because you think that I'm treating you like a ho simply because I won't ask Nicole to take part in a threesome, yet I would be willing to get you involved in one. But see that's because I know how religious Nicole is, and I know that she wouldn't compromise her faith in God for something like that."

"Oh, and I'm a spin doctor? Lance, you know what? We don't even have to take the conversation back there. I'm just gonna take you up on your offer, an offer that I now realize is in my best interest, and I'm gonna leave you alone."

I didn't know if Scarlet was playing mind games with me or what, but I was feeling mad confused. In fact, I was starting to feel hurt. Yeah, it's true that for the sake of my marriage I had decided to leave Scarlet alone, but the end of the relationship clearly had to be on my terms, otherwise I knew future problems would lurk because of the lack of closure I would feel.

"Scarlet, listen—"

"No, Lance, you listen. Enough with all the games. I'm gonna give you what you want and what you requested. I mean, you might be used to having your way with Nicole, but I am not Nicole, so if you're gonna be with me, you can't be playing me for a fool, and that's exactly what you're trying to do."

As Scarlet said that, she reached in her pocket and pulled out a drug dealer–like wad of cash. She peeled off twenties and tens and said, "Here. This is five hundred dollars. This is for your tire that I slashed."

Yo, this chick is dead serious, I thought. As I gave a very insecure laugh I said, "Scarlet, put your money away. Why are you trippin'?"

"Lance, just take the damn money. And I am not trippin'. What is wrong with you? Isn't this what you wanted for some time now? So I'm simply granting you your request, so the real question is why are you trippin'? Now here, take this money."

I reached out, and I took hold of the cash and put it in my pocket. "Scarlet—"

"Lance, there really isn't much else to say. Things were real, we had some fun times and some real good sex over the years, but all good things must come to an end. So you make sure you take good care of yourself. Okay?"

"Scarlet, you are really buggin' out," I said, sounding very astonished.

From the drift of that conversation, you can get a clear understanding as to why my ego was crushed. The remainder of the conversation continued in a similar manner. I began to wonder if Scarlet had linked up with some other cat who was breaking her off with better pipe game than mine or if she was really just fed up with me. I mean, man, I hadn't even really done anything wrong. All I did was have sex with Toni one time, so I didn't know why she was trippin' the way she was.

I wasn't one to get dumped and get played, so I knew I would have to bang Scarlet at least one or two more times in order to put some real closure to the situation. When I set a goal, I don't stop until it is attained and fully achieved.

I also knew that I had to quickly correct the situation of neglect I had been dishing Toni's way. I guess my confidence was slumping so bad to the point that it had become one of the main culprits as to why Toni and I had only been managing to speak on the phone. Unfortunately, we had only been able to see each other once since we had sex. In my heart I felt as though Toni not only wanted to see more of me, but rather, she needed to see me more. I felt like I owed my presence to her, and since Scarlet had basically dissed me, I, too, was starting to feel like I needed to see more of Toni in order to confirm in my own mind that I was still "the man."

The day after we had sex, Toni, in her own way, expressed to me that she wanted to be around me as much as possible. I had finally gotten a chance to ask her why she had remained dead silent right after our sexual encounter. What she told me was that although she was physically feeling real good, mentally she was actually feeling worthless, cheap, and dirty at that point. Yeah, she confirmed what I knew, which was the fact that I'm a great lover, but she also added that sex was more than just a physical thing to her.

Toni went on to explain that she had never made love to anyone without first getting to know them for a very long time. She added how she really trusts me, but at the point right after sex she felt vulnerable in the sense that she knew that I could hurt her like she'd never been hurt before. All I had to do, she explained, was never speak to her again and go on with life thinking that she was some cheap trick. Toni also wondered if I would drift out of her life just as quickly as I had drifted into it.

She had me completely misunderstood. See, yeah, I'll admit that the day after we had sex, that I was second-guessing myself and wondering if Toni was just some nice-complected, good-hair ho. Or if she'd really felt so good about me that she just felt an urgent need to express her feelings by letting me have some na-na.

During our conversation the day after sex, I made sure she didn't have me misunderstood. The first thing I explained to her was that if sex between the two of us wasn't supposed to have happened, then it would not have happened. I assured her of the fact that since we did in fact *make love,* it said a lot about how we feel about each other. I explained to Toni that, in the same way, she probably couldn't explain why she'd gone against her normal rules and made love to me. I, too, was unable to explain why I'd gone against moral rules to be with her.

With that in mind, I also explained to Toni that there was no way in the world that I was ever going to look at her as just some cheap trick, just as I was confident she wouldn't look at me as a typical male dog. I gave Toni my word that I was going to sincerely do everything I had to do in order to allow the trust she feels for me to get stronger and stronger.

There existed a catch-22 in the sense that if I started over-compensating to make Toni feel good, then my wife would be neglected and vice versa. To combat this dilemma, I came up with a well-thought-out plan of action. Actually, it turned out to be a no-brainer. To solve my dilemma, all I had to do was switch my work schedule. Or at least I should say all I had to do was create the illusion in my wife's mind that my schedule was going to be changing.

I was prepared for Nicole to flip out, but I knew that if I wanted things to work out then I would have to be straight-forward with her. When she came home from work, I told her, "Honey, I know you're not going to like this, but I've thought about it, and I realize that it is gonna be the best situation."

Nicole prodded as she asked, "What are you talking about?"

Being confident and straightforward, I blurted out, "I switched my schedule at work. I'm gonna be working the graveyard shift for about a month or so."

Nicole raised her voice as she asked, "You mean twelve at night until eight in the morning?"

"Yeah, that's what I mean. But like I said, it's only going to be for a month or so. Actually, it might be less time than that."

"Lance, why didn't you speak to me about this before you actually did it?"

Lying through my teeth I answered, "Well, baby, I knew that you would have objected. And . . . but, honey, listen . . . I already worked everything out. The bus will pick LL up in the morning so that's not a problem, and I'll still be able to make it to Bible class and all."

Nicole shot back, "Well, when am I going to sleep with you? We're married, and we should be together at night."

In my head I was like, *Oh, boy. Here we go again.* My wife isn't a nag, but lately she had been getting on my nerves, constantly objecting to this and that. I could already see that that was one good thing about Toni in comparison to Nicole. Toni seemed like she would be more than willing to let me wear the pants in the relationship. She seemed like she knew her place and would be more submissive.

I put my wife's fears aside and told her that we would spend our nights together on the weekends. Again I let her know that it would only be for a few weeks. Unfortunately the new nag in Nicole wouldn't let things die as she stated, "Well, I don't . . . I mean, you still haven't told me why all of a sudden you decided to change your schedule."

Enough with this nagging, I thought. I calmly but sharply snapped at Nicole. "Look, Nicole, I'm switching my hours, all right? That's it. If you want to know why I'm changing my schedule it's because I need to spend more time by myself. I figured when I get off work in the mornings I'll be able to relax by myself. I can hang out, sleep, or do whateva it is that I want to do by myself."

Nicole was about to cause me to drive my fist through the kitchen wall as she would not let up. "Oh, so you're trying to say that I'm stressing you out? Oh, what, you would rather spend as much time away from me as possible? Is that it?"

I looked toward the ceiling and slowly counted to ten before I responded. I didn't want this to escalate, and I knew that it would if I kept adding fuel to Nicole's fire. I calmly answered in the softest tone of voice that I could muster, "No, honey, that's not it at all. Listen, I don't want this to escalate into a big argument or anything. All I'm saying is that I want to spend some time alone for a few weeks."

Nicole sucked her teeth and asked, "Well, when do you start this new shift?"

"Sunday night," I replied. "I'll be working it Sunday nights through Thursday nights, and we can still spend Fridays and Saturdays together."

My wife didn't respond, and I was glad she didn't. I was expecting Nicole to remind me of the fact that I have a son who I should have thought about before I made my decision to switch shifts. Man, I was getting all this static, and I hadn't even cleared things with Toni. See, what I really planned to do was continue working my normal 8:00 a.m. to 4:00 p.m., Monday through Friday schedule. But see, Nicole would be thinking that I was home during those hours. When in actuality I'd be coming home from work like normal at four o'clock and go about the remainder of my day like I would on any other day. Then at night, all I would have to do is get dressed like I'm going to work and head straight for Toni's crib and spend the night there every night. Yeah, I know it's a brilliant plan, one that only a dog in heat could think of.

One of my biggest concerns was the fact that I wondered if Toni's parents would object to me spending the night with her every night. I knew from experience that Haitian parents are mad old-fashioned and strict. However, my concerns were eased as I remembered that Toni had already told me how hard her parents work. They were rarely home during the week, and when they were, they usually came in very late, ate, and went straight to sleep. So in reality it's like Toni lived by herself, especially considering that she had a separate apartment and a separate entrance. Therefore, I doubted that her pops would even be home to object to anything.

Chapter Sixteen

Steve and I hadn't hung tight in a while, so when Friday rolled around, I decided to go by his crib after work and kick it with him. When I reached Steve's house I put him up on all of the latest details between Toni and myself. I especially made sure to tell him about the sexcapade that Toni and I had. To my full satisfaction, he admitted that he was grossly jealous. Although Steve gave me my props, I made sure to remind him of how, only a few short weeks ago he had been laughing at me. Revenge is so sweet, because now I was the man.

As I gloated and rubbed my success in Steve's face, there was one thing I didn't like. That was the fact that Steve, from out of nowhere, started talking subversive. He began talking like I'd never heard him talk before. Granted, he asked me about every nook and cranny of Toni's body, including wanting a detailed description of her vagina, but that was only normal for him. Then Steve totally flipped the script.

He started kicking this mess about how he was really starting to feel for Nicole. He asked me had I ever really considered what I was doing to my wife. Steve also managed to throw in a bunch of "what if" statements to the effect of, what if Nicole happened to find out about me and Toni or me and Scarlet?

For the first time that I could remember, I felt like col' punching Steve right in his ugly mouth. I mean, from one playa to another, Steve was breaking all kind of playa rules. I knew that he was probably just jealous 'cause he didn't have the ability to scoop women like I did. Then I started thinking, *What if Steve had plans of snaking me?* Yeah, he probably saw how easy I tapped Toni and had secret thoughts of doing the same.

If there's one thing I hate, I mean hate to the core of my insides, it's jealous, envious niggas. As I spoke to Steve I was getting more vexed by the minute. He was sounding worse than those male-bashing women in Toni's beauty salon. Steve was just ripping into me and totally blowing up my spot so bad that I almost blew my top.

For a split second, I really had thoughts of murdering Steve. Not because he might be trying to snake me for Toni, but rather, what if Steve was trying to backdoor me and play in my own backyard? Yeah, Toni is all that, but Nicole is my true dime piece. I knew that Steve, like any other of my so-called homeboys, if given the chance, they would run all up in my wife.

After Steve had gotten all of the pertinent details he needed in order to satisfy his own innate desires, such as asking about Toni's nipples, he once again, uncharacteristically began ripping into me about how I should be thinking about LL. He started saying that although LL is young, he still probably understands what is going on with me and Toni. He asked me if I wanted LL to grow up and do the same things I was doing.

I couldn't take it anymore. Who the hell did Steve think he was? I'm sayin', he was coming at me all self-righteous and all. Sounding ticked off, I asked, "Yo, Steve, get at me. Where the hell is all of this coming from?"

Steve, seeming as if he had no idea what I was talking about, asked, "Where is what coming from?"

"Steve, don't play stupid," I barked. "I ain't never heard you talk like this in my life. Now all of a sudden you trying to label me as a dog or something."

Steve immediately came on the defensive. "Yo, Lance, come on, man. You know you my boy. Why you trippin'?"

I yelled, "Why am I trippin'? What do you mean why am I trippin'?" Now I was really beginning to believe that Steve was hiding something from me. I yelled, "You know exactly why I'm trippin'."

Steve raised his arms in the air to show surrender. He proceeded to acknowledge me by my street name, "Yo, L, what's up? You lost me, brotha. All I'm saying is that sometimes as men we have to—"

I interrupted Steve 'cause I knew exactly where he was headed. With a screw face, I angrily said, "Yo, Steve, check this. I ain't stupid, man. Nicole is bad! She's got a big butt and all that. Her head is on her shoulders, and she's making dough. I see the way you be looking at her—"

Steve swiftly interrupted me, as he yelled, "Oh, hold up. Hold the hell up."

Like a lion, I roared right back, "Nah, you hold up." After Steve realized I was a more powerful lion, he backed down. With his lips twisted, he looked at me and didn't speak.

I continued, "Steve, I'm sayin'. I see the way you be looking at my wife. But see I always let it slide 'cause I know that she has a bangin' body and niggas probably can't help but to look. But Steve, I'm sayin', I never thought twice about you back-dooring me."

Steve, who now was seething with anger, yelled, "Lance, I know exactly what you're thinking, and I can't believe you would—"

I cut him off again. "Yeah, you can't believe I would think you would try to snake me, right? Steve, come on, man. I'm a man, and I know how men think."

I got closer to Steve, and in an attempt to intimidate him, I let him know straight up, "Steve, I don't know where all this 'I should think about Nicole crap' is coming from, but let me tell you this, if you ever try to snake a nigga, I'm telling you, I'll murder you. Word is bond."

I prepared to leave Steve's crib, and I could have cared less if I ever spoke to him again. As I made my way to my car, I knew that, like a woman, Steve would be determined to get in the last word. I was about two seconds from knocking him flat on his back, when he added, "Lance, man, you don't even know who your boys are anymore. All I'm saying is that I personally know that I ain't ready for marriage, but it comes a time when we have to just stop thinking about the booty, 'cause there's more to life than that."

"Yeah, whateva," I snapped back.

I jumped in my car and was about to pull off. Just as I figured he would, Steve made sure to throw in the last statement as he said, "Lance, all I'm doing is telling you the same words that you used to kick to me. And I know you know exactly what I'm sayin', 'cause remember you're the one who used to kick all that religious holy-roller BS."

With Steve having dropped his final line, I took off in my car. I made sure to make the loudest screeching-tire sound my car could muster. I couldn't believe Steve was acting so shady. Although I knew that he might have been right, all I'm sayin' is he shouldn't have come at me like that. I mean, I don't think he has plans for Toni 'cause he knows that she's out of his league, but I know he might have had plans of creeping with my wife. I was just making sure that I had deaded any of that before it began. As for our friendship, I really could have cared less if I didn't speak to him again.

Steve had me heated, but I wasn't gonna let that situation undermine the rest of my evening. Later on, while it was still early, I played Nintendo with LL for about a half hour.

I couldn't play Nintendo with LL for very long because Nicole and I had to drop him at my in-laws. The reason being, we had tickets for the Kenny G/Toni Braxton concert. The concert, which was being held at Radio City Music Hall, was scheduled to start at eight-thirty. By the time we left my in-laws, who live in Brooklyn, it was 7:45. Believe me, when you are driving into Manhattan, a forty-five-minute cushion is nothing. So to say the least, we were running late.

I have a bad habit of getting angry whenever I'm running late for something. That anger usually leads to a lot of horn-honking, reckless driving, which Nicole hates. The fact that I was still kind of ticked off because of what had transpired between Steve and me, coupled with the fact that we were now running late. I had to make a concentrated effort not to let my anger show. I simply focused on how great it was that Nicole and I were actually going out on a date.

With the Manhattan skyline in full view, we drove across the Brooklyn Bridge, and my wife commented on how beautiful the New York City skyline looked.

I joked as I said, "Honey, do you realize that every time we come into the city you say the exact same thing?"

Nikki replied, "Well, it's true."

Then from out of left field, I asked, "Baby, do you ever think about cheating on me?"

Taken aback, Nikki asked, "What? Where did that come from?"

I tried to downplay things with laughter, as I added, "Not that I'm accusing you of anything, but I just be thinking sometimes about whether or not I'm good enough for you. I mean, I know every day you have to interact with successful judges and lawyers and what-not. I just be wondering if you ever thought about . . . well, you know . . . cheating on me."

Nicole frowned as she sincerely replied, "Lance, I would never ever cheat on you. Never. You mean everything to me."

Although I knew that Nicole would never really stoop to the infidelity level, I just wanted to hear it from her lips. Her words relieved me a great deal. Then Nicole blew up my spot and asked, "Well, since you brought it up, have you ever thought about cheating on me?"

I wanted to blurt out the fact that not only had I thought about it, but I had come full circle with it. As I continued to drive, I thought that it probably would have been better for me to jump into the East River and commit suicide than to come clean with Nikki.

So as not to lie, I answered my wife's question truthfully. "Yeah, baby. As a matter of fact, I have thought about it. That's why I asked."

Nicole seemed shocked as she said, "What?"

With Nicole staring at me and waiting for me to expound, I began thinking, *Man, why did I open up this big can of worms?*

Nicole asked, "Well, is there something wrong between us? Something that would make you think about cheating?"

Being a master of deception, I managed to twist my words around, but even I didn't expect to smoothly get out of this one.

"No, no, baby. I'm not talking about myself having thought about cheating on you. I was trying to say that I've really been thinking about whether or not you've cheated on me."

Nicole looked at me with a serious expression. I remained silent, and I guess my silence caused Nicole to feel a little uncomfortable. Then she laughed and asked, "Lance, what's going on?"

As I blew air out of my cheeks, I replied, "Okay, baby, I'll just put it out there."

"Yes, please just put it out there so I'll know what you're talking about," Nikki begged.

Backing myself out of an almost fatal situation, I explained, "Well, baby, today me and Steve got into this big yelling match. I screamed on him 'cause I noticed that he looks at you a little too close, like he be wanting to do you or something."

When I was done speaking Nicole burst out into tear-jerking laughter. She could barely get the words out of her mouth as she said, "Lance, you thought that? *Ha, ha, ha, ha.*" Again, she began laughing. She laughed so much until she caused me to start laughing.

Then finally, after wiping her tears away, my wife said, "Lance, you got me laughing so hard that you're causing my makeup to smear." She laughed again as she said, "I can't believe that y'all are best friends, and y'all got into a shouting match over me. Baby, listen to me. I'm flattered that you still get jealous over me, but come on now. Steve? Baby, I would never cheat on you, especially not with your best friend, a best friend who happens to be a dog at that. Lance, you should know me better than that."

Yeah, I began to feel extra stupid about how I had acted toward Steve, but there was no time to dwell on that. We were practically right around the corner from the concert, and it was already eight-thirty. I had to park in one of those expensive-as-hell parking garages that are found all over New York City. But it was either pay through the roof and park in a garage or have no peace of mind at all and risk getting your car towed by parking on the street.

Fortunately for us, we were able to park the car and make it to our seats before the show started. Nicole and I were both excited like little kids. There was a buzz of anticipation that filled the air in Radio City Music Hall. Being a man, I had to hold back some of my excitement because I didn't want to seem soft like a sissy, but I was thoroughly enjoying the atmosphere of the concert. It was a mature crowd, and everyone was dressed up. Sadly enough, I couldn't help but think how my mistress Toni would have greatly enjoyed an evening like this if she were with me.

It was nearing 8:45 when the people running the show informed us that it would be starting in about ten minutes and that everyone should take their seats. I used the ten minutes to hug and kiss on Nicole. I also sweet-talked her and whispered sweet nothings into her ear. Nicole was very giggly and happy. The whole time reminded me of how it was years ago when we first met.

The ten minutes flew by. Before long the curtain on the staged parted and the diva, Ms. Toni Braxton, came strutting out onto the stage with her dancers while singing her hit song "You're Making Me High." The crowd went crazy. The first thing I began thinking about was how good Toni Braxton was looking. She is sexy as hell as it is, yet she had the nerve to have on a dress with a split that was about up to her hip bone. Every time she walked, all you could see was thighs for days. In my head I was like, *Yeah, kid.* Of course I was singing and cheering like the rest of the crowd, but I definitely was cheering her body more so than her voice. One thing that I hated was the fact that she'd let herself lose so much weight. I mean she is still the bomb as "Bony Toni," but she was all that when she had weight on her.

The concert was on point. Kenny G ripped it down as did Toni Braxton. Nicole and I had a bomb time the whole night.

On the ride back to Queens with Nicole, I made sure not to spark any more dumb conversation. I really didn't have to worry about that because Nicole, who was out of her seat belt and all over me, definitely had my mind preoccupied. Very uncharacteristically my wife had unzipped my pants and was playing with my goods as we drove. A couple of times she almost caused me to crash, but I managed to keep my composure. Just the thought of having sex in any unconventional location with Nicole had always been a running fantasy of mine, and what better time to fulfill it than now?

In the worst way I wanted to pull over on the side of the highway and do her right there, but I was scared she might view me as a super freak, so I put my desires aside and waited until we were in the privacy of our own home.

Chapter Seventeen

Over the next few days, I set aside time so I could read the Bible. I have a very good knowledge of what the scriptures are all about, but I had been reading so I could try to understand how I should deal with my adultery affliction. No, I was not just reading the Bible as a spiritual front for my wife. Rather, I was trying to search the scriptures to see what on earth was wrong with me.

I realized that in the case of adultery I had many Biblical companions who had been plagued with the same affliction. I was shocked when I read the story of how King David had committed adultery with Bathsheba. King David not only was pulled down by his own lustful desires, but his desires for Bathsheba led him to lie and cover up what he'd done. He also went as far as having Bathsheba's husband murdered.

As I studied King David's ordeal, I saw many similarities in comparison to mine. See, the scriptures refer to King David as a man after God's own heart, yet he was still afflicted by the same thing I was going through. I justified in my mind that if someone as righteous as King David had been creeping around with women, then I must not have been as bad as I thought I was.

When Sunday rolled around, I found it very ironic that the pastor's sermon was about the exact same account of King David and Bathsheba. I could hear that voice inside of me telling me God was trying to say something to me. No, I'm not superstitious, but sometimes I think things happen for a reason. I definitely felt it was no accident that the pastor's sermon was about adultery. People always say the best sermons are the ones that seem as if they are being spoken directly to you and specifically for you to hear.

When service was over, I realized with even more intensity that I could relate to the dirt that King David had done, but in no way, shape, or form did I fear God like King David had, nor was I as repenting as King David had been.

Sunday night was quickly approaching, and faced with the choices of doing right or continuing with evil, I didn't know which way to turn. I found myself in that gloomy state of mind that I am usually in just before I get depressed. There was no way in hell I was gonna let myself get depressed. I knew I had to confront my demons head on and start correcting the nonsense.

Toni had already consented to the idea of me spending my nights with her. That present Sunday night was supposed to be the first of many I would start spending with her. Reflecting on what I had learned from the Word of God and remembering the piercing words that Steve had spoken to me, in my mind I was like "forget Toni." Enough damage had been done. I convinced myself that there was no way I was gonna be at Toni's house Sunday night or any other night for that matter. Scarlet had basically removed herself from the picture, so now was a perfect time to just make a clean break from Toni, and I could be done with all of the drama, lies, and cheating.

Yeah, although I'd promised Toni I would start spending more time with her, I would just have to let her know that I would now be reneging on the spending the nights thing. I convinced myself to not worry about the fact that Toni might think I'd just gamed her for a piece of butt. I had to really get angry with myself for feeling that I owed something to Toni. After all, she was a responsible adult, and she should have known the consequences before she opened her legs for me. I laughed to myself as I thought, *Word up. I don't owe that ho anything.*

My gloomy mood was starting to subside, and I prepared to eat dinner with my family. Being that my schedule had never really changed, I knew that it would be very easy to tell Nicole that I'd come to my senses and decided not to work the graveyard shift. I knew I could gas Nicole by saying to her how I realized that being home with her was more important than spending time by myself. I thought I could really get in good with Nicole if I also mentioned that I realized it was important for LL to see me and the graveyard shift would hamper that father-and-son time.

Right before we started to eat, I made sure to turn off my pager. I also turned off my cellular phone. Therefore, Toni wouldn't be able to get in contact with me at all. Finally, I was beginning to realize that the only way to be rid of Toni was going to be for me to go cold turkey and have no kind of contact with her whatsoever.

During dinner that evening, my wife reminded me of the conversation we'd had on our way to the concert the other night. She tied it into the sermon we'd heard earlier in the day. She told me how she felt that it just didn't make sense to cheat, because just like with King David, cheating only leads to lying and a whole host of other sins.

Our conversation was flowing very smoothly. I was agreeing with my wife, and I was letting her know what particular points I had managed to pick up from the sermon. As we ate, I wondered if I would ever tell Nicole about Toni. I knew that I would want her to know one day, but I had no idea how I would tell her.

The food Nicole cooked was definitely hitting the spot, and I was in such a good mood because I finally felt, even if just on a small scale, a sense of freedom from my distorted sexual desires. I was just about to drop the surprise on Nicole and let her know that I had decided against the graveyard shift when the phone rang.

Sounding upset, I said, "Man! Can't we ever have a peaceful moment without the phone ringing?"

Nicole shot back, "Don't answer it. Just let the answering machine pick it up. If we keep answering the phone at all times of the day and night people will think that it's okay to call here whenever they want."

The answering machine usually picked up after the fourth ring, and our phone was already on its fifth ring.

"Man, the answering machine ain't even on," I said, sounding disgusted.

"Just let it ring," Nicole instructed.

The phone was approaching its tenth ring, and I was getting very annoyed. I told Nicole that I would answer it because it had to be important if someone would let the phone ring for that long. I pushed my chair from the kitchen table and proceeded to answer the phone, which was hanging on the kitchen wall. Although the phone had ticked me off, I didn't want my anger to come across when I answered the call.

I commented to Nikki, "Watch them hang up as soon as I get to the phone." Picking up, I politely said, "Hello."

To my complete surprise, Toni was on the other end. Inside my head I was like, *Ah, man.* My heart raced, but I played it cool as she spoke and said, "I didn't think you were home 'cause the phone rang so many times."

I replied, "Yeah, I was eating dinner."

Toni apologized for interrupting my meal. I told her not to worry about it, then she proceeded to ask all kinds of personal questions, like why my cell phone and pager were off. I lied and simply told her that I didn't know they were off. Toni was kind of annoying me. Here I was with my wife standing right beside me and practically breathing down my back, and Toni was running off at the mouth. I was hoping that she'd hurry up and get to the point of her call. Then it happened . . . Toni melted me with her words.

She seductively said, "Baby, when I couldn't get in touch with you I got scared. I started thinking that you might be trying to avoid me or something."

Talk like that was not what I needed, so I said, "Oh, no. Nah, I'll be there."

Toni asked, "So you are still coming tonight, right?"

"Yeah, definitely."

"So what time are you coming? Lance, I miss you. It feels like I haven't seen you in so long, and . . . I don't know why I'm telling you this but, it's like I can't stop thinking about you."

Trying hard to not get totally wrapped up into Toni words, I responded, "I'll be there at eleven-thirty."

Toni ended by saying, "Okay, just don't disappoint me."

I hung up the phone, and just like that, I had been roped back into my destructive cycle. I know that I've said and felt like this before, but this time I really and truly felt like a crack addict, and to me, Toni was that big, bright vial of crack.

As I hung up the phone, my wife asked, "Honey, who was that?"

In my true dog form, I replied, "Oh, that was my supervisor. He was reminding me that I had to come in at twelve tonight."

I could hear the disappointment in Nicole's voice as she sucked her teeth and dejectedly said, "Oh, yeah, I forgot you were starting that new shift tonight."

Luckily Nicole let the issue rest. She did suggest that we put LL to bed and go make love before I left for work. Wanting to satisfy Nicole's every need, I complied with her wish. Yeah, my wife and I made love that evening, and I made sure to put an asterisk next to that night's sexual performance. The reason being, I almost cried while making love. See, Nicole literally burst out into tears as we were having sex, and I didn't know what was wrong. As my wife rode on top of me, her tears trickled off my chest. The tears were flowing from Nicole's eyes like a leaky faucet. With her voice cracking from emotion, Nicole told me that she'd just became overwhelmed with joy because she was feeling so close to me and in love with me at that moment. She also added that the tears were because, as she put it in her words, she "just loves me."

Like I said, I, too, almost came to tears. I'm rotten to the core, but I did have some human feelings in my body. I wanted to cry because I knew that without a doubt I was still gonna listen to that demon inside of me, and in about an hour or so I knew that I would be cuddled up with Toni and possibly getting my freak on with her.

Chapter Eighteen

When Toni greeted me at her door I could tell she was jubilant over my presence. Toni, who smelled fresher than a bed of roses, had on silk pajamas. She hugged me and wouldn't let me step into her apartment until I'd first kissed her. Although her mouth felt very refreshing, I just wasn't into the kiss. I had been thinking about my wife's tears of joy for the entire ride over to Toni's crib. Sadly enough, Nicole's tears weren't enough to make me turn around and go back home.

Yeah, I was already at Toni's, and I figured I might as well make the best of it. Toni could sense that something was wrong with me, I guess because I wasn't acting as happy to see her as she was to see me. When she asked for the reason for my somber mood, I lied and told her that everything was A-OK. To myself I was like *Come on, what does she think is bothering me? She knew that I was a married man. Couldn't she just put two and two together and figure out what was troubling me?*

One thing about Toni that I noticed as of late, was the fact that since our sexcapade, Toni hadn't mentioned Nicole's name or anything about me being married at all. I wondered if she'd just decided to block out the fact that I was married.

Toni was smelling good and looking good. She was also playing the role of an adulteress to a tee. As all kinds of thoughts were running through my head, Toni was busy sweet-talking me and making me feel like a king. Before I knew it, she had my shoes off, and she was feeding me grapes. Toni also took it upon herself, as she put it, to relieve me of the stress that I was feeling. Roles were drastically reversed compared to the last time I was at her place. Now it was I who'd become the recipient of the massage.

Toni was doing a very good job on my shoulders as she reminded me once again of how much she'd missed me. Then before I knew it she was on my lap and we were kissing. Again, roles were reversed as Toni began kissing my neck and my ears. I'm human, and to boot, I'm a man, so I was definitely getting turned on. Toni was operating smooth as hell. Like magic, she had my shirt off quicker than I could blink.

I couldn't believe it. Here was Toni, feeling all over my muscles, and I hadn't done a thing to try to turn her on. I knew Toni wanted to establish a relationship with me, but now I was beginning to have some serious reservations. All this time I had been thinking Toni was a respectable, high-maintenance lady, but lately all she'd been revealing to me was that she was nothing more than a two-bit ho.

The thought ran through my head that maybe it would be in my best interest if Toni proved to be a ho 'cause then I wouldn't feel as bad if I were to dump her. Plus, who was I fooling? I knew I wasn't gonna marry her or nothing like that, so actually I should have been happy that she appeared to be a ho.

One thing that I decided to do differently as compared to the first night Toni and I made love was to take my time. I sat back and began to really enjoy every touch that Toni placed on my body. I caressed and squeezed all over her body as well. We weren't like two rabbits in heat 'cause we did manage to converse as we made out. I definitely felt more at home this night as opposed to the last evening I'd spent with my beautiful, sexy mistress. This time I was no longer on her living room couch. Rather, on this late evening, I found myself stretched out across Toni's bed.

I don't remember where Toni's silk pajamas had disappeared to, but my plans of taking my time and enjoying things quickly went out the window. The smell of Toni's coochie juices set me off. Before long, and like a deranged sex addict, I couldn't believe what I'd brought myself to do next. But one thing is for sure, and that is, I was enjoying every moment of what I was doing.

The sex lasted just about as long as it had lasted the first time we performed together. This time, though, things were much different on Toni's part. When we were done having sex, she placed her head on my chest, and she expressed how she was starting to fall in love with me. To myself I was like, *Oh, boy, here we go.* Why does it seem that after performing oral sex on a woman, they start talking about love? Maybe they confuse multiple orgasms with love, I don't know.

However, I knew that it was just a matter of time before that topic of love would come up. In a way, I was prepared for it, so I just made sure not to respond.

As we lay in her room with the lights off, Toni expounded on her statement. Talking in a quiet and still tone of voice, Toni said, "Yeah, baby, I've just been really thinking. I mean every day you're the only thing on my mind. Lance, it's like you have a spell over me or something."

My ego couldn't help but feel gassed as I chuckled like a pimp.

Toni quieted me by saying, "No, Lance, I'm serious. I really have been thinking about our whole relationship. See, after we made love the first time, I didn't know what to think or how to continue in this relationship. I was thinking about just not allowing things to go on any further between us. But I realized that would have been too hard for me to do."

As Toni spoke, I managed to remain quiet because I wanted to let her speak her mind. It's sad, but I was feeling so good about all that Toni was saying. Yet at the same time I felt like the game was over. I had captured my kill and devoured it. To me, the hunt was always the most enjoyable part of the game. Unfortunately, in Toni's case, that was over.

Toni continued, "Lance, I know you're married, and I don't even like thinking about that. But I have to think about it because it's a reality. Lance, I wanna know, have you ever thought about me in the ways that I think about you?"

What the hell? I decided to just blurt it out. I mean I had done enough dirt, so why try to clean it up now?

"Toni, when I first saw you, I knew that something special was gonna develop between the two of us. Matter of fact, I even told you that. And you know what? That something special is developing as we speak. Baby, without a doubt, I know that I love you. I'm past that stage in my life where I just have sex to be having sex. I've been making love to you, not just sexing you, so you should know that I love you."

Toni, who had to be excited by what I was telling her, tried to keep a serious face as she asked, "Well, where do you see our relationship going?"

Toni stumped me with that question. But I knew that I owed her an answer. I understood fully that Toni was just like any other female. She was holding on to all of that emotional female crap. She needed her emotions to feel at ease.

"Toni, I'll be honest. I'm not gonna just say this just because I know that this is what you wanna hear. I'm saying it because it's how I feel about you. I know you said you hate talking about the fact that I'm married, and so do I. Now I'm not saying right away or anything like that, maybe in a year or so, but I know things are gonna end between me and Nicole. When that happens, it'll make room for me and you to be together the way we want to be."

I was waiting for Toni to respond, but she didn't. I didn't know why I'd said what I just did because I didn't mean it at all. I knew that if I kept talking I was bound to keep putting my foot in my mouth. Trying to put a lid on all of the love talk, I hugged Toni and asked her if she really believed that I loved her. She told me she did, and with the snap of a finger, we were kissing. When we paused, Toni let me know that she had been anticipating making love to me for the past week. She smiled like a little devil and told me that the reason she'd let my phone ring for so long was because of that same anticipation of having sex with me.

I began laughing as I said, "Oh, so you used me." Then I playfully pulled the bed sheets up to my chin and said, "I feel dirty and cheap."

Toni slapped me and laughed as she said, "I'm just trying to keep it real. A sista does have her needs, and Lance, you know you got that butta love."

We both began laughing, and Toni turned on the bedroom light. With the room bright, she informed me that she was going to the kitchen, and she asked me if I wanted anything to drink. I asked for a glass of water. After placing my order I watched as Toni walked naked toward the kitchen, feeling like the man. When she returned with my water, she sat on the bed, and after thanking her, I reminded her that I still had to wrap her hair for her so she could see my skills.

Sounding excited, Toni replied, "Oh, that's right. I have to see what kind of skills you got. You're coming over tomorrow night, right?"

"Yeah, I'll be here."

Toni added, "All right, bet. Tomorrow night I'm gonna see what kind of skills you got. Tomorrow it's on."

Toni and I talked until about three in the morning. She didn't have to get up for work the next day, but I did. I knew that I would only get about three good hours of sleep, so I was definitely ready to hit the pillow and be out.

By the time I laid my head on the pillow for the night, it was five past four in the morning. I was hoping that two hours of sleep would be enough to carry me through the next day. So far, my adultery plan with Toni had been working to the tee, but the all-night sex thing was bound to wear a brotha down.

Chapter Nineteen

The guilt of not having my wife by my side as I slept every night lasted for about three days. It was replaced with the rekindled excitement of being around Toni. For the past two and a half weeks, my plan continued to work like a charm. Nicole hadn't suspected a thing. The fact that Nicole was still in the dark as to my affair with Toni was a testament to my split persona and skilled acting ability. As for Toni and me, we managed to enjoy each and every moment that we spent together.

Although the majority of the time I spent with Toni had been at night, we still lived it up. Our nights together included activities such as romantic strolls on the boardwalk out at Long Beach, sex on the beach, weightlifting, the twenty-four-hour bowling alley, rollerblading, the movies, and much, much more. I also proved to Toni that I did, in fact, possess a few skills in the cosmetology department. A couple of our nights were spent with me experimenting on Toni's hair and eyebrows.

Over the past few weeks, I'd also come to learn so much about Toni, things that almost turn me on in the same way her looks turn me on. There is one thing that I was convinced of, and that is Toni is definitely far from a homewrecking ho. Toni's mind wasn't on materialistic things. I'm not saying that she didn't appreciate the finer things in life, but she did-n't let material things consume her. I remember thinking to myself how Toni's non-materialistic quality was such a sharp contrast to Scarlet, who was always talking about how she had to buy the latest and top designer clothing and accessories. It was always "Gucci this" and "Gucci that," or "Prada this" and "Prada that," Manolo, LaPerla, or some nine-hundred-dollar snakeskin boots or something expensive. I mean, there is nothing wrong with wanting nice things, but it can't be the only thing you talk about, and in Scarlet's case, it seemed like materialistic talk was always on her brain.

I explained to Toni how I'd been making over forty thousand dollars a year since I was nineteen years old, and how I now, with overtime, made close to seventy thousand dollars a year. Toni was shocked to realize that I make as much money as I did, considering what I did for a living. But at the same time she was not all that impressed. I tried hard to impress her by explaining how I used most of my paychecks to invest in Con Edison stock. Speaking like a certified financial planner, I described to Toni how if I kept investing the way that I'd been doing, that I should be a millionaire by the age of forty. I was also sure to let Toni know how young I was when I'd bought my house.

I rambled on and on with materialistic mumbo-jumbo that most chickenheads would have been salivating over, but Toni wasn't that concerned. In a polite way she told me that if she wanted to, she could have whatever she wanted by simply asking her father to purchase it for her. However, Toni told me that she never wanted to get by in life based on the level of success that her parents had achieved. Rather she wanted to go after her dreams and create a legacy of her own.

Besides the fact that Toni wasn't about money, one other thing in particular that impressed me about her was her expression of a genuine desire to help children. Toni told me that she was in school studying to be a special education teacher and she only wanted to teach in impoverished neighborhoods.

I was curious to know why, with her father being a doctor and all, she want to pursue a career such as teaching. Toni informed me that her father tried to instill in her since she was little that she had to become a doctor. She even wanted to be a doctor, but after failing miserably in school when she was young, she got turned off to the medicine thing.

Toni wasn't embarrassed at all to let me know that she had suffered from dyslexia as a child. She told me that she grew up privileged and rich, yet at times she still felt useless because she had a learning disorder. She explained that if as a rich kid she still felt useless, then she could only imagine how low the self-esteem levels could drop in terms of learning-disabled children who are poor. Toni added that ever since her problem was diagnosed, it has been her mission to help educate those who were like her but only less fortunate.

With the way Toni was impressing me, and with the fun we'd been having, it was sad to say, but I had seriously been entertaining the idea of bouncing on Nicole. I thought if things were this great between Toni and myself, I could only imagine how they would be if we were spending all our time together. Plus, Toni is crazy about LL, and LL is crazy about her. She'd bought him exactly what he wanted for his birthday, and he was officially hooked on her from that point on, so I knew he would have no problem making the transition.

I had been maintaining my sanity throughout this whole spending-the-night ordeal, but I was dog tired. In fact, during the week there was one twenty-four hour episode in particular that really drained a brotha, but I guess in a sick kinda way it was more than worth it. Somehow within that time, I managed to have sex with Toni, Scarlet, and Nicole, all at separate times, which was a record for me. I would have to say that that was probably my most crowning and defining day as a dog, and at the same time I had probably never felt more disgusted with myself.

Mainly what fueled me was, well, it was just something that I wanted to see if I could pull off, and I did. Doing both Toni and my wife was a relatively easy task. But hitting Scarlet's skinz that one last time was the only minor hurdle I had to overcome. It wasn't as easy as I thought it would be. I just had to have Scarlet one last time so that I could prove to myself that I was still the man and so that I could also end things with her on my terms.

Like I said, sexing Scarlet proved to be a little tough. I had basically popped up at Scarlet's crib during my lunch break at work. She was surprised to see me, but she kept up her defiance in terms of forcing herself to not get close to me. She was properly allowing room for the permanent space, which, of course, was something I had originated and requested. We talked about this and that—basically it was a lot of small talk—but I was straight up with Scarlet and I let her know that I hadn't stopped by to just talk, but I wanted to get some booty. I wanted a quickie.

Scarlet was really ticking me off because even after express-ing to her that I wanted her, she managed to keep up that wall. I had to kind of force myself on her. Yeah, I had to because she wouldn't kiss me or anything. In my mind I was like, *Yo, why is she bugging out?*

I really had to get physical with her, and we had basically come to a point of scrapping with each other like boxers and wrestlers. Of course I was stronger than she was, so I basically managed to overpower her and get my way. Actually it was more like she finally stopped resisting me.

So when she stopped, I literally ripped the zipper on her jeans while ravenously pulling her pants down to her ankles and then I did my thing. Scarlet was not her usual self, and I could sense that she wasn't into the sex at all. It wasn't even one of those love-hate-rough-but-good-psycho-break-up-sex type of episodes that we'd had on a past occasion. Although I did manage to enjoy it while I was pounding it, after I nutted and I was done, I began asking myself, *Was this just some rough sex or did I just rape this woman?* My mind was really buggin' because I couldn't tell.

Scarlet managed to pull her jeans back up, and she buttoned them in spite of her broken zipper, and she looked as if she was confused and truly heated, but she kept silent. I guess I felt better about the whole situation when Scarlet consented to my request for a kiss. Despite the fact that she had given me a cold and quick non-wet good-bye kiss, which included no tongue action at all, it was still a kiss.

I don't know if she gave me that kiss because she wanted to really kiss me or if because she just wanted me to get the hell out of her crib. But I do know that when I left her crib and continued with my workday, I was basically feeling like, *Okay, now I am definitely finished with Scarlet. Definitely.*

Yeah, that twenty-four hour period had really drained a nigga both physically and mentally. Mentally I was all screwed up because now I was feeling like an adulterer and somewhat like a rapist, which was definitely no easy thing to sit with.

But like anything and everything else, I had to just block it out and not worry about a thing and simply keep things moving. Physically I had never had so much sex in such a short period of time, and I was just worn out.

I informed Toni that Thursday I was gonna be going back to sleeping at home for a couple of weeks just to make sure I didn't wear down my body. Toni had no objections. But at this point in our relationship she had become more than attached to me. I could tell that, unlike before, Toni was now more insecure with the fact that my wife was still in the picture. Toni had been making comments such as, "I know you'll probably dump me and go back to only being with Nicole."

She'd been asking so many "what if" questions. She wanted to know what was gonna happen when she went back to school in August for her last semester. She was convinced that when she was to leave for school I would automatically revert to Nicole forever.

As a matter of fact, I think it was Toni's insecurity that led her to allow us to have unprotected sex during the past week. I had mentioned to her how sex with condoms just didn't feel as good as sex without them. Toni immediately wanted to know if Nicole and I used condoms. After telling her no, I think she thought I was trying to imply that sex with my wife was better than sex with her. In no way was I trying to imply that, but from that point on, Toni and I didn't use any protection. I know I was being beyond foolish, but, hey, I'm just sayin'.

Chapter Twenty

I don't know how on earth I had managed to slip up, but I had made a major, major error. When I walked through the front door of my house I thought the world was coming to an end. My heart dropped to my knees as I immediately thought my wife had somehow found out about my multiple affairs. Why else would she be so angry? After all, as far as Nicole was concerned, more than a week had passed since I'd returned to my normal schedule and plus, I'd been on point spiritually.

"Lance, what is this?" Nicole yelled while holding up a videotape.

I thought, *Oh my God. I know Toni didn't set me up and videotaped me. Scarlet del Rio. It had to be her ghetto Brazilian ass.* For a split second, I thought that maybe Nicole had some private investigator tailing me during the past few weeks.

I began my defense. "Baby, calm down. I don't know what that is. I mean it's a VCR tape, but—"

Nicole interrupted me, "Lance, don't play stupid. Now I asked you a question. What is this? And why is this garbage in the house?"

At that point my heart began beating terribly fast. I was about 99 percent sure as to what my wife was talking about.

"Let me see that tape," I said, taking it from Nicole's hand. "Oh, this," I said very nonchalantly.

"What do you mean, '*Oh, this*'?" Nikki barked.

"Nicole, calm down. It's just a porno tape," I said while trying to diffuse the situation.

"Lance! Just a porno tape?"

Still trying to downplay the situation, I said, "Yeah, it's not like I watch it or anything. One of the guys on the job gave it to me."

"Lance, first of all, stop lying. 'Cause you would not have the tape if you weren't watching it. Second of all, do you know I caught your five-year-old son watching this crap? Do you know what this stuff will do to him?"

At that point, all of the energy in my body left me. I felt like I was at a funeral looking into the casket of a dear family member. I think I was feeling that way because I was wondering if I had just killed LL. Did I just kill my son in the same manner pornography had managed to kill me? I have been a resurrecting sex addict since I was nine years old. And that can mainly be attributed to my early childhood exposure to pornography.

Nicole was furious and rightly so. With my head bowed from embarrassment, I began speaking in a very low and humble tone. "Honey, I'm sorry that was in the house. Where is LL? I wanna speak to him."

Nicole ripped into me again, "And Lance, what about all of those magazines? God only knows how long LL has been looking at those things."

"Honey, I told you that I'm sorry. They should not have been in the house, and I'll definitely throw them in the garbage. But where is LL? I wanna speak to him."

Nicole sucked her teeth, looked at me, then she told me that LL was in his room. I quickly rushed up to LL, and when I stepped into his room, the first words out of LL's mouth were "Daddy, I'm sorry. I'm sorry, Daddy."

After watching LL cower into a corner with his hands up, I almost broke down and started crying because he reminded me of a kid who gets physically abused and is anticipating a butt whipping.

Mustering up as much mercy and compassion as I could, I immediately began to console LL. I picked him up from the floor and I set him on my lap. LL was crying, and I knew that he felt extremely guilty for what he had done. "LL, Daddy is not mad at you. Look at me," I instructed.

LL wiped away his tears, and he looked at me. I continued to speak, "LL, I know that your mother probably yelled at you, and she yelled at you because what you were watching is not good for you. See LL, when a person is your age, they shouldn't watch what was on the tape or look at the pictures in those magazines because it's not good."

LL was just about done wiping away his tears, and he asked, "Daddy, those are grown-up tapes, right?"

I nodded in agreement. With his cheeks still wet from tears, LL asked a very convicting question. "Daddy, if it's bad for little kids to watch those tapes, why isn't it bad for grown-ups to watch them? You were little before too."

At that point I couldn't help it anymore. I wasn't gonna try to put up a front. If I wanted the cycle to end, I had to keep it real with LL. Starting to shed tears of my own, I insecurely laughed, and I asked LL if he had ever seen me cry before. He was very wide eyed as he shook his head no.

"LL, Daddy is crying because I love you so much. You might not understand what I'm about to tell you, but just listen closely. LL, do you remember how I told you that drugs are a bad thing and you should never use them or take them from anyone?"

LL answered, "Yes."

I continued, "LL, the reason I told you to stay away from drugs is because there are people who take them, and they might want to stop taking them, but they can't because they get addicted to the drugs."

I continued, "See, LL, when you're addicted to anything, whether it's to drugs or cereal, it's no good because being addicted makes you do things that you know are wrong. You know certain things are wrong, but when you're addicted you do them anyway. LL, when you do things that are wrong, you start to hurt people who love you, and you also hurt yourself. Do you understand me?"

LL said, "Yeah, because if I was addicted to Fruity Pebbles then I would get sick, and you and Mommy would be hurt because I didn't listen, right?"

I smiled and replied, "Exactly. Now LL, the reason I'm telling you this is because when I was your age, maybe a little older, I looked at magazines and certain pictures that I wasn't supposed to look at. Just like you, I sneaked into my daddy's things. The things I saw were just like the movie you watched and the pictures you saw. But see LL, my father and my mother never caught me. As a matter of fact, nobody ever caught me, so I would look at those things whenever I got the chance. I did it because I liked it and it made me excited. But LL, I didn't know that those things were bad for me. They were bad for me in the same way that drugs are bad for a person. LL, you know what? When I got older I realized that I was addicted to the pictures and to tapes like the one you saw."

As I spoke, LL looked intently at me. I began welling up inside, and before I knew it I was bawling in tears. I made sure Nicole didn't hear me, and I was hoping she didn't walk in the room. Literally, for the first time in my life I was being real with someone and admitting that I had a problem with sex. I was trying like crazy to hold back my tears. I told LL it was not right for a grown-up to look at the pictures or watch the tape he'd seen. I explained to him that grown-ups sometimes make mistakes just like little kids.

"Daddy, you mean like it would be wrong for me to keep eating Fruity Pebbles, but if I was addicted I wouldn't be able to help it, and I would eat it anyway . . . and, and . . ." LL paused then he continued, "and it's like, it's wrong for you to watch the tape, but you are addicted?" LL ended his statement in a tone that said he wasn't sure if he was saying the right thing. But I knew he understood.

"LL, that's exactly right," I told him. "LL, now tell me the truth. How many times did you watch that tape and look at those pictures? Whatever you tell me, I won't get mad at you."

LL paused and looked toward the ceiling. Then he held up three fingers.

"You watched it three times? Are you sure that was it?"

LL answered, "Yeah, I'm sure 'cause when you were working in the nighttime, Mommy was on the phone, and I was in the basement playing and that's when I found it."

"What did you think when you saw what was on the tape?"

LL shrugged his shoulders, put both of his hands in the air, and he said, "I don't know. I thought it was like when you kiss Mommy. And like when I got my haircut and you hugged Toni."

Man! I knew I'd been sending LL some damaging messages, and I had to change. I only hoped that he hadn't been permanently scarred.

"LL, now I want you to look at me. LL, I promise you that I will throw those tapes and those magazines in the garbage. Just like I made you promise me that you would stay away from drugs, I want you to promise me something else. LL, promise me that you will never, ever watch another tape like the one you saw and that you will never look at pictures like the ones you saw."

LL promised me he wouldn't. I slapped him five, and told him he didn't have to tell his mother what we'd talked about and I would make sure that she didn't yell at him for what he'd done. I didn't mind if LL knew about my perverted past, but I didn't want to expose myself to Nicole just yet. I knew that I was gonna eventually have to come out of the closet and tell her about my sexual addictions, but I just didn't know how she would look at me.

I wished like heck that LL was older so I could explain to him how, indirectly, my addictions were hurting his mother and she didn't even know it. I thought if I could just be open with someone about my feelings then maybe I could stop creeping around and lusting the way I did. At least I had the courage to speak to LL.

After LL and I finished talking, I went to make peace with Nicole who was on the telephone in the kitchen. I quietly overheard her yapping all this mumbo-jumbo about how she couldn't believe I would even have that garbage in the house. After eavesdropping for five minutes and listening to her bash me, I didn't know if I felt like crying or screaming out in anger. I proceeded to abruptly walk into the kitchen, and I asked Nicole if she could get off the phone.

She ignored me, and she spoke on the phone for another two minutes. Then when she was ready—and only when she was ready—she told her sista that she would call her back.

I was frustrated, but I had to keep it inside of me, and I reminded myself that Nikki had no idea of what I'd been through in my lifetime in terms of my distorted sexuality. And there was no way that I was gonna be able to convey that to her at the moment.

"Nicole, do you have to be on the phone running your mouth to your sista about everything that goes on in this house?" I barked.

Nikki, who seemed ticked off, replied, "Lance, don't even go there, all right?"

"Nikki, all I'm saying is that I was wrong, but we haven't even spoken about this, and you're already spreading my business."

Nikki added, "What do you mean we haven't spoken about this? There is nothing to speak about. You're getting rid of those tapes, and that's it. It's final. I mean, if you find those whores on those tapes more appealing than me then that's another story."

Thinking to myself, *Oh, boy,* I said, "Nicole, it has nothing to do with finding those women more attractive than you or anything like that."

Nicole added, "Women? You mean sluts." She paused then she sucked her teeth and said, "Well, whatever. Did you speak to your son?"

"Yeah, I spoke to him, and everything is cool. I explained to him how it was wrong for me to have pornography in the house and how I didn't want him looking at things like that anymore. Nicole, he promised me that he wouldn't look at them anymore and he told me that he'd only looked at it three times."

Nicole yelled, "Three times. Lance do you realize how smart LL is? He knows how to operate that VCR and everything. Who knows how many times he actually watched that garbage? I have a master's in psychology, so I know how damaging just one glimpse of that stuff is."

"Nicole, look. He watched it, and it's over, a'ight? It's not gonna happen again, and that's the end of it. I don't wanna hear another word about this."

As usual, Nicole had to get in the last word and she uttered, "I don't know what kind of Christian you call yourself."

With that sarcastic remark, rage ran down my body. I just wanted to run and grab my wife and ram her skull upside the kitchen wall. She had no right to be making statements like that, especially since she didn't know the amount of years that I'd struggled with pornography. As far as I was concerned, my struggles had no bearing on my Christianity and neither did they have anything to do with my degree of love for Nicole and

LL. Nicole's sarcasm had me bent. I felt like storming out of the house, but I knew running wasn't gonna change anything.

For the remainder of the night I chilled out with LL, and I thought about coming clean with every sexual sin that I'd ever committed. I was trying to see how I could tell Nikki everything about my sexual past, up to and including Toni. As I sat and pondered, I realized I really didn't care about a divorce and all that nonsense. I just wanted to be set free from my skeletons and demons. I could pray to God and I could go to church, but I knew I would never be set free until I truly confessed my iniquities to Nicole, who is my heart and soul.

Later that night when Nicole and I lay in bed, my heart was racing. I thought about at least telling Nikki about some of my past. Yeah, maybe it wasn't the right time to hit her with the reality of the affair, but at least I could start unlocking the door to my horrid past.

As I was gearing myself up to voice the sounds of confession, my wife asked me a question.

She asked, "Lance, I don't know how to say this, but, is there anything on those tapes that you see those porno queens doing that you would like me to do?"

Once again, all of the strength left my body. As I was getting ready to respond to Nicole, she abruptly added to her statement, "Lance, I just don't ever want you to think about the whores on those tapes more than you think about me. I mean, I can dress up in high heels and garters and all that. I'll strip for you or whatever. Lance, if there's some special sexual favor that you want me to perform, just let me know."

I began feeling dejected as hell because Nicole simply didn't have a clue. I guess she was only asking the normal questions that any woman would ask after finding out that their husband has been secretly watching pornography, but still, she was clueless.

Sounding despondent, I replied, "Nah, baby, believe it or not, I'm satisfied. Just keep doing what you've been doing."

Chapter Twenty-one

To me, LL is the most important person in the world. He is my seed, and I didn't want my seed to grow up and bear rotten fruit. For LL's sake, I knew it was time to go cold turkey and put an end to all of the foolishness. When LL gets older, how am I going to teach him that certain things are immoral if I myself have not abstained from them? One thing I know for sure is that actions speak a whole lot louder than words.

My actions over the past month have been phenomenal. It's been hard, but for LL's sake, I managed to stop going to the strip clubs. I cut down on the number of times I masturbated, and I have thrown away and stopped looking at all forms of pornography. I even threw away phone numbers of females I've flirted with. My lusting was also on the decline.

I managed to see Scarlet a couple of times, but that was because I wanted to make sure that she was okay, both physically and mentally. I mean, I had kind of forced myself on her the last time I was with her, and that just wasn't sitting right with me. Little did I know, but I had managed to reopen a whole other can of old worms and emotional baggage and skeletons that were in Scarlet's past as it related to sexual abuse and rape. It was like although I had promised myself that there would be no more sex between Scarlet and me, I knew that now she needed me to be around her because of the old wounds that I had managed to reopen. Plus, I felt guilty. But yeah, I guess that was all just a minor setback in my quest to free myself from my cheating ways.

On the flip side, I would say my biggest accomplishment was that I went a little over one month without visiting Toni. Yeah, Toni and I spoke on the phone, but even that was been limited to short conversations. Toni was no fool, and I knew she realized that I've been purposely trying to distance myself from her. LL's future sexuality played a major role in me abstaining from Toni, but there was another major scare I had that also told me enough was enough.

About a week or so after LL got busted watching the porno tape, I noticed something odd about my wife's vagina. Nicole had this sort of thick and slimy discharge coming from her. Needless to say, she wasn't exactly smelling like a bed of roses down there either. In fact, Nicole's vagina smelled a lot like the low tide at Jones Beach. Anyway, I noticed the discharge before my wife did. I wanted to bring it to her attention, but I was scared as hell.

The first thought that came to my mind was that I had contracted some sexually transmitted disease from Toni and had infected my wife. Man, I was panicking like crazy. When I saw that discharge, I immediately wanted to get on the horn with Toni. But at the same time I didn't want to jump the gun and automatically assume that Toni was at fault. I also wanted to run to the doctor to get myself checked out, but I was too damn scared to do that. What I did was I simply remained quiet.

Nicole and I hadn't used condoms since our first year of marriage, but due to fear of the unknown, I felt that it was time to revert to the old way of doing things. I had no clue as to what kind of disease Nicole had or if I had given one to her, so I figured by using condoms it would at least keep a bad situation from getting any worse. I was creative in my reason as to why I wanted to start using condoms again, and fortunately for me, Nicole shrugged it off and didn't object to it.

About a day or so after I noticed the discharge, Nicole started to complain that her private area was very itchy and irritated. To my surprise, she informed me that she, too, had seen the discharge but didn't know what it was. In my heart I knew that Nicole, although she didn't show it, was very alarmed. I was thinking that with this whole pornography episode now lurking in my past, that Nicole surely wouldn't have put it past me to go behind her back.

Surprisingly, I'd managed to be upfront with Nicole. I explained to her that I had noticed the "white stuff," but I'd chosen not to say anything. I also told her the discharge had alarmed me and that was the true reason I'd decided to bag up and wear a condom. Nicole was concerned, and so was I. So without delay we marched our butts down to the doctor's office.

I was never secure with the fact that Nicole's gynecologist is some middle-aged handsome black dude. But hey, she had to see him in order to figure out what was wrong. What ticked me off was the fact that when we got to his office he seemed to be a little extra friendly. Granted that Nicole hadn't been to see him in quite a while, but at the same time it's not like he knew her all that well on a personal basis.

His name is Doctor Timothy Wine, and when Dr. Wine came out to the waiting area to greet us, his face lit up with a huge smile.

"Oh, Nicole? How have you been?" Dr. Wine happily asked, as he extended his hand to Nicole for a handshake.

Nicole, with her ever-pleasant smile, accepted his hand-shake and replied that she had been doing fine. It's funny how he'd forgotten my name as he asked, "And your name again, sir?"

I just turned my lips and looked the other way so that he would know that I was purposely trying to diss him. For the sake of peace, Nicole interjected and reminded him of my name. Although there wasn't a damn thing funny, Dr. Wine started smiling and laughing this fake laugh as he patted me on the back and said, "Oh, that's right. Lance." After he realized I had a very serious face and he was the only one laughing, he quickly donned a serious expression and tried to change the subject as he asked, "And how's the little one?"

That was it, I'd had enough of this punk-ass, brown-nosing doctor. I rudely blurted, "LL is fine. Now, Doc, if you don't mind, can we get started?"

Dr. Wine took the hint, and he requested that Nicole follow him into his office. I made sure I followed right behind the two of them. Nicole pushed me as she tried to persuade me to go back into the lobby, but that wasn't happening. Then Dr. Wine tried flexing his authority as he told me that no unauthorized people were allowed into the examination area.

I quickly stepped up and flexed my authority, and I explained the fact that I'm married to Nicole gave me the authority to go with her. To Nicole's extreme embarrassment I added that, furthermore there wasn't a man in the world who could poke and probe my wife's vagina without me being present.

When I was done flexing on the doctor, his position had changed. Without any further delay, the three of us found ourselves sitting in his office. Nicole explained to him her symptoms, and he took very studious notes. The doctor then explained to Nicole that he was sure that she had nothing more than a yeast infection.

While Nicole was dropping her pants, the doctor explained that when women have their first yeast infection, it is very often mistaken as an STD. He advised that, just to be sure, he was gonna perform a pap smear, and he was also going to draw some of Nicole's blood and have it tested for STDs.

The doctor slipped on some plastic gloves and began pulling back skin, poking, sticking, swiping, and trying to peek at every crevice of Nicole's private parts.

When he was done, he told Nicole that based on his years of experience, he was certain that she only had a yeast infection. He prescribed her some medication that she had to inject into her vagina for three days. He added that in time, everything should be back to normal.

Man, I can't begin to explain how relieved I was when after a week had passed Nicole told me that the results from her pap smear were normal and her blood test showed that she didn't have any STDs. Without Nicole's knowing, I, too, had run out and gotten tested just to make sure everything was on the up and up with me, which, thank God, it was.

That whole yeast infection episode just made me think. I realized even more that it just wasn't worth it for me to be running around sexing different women and risking my life—and my wife's life at that.

Chapter Twenty-two

By the time the middle of August rolled around I found myself being tempted by some of my same old demons. I had no porno tapes at my disposal, but sad to say I found myself watching the X-rated channel on cable TV. No, my wife and I weren't subscribers to that channel. But see, I went as far as watching the channel even though the screen was scrambled. I couldn't even get a clear shot as to what was being displayed on the screen. To me just hearing the sounds of people having sex was enough to wet my appetite. On a good night, every now and then the picture would clear up for about three seconds, which enabled me to see all of the meat and potatoes.

Like a fiend, I was exhausting all of my options. I found myself on the Internet looking at all kinds of X-rated material and talking to people in sex-oriented chat rooms. During my sexual excursions on the Internet, I came to realize that there are some major sex freaks in this world. I was actually able to meet people kinkier than myself. With me exposing myself to new forms of sexual material, I again had to combat that age-old demon of mine, which was masturbation.

I had also been seeing Scarlet more frequently. We had kind of worked out a new arrangement where we both agreed to limit our sexual contact with each other to just oral sex. It wasn't just selfish oral sex where only I benefited, but I also returned favors to Scarlet. It was a good arrangement because oral sex was not really cheating—at least not in my mind. Plus, my relationship with Scarlet was just *different,* so slipping up with her wasn't too bad, because like I have been saying from day one, what I have going on with Scarlet isn't really wrong—at least, in my mind it isn't.

I was able to toot my success horn in one area, and that was the fact that I continued to stay away from Toni. However, with each passing day the urge to see her grew stronger and stronger. I'd been praying to do the right thing, and for the most part, I was. But I knew that until I actually opened up to my wife and told her the truth about my past, I'd continue in my same sad pattern of behavior.

I called Toni just to see how she was doing. When I spoke to her, it was as though I had been hit by a moving train. See, to my disappointment, Toni told me that she was leaving for D.C. in three days. The fact that my real-life fantasy was about to end, well, that didn't sit well with me. Immediately I thought back to the first time I saw Toni. I thought back to pulling her over and asking her to cut LL's hair. I thought about the numerous times I visited her in the shop. I thought about all the sexy outfits I'd seen her in. I reminisced about the first time we kissed. I got chills thinking about the first time we made love. I tried to go back in time and relive the nights I'd spent sleeping over at Toni's crib, and all the fun we had.

Although common sense had already told me that Toni would eventually have to go back to school for her final semester, it was still an unpleasant dose of reality to have to swallow. I looked back on the last month and a half and realized what a fool I was to have let all that time pass by without even seeing my girl. Sad to say, I knew I had let Toni slip out of the grip of my paws. I also knew that very soon she would be fair game to any cat she would meet in D.C. Inside my heart, I agonized as I wished that I could just always have Toni in my hip pocket and pull her out whenever I needed a hit of her.

My obsessive feelings for Toni overrode my common sense. Two days after calling her, I managed to find my way back over to her place. I unexpectedly popped up at her crib. When Toni answered the door, her jaw dropped to the ground. She seemed shocked and excited to see my face. Although it had only been a little over a month since I'd last seen Toni in person, she looked as if she had matured for the better. She had a slammin' new short hairstyle and her eyebrows were done up in a very exotic way.

In the doorway of her crib, I hugged Toni. Feeling how good her body felt made me want to kick myself for not having experienced more hugs and sex from her. I asked Toni, "You didn't think that I was gonna just let you leave without saying good-bye, did you?"

Toni replied that she knew I would call her, but she had no idea that I would take the time out to come by.

"Toni, I hope this doesn't mean good-bye forever." Toni remained quiet. She didn't know what to say. Then I asked, "It doesn't, right?"

Toni, who was in the midst of packing her clothes, unzipped a suitcase and said, "Lance, I can't front. I'm crazy about you. Like I told you in the past, in the short time I've known you, I've found myself doing things that I can't believe I let myself do. I don't regret the time we had together, but Lance, come on . . . I mean, I haven't seen you in like almost a month and a half, and I think I know why."

I hated hearing that type of talk from Toni. I wanted to put a halt to it. I walked over to her, and I tried to hold her. I was trying to make a move to kiss her, but I think she knew what I was up to. Toni pushed me away as she told me no.

"Come on. What's wrong?" I asked.

"Lance, I'm not gonna kiss you because I realize that all I'm doing is letting my emotions dictate how I feel about you. I have to start exercising some common sense."

Playing dumb, I asked Toni what she was talking about.

She replied, "Lance, I don't have to explain because you know exactly what I'm talking about. For the past month and a half, I've desperately wanted to speak to you and see you every day. My heart was telling me to do whatever I had to do to be happy, but my mind was telling me that I had no business whatsoever wanting you like that. Lance, I don't think that I have to tell you that this *is* good-bye forever, because you should already know that."

Feeling like a kid who was told he couldn't have a new toy, I said, "Toni, I know what you're saying, but all I'm saying is that I want to keep in touch with you."

"For what?" Toni asked in a somewhat rude manner.

I knew that this conversation wasn't going well, so I tried switching subjects. "Okay, Toni, listen, at least let us depart on a good note. I tell you what, why don't I help you pack?"

Toni answered, "Actually, Lance, I'm almost done, and I really don't need much help. Plus, I have to get dressed 'cause me and Kim are going out tonight."

Feeling like an unwanted roach, I replied, "Oh, okay. Well, where are y'all going?"

Toni handed me a flyer with pictures of two cock-diesel male strippers. When I saw the flyer I got so vexed that I almost wanted to crumple it up and throw it at her.

I barked, "Strippers? Y'all are gonna go see some male strippers?"

Although I wasn't fond of the idea, Toni expressed her excitement, which drove me absolutely bananas. She took the flyer from my hand and held it up in the air and began twirling it around as she, being happier than a peacock, said, "Yeah, we're gonna see Mandingo and oooh, I can't forget about Flava. Both of them have got it going on."

I was so heated. Here I was trying to spark the last bit of passion between Toni and myself, and she was running off at the mouth about Mandingo and Flava, two male strippers who had her salivating. Trying to hold back anger, I asked, "So that's how you're gonna spend your last night in New York?"

Toni continued packing her clothes, and she nonchalantly responded, "No doubt. I'm young and I gots to get my groove on. You know what I'm sayin'?"

Man, I didn't know what to make of the situation. I have to admit that I was jealous like crazy, but what could I do? I wanted to grab Toni's full attention for one more night. I thought about bringing the conversation toward God and asking Toni about her spiritual life, but how absurd and hypocritical would that have been? I was convinced that Toni still had feelings for me, but she seemed as though she had made up her mind to erect this emotional wall in order to leave me out of her life.

I had overstayed my welcome, and Toni began hinting that it was time for me to leave. As I hesitantly made my way to the door, I asked one last question. "Toni, look . . . I know that you're gonna be turning twenty-five in a couple of weeks. Can I at least have the privilege of having your address in D.C. so I can send you something nice?"

Toni looked at me and smiled as she nodded. I wanted to let out a sigh of relief. At least she wasn't telling me that she absolutely, positively didn't want to have anything at all to do with me. Toni quickly jotted down her address and handed it to me. I looked at her and wondered if that would be the last time I would ever actually see her.

"Can I have one last hug?" I asked.

Toni quickly complied and gave me a very warm hug that lasted for about thirty seconds. That hug proved to me that Toni was going to be torn on the inside after I'd ceased to be a part of her life. I didn't want the two of us to depart feeling awkward, so I decided to make the situation funny and relaxed.

"Toni, take off your socks," I commanded. "What?" she asked as she started laughing. "Take off your socks. If I never see you again, I wanna make sure that I remember exactly how your toes look."

Toni continued laughing as she said, "Lance, you are so crazy." She then did as I requested and took off both of her socks and wiggled her toes around. "Are you happy now?" she asked.

"Very happy," I replied with a smile.

Then I gave Toni one last hug and a peck on her ear. While still hugging her, I felt like shedding a tear as I told her that I was going to truly miss her, after which she looked me in my eyes and told me she was going to miss me too.

I sadly left and headed home.

Chapter Twenty-three

With Toni off to D.C. and out of the picture, the relationship with my wife was so much more pleasurable. Spiritually, I'd been doing better than ever. I'd been able to spend much more quality time with LL. Also, I'd been combating many of my sexual hang-ups. But I have to admit that since Toni's departure, I still felt the need to be with her. I greatly perceived a need to make love to Toni one last time. It was like in my mind things just wouldn't be complete between the two of us until that happened.

I had been trying to come up with all kinds of excuses to tell my wife why I would have to take a trip to Washington, D.C. Unfortunately, I hadn't been able to come up with a plausible one. I figured that my only option would have been for me to take a plane to D.C. early one Saturday morning, spend the day with Toni then fly back to New York around eight or nine in the evening. But see, I still had another hurdle to leap over: Toni. My gut feeling told me she'd object to the idea simply because she was trying to put me behind her.

To me, jumping a hurdle was not that big of a deal because if I didn't make it over, I'd simply try again. I'd keep trying until I was successful. Yeah, I might fall and scrape my knees, but even the pain of that would eventually subside. I had to remind myself that women are an easy hurdle to jump if you get at their emotional side. I couldn't think of a better way to get at Toni's emotional side than to write her a love letter. I'm not the best one with words, but I at least had to try. So writing her is exactly what I did. My letter went:

> *Dear Toni,*
> *I know that you are probably surprised to be receiving a letter from me, but I just had to write you. Toni, I don't know if I made it clear to you when you were in*

New York, but so that you know, I'll tell you now. Toni, I love you. I'm not trying to run game on you. I hope that you don't take offense to me saying that I love you, but I really feel as if I do.

I understand what you were saying when you told me that you didn't want to be led by your emotions. I'll admit when we first met I was definitely driven by my hormones and emotions in the sense that I was only physically attracted to you. Toni, I'll even admit that maybe it was a mistake for us to have made love as soon as we did. But the fact remains that we did make love several times, and, Toni, each time I felt that much closer to you.

Toni, I didn't fall in love with you based on superficial reasons. Rather, what I learned is you are more beautiful on the inside than you are on the outside. Toni, it was during the three weeks or so when we spent every evening together I learned what a special person you are. I found out what drives you, and you are far from shallow. I could go on and on in terms of how much I'm drawn to you, but I don't want you to think I'm trying to sell you something or trying to gas you.

I know that you probably feel the same way about me as I feel about you. Toni, you have to be honest with yourself in the same way I had to be honest with myself. What I mean is, could only our hormones and emotions be pulling us toward each other, or is there something that goes deeper than the surface? Could that something deeper be called love?

Toni, it's funny how it's been like two months since we've really hung tight with each other, yet we still have strong feelings for each other. What I'm trying to say is, I know it was me who chose to distance myself from you. I also know that you said before you left that it meant good-bye forever, but I can't go on if it really means good-bye forever. You told me you would be finished with school this December and you would be coming back to New York to live. Well, Toni, December is only a few short months away.

I take the blame for letting you slip out of my life, but now I want you back. Toni, I also want to fly to D.C. one Saturday and see you. That's if it's all right with you. Let me know. You have the number, and you don't have to be afraid to call.

Love, Lance

P.S. I know that you told me that you make good money doing hair in D.C. because women down there get their hair done like it's a religion, but I want you to keep the three hundred dollars that I've sent along with this letter. Keep it as a birthday present. Thought I forgot, didn't you? Happy twenty-fifth birthday.

About a week passed since I'd mailed Toni that letter, and she hadn't called me or anything. I was wondering what on earth was going on. I began to think that she really did just want to end the situation between the two of us. In a way I needed Toni to hammer it through my thick skull that things were over, finished, kaput, period, end of story. See, if Toni didn't end it, I knew I was too weak to even try.

As the days strolled along, I began to look back, and I realized that my obsession with Toni was causing me to lose focus on what was important in my life. Take my relationship with my friends as an example. It had been a while since Steve and I had our falling out, yet I was more worried about Toni than I was about mending things with Steve. I was more focused on which airline had the cheapest airfare to D.C. as opposed to which restaurant I should take my wife to on Saturday night. I realized I was a sick man, but that's just me.

When Saturday afternoon came upon me, I found myself mowing the lawn. Again, just like the past couple of days, I was eagerly anticipating a phone call of some sort from Toni. The phone rang off the hook all morning long, but Toni never called. Even as the early afternoon was in full gear the phone continued to ring, yet no Toni.

Early Saturday afternoon did, however, bring one thing. It brought the mailman to my house with a handful of bills. Along with the bills, there was a small envelope that was addressed to me. Despite the fact that the letter was in a small envelope, what was odd was that it didn't have a return address on it. I knew that many junk mail letters came in that fashion just to throw people off. I was tired of receiving junk mail, and I was just about to throw the letter in the garbage, but something told me to just open it.

To my complete shock and surprise, when I opened the envelope I realized that it was a letter from Toni. I quickly turned off the lawnmower. I put my rake to the side, and with my dirty hands I began to read what Toni had to say.

What's up, Lance?

I hope that you are reading this letter and that it didn't get into the hands of the wrong person. For obvious reasons I left out the return address information. Lance, I was glad to have received a letter from you. I've been meaning to speak to you for quite some time now. Actually, I wanted to speak to you before I left to come back to D.C., but I didn't know how to approach you.

Before I get into what I want to say, let me say this. Lance, I believe you when you say that you love me, and I believe I love you too. But one thing is for sure and that is we can't have a relationship that goes beyond just being friends. I've thought things over, and I feel that we should definitely remain as friends. However, Lance, there is something that is probably going to pull us to be closer than friends.

Lance, I'm going to get straight to the point. I have been extremely troubled by something. Like I said, I wanted to tell you. But I didn't know how, and when you wrote me, I figured that putting my words on paper would be the best way to tell you. Lance, I'm two months pregnant, and I am positive the baby is yours.

I took a pause from reading the letter. I took a deep breath, and I slowly re-read what I thought I'd just read. *Oh, man,* I thought. *Toni better be joking or else I have some serious problems on my hands.* I had to take a seat on my front steps just in case I fainted or something. When I sat down, I quickly scanned the letter one more time. I was looking for the spot where Toni would tell me that she was just joking. When I realized there were no references to a joke, my heart started beating a hundred times per second. I felt a fear I had never—and I mean never—felt in my life. Before I continued reading, I thought about what I had just read: *Two months pregnant, and it's my baby.*

So Lance, to answer a question that you asked me in reference to coming to visit me, I think that you know you have my approval to come to D.C. Lance, I am so sorry I didn't tell you this when I suspected it in New York. But please don't be upset with me. I just want us to speak about this face-to-face.

Lance, I am so scared. I am worried, and I am confused. I know I have to keep this baby because abortion is not in my vocabulary. I just don't know how I'm going to work out a lot of other personal issues. I know my father is going to disown me, but in time that'll work itself out. I don't have the slightest idea as to what I'm going to do about starting my career and all that. I mean, I won't have to leave school or anything like that because I'll be done with school in December, but I don't know what I'm going to do in terms of working and taking care of a baby.

Lance, I hate to be telling you this, but it's real, and I would never joke with you like this. I know one thing, and that's the both of us can't really worry about what the past has meant or how this or that should have been different. What we have to do is concern ourselves with what we are going to do with the future. Lance, call me as soon as you read this letter.

Love,
Toni

P.S. My number is . . .

I memorized the number and quickly shredded all of the incriminating evidence. I had never felt worse than I was feeling after reading that letter. It was so weird how just that quick, all my talk about how I loved Toni and how I wanted to see her had vanished. As scared as I was feeling, I knew that there was no way on earth I could truly love someone and then in a split second view them as if they had the bubonic plague. Forget about catching a red-eye to D.C. I felt like catching a plane to the nearest desert where I could be alone and not have to deal with all of the drama.

Although the grass was not yet complete, I managed to wrap things up. A beautiful lawn was the last thing on my mind. While putting the lawnmower away, I almost broke out into a cold sweat as I thought about my wife. I began to hyperventilate just thinking how I was going to tell Nicole. She wasn't home, and although I was terrified to pick up the phone, I had to call Toni just to make sure I wasn't dreaming.

When I dialed Toni's number, she picked up on the first ring. I left out all that "hello, how are you doing" crap. I wanted to get down to business. Breathing heavy due to my nervousness, I said, "Toni, I just read your letter. Tell me you're not serious."

Toni quietly replied, "Lance, I wish I could, but I can't."

I cried out over the phone, "Oh, no. Toni, don't tell me that. Please, Toni, don't tell me that. Don't you know that I'm married?"

Toni quickly became apologetic as she said in a velvet baby tone of voice, "Lance, I wish I could tell you I was lying. I wish I could, but I'm really pregnant, and I know it's yours."

There was dead silence on the phone for about a minute. I contemplated what I should do. All kinds of thoughts ran through my head. I wanted to ask Toni why she had waited so long to tell me. I also wanted to demand that she get an abortion. In the worst way, I wanted Toni out of my life, but now more than ever, she was a very big part of my life.

Toni broke the silence and said, "Lance, I'm sorry."

I sucked my teeth and said, "Toni, you don't have to be apologizing. Listen, next Saturday I'm coming to D.C. I'll call you and let you know what time to pick me up from the airport."

Toni agreed to the plan. We spoke for another minute or so then we hung up.

I had never felt so lonely in all my life. I felt as if I had nowhere to turn. I couldn't call Steve. I couldn't talk to my wife. LL was too young to give me any advice, and I definitely couldn't call anyone from the church. Also, I hadn't analyzed the situation enough to speak to any of my immediate family members. Feeling hopeless and with no options, I began sobbing like a baby. Through my tears I glanced at the family photo of my wife, LL, and myself. How on earth was I gonna drop this bomb on Nicole?

I immediately dropped to my knees and began praying to God because I really felt like slitting my wrists. The only thing that stopped me was that I didn't want LL to come home and see such a gruesome sight.

Chapter Twenty-four

Although I was deeply bothered as to how I was gonna handle this baby situation, I knew that the sooner Nicole found out, the better things would be. There was no way to make this situation easy for anyone involved. Two days after I'd found out that I was a father to be for the second time—and under some real thick conditions I might add—I started hinting to Nicole that I had something important to tell her. Nicole begged to know what was on my mind, but I had to keep her in the dark until I had all the details. It was sad because Nicole thought I was hiding some sort of pleasant surprise from her. If she only knew.

I managed to put my pride aside, and I trooped over to Steve's crib. Steve didn't even want to open the door for me, and I can't say I blamed him. I spoke to Steve through his front door, and I begged him to hear me out. I told him I was sorry for having played myself. I also apologized for yelling at him.

Fortunately for me, Steve opened the door, and he reluctantly entertained my sob story. I reached to give Steve a pound, but he just looked at my hand and did not extend his in return. "Yo, Steve, I'm sorry for flipping on you like I did. You don't have to say anything, and I know you probably don't even feel like talking to me, but, Steve, I'm in big trouble."

Steve, who has been my man for years, couldn't help but be concerned. Although he tried to disguise it, he looked away and mumbled, "What's up? Get at me. What are you talking about?"

I shook my head, but I didn't say a word.

Steve then asked, "Yo, L, what's up? You got beef with somebody or what? What's up?"

I answered, "Now Steve, we've been tight for years, and I know I was in the wrong and I should've come to you and apologized earlier but—"

Steve interrupted me and said, "Yo, Lance, I ain't sweatin' that. Now what's up, man? Get at me."

I made another attempt to let Steve on to what was bothering me. "Steve, promise me that what I tell you is gonna stay between me and you."

"Lance, come on. You're my man."

"A'ight check it. Remember that chick Toni?"

Steve sarcastically replied, "Nah, I'm not sure if I do. . . . Help me out. How does she look again?"

I paused and then I let it out, "Yo, she's pregnant, and guess who the father is?"

Steve looked at me and said, "Nigga, you have a . . . ah, man . . . Yo . . . Yo . . . kid, are you serious?"

"Hell yeah, I'm serious."

Steve replied, "Ah man, I'm sayin' . . . Man, you ran up in that piece raw, dawg?"

If this had been normal circumstances I would have been bragging at this point. But not today. I sadly had to admit that yes, I had run up in Toni with no protection.

"Steve, man, what do you think I should do?"

"Well, I'm sayin', if I was you I'd give her the dough and tell her to get rid of it."

"Yeah, but she wants to keep it."

"What? She knew a nigga was married. Yo, was she trying to trap you or something?"

"Nah. Yo, she ain't like that. It just happened."

Steve shook his head again and said, "Yo, all I can say is that if she wants to keep that kid then, I hate to say it but, you can hang things up with Nikki."

Scared as hell, I wanted Steve to confirm what he'd just said, "Word? You think Nicole is gonna flip?"

"Nigga, what do you think she's gonna do? Imagine her coming home and telling you that she's pregnant by some other cat. What would you do? It would be over, right?"

I knew that Steve was right, and that's why I'd started to plant seeds in Nicole's head.

"Lance man, how many months pregnant is she?"

"Two months."

"Two months? Man, you got time, but I tell you what, just ask for a divorce. Don't mention anything about a baby or anything like that. Just tell Nicole that you aren't happy anymore and it's time to end things."

I jumped in, "But everything is on the up and up with our marriage, and plus, what about LL?"

"Lance, listen. You ain't working with too many options. Matter of fact, if Nicole finds out that you got someone else pregnant, she's probably gonna do a Lorraine Bobbit on a nigga and slice your dick off. I know Nicole is religious and all, but watch how quick she'll lose her religion when she finds out what you did."

Steve had a point. See, the main reason I was so filled with anxiety was due to the fact that I didn't know how Nicole was going to react. But one thing was for sure, and that was the fact that her reaction toward me wanting to get a divorce was sure to be less volatile than her would-be reaction to the news that I'd impregnated another woman.

Before I knew it, I found myself getting off Flight 702 at the Reagan National airport. It was 8:30 on a Saturday morning. Toni was waiting in baggage claim for me when the plane arrived. When I stepped off the escalator, I saw Toni wearing a jean jacket and some jeans along with a pair of the new Air Jordans. Although I was a mental wreck, I immediately became happy when I saw Toni's beautiful face.

Toni ran over to me and gave me a kiss on the cheek.

"How was the flight?" she asked.

Due to the changes in altitude, my ears had clogged. I hated that popping feeling to them. But I didn't comment on that, I simply replied, "It was short and quick. It was like before I knew it I was here. I mean they didn't even serve us any food. They just gave us some peanuts and a cup of soda."

Toni laughed, and she advised me that she had food in her apartment if I was hungry. We both walked to the airport parking lot where we hopped into Toni's car and headed to her apartment. In the beginning of the ride we both were silent, so to break the tension Toni popped in a CD into her car's stereo system. It was a bass-thumping hip-hop mix tape. I wasn't really in the mood for hip-hop, and asked if she could put on something a little softer. Toni complied, and while she was switching CDs, she asked what time was I planning to head back to New York.

"My flight back leaves at five-thirty this afternoon," I informed.

"That soon?"

"Yeah. I told Nicole that I was working overtime today, so I have to be back at a reasonable time."

Toni understood, and as we drove, she informed me that she had to stop at a store to pick up some orange juice. When we reached the supermarket I stayed in the car and Toni jumped out and ran inside the store. I started to run in behind her and ask her if we could stop at a pharmacy and pick up a ho pregnancy test—I mean a home pregnancy test. After all, what if she was just gaming a nigga? I decided against asking her because if she wanted me that bad she knew she didn't have to stoop as low as telling me she was pregnant.

It's funny because whenever I go to another state it just seems so much more peaceful as compared to New York. I always have thoughts of what it would be like if I actually picked up and moved. The horrid thought of me just breaking out on my family and moving to D.C. crossed my mind. As I sat in the car and waited for Toni, I really began to consider that as a natural solution to all of my troubles. I didn't want to be tied down in another marriage, but I could definitely see myself living in D.C. with Toni and raising the baby.

Before long Toni had returned to the car.

"That was quick," I said. "A woman never comes out of any store that fast."

Toni smiled and reminded me she had only gone to buy orange juice. She then advised me that we were only like two minutes away from her apartment.

"Lance, do you eat omelets?"

I replied, "As hungry as I am, I'll eat anything."

Toni laughed, and she let me know she was gonna cook us some French toast and omelets. As Toni slowly maneuvered the car over two speed bumps I realized that we must have been at her apartment complex.

I asked, "Is this where you stay?"

"Yep," Toni informed me as we pulled into her personal parking spot.

The complex was very nice. I would say that it held fifty or so apartments. It wasn't a high-rise complex—it was only two stories high. When we walked into Toni's apartment I immediately noticed that she kept the place just as immaculate as she'd kept her apartment in New York.

"Toni, your apartment is just as nice as your place at home."

"Oh, you like it?"

"Yeah, it's cool, but you need to take down that poster of Maxwell."

"Maxwell is the man," Toni laughed.

Toni began to show me around the place, and when we reached her bedroom I flopped onto her bed, and let out a groan. Who was I fooling? Since the airport I had been behaving as if I was seeing Toni on an ordinary visit. But I knew and she knew that this was no regular visit.

After groaning, I smothered my face into Toni's pillow and I asked, "Toni, what are we gonna do?" Being that the pillow was muffling my voice, Toni couldn't make out what I had asked. I sat up, removed the pillow from my face, and I looked at Toni and asked again, "What are we gonna do?"

Toni sat next to me and suggested we talk over breakfast. I agreed, so as Toni went to the kitchen to cook I stayed in her room on the bed and rested. Again, a stupid thought passed through my mind. With everything going on, I still managed to think about realizing the possibility of having sex with Toni one last time. My rationale was that I was already in her apartment, and sex would be a great way to relieve some of the stress I was feeling.

While I was thinking, Toni yelled from the kitchen and asked me to come join her. I sluggishly made my way to the kitchen and Toni remarked, "What's wrong? You scared of me or something?"

Toni was standing in front of her stove, and while I pulled out a chair to sit in, I said, "Nah, I'm not scared of you. I was just trying to get some more rest. With all that's been going through my head lately, I haven't been able to get a lick of sleep at night."

Toni sympathized with me, which led us into deeper conversation.

"Toni, I've been thinking this whole thing through, and I have to admit something. When I read your letter, I knew right away you weren't lying, and I got mad scared. People usually think irrationally when they're afraid. And to be honest, the first thought that came to my mind was I wanted you to get an abortion."

Toni, who was sautéing onions, immediately interrupted me and said, "Lance, I already told you in the letter that I ain't getting no abortion. I don't believe in that."

"No. Nah, I understand that. I'm just sayin', that was the first thought that came to my mind when I initially found out. I mean, I don't believe in abortion either. It probably doesn't seem like it, but I'm a Christian."

Toni took a pause from preparing the food, and said, "Lance, you know what? I can't even believe we're discussing this. For real, I mean, in my wildest dreams I never thought I would be mixed up in something like this. In the past whenever I watched *Jerry Springer* or some other trash talk show, I always wondered where on earth they get such jacked-up people from. Now here I am having a married man's baby. I need to call one of those trash talk shows and try to get on."

Although Toni was being sarcastic, I could hear a sense of pain and some regret in her voice. "Toni, believe me, this episode that we're going through is not going to be anything like *Jerry Springer*. But on the serious tip, what I was thinking was, I'm just gonna divorce Nicole before she even finds out anything about this baby."

Toni again took a break from preparing the food, and she commented, "See, Lance, that's exactly what I'm talking about. I never could have pictured myself as a homewrecker. And that's exactly what I feel like I am."

"Toni, you ain't no homewrecker. This whole thing is my fault. I dragged you into this hook, line, and sinker. You didn't have any intentions of messing with me. That's the difference. See, a homewrecker sets out with a motive of destroying a family, and you never had those intentions."

"Still, but, Lance, I don't want you getting a divorce."

Raising my voice a bit I asked, "Why not? What do you expect me to do? When you have this baby, it's not like I can just bring the kid home to play with LL. I want to be around any baby that I helped create."

Toni became defensive. "No, Lance, I understand that you would want to be around the kid, but I don't know . . . Just forget it, I don't even know what point I was trying to make."

I was ready to comment but Toni quickly retracted and said, "Oh, okay, I know what I wanted to say. Lance, I know things are gonna be difficult, but all I want from you is to help me financially with the baby. You don't have to get a divorce in order to do that."

I turned my lips and just looked at Toni for a few seconds. I was disgusted as I said, "Toni, what is wrong with you? I don't know about you, but my idea of helping to raise a kid isn't just sending money for some new sneakers."

Toni looked at me but didn't respond. Both of us stayed quiet for about two minutes. The wheels were spinning in my head, and my blood pressure was starting to rise because of the silence.

Toni finally cut into the quietness as she said, "All right. I guess I can see where you're coming from. But, Lance, one thing that I say is you should just tell Nicole what's going on. I'm a woman, and all I'm saying is that from a woman's point of view, I know she would much rather know."

I remained silent, and I thought about what Toni had just said. Toni then added, "I know that it's going to be a hard thing to do, but, Lance, there isn't any easy way around this whole thing."

I continued in my silence. I guess Toni was feeling uncomfortable because she continued to break the silence. "Lance, I don't know how I would do this, but if anything, I mean I'll tell Nicole what happened. I'll apologize straight up, woman to woman."

My silence was finally interrupted as I replied, "What?"

Toni reaffirmed what she had just said.

"Toni, if that is not the dumbest, most ass-backward thing I have ever heard in my life." I began to use some of Steve's logic as I added, "Nicole is religious and all, but I don't know if there is enough religion in the whole world that would keep her from murdering you if you told her that you're pregnant by me."

Toni was just about done preparing breakfast. She added, "See, Lance, I know that I'm here in D.C. cooking breakfast for you, and it's easy for me to say that I'm willing and actually would want to speak to Nicole and all that, but I know if I were ever face-to-face with her I wouldn't expect the situation to be a calm one. Lance, I stepped way beyond my bounds. I slept with another woman's man—better yet, another woman's husband. That's not something I'm proud of, but I'm woman enough to sincerely apologize to Nicole's face, and regardless if she accepts my apology or not, I would at least feel a bit more respect for myself."

Both of our breakfast plates were prepared and on the table. I took a sip of my orange juice, and said, "Toni, look. I guess I see where you're coming from. I mean, deep down I know I have to tell Nicole what the deal is. Somehow I'll muster up the courage to tell her because I couldn't respect myself if I didn't. The main thing that has been eating at me lately is the fact that I feel that Nicole more than deserves to know the truth. I know my marriage will most likely end up in divorce court, but I have to keep things real. I can't just hit Nicole with divorce papers. First of all, if I did that, I would have to literally become the most cold, angry, and split-personality person in the world to really pull the divorce thing off. Second of all, by me just hitting Nicole with divorce papers it'd be like I'm trying to hint that I want to end the marriage because of her when in reality I'm the one who did the dirt."

Toni had her mouth full of food, so she nodded to show her agreement of what I'd just said. I then informed Toni that it would kind of be out of place for her to speak to Nicole.

However, if she insisted that she talk to Nicole, then at least let me tell Nicole first. Toni agreed that I should definitely be the first one to speak to Nicole, but she also insisted that she be allowed to apologize.

The breakfast was on point, and I complemented Toni on it. I wanted to switch the conversation to a more relaxed tone, so while switching gears, I smiled and said, "Toni, even with all the turmoil going on, the fact remains that there is a child inside of you. The baby has nothing to do with the mess we caused, and that's why I'm not shy to admit I would love to have a little girl who looks just like you."

Toni laughed and asked, "Lance, how could you be thinking of that now?"

"I'm sayin'. What's wrong with thinking like that? I'm keeping it real. I want a baby girl who is the spitting image of you. I can picture a little girl in one of those white dresses with white shoes, and those ankle-high white-lace dressy socks that little girls wear."

Toni began laughing, and she said, "Lance, you are so crazy."

"I'm crazy?" I asked. "Come on, Toni, admit it, you know it would be fly to have a little girl walking around trying to be as sophisticated and sassy as you are."

"Sassy? Who you calling sassy?" Toni asked.

I smiled and said, "You know I'm just playing."

Toni finally gave in and admitted she did in fact want a little girl. She explained that she'd always envisioned having a girl before having a boy. Her desire for a daughter was due to her reasoning that with little girls, there is so much more to do, such as creating new hairstyles and the like. I informed Toni that the only reason she thought like that was because she's a beautician. We both were just about finished eating our food. As we prepared to do the dishes together, I wanted to make sure the mood remained upbeat.

"Toni, do you have any candy or gum?" I asked.

Toni pointed to the top of the refrigerator where there was a bowl full of candy. I reached in, and I got a peppermint ball. As I made my way back to the sink to help Toni, I made sure to hand her the candy. Toni smiled and asked what it was for.

"No offense, baby, but I'm sayin', the onions in that omelet didn't do you any justice."

Toni broke out into laughter. She covered her mouth and slapped me on the arm.

I continued, "Well, you wouldn't have wanted me to let you walk around with stink breath, now would you? Just like if I had a booger or something I would want you to tell me."

Toni continued laughing. She was embarrassed as she said, "Oh my God, I can't believe you played me like that." Toni then ran out of the room.

"It's all good, baby. Don't sweat it," I yelled to her.

While Toni was out of the room, I continued washing the dishes. See, although I was in D.C. for a serious reason, there was no need to not be loose. After all, there was going to be plenty of time for seriousness in the future.

Toni returned to the kitchen, and she blew her breath in my face. "You happy now?" she playfully asked.

As I was forced to inhale a whiff of Toni's breath, I realized she must have gone to brush her teeth and rinse her mouth with mouthwash.

"Yeah, you're good now," I replied. "Your breath isn't as hot. You're good."

Toni then handed me the bottle of Scope she had used, and recommended that I use it as well. I took the mouthwash, and we both began laughing. In an instant we'd both totally forgotten about the dishes, and we started snapping on each other and telling mother jokes.

The mood was definitely where I wanted it and where I preferred it. In the back of my mind, I knew that I could get some butt from Toni if I pushed up. As we made our way to the living room, the thought of having sex with Toni became even more compelling. I decided to keep the mood relaxed by continuing to joke with Toni. I asked her if she knew my uncle had invented nacho cheese.

She looked at me and twisted her lips.

"He did," I exclaimed.

"Yeah, right."

As Toni looked at me and smiled, I said, "A'ight, you don't believe me, so I'll explain to you how it happened and prove to you that I'm not lying. See one day my uncle was in the park eating crackers and cheese. Then from out of nowhere this bum comes up to him and asked him for the time. He gave him the time, and the bum walked off. So my uncle continued eating his crackers and cheese. Then about five minutes later the bum came back and asked for directions to somewhere. My uncle gave the bum the directions, and the bum walked off. My uncle continued eating his crackers and cheese, and before you knew it, the same bum came back a third time. My uncle who was sitting on a park bench asked the bum what he wanted this time. The bum didn't say anything. He just kept walking around the bench like he was plotting a scheme. My uncle paid him no mind, and before you could blink, the bum had snatched my uncle's cheese, and he ran off. So my uncle, who was left sitting there with only crackers in his hands, stood on the park bench and yelled real loud, 'Hey, come back here. That's not yo' cheese.' And with that came the invention of nacho cheese."

After verbalizing the punch line of that joke, I fell out in laughter. Toni looked at me, and I could tell that she wanted to laugh simply because the joke was so corny. However, she managed to hold it in. I, on the other hand, was balled over in laughter.

"Toni, you know you wanna laugh," I said.

Toni looked at me like I was stupid. I ran over to her and began tickling her. "Oh, you're gonna laugh. You're gonna laugh. . . ."

Toni finally gave in, and she started laughing.

"See, I told you that you were gonna laugh," I said as I continued to tickle her.

Toni replied, "Yeah, but I ain't laughing at that stupid joke. Lance . . . ha, ha, ha . . . Lance, stop tickling me. *Ha, ha, ha* . . ."

As we were both laughing, I decided to stop tickling her. I didn't want to be too childish. The two of us paused and caught our breath, after which we headed to the living room to watch *Soul Train*. As we made our way, I stopped and pulled Toni close to me, and I hugged her.

"Toni, we don't have to act like we both have some kind of disease or something. We can still get close to each other."

Toni tried to push me off as she explained that getting close was exactly what had gotten us in the mess we were now in.

"Baby, don't fight me. All I want to do is kiss you. I mean, we both have fresh breath and all, so what's the problem?"

As Toni began to smile, I made my move and kissed her. As we kissed, I began feeling all over her body and kissing on her neck. I knew she was enjoying it, but she pushed me away. I moved closer to her, and I whispered in her ear that it had been such a long time since we'd done "it."

The look on Toni's face after I'd whispered those words told me she wanted to go further. Unfortunately, she exercised self-control. Reluctantly, I, too, told my hormones to calm down and we both sat and watched *Soul Train*. As we watched, I was commenting on all of the slammin' female dancers who were on the show. With Toni right next to me, I found myself getting a little too excited due to the tight and revealing clothing the dancers had on.

When a commercial came on, Toni took the remote and turned off the television. "Lance, you came here so we could talk, and we aren't doing that, so what's up?"

Realizing that Toni was right, I paused and thought for about a minute. I sighed and said, "Okay, this is the deal. When I get back to New York, I'm gonna make sure I tell Nicole what's going on because I want to get this off my chest. Matter of fact, if I don't get this off my chest, I'll probably have a stroke or something.

"Now after I tell her, I have no idea what her reaction is gonna be, but if you still want to speak to her, then by all means go ahead. But, Toni, one thing that I want you to know is no matter what happens between Nicole and me, I'm going to make sure you and the baby are always taken care of. I can't promise how much time I'm going to spend with the kid, but I can promise I'm going to make the best effort possible to be a big part of the kid's life."

Toni and I continued to hammer out "what if" scenarios. We came to the conclusion that at this early stage, it was gonna be hard to predict just exactly how all the little details would be handled. Regardless of whether the future would go according to how we envisioned it, we both simply solidified the fact that we were going to be committed as a team to giving the best of everything to the baby.

The remainder of the day flew by. When it was all said and done, I found myself on the plane heading back to New York. Yeah, I was wondering how I was gonna tell Nicole. I didn't know how I was gonna bring myself to open up to her or where I was gonna get the courage, but at least I had achieved one moral victory for the day. Although I'd wanted to hit it, Toni and I had managed to keep our pants on.

Chapter Twenty-five

When Sunday arrived on the scene, I found myself in church. However, I couldn't even concentrate on what was going on. Everyone seemed to notice that something was troubling me, but I played like all was okay. Nicole also noticed I wasn't my normal self, and she wanted to know if it had anything to do with what I had to tell her. At that point, there was no sense in lying, so I told her that, in fact, that was the reason I was in such a lethargic mood. Nicole begged and pleaded to know what was going on, and I told her in a couple of days she would definitely know. Nicole was upset, and rightly so, due to the fact that I was hiding something from her.

Monday after I'd picked LL up from the day care center, I found myself at my sista, Tiffany's house. I had already called and told her I had something very important to discuss with her, so she was expecting me. When I got to Tiffany's house, I put LL in another room where he could be entertained by the television while she and I spoke.

I looked away from my sista as I said, "Tiffany, I know that you aren't going to believe what I have to tell you, but it's the truth. Matter of fact, I don't even know how to say this to you."

Tiffany knew I had something serious on my mind, and she said, "Lance, I'm your sista so you know that you can tell me anything without worrying about me trippin'."

I continued to look away from my sista as I said, "A'ight, I'm gonna be straight-up real and just spit it out." I sighed and I felt myself beginning to form tears, as I said, "Tiffany, you know how much I love Nicole . . . that's why this is so hard."

"Lance, what? What is going on? Are you and Nikki having problems?"

I sighed again and then I let it out, "Tiffany, I messed up big time. Nicole has been on point since the day we got married, and there was no excuse for me to do what I did, but I . . ."

"Lance, but what?" Tiffany eagerly questioned.

I spat out, "But . . . I got this other woman pregnant."

With sounds of disbelief, Tiffany covered her mouth, which was wide open. Her eyebrows were also raised as she said, "Lance! I can't believe what you just said."

Tears ran down my face as I finally looked my sista in her eyes and said, "I can't believe it either."

Tiffany, who knew that I wasn't lying, asked how this all had come about.

"Tiffany, I don't really want to explain all of that. I mean I'm a dog, and I messed up. It's as simple as that."

Tiffany then said, "Lance, like I told you, I'm your sista, and I'm glad you came to me with this. But is there anything specific that you want me to do to help you? Because really, I don't know what to tell you, but I do want to help you out if I can."

Wiping my tears away, I said, "Tiffany, I haven't told Nicole yet. I have no idea how she's gonna react, and I don't even know how I'm gonna drop this on her. I just want you to be there when I tell her."

Tiffany assured me that was not a problem. All I had to do was let her know when.

I then added, "See, what makes this so hard is the way people are going to look at me and Nicole. I mean, I know I'm gonna have to deal with people calling me a hypocrite. I know people are going to be sayin' I'm supposed to be a Christian and all that and I'm always kicking this religious crap, yet I'm running around cheating on my wife. Plus, Tiffany, it just makes Nikki look bad. She's been the best wife in the world, and I messed up. What's gonna make things even harder is the fact that there have always been people, especially some of Nicole's friends, who have been jealous of our relationship since day one. We're educated, we have careers, the house, the cars, and the kid, and to everyone we seem like we're totally in love. Now all of those jealous people are going to be laughing and feeling some sort of redemption. But Tiffany . . ."

As I stopped speaking and I started to cry, my sista came and sat right next to me and began to console me. Tiffany and I were never very affectionate toward each other, and I was surprised she put her arm around me and rubbed my shoulder.

"Lance, let me tell you something. I don't know all of the details, and I'm sure you know as well as I do that what you did was beyond wrong. But this is between you and Nicole to work out. If you start worrying about what everyone is going to think, Lance, you'll drive yourself crazy. I'm here for you if you ever need anyone to talk to, and I'm not going to look at you in a judgmental way."

I remained silent. Although I would be turning twenty-eight years old in two months, I had never felt so young and pitiful. I felt like I was reliving a scene from my youth. Here I was crying and being consoled by my sista due to a mistake I had made. Tiffany went and got me a moist paper towel so I could properly wipe my face, then she asked when I planned on telling Nicole.

I paused and thought for a moment, then I said, "I figure it's just like taking medicine. It's disgusting and all, but you just have to swallow it and get it over with. No matter how bitter it might taste, if you ever want to feel better then you have to go ahead with the process. So I was thinking that maybe tomorrow I should tell her, if that's okay with you."

Tiffany agreed. I finalized things by letting Tiffany know I would call her the next day once Nicole came home from work.

"Tiffany, I just hope everything works out. I never wanted to hurt Nicole."

"Lance, let me ask you something. You're religious and all, right?"

Having no clue where my sista was going with her line of questioning, I said, "Yeah, why?"

Tiffany added, "I mean, you're not just religious on the surface, are you?"

The truth of the matter was, as of late, I, in fact, had been just religious on the surface. Who was I fooling? For the past six months or so I had definitely been Satan's child. Although I was starting to realize it was time to get serious about repenting and truly representing as a child of God, I didn't want my sista to know my religious ways of late had been very hypocritical, so I answered her, "Tiffany, you know I'm not just religious on the surface. What's up? What are you getting at?"

"Lance, all I'm saying is that I'm not as religious as you are, but one thing I know is God wants us to come to Him when we're feeling troubled or anxious. Lance, you probably know this better than I do, but God is not like your friends on this earth. Your so-called friends will sell you out in a second. They'll let you come to them with your problems a couple of times, but if you keep coming to them they'll soon want nothing to do with you. Lance, God is exactly the opposite. He'll never sell you out, and He'll never get tired of you. See, sometimes religious people forget the hope they have in Jesus. Lance, I'm going to stop preaching to you, but what I want you to do is go home, get on your knees, and pray about this whole situation. Pray like you've never prayed before." Tiffany paused then she added, "Lance, I can't tell you how Nicole is gonna take this, but I can tell you that with God, all things are possible. So if you earnestly pray about this, God will see to it things work out. I promise you that."

I took to heart everything that my sista had just told me. I hugged her and thanked her for being there for me. LL and I departed, and we made our way home.

The remainder of the evening went like any other typical one. Nicole, LL, and I ate dinner like a loving family. Nicole and I watched a movie after dinner, and we talked. I was glad that not once did Nicole ask me about what it was I had to tell her.

When the lights were out, and after Nicole was fast asleep, I snuck out of the bedroom and made my way to the basement. I dropped to my knees and prayed with every ounce of feeling and emotion that I had in my body. When I was done praying, I sat on the floor and just meditated in the dark. Since this whole ordeal began to unravel, I'd never felt as peaceful as I did after that prayer.

When I was done meditating, I made my way back upstairs and into my bedroom. Nicole looked so peaceful and beautiful as she slept. I knew telling her what I had to tell her would be as difficult as driving a knife through her heart, but I had to do it.

Chapter Twenty-six

The last time I had butterflies this bad had to be the night before my high school city championship basketball game. It's ironic that Nicole was a cheerleader in that game. In fact, it was Nicole, my high school sweetheart, who told me to relax and concentrate just before I took the game-winning free throws.

My current real-life crisis far exceeded the pressure and drama of any high school basketball game, and I definitely wouldn't have Nicole in my corner cheering me on. I made those two game-winning free throws the day my high school won the city championship, but the question now was how I was gonna fare in the present moment under the intense pressure of admitting to adultery.

For the most part, I'd been holding up well throughout the day. I'd already called Nicole at work and told her that Tiffany would be coming by for dinner. Nicole didn't object. As a matter of fact, she was kind of annoyed I would even go out of my way to call her and tell her Tiffany was coming over. See, she and Tiffany are pretty close, so Tiffany could drop by unannounced anytime she felt like it. I knew Nicole wouldn't object to Tiffany coming over, however, I was just trying to cover all of my bases. I didn't want this to be a night where Nicole decided to go to the mall after work or what have you.

When I got home, I was crazy antsy, but I remembered my sistas words, so every time my anxiety became overwhelming, I began to pray. The prayer therapy was working, but I decided to cook in order to keep myself busy to keep my mind off the adulterous topic. I couldn't remember the last time I had cooked dinner for Nicole. I didn't go all out with a gourmet meal, but I made baked chicken wings, baked potatoes, and some broccoli.

By the time 6:45 rolled around, Nicole was walking through the door. My heart was pounding as I greeted her with a hug and a kiss. I took her jacket and put it on a hanger.

"Lance, what's that smell? It smells like food."

I chuckled and said, "It is food."

Nicole sarcastically replied, "No, but I mean it smells like it's coming from this house."

"Baby, stop playing. I decided to cook today," I informed her.

Nicole's mouth dropped wide open as she walked toward the kitchen to confirm the unbelievable. Before I knew it, I heard a scream come from the kitchen. I ran to see what was going on. When I reached the kitchen Nicole was smiling and standing with her arms wide open, waiting for a hug. After the hug, Nicole expressed her gratitude for me having helped out with dinner. Then she became suspicious. "Okay, so what's the occasion?" Nicole asked.

I was still feeling nervous as I said, "Why does it have to be an occasion? I'm sayin', I just felt like cooking for you today."

Nicole informed me she was going to change her clothes, but before she left the kitchen, she said, "Lance, I know something is going on. You haven't cooked dinner in I don't know how long, plus your sista is coming over. Do you want to tell me now and get it over with?"

My heart was in the bottom of my stomach, but I side-stepped everything. I slapped Nicole on her butt and said, "Nicole, just go and change your clothes. I'm sayin', can't a brotha cook for his wife once in a while?"

When Nicole left the room, I immediately grabbed the phone and called Tiffany. I frantically instructed her to hustle her butt over to my house so I wouldn't lose the nerve to spill my guts. My sista pleaded with me to calm down, and she informed me she would be at my house within the next half hour.

While I waited for Tiffany to get there, I began to think about how I was going to spill the beans. I rehearsed comments in my head, but nothing was coming out the way I wanted it to sound. Thinking of what to say and how to say it was really making me nervous. I decided to just block that issue out of my mind as I realized the best thing to do would be to concentrate and remain calm.

When Nicole returned to the kitchen, she walked up to me and gave me a kiss. She also took my hand and suggestively put it inside her pants. I don't know why I was shocked by Nicole's actions, but I was. Feeling as though I was doing something wrong, I snatched my hand away.

Nicole frowned and asked what was wrong.

"Nothing," I quickly replied.

"Well, why did you pull your hand away like that?"

"Oh, because I want to hurry and fix LL's plate so he can eat his food now."

"Lance, why don't you just let LL eat with us? Tiffany is still coming over, right?"

At that point, I told Nicole I didn't want LL to eat with us, the reason being that tonight I wanted to tell her what it was I had to discuss with her.

As I prepared to fix LL's plate, Nicole came close to me and kissed me on the neck. She was trying to get frisky, but sex was far from my mind. I mean as nervous as I was, I probably wouldn't have been able to get it up anyway.

I was glad that Nicole was behaving frisky because it took her mind off asking me about what we were going to discuss. Nicole whispered in my ear that she had been thinking about me all day long. She then kissed me and playfully told me how turned on she gets when she sees her man making his way around the kitchen.

Nicole had on sweatpants and bare feet. That combination usually turned me on like crazy. Normally, with the way Nicole was dressed, coupled with the way she was coming on to me, we would have been in our bedroom with the door locked and going at it like two horny rabbits. But at that present time I was functioning only on one track like I had tunnel vision. I kept declining my wife's advances, and I quickly got LL's food.

I called LL into the kitchen and informed him it was time to eat. While he was eating, I made sure to remove myself from the kitchen. I went upstairs to the bathroom and locked the door. I was trying to stall and give my sista time to get there. While I was in the bathroom, I sat at the edge of the tub and said another prayer for courage.

When I was done praying, I sat in the bathroom, and again I tried to rehearse what I was gonna say and how I was gonna say it. While I was pondering, I heard Nicole laughing and talking real loud. She sounded like she was having one of those sista-girl conversations. I knew that could only mean one thing. I made my way out of the bathroom and downstairs where I saw Tiffany and Nicole talking.

"What's up, sis?" I asked.

Although Tiffany had only been in our house for about two minutes, she was heavy into dialogue with Nicole, and she basically paid me no mind.

I yelled, "Hello, Tiffany."

Realizing that I had been trying to get her attention, Tiffany stopped in mid-stride of her conversation and began laughing as she said, "Oh, Lance, I'm sorry. How you doing?"

I smiled and shook my head as I said, "I'm fine, but man. . . . How on earth could the two of y'all be into such a deep conversation that quick?"

The three of us began laughing. With a million butterflies floating around in my stomach, I suggested we go to the kitchen and start eating. LL was basically playing with his food, and I wanted to tell him he could leave, but Nikki beat me to the punch. She yelled at him and told him that he couldn't leave the table until he had eaten everything, broccoli and all.

So as LL toyed with his meal, Tiffany and I sat at the table and Nicole politely fixed our plates for us. When we were all sitting, I said grace, and we began to eat. Tiffany began to talk about how stressful her job as a schoolteacher was. I was glad the ice had been broken in that manner because it allowed things to flow naturally. Before I knew it, Nicole began talking about events that happened on her job. Just that quick the two of them were again engrossed into another lively conversation.

I let the two of them converse, and I tried to eat, but I was behaving worse than LL. I was so nervous that I couldn't even eat. When there was a pause in Nicole's conversation, she sort of noticed my nervousness and commented on the way I was handling my food.

Nicole said, "Lance, you're acting worse than LL with the way you're playing with that food." Then she joked and asked if my own cooking was so bad that I couldn't even eat it.

Realizing that it was time to get serious, I didn't laugh or acknowledge my wife's joke. I told LL he didn't have to finish his food and he was excused to go to his room and play. LL knew he had to quickly capitalize on that opportunity, so he didn't hesitate. He bolted from the table and made his way to his room. With LL out of the way, I told myself, "Now or never."

My heart was pounding, and my hands were ice cold. My palms were extremely sweaty. I pushed my chair away from the table and looked toward the floor. After bracing myself, I spoke up.

"Nicole, I know that I've been hinting to you that I have something to tell you, and I'm about to tell you right now." I wanted to be a man and look Nicole in her eyes, but I knew if I did, then I would surely break down and start weeping. The room was silent, and all eyes were on me. Although my heart was pounding, it was as if I could hear Nicole's heart rate beginning to pick up as well. I inhaled very deeply. After slowly exhaling I began to talk. "Nicole, before I say anything, let me start by saying that I love you, and you mean everything to me."

Nicole started to get nervous as she apprehensively asked, "Lance, what is going on? Just spit it out. Tell me what's up."

Still beating around the bush, I said, "Nicole, I already told Tiffany, and the only reason she's here is because I didn't know how you would react to what it is I have to tell you."

Nicole started to get ticked off, and she said in a stern tone, "Lance, spit it out. Stop stringing me along."

I finally mustered up enough courage to look Nicole in her face. She had the most concerned look I had ever seen in my life. I could see her chest rising up and down as she was nervously but eagerly anticipating what I had to say. Tears came to my eyes, and I went back to looking at the kitchen floor. As I shook my head, I simultaneously rubbed it with my left palm.

Nicole then began to raise her voice as she asked, "Lance, what's wrong? Did you get diagnosed with some sickness? No, wait a minute, did somebody we know pass away? Lance, you're driving me crazy. Just tell me what's going on."

Through my tears and while looking toward the white tiled kitchen floor, I mumbled, "A'ight. Oh, man. Oh God . . . Nicole . . . baby . . . I cheated on you."

Nicole screamed out, "What? Lance, what did you say? Speak clearly. I can't hear you if you're mumbling."

Mustering up a bit more courage, I again exhaled and said as clearly and coherently as possible, "Nicole, I cheated on you." Trying to be brave, I gave Nicole a "thug-life" look, as if I was preparing to scream out, "Yeah, I cheated on you. What?"

Nicole insecurely looked at Tiffany, then she looked at me. She'd definitely heard what I said, but she rhetorically asked with a frown on her face and a little ghettoness in her voice, "Lance, repeat that for me one more time."

I immediately went on the defensive as I said, "Baby, I'm so sorry. Please just let me finish." Nicole was breathing hard, and she was at the edge of her seat. I continued. Through my tears, I added, "Nicole, I cheated on you, and there is no easy way to say this . . . but, Nicole . . . the other person . . . Nicole, I got someone else pregnant."

Nicole immediately and violently stood, and in disbelief, she looked around. Not really knowing what to say, she asked Tiffany if I was joking. With the somber mood of the room, Nicole had to know I was telling the truth. Tiffany confirmed the matter.

Then Nicole calmly, but in a desperate-sounding tone said, "*Pregnant?* Lance, I can't believe you."

Within a split second Nicole went crazy. She flipped her plate of food into the air, and she began screaming and crying and asking, "Lance, how could you do this to me? Lance, how could you do this? I trusted you. How could you do this?"

Nicole then picked up my plate of food and threw it at me. I attempted to shield myself from the plate. I, too, was crying, and I tried to explain, "Nicole, I'm sorry. Baby, I am so sorry. If there was anything I could do to change this, I would."

Nicole looked at me through her tears, and she had a look of death. She charged at me and started kicking me and punching me as she continued to ask, "Lance, how could you do this to me? What about your son?"

Tiffany tried to separate the two of us, but I wanted Nicole to hit me and let out all of her frustrations. I kept yelling and telling her that I was sorry. The whole scene was like a very dramatic and climatic movie scene.

"Sorry? Sorry? Lance, sorry doesn't count now. Are you trying to ruin my life? You must want to ruin my life. Answer me. Are you? I can't believe you. I'm gonna ask you again, what about LL? Did you think about him? How could you do this to us?"

Fortunately Nicole had stopped trying to hit me. She had given in to Tiffany's restraints. I didn't know what to say or do, so I remained silent. Then Nicole asked, "Who is the bitch?"

I was shocked because I rarely heard Nicole use a curse word. But what did I expect? Nicole was truly heated—she was breathing heavy. She looked as if she had just been in some type of street brawl. Her shirt had become slightly wrinkled, and her hair was a bit messy. Nicole demanded to know who my mistress was.

"Lance, who is she? Who the hell is she?"

By this point my tears had subsided, and I mumbled, "Toni."

In disbelief, Nicole screamed out, "What? I know you are not talking about that bitch you brought to my house. Lance, I know you are not talking about her. Don't tell me you disrespected me like that."

I remained silent, which confirmed I indeed was talking about "that bitch" I had brought to the house.

Nicole began to wail and weep very loudly as she threw a ceramic cup at me. It clocked me right upside my head, and it hurt like crazy. The cup shattered to pieces as it landed on the kitchen floor.

"Lance, you had that whore around my son. You even had her in my house eating my food and talking to me."

Nicole paused. I didn't say a word, and I didn't dare to look at her. Then I heard the sound of a person who was coughing and choking. I looked up, and I saw Nicole standing over the garbage can holding her stomach. A split second later she began to throw up right into the garbage can. Tiffany ran to Nicole's aid, and I began to cry again. I didn't think things would get this ugly. I wanted to console Nicole, but I knew she didn't want me touching her.

While trying to wipe the spit that was hanging from her mouth, Nicole spoke again, this time in a very despondent tone and while sobbing, she said, "Lance, look at me. How could you do this to me? I thought I did everything I could to please you."

Nicole finished vomiting, but she was still crying. When she'd gathered herself, she managed to tell me to get the hell out of the house and she didn't ever want to see me again. She also threatened I would never see LL again.

I tried to run upstairs and speak to LL because I knew he had to have heard everything that had transpired, but Nicole was insistent that I leave right away. She made it clear that I couldn't get a lick of clothing or anything. She just wanted me out.

At that point I felt the least I could do was to comply with Nicole's wishes. I searched for my shoes and my jacket. When I found them, I slipped them on, and I prepared to leave. I walked past the kitchen one last time, and I saw my wife sobbing with her head buried in the kitchen table. Tiffany was caressing her back, trying to comfort her.

I motioned for Tiffany to walk me to the door. When we made it to the front of the house, I asked her if I could stay at her place. She said it wouldn't be a problem. Tiffany also told me she would probably spend the night with Nicole just to make sure she would be all right.

My life was a mess, and I looked like a mess. Before walking out of the house, I hugged and thanked Tiffany for being there for Nicole. I didn't want to let go of that hug, but Tiffany told me to get going. She also sternly reminded me to pray.

Chapter Twenty-seven

It had been two weeks since I'd last seen either Nicole or LL. Thankfully, Tiffany had kept in contact with the two of them, and they were doing fine. Tiffany had been reporting to me on Nicole's emotional state of being. This entire ordeal had been affecting Nicole like I wouldn't believe. Tiffany explained to me that Nicole could get over the fact that I'd been unfaithful, but just the mere thought of another baby was too devastating for her to handle.

Like me, Nicole had also been dipping in and out of depression for the last two weeks. Tiffany told me that Nicole went as far as taking a week of sick leave from her job. She wanted to use the time to get her head straight. Unfortunately, I didn't have the same luxury. But even if I had, I probably would have declined to do so. I couldn't see myself taking a week off, because that would have given me too much time to think and condemn myself.

With no surprise to me at all, I found out everyone on Nicole's side of the family had been updated with the news and details of my affair. The consensus of her family was that I was a no-good man and Nicole should leave me, but not before she took me to court and sued the pants off me.

My most dominant thought of late had been in relation to my son. In my wildest dreams I never imagined that LL would grow up without a daddy. It saddened me deeply just thinking I would only be able to see him every other weekend. Since he was born I'd dreamed about taking him to the park and teaching him how to be the next Michael Jordan or the next Reggie Jackson. With being limited to seeing him every other weekend, I told myself to wash those aspirations down the drain.

With everything that had been going on, I'd managed to speak to Toni on a few occasions. I made it crystal clear to her that in no way, shape, or form did I want her to speak to Nicole. I guess Toni had noble intentions by wanting to personally apologize and all, but come on. With Nicole agonizing over this ordeal, I really didn't think her hearing Toni say sorry was going to help. If anything it would just help to inflame the entire situation. Toni understood, and she gave me her word she would keep her distance. I assured her that when the time was right she would have an opportunity to apologize to Nicole.

During the past two weeks, I'd say that I'd been down, but at the same time my thoughts had been extremely sober in the sense that for the first time in all of my years of being a dog, I was beginning to realize the emotional devastation that dogism can cause. Yeah, I always knew adultery was wrong and pornography, lusting, and the like were not good for me, but I never understood the depths of devastation the destructive mental programming from those acts could bring to the lives of others.

My sober thoughts caused me to look at myself as a murderer. See, it's easy for a murderer to pull a trigger, shoot someone, and walk away with no remorse because that murderer has no real emotional connection to the victim. But if you take that same murderer and let him feel the pain of the murdered victim's family members then everything changes. Force that murderer to sit through the funeral service of the one he has murdered, and suddenly it's a whole new ballgame. When things become real and attached to that murderer and he can make an emotional connection, he can no longer simply remain a coward and continue to hide behind the trigger of a gun. Now he has to face the reality of what he's done. I'm convinced that if everyone who was ever convicted of murder had the opportunity beforehand to feel the emotional devastation murder produces, then the number of murders around the world would be a fraction of what they already are. And the same holds true for cheating and adultery.

***

In two days, it would mark three weeks since I'd last spoken to Nicole. I was convinced she really didn't want to have anything more to do with me. I hadn't even dared to venture home in order to retrieve some of my clothing. During the past three weeks, I'd spent almost four hundred dollars on new clothes. However, that was not my main concern. LL was. I'd spoken to Tiffany and asked her if she could speak to Nicole on my behalf and try to persuade Nicole to let me see my son.

Fortunately for me, Nicole didn't flex her position of authority when it came to allowing me the right to visit LL. Nicole's pain probably would never go away, but I was grateful that she hadn't allowed it to block me from seeing LL. She okayed my request, and when Monday night rolled in, I found myself feeling very uncomfortable as I approached my own house.

The door locks on the house had not been changed, so I was able to freely let myself in. I wasn't nervous per se, but at the same time I didn't know what to expect from Nicole. When I walked in, I went straight to the kitchen where I found a mountain of mail and a stack of bills that had gone neglected during my absence.

LL must have heard me because he came running downstairs. When he realized it indeed was me, he screamed out, "Daddy!" The biggest smile was plastered across my face as I knelt down to hug LL. He ran and jumped toward me. After I caught him, I picked him up and just looked at him.

I hugged him as I told him, "LL, Daddy has missed you so much."

LL asked where I had been.

"I've been staying at your aunt Tiffany's house."

"Why?"

"Well, LL, remember how you used to tell me stories of kids in the day care center who got into fights over toys and things like that?"

LL nodded and replied, "Yeah."

Then I explained, "Well, I did something that was very wrong. It was something your mother really didn't like, so just like those children at your old day care center, your mother and I got into a fight. LL, arguing and fighting are wrong. I want you to know that. I also want you to know that Daddy was completely wrong, and your mother was completely right. LL, Mommy was so upset with me that she told me I couldn't sleep here anymore."

LL replied, "But Daddy I want you to sleep here. Please Daddy, I don't like it when you're gone."

Statements like that were what I had been dreading to hear. I had no idea how to respond, so I said, "LL, listen to me. I can't promise you that I'll be able to stay here, but you have to promise me you're going to take care of Mommy. Okay?"

LL whined as he said, "No, Daddy. I want you to come back home. Daddy, I promise I'll be good if you come back home. I promise."

LL was bringing tears to my eyes. For some reason I think he felt as though he might have been the cause of the breakup. I had cried in front of him before, and there was no need for me to hide my tears from him at the moment. As I continued to hold him, I looked at him and I kissed him on his cheek. Through my tears I said, "Okay, LL, I'm gonna see what I can do."

I put LL down, and I asked him where his mother was. He told me that she was in her room.

"LL, go to your room and turn on PlayStation. I have to speak to your mother, and then I'll come to your room to play with you, okay?" As I wiped my eyes with a piece of tissue, LL nodded, then he darted to his room.

Looking over the pile of bills that had come, I separated the overdue ones from those that didn't have to be paid right away. While doing that, I contemplated what I was gonna say to Nicole. While I was thinking, I remembered my sista's words, and at that moment, I said a short and quick prayer.

When the prayer was over, I put the bills on the table and proceeded to walk to my bedroom where my wife was. By this time, Nicole had to know I was in the house. But I guess she figured I had only come to see LL, and therefore she probably didn't want to interrupt our time together. As I approached the entrance of our bedroom, I could hear the sound of the television. I walked as quietly as I possibly could, then all at once I became very nervous. My heart started pounding, and I thought about just bypassing the bedroom altogether. Instinctively I knew I had to at least say hello to Nicole.

I braced myself for the worst. As I stood at the entrance of the bedroom I saw Nicole sitting on the bed. Her back was cushioned by a pillow, and she was leaning against the headboard, and her legs were bent at her knees. Nicole looked as if she was reading something related to her job.

In a shy, humble manner, I said, "Hello, Nikki." My heart continued to race as I waited for a response.

Nicole looked up from the papers she had been reading. She slowly turned her head and looked my way. I wanted to cringe because I just felt so uncomfortable. There was a brief deafening moment of silence.

Then Nicole sort of mumbled the words, "How are you doing?"

Her words were followed by more deafening silence as she continued looking at whatever it was she had been reading. Nicole could have just totally ignored me, but she didn't, so I figured that we were at least still friends.

Still feeling extremely self-conscious, I took two cautious steps into the bedroom and I asked, "What are you reading? Is that something for work?"

Nicole was very cold and slow to respond, but she did reply, "Yeah, it's for work."

Realizing that after three weeks, I couldn't just pop up and hold a conversation like things between us were normal, I shifted gears. "Nikki, I don't know about you, but I feel extremely awkward, and just being around you is extremely difficult for me. I'm glad you let me come see LL, and that's why I came. I don't want to interrupt you or upset you, but Nikki, I just want to say one thing."

Nicole made sure to ignore me and not look in my direction.

"Nikki, please, can you just look at me?" Again, Nicole didn't respond. So again I asked the same question, only this time I asked in a very meek manner. "Nikki, can you please look at me?"

Nicole pondered my request, and after thirty seconds or so, she looked my way. Nicole was still as pretty as ever. As I looked at her, I remembered Steve's words and the words of so many other men, which were, "Why would I cheat on that?"

With Nicole's attention, I said, "Nikki, I just want to tell you that whatever decision you choose to make concerning us, I just want you to know that I won't try to fight it in court. Whatever you feel is best, that's what I'll abide by." I paused, and a tear came to my eye. If this had been a movie, I would have won an award for Perfect Timing of a Tear. But this was no act. It was a real tear. I continued, "But Nikki, I just want to beg you, and I ask you to please give me the chance to properly apologize to you."

Nicole sucked her teeth, twisted her lips, and looked away from me.

I quickly commented, "No. Nikki, please don't brush me off like that. Please. See, what I'm talking about is me and you and a neutral third party sitting down so I can apologize to you and let you know some things about me that I never told you."

Nicole sarcastically commented, "Yeah . . . um . . . I'm not sure, correct me if I'm wrong, but I think we already did that about three weeks ago."

"No, Nikki, come on, please. I'm serious. What I'm trying to say is what if we go through some sort of counseling session or something like that?"

Harshly, but in a subdued manner, Nicole responded, "Lance, listen, I went to school to learn how to counsel people. I am not going to spend money just so I can tell some therapist that my husband is a dog. What black people do you know who actually pay to go see a therapist? Now if you want to apologize, you can do that right now. We don't need a marriage counselor."

Nicole was still very bitter, and I completely understood. "Okay, Nikki, I didn't come here to upset you. I just came here to see LL. But Nikki, believe me, all I want to do is apologize the right way. I feel that I at least owe that to you. To me that means more than just saying 'I'm sorry.' Again, I came tonight to spend time with LL, but right now I'm just asking you if I can come by tomorrow and apologize. Is that all right?"

Sounding kind of disgusted, Nicole replied, "Lance, just go see your son."

I wanted to make sure that I was persistent, so I asked again, "Nikki, can I come by tomorrow and talk to you?"

I could hear the annoyance in Nicole's voice as she said, "Lance, there's no need for you to come here tomorrow with a rehearsed line of crap you've had three weeks to make up. Now if you want to apologize like you say you do, you're more than welcome to pick up a phone and call me. Honestly, just seeing your face makes me wanna just kill you."

Working with what Nicole had given me to work with, I replied, "A'ight, so I'll call you tomorrow."

I walked out of Nicole's presence and made my way to LL's room. Before I reached it, I paused and said another quick prayer. I needed God's help so I could block out the problems between Nicole and myself and focus solely on LL.

LL and I had a ball together. While we were playing video games, I marveled at his innocence, and I became envious of him. I thought about how I didn't know what the future held in terms of a divorce, visitation rights, and all that, but I was determined to make sure LL maintained his innocence. I realized that the loss of youthful innocence is what helps breed dogism. I couldn't wait until LL was old enough to understand things such as sexuality because I wanted to give him the proper per-spective on the subject. Yeah, I was never taught how to deal with that subject, and it was my ignorance toward my healthy sexuality that probably led me to my doggist ways. Similar to the way ignorance of true love and humanity is the root of racism. As far as my immediate family, I was determined the dogism was gonna end with me.

When it was time for me to leave, LL wept and pleaded for me to stay. It broke my heart to see him like that. Why did he have to suffer because of what I'd done?

As LL cried, I tried to persuade him to understand. "LL, I need you to stay here and protect Mommy, okay? I can't stay with you, but I promise you I'm going to see you as much as I can. What I want you to do is go get your sword you got from the circus and keep it by your bed. This way you can protect your mommy for me. Okay?"

With tears streaming from his eyes, LL did what I said.

When he returned with his sword, I instructed, "Now LL, go kiss your mommy good night—give her a kiss for me too—and after you do that, I want you to get ready for bed. You're in kindergarten now so you have to be well rested for school."

The saddest thing in the world was looking at LL as he walked off to kiss his mother good night.

As I drove back to Tiffany's house, all I could picture was that toy sword in LL's hand and him walking toward his mother's room.

Chapter Twenty-eight

Tuesday afternoon when I got off work I headed to the supermarket and purchased about a hundred dollars worth of food for Tiffany's house. Tiffany has such a good nature that she would easily let me stay in her house for as long as I wanted and not pay her a dime. I am not one to freeload, so buying food and paying for the phone bill was my way of earning my keep.

Somehow, with Toni three months pregnant, my marriage in shambles, and my son crying for his daddy, I found myself making the same stupid mistakes from the past. No, the mistakes didn't have anything to do with Scarlet. I guess it was more subtle than that.

When I reached Tiffany's house, I carried about three bags of groceries into the kitchen. Tiffany and a female friend of hers were in the living room discussing a few things. They saw that I was having trouble carrying the groceries, and they came to my aid. Being that there were about ten more bags in the car, they came outside and helped me with those as well.

I don't know if it was because I hadn't had sex in a month, or if it was because Tiffany's friend was slammin', but her friend instantly turned me on. When we were done carrying the groceries into the house, Tiffany introduced me. Her name was Naomi. Naomi was more bangin' than Naomi Campbell. I have nothing against dark-skinned women, but I usually don't find myself attracted to them. However, Naomi was dark-skinned, and she had it going on. Her body was on point, as was her hair, but I think it was her sexy lips that took the cake. Although I didn't know her from Adam, I wanted to just walk up to her and slob her down right in front of Tiffany.

After we were introduced, Naomi remarked on how I looked so much like my sista. Tiffany replied that everyone who meets us always says the exact same thing. I, on the other hand, wasn't trying to get into small talk. I held back no punches as I charmingly said, "Naomi, I'm not trying to be obnoxious or anything, but I just have to give you a compliment. You are a very, very gorgeous woman."

Naomi smiled, and I know she was a bit embarrassed as she thanked me for the compliment.

Tiffany looked at me with an annoyed expression, and she abruptly interrupted by saying, "Anyway! Um, Lance, Naomi and I have a project we have to get done by tonight, so if you don't mind, can you please give us some privacy?"

I complied with Tiffany's wish and vanished to the bathroom. As I took a shower, I plotted as to how I was gonna make my next move on Naomi. I knew I had scored with that compliment, so I just had to back it up with one more move, and I would be in there like swimwear. I thought about doing some pushups to get my muscles stimulated and perky, then all I would have to do was take my shower, wrap a towel around my waist, and accidentally but on purpose, walk into the living room and ask Tiffany if she wanted me to start cooking dinner. If Naomi were to see my sexy body still slightly wet from the shower, she would be salivating over me.

As I showered, I was thinking about Naomi. As I thought about her attractive attributes, I started receiving rushes of excitement. Then before I knew it—and thank God, 'cause it helped me to wise up—I felt as if a cinderblock had hit me square in the head. I couldn't believe I had just flirted with another woman. *What is wrong with me?* I thought.

As if all I'd been through wasn't enough, here I was contemplating exacerbating the situation with another female. That little demon in my head was trying hard to convince me I would soon be getting a divorce so it really wouldn't matter if I kicked it to Naomi. I decided to be wise, and I listened to the voice of the angel who told me that it wasn't about being divorced. Rather, it was about exercising self-control, and if I knew what was good for me then I had better stay as far away from Naomi as possible.

Realizing how pitiful I was, I remembered to just pray. So right on the spot, with my body lathered in soap, I prayed for God to give me some self-control, which He did. When I was done washing the filth off my body and my soul, I headed straight toward Tiffany's room where I changed my clothes. When I was done, I started watching game shows, but in the back of my mind I knew I had to call Nicole. Without hesitation, I picked up the phone and dialed my home number. I didn't know what I was gonna say, but I did know I was just gonna shoot from the hip. I was prepared to lay out all of my dirty laundry for Nicole to see.

Nicole answered the phone and I said, "What's up, Nikki?"

She obviously knew my voice, so she didn't ask who was calling. She simply said, "Yeah."

"Nikki, it's me Lance."

Nicole rudely blurted, "And?"

It didn't take a rocket scientist to figure out that Nicole really didn't want to talk, but I was perfectly capable of mustering up enough things to say that I didn't need any responses from her.

"Nicole, I know you don't want to talk, but, please, just hear me out." I paused, took a deep breath, and continued, "Nicole, I want to say I'm terribly sorry for what I've done to you and LL. What I did was foolish, it was selfish, it was stupid, and it should never have happened. Nicole, I know I can't even begin to imagine the pain you must feel, but believe me, I know I hurt you very bad. Baby, I am sorry. What I've been doing in order to sympathize with you is I've put the shoe on my foot and wondered how I would feel or how I would have reacted if you told me you had cheated and you were carrying someone else's baby. Nicole, I would be beyond devastated to say the least, and I know that you're devastated.

"I've been praying that God can make this as easy on you as possible. Nicole, I know things are over between us. I mean, even the Bible tells us once the bond of marriage is broken due to adultery, then, and only then, is it justifiable and permissible to get a divorce. Baby, I wasn't loyal to you, and yet you always treated me like a king. I just want you to know

now more than ever, I appreciate all we had. I appreciate all you've done and all of the sacrifices you've made for the sake of our marriage. Nicole, believe me when I say I've put my mind through torment while trying to figure out a way to change the mistake I made. Unfortunately, I just can't change it. I can't change the past.

"Baby, yesterday you said something to the effect that I've had a lot of time to prepare a line of crap. But Nicole, listen, I'm not dropping a line of garbage to you. I just want to tell you some things you never knew, things that might shed light on this entire mess."

I took another deep breath, then I continued, "Nicole, ever since I was about ten or eleven years old, maybe even younger than that, I've been sneaking around and looking at anything that was pornographic. I started by finding my father's dirty magazines, and as I got older, the VCR became a big thing, and I started sneaking and watching porno movies. Nicole, even as a kid I knew it was wrong, but I loved it. My mind, body, and soul craved it. It was like a drug. Looking at pornography gave me the biggest rush in the world. By the time I was eleven years old, I started masturbating. Nicole, forget about it. When I discovered masturbation, it was over. I became deeply addicted to it.

"Nicole, when I say addicted, I mean at thirteen years old I was masturbating as much as three times a day. I knew it was wrong, but I loved it. No one in my house knew what I was doing, and I figured I wasn't hurting anyone, so I kept doing it. As I got older, that same pattern continued. In fact, it intensified. I would try to go cold turkey and stop masturbating, but like an addict, I just couldn't stop. I would go for a maximum of two weeks without doing it, but then I would be caught up right back into it."

As I continued to explain my ordeal, I began to cry. Never before had I opened up and exposed myself to an adult in the manner in which I was now opening up. I was hoping that Tiffany didn't walk into the room.

Through my pain and tears, I added, "Nicole, when I got older, things got much worse. I mean I started going to strip clubs and getting blow jobs from hookers and just wildin' out.

Baby, it hurts for me to even tell you all of this. I mean I never wanted to let anyone into this dark closet of mine. But baby, I now realize because I've kept that closet closed for so long it only made my problem intensify. Baby, I'm so sorry. I didn't mean to hurt you. It's just that I'm so messed up, and you never knew. . . ."

At that point, I broke down and started weeping harder. I'd finally broken through Nicole's wall of defense as she said, "Lance, I believe you. Believe me I do, but why didn't you ever tell me any of this? We're married, Lance. We don't have to hide things from each other, no matter how bad it may seem."

I continued to cry as I explained, "Baby, you don't know how shameful I've felt all of my life. I mean, it was only like a year ago when I realized other people actually masturbate. Since I was young I've always felt so ashamed because I thought I was some kind of sexual freak or something. I mean masturbation and taboo things like that are something people never discuss. Since it wasn't ever being talked about, for like twenty-something years I felt as though only I had that problem.

"And baby, it even hurts me to tell you any of this. See, another reason I hid things from you was because I always knew if I told you about my past I would have to tell you everything."

Nicole asked what I meant.

"See Nicole, we've been together for God knows how long. I mean we met in high school for crying out loud. I know that when we met we were both virgins and all that. Although we had sex before marriage, things were still special because neither you nor I had ever been with anyone else." I paused as more tears were shed, then I kept flowing with my history. "Nicole, what I meant by I would have to tell you everything is that I cheated on you before we were even married."

In disbelief and astonishment, Nicole said, "What? Lance, how could you? I've been trying to handle this pregnancy thing, and you mean to tell me this whole ordeal gets worse? Lance, what in the world did we ever have? It definitely wasn't a marriage."

As Nicole sighed, I could sense she was getting ready to start crying. Before she broke down, I wanted to make sure I got everything I wanted to say off my chest.

"Nicole, I'm gonna let you speak, but please just let me finish. This is very hard for me, and I just want to get it all out. Nicole, we were young when we met, and we were young when we got married, but ever since I graduated from high school I've always had money and a nice car. Baby, back in the day, none of my friends were married or even thinking about settling down. They were all about hanging out, partying, and hoing around. Now Nicole, I'm not saying my friends made me do anything, but just being around them put me in situations where I met other women and things happened."

Nicole was now crying, and at that point, she asked, "Lance, what kind of things?"

I sighed and said, "Nikki, I mean, well, I'm sayin', I had sex with like thirty different women before we got married."

Nicole said in disbelief and through her tears, "Lance! Thirty? But we've been together since high school, so how, Lance? How?"

"Nikki, just hear me out. Like I said, I was young, had money, and my mind was already screwed up sexually. I just went ahead and did stupid things. I've read many books, and I realize pornography had my mind so screwed up that I was trying to live in the fantasy world that pornography portrays. See, baby, most people, especially women, have to connect emotionally before they can have sex with someone. But as for me, pornography had my head so screwed up I lost all sense of the emotional connection that goes along with sex. For me, sex has always been purely physical. I didn't love any of those women I had sex with. Nicole, I've always loved you and only you. See, pornography made sex seem so easy and harmless. With every porno movie I watched, I would see women walk into a room, take off their clothes, and with no kind of attachment they would start getting it on with some nigga.

"Nicole, I tried my best to live out what I saw in those movies. The funny thing is I didn't even realize what I was doing. I mean, subconsciously I was making decisions based on sexual fantasies that I wanted to play out. Nicole, you just don't know how bad it was, the struggle between wanting to do good and having evil right there tugging at me. It still is bad at times."

Nicole, who had stopped crying but was still sniffling a little bit, asked, "Lance, before this chick Toni, did you ever cheat on me with anyone else during our marriage?"

"Nicole, no," I immediately responded.

Nicole raised her voice as she demanded honesty. "Lance, tell me the truth. Did you?"

"Baby, no. I'm telling you the truth. I never cheated while we were married, not until Toni. Nicole, if I had done anything at all, I would tell you now. I wouldn't hold anything back, not at this point."

I could hear the pain in Nicole's voice as she added, "Lance, I really can't believe what you're telling me. I mean with everything that has been going on, this is a lot to swallow. One thing I realize is I've never known you, Mr. Lance Thomas. Who are you? I mean I've been in the same house with you, I went to school with you, I've eaten with you, I've slept with you, I've given birth to your son, but I still have never known who the hell you were. I thought I knew you, but I only knew the top layers of you. I now realize I've never gotten inside you. The funny thing is I thought I knew you inside and out, but I didn't. I don't know . . . I mean . . . all I can say is it's sad, it's really is sad to say, but you are good. I don't know how you pulled it off for all this time. You must be two people 'cause I don't know . . ."

"Nicole, let me say this, I know that I have a remarkable talent, remarkable, but at the same time horrible. That being I can deceive anyone. I can do such a good job at it, that at times even I forget I'm being deceptive. I have another ability to just block out my feelings. Like in the past when I cheated on you, I never consciously and deeply thought about how you would feel. If I had, then I wouldn't have been able to go through with my dirt. What I would do is I would always block the thought of you and LL out of my mind, and I would proceed to do that which I knew was wrong."

When I was done speaking, Nicole didn't say a word, she just blew some air into the phone.

"Nicole, it's the same thing with God. I mean I love God and I love the church, but at the same time I would block out what was morally and spiritually correct and do that which I knew was wrong. Baby, it goes so much deeper than you could ever imagine. I mean, my sexuality is so jacked up it's like my every thought is of something sexual. I think about sex twenty-four seven. If I see a woman's toe, that can turn me on and spin me out of control—the slightest things are like poison to my mind. Nicole, all the working out and the weightlifting, that's all done so women will lust over me in the same way I lust over them. Yo, Nicole, I laugh because back when that book and the movie was really popular, women would talk about waiting to exhale, but men are also waiting to exhale. I say that because, nine out of ten men are going through what I've been through. Maybe not on the same level as me, but most men have a screwed-up sexuality, and they aren't letting anyone on to that fact."

Nicole then sighed and asked, "So, Lance, what does all this mean?"

I answered, "Honey, I really don't know what all this means, but I'll tell you one thing. Right now I feel so light. For my entire life I've been carrying around so much baggage and guilt. The guilt always intensified as each day passed, and it just kept me seeking more and more immoral behavior so I could sort of get high off it, but then, right after the high would wear off, the guilt would return. It was like a vicious cycle. But finally I've let it out. Finally I feel free. I still have sexual problems I have to work out, but just knowing that I've opened up to someone, especially to you, is going to help me so much."

Again my wife blew air into the phone's receiver. I knew she probably had a million and one thoughts running through her head. I had already said my piece, and I didn't want to annoy Nicole by keeping her on the phone.

"Nicole, I'm not gonna keep you on the phone any longer. But I just want to tell you this one last thing." My voice cracked with emotion as I said, "Again, Nicole, I know what I did was horrible, and I can only imagine the pain that you feel. I wish I could change the past, but I can't. All I know is that I can try my hardest to positively affect the future. Nicole, I'm sorry for putting you through this, and if it takes fifty years for you to forgive me, I'll understand. I mean even if you never forgive me I'll understand. But baby, I say this with the fullest sincerity, God doesn't make women like you anymore. Honey, I know I've thrown away the best thing that this side of life has to offer me, which was having you as a lifetime mate. But Nicole, please . . . please, no matter what happens, please let me continue to be a part of my son's life. Please."

Nicole responded to me in a very soft and gentle tone. She sounded as if she was beginning to develop a sense of closure. "Lance, I'm gonna hang up by saying this. I believe what you've told me, and I'm glad you told me all of this. I do wish you hadn't waited so long to tell me, but I mean, I guess now that's neither here nor there." Nicole paused then she added, "LL should never get caught up in our problems. You know I'm a rational person, so don't worry about me removing him from your life. That wouldn't be fair to him."

I smiled as I thanked my wife. After I hung up the phone, I regretted that I hadn't ended the conversation by telling Nicole that I loved her. For all I knew that could probably have been the very last time I would have had the opportunity to tell her.

Anyway, after hanging up the phone, I got dressed. I was in the best mood I had been in in weeks. I walked into the living room, and I let Tiffany know I was stepping out for a minute. Tiffany acknowledged me. I also told Naomi that it had been nice meeting her. She smiled and said likewise. I made sure not to flirt with Naomi, and I kept it moving as I walked out of the house. I realized how easy it was for me to exercise self-control if I just simply focused.

Still feeling as if the weight of the world had been lifted off of my shoulders, I jumped in my Lexus and I blasted music as I cruised the streets of Queens. The radio blared, and as I listened to Funkmaster Flex spin on the ones and twos, I felt so elated.

Yeah, the music was slammin', but I was elated because finally, a huge floodlight was placed into my dark closet of skeletons. True was the fact that my marriage was practically shipwrecked, but I felt like at least I had managed to fight off the angry waves and was able to make it to the peaceful shore.

Chapter Twenty-nine

I had made plans to hang out with Steve on Saturday so we could go to this comedy/jazz club. When Saturday arrived, I found myself at Steve's crib. It had been a mad long time since the two of us hung out. I took the blame for that. Anyway, as Steve was getting dressed, I began to fill him in on all that had been transpiring between Nicole and myself. Steve was adamant about the fact that I should have never told Nicole about the baby and I should have just gone through with the divorce.

I explained that I was trying to turn over a new leaf. I let him know my new leaf would no longer contain the drama, lies, and deception of old. Unfortunately, I didn't get any encouragement from Steve.

His outlook on the situation was somber. He asked, "Lance, do you like having money in your pocket?"

"Of course," I replied. "Who doesn't?"

Steve added, "Well, you certainly must not because you're gonna be a broke man in about six months to a year."

I knew exactly where Steve was going with his line of thinking.

He continued, "First of all, you know all that money you have in stocks and in that 401(k) crap?"

"Yeah, what about it?"

Steve explained, "Well, Nicole gets half of that. Oh, yeah, and that nice house you have in Cambria Heights, guess what?"

Sarcastically I asked, "What, Steve?"

"Oh, nothing really, I mean I just wanted to let you know that you will no longer be living there. That goes to Nicole as well. You'll probably be living in some one-room flat. Lance, you're gonna be mad as hell when you go to visit your son and you see some big-belly nigga with crusty feet laying up in the bed you used to sleep in."

"Anything else, Steve?"

Steve replied, "Oh, yeah. Um, those fat paychecks you're used to, well, they're going to get small very quickly. Nicole will be getting something like seventeen percent of your paycheck for LL. And that bad chick, uh, I think her name is Toni. Yeah, that's it. Well, when she spits out that kid, she'll also be getting seventeen percent of your check. That money comes straight off the top. It goes directly from Con Edison and right into their bank accounts before you even see it."

"Yeah, whateva. All I know is I'm not even thinking about that. I'm sayin', like I told you before, I'm turning over a new leaf. But Steve, you know what? With everything that's been going on, I've still never felt so peaceful in all my life." After I said that, Steve began laughing with this loud, long, drawn-out laugh. He sounded like he was some wino on the street corner who was hoarse and trying to cough up phlegm.

Through his laughter, Steve replied, "Peaceful? Nigga when them pockets get empty, we'll see how peaceful you are. All I know is Toni was one expensive piece of butt. Man, you're gonna be paying for them few nights of booty for the next eighteen years. You better start getting Scarlet to hit you off with some cash because you are definitely gonna need it in a minute."

Steve just didn't get it. He didn't fully understand that I was done with the cheating, the lies, the deception, and the strip clubs and all of that. I was completely done with it all, including Scarlet.

Steve continued his laughter as he added, "Lance, you're gonna be just like the rest of those New York cats. Yeah, you're gonna be riding around flossing in a fifty-thousand-dollar car, but you're gonna be broke as hell living in a one-bedroom basement apartment."

With more sarcasm I remarked that we didn't have to go to the comedy/jazz club, for the simple fact that Steve was funnier than any comedian we were gonna see. Steve added a few more of his one-liners, but we finally did manage to depart for the club. Before we got there, I made sure to tell myself to keep the right focus for the evening. During the entire ride to Manhattan, I kept telling myself, *Lance, have some self-control tonight.*

When we reached the club, there was no doubt the honeys were in full fly mode. The jazz music made the atmosphere on point. The club was definitely a prime stomping ground for picking up a couple of high-maintenance chicks. Steve was true to form with his game. As soon as we stepped into the place, he found himself at the bar buying a drink for some bad-ass-looking chick.

I just parlayed and did my own thing. I even surprised myself when I ordered a plain orange juice. I just didn't want to get alcohol flowing through my body. I knew if I were to start drinking, I would quickly loosen up and start doing things I would live to regret. I was trying hard to maintain, and at the same time I was thinking, *What the hell am I even doing in here?* It was places like this one, along with the parties and the hanging out until the wee hours of the morning without Nicole, that had added to my doggish mentality. Thankfully, the comedians were very funny, so they took my attention away from all of the good-looking women.

Before long, the club started to get too smoky from all of the cigarette smoke, and I really wanted to bounce. I couldn't fake it. I mean, my mind just wasn't feeling that playa nonsense. I hated playing party pooper, especially considering we had only been there for about a little more than an hour. Although I knew Steve wouldn't be ready to leave, I didn't care because I'd had enough, and I was ready to bounce.

I spotted Steve coming toward me with this mack daddy, big baller look in his eyes. When he reached me he was like, "Yo, Lance, you see those two chicks over there, the ones with the white high heels on?"

"Yeah. What about them?"

"Yo, playa, I'm sayin', the one on the right is all on my biznalls! And yo, her friend was checking you out, so I'm sayin' go kick it to her, get the digits from her. I think we can probably take them both back to my crib and hit that tonight. You know what I'm sayin'?"

Steve held out his fist for a pound. I didn't acknowledge his hand, and I replied, "Yo, Steve, shorty has definitely got it going on, but I'm just trying to maintain right now. Matter of fact, I was thinking about bouncing up outta here."

In disbelief, Steve replied, "What? Yo, do you see the thickness on those chicks? And you ready to leave? Man Lance, are you crazy? Yo, you better hurry up and get over that Toni and Nicole nonsense."

Steve looked at me and waited for a response, but I simply ignored him.

After sighing in disgust, Steve angrily said, "Man, I'm sayin', I ain't leaving, so if you wanna act like a homo then go right ahead, but you gonna have to bounce on your own."

I was sitting at a small lounge table, and I took one of the toothpicks from the dispenser that was on the table. I slowly placed the toothpick inside my mouth, and I twirled it around. I contemplated what I should do. I looked over at the chick Steve was talking about, and I confirmed that she definitely had it going on. She was thick in all the right places, and she looked good. She waved at me, and I knew that was my cue to get up and go over and kick it to her. So I exhaled and stood up. . . .

"Yo, Steve, I'm out, kid."

"What? Lance, I'm sayin', at least go speak to her. You're gonna make me look bad in front of them."

As I made my way to the coat check, I looked at Steve and said to him, "You'll be a'ight. Just tell shorty that I'm a married man."

After retrieving my coat, I headed out the door.

Steve replied, "Ah, man! See that's that BS. Nigga, what's wrong with you?"

I paid him no mind. I kept my focus, and I kept on walking. I was in midtown Manhattan and being that I had ridden to the club in Steve's car, there was no way I was gonna hop on a train at such a late time of night. Although it was gonna be expensive, I attempted to hail down a yellow cab. When one stopped to pick me up, I asked how much would it be to take a brotha to Queens. I could barely understand the foreign cabdriver's accent, but it sounded like he said fifty dollars.

I had a feeling that the fare would be in that range, so I just hopped in the cab and headed to Steve's house.

When we reached Queens, I directed the cabdriver to Steve's house. I paid him the fifty bucks, and I jumped into my Lexus and headed back to Tiffany's crib, taking the scenic route, which led me past my house in Cambria Heights. When I drove down my block, I really wanted to just park the car and go inside my house and cuddle up next to my wife. I couldn't remember the last time Nicole and I had made love.

I pulled up in front of the house, and I noticed that all of the lights were off. The house was in total darkness. "Nah." I decided against going inside. I didn't want to wake up anyone.

I chuckled as I imagined myself walking into the house and trying to sneak into the bed with Nicole, only to be confronted by LL and his toy sword. I chuckled once more, then I shook my head in sorrow. Yeah, it was like one o'clock in the morning, so I decided to just head to Tiffany's and call it a night.

When I reached Tiffany's, I made sure to be as quiet as possible so as not to wake anyone. From the time I started staying at Tiffany's I'd been sleeping on the sofa bed in her living room. So after I took off my clothes and brushed my teeth and took a shower, I made my way to the living room. As I attempted to open up the bed, I saw a note that was left for me on the cushion of the couch. I picked it up and read it:

> *Lance,*
> *Nicole called around ten-thirty tonight. She told me to tell you that she expects to see you in church in the morning.*
> *Good night.*
>
> *Love,*
Tiff

I was overwhelmed with joy after reading the note. I realized that I desperately needed to be going to church, especially considering I hadn't been since I'd told Nicole about Toni's pregnancy. I guess I'd kinda forgot about worshipping God. Or should I say, I stopped going to church because I feared the embarrassment I would feel from having my business publicly exposed? I was sure by now Nicole had let someone in the church know what was going on between us. Even if Nicole had only told one person in the church, that would have been the same as telling the entire congregation.

As I continued to prepare my bed, I thought about not facing up to the embarrassment of seeing church members. Then I quickly realized all my life I'd been afraid of being exposed. In fact, it was that fear of exposure that helped wreak such havoc on my sexuality.

I paused and thought for a moment. I pondered about how exposure to air helps to heal wounds. If a wound is consistently hidden under a Band-Aid then it leaves the sore less of a chance of ever developing a scab. Without exposure, an ugly scab would not form, and if there is no scab, then proper healing cannot take place. I needed to forget about using Band-Aids in my life, those Band-Aids of two-faced living. *So what if I'm exposed?* I thought. *At least I'll be free.*

I sighed and convinced myself to be like a sore that was in need of exposure. I continued to talk to myself as I said, "Lance, go to church so you can help that scab to form and begin the *true* healing process."

Before I laid my head on the pillow of the sofa bed, I got on my knees and prayed to God. I just thanked Him for so much, and I repented for so much wrongdoing. I especially made sure to thank God for sending me my own angel in the form of Nicole.

As I waited to fall asleep, I realized what separated Nicole from all of the other women I'd either been with or fantasized about being with was Nicole always held my best interest close to her heart like no other person could or would attempt to do. Even with everything we'd been going through, my wife was still willing to put her pride aside in an effort to ensure that I wouldn't turn my back on God at a time when I needed Him most.

Man, I just wished I hadn't screwed up such a good thing.

Chapter Thirty

I purposely arrived to church ten minutes late. The reason being, I didn't want to have to answer a million questions from people who hadn't seen me in a while. I also arrived late because I wanted to sit toward the back. Although I didn't know what kind of reception I was going to get from Nicole, I still felt very good about coming to church.

When I walked through the doors, I immediately saw a brother I knew. Like I'd guessed, he started right away with the questions. He wanted to know where I'd been and if everything was all right between Nicole and me. In a polite manner, I brushed him off by telling him I would get with him later. As I continued to make my way to the pews I saw another cat I knew. He wasn't in close proximity to me so he put his fingers to his mouth and ear, signaling that he wanted me to call him. I nodded and just walked to my seat.

When I reached it, I looked in the direction of where I usually sat, and there I saw Nicole. She was sitting in the exact same row and the exact same seat she usually sits in. LL was seated to the left of her. Someone was missing from that picture, and I knew it was me. I contemplated taking a seat next to Nicole, but I just didn't know if she wanted me to be next to her. I mean, yeah, she'd requested I come to church, but that didn't necessarily mean she wanted to be seated next to me.

Five minutes went by, and I realized I wasn't paying any attention to the church service. My mind was completely distracted by Nicole's presence. I braced myself, blew some air from my cheeks, and proceeded to make my way to my normal seat. When I reached the pew Nicole was in, I tapped her on the shoulder to request that she scoot over and make more room for big daddy.

Nicole's face lit up with a smile as did LL's. He waved and excitedly whispered, "Hi, Daddy."

I smiled, then I stuck out my hand for LL to slap me five. Whispering, I asked him, "What's up?"

LL excitedly asked his mother if he could sit right next to me. Nicole complied, and LL planted himself right smack in the middle of me and Nicole. LL used his left hand to grasp my right one, and with his right hand he took hold of his mother's left one. LL's legs weren't long enough to reach the ground, so as he sat he freely swung his legs back and forth. I knew exactly what LL was trying to do. It's so funny how kids instinctively know what love is. They are smart enough to realize when the love between their parents is fading and when it's peaking. LL was doing his best to bring the love between his parents to its highest point.

Nicole reached over LL, and she planted a kiss on my cheek. Goose bumps ran up and down my body.

My wife whispered and said, "I thought you weren't gonna make it."

I smiled and said, "Nah. I'm here."

After that kiss on the cheek, I felt so relieved. Throughout the service I felt as if I was on cloud nine. Sadly, I don't remember what the pastor was preaching about, but I really didn't sweat it. I was more concerned as to what would happen once the service was over. One thing I was going to suggest was that Nicole and I take LL to get some ice cream. I knew if I asked Nicole right in front of LL, she would be hard pressed to say no. After all, she was the one who told me LL shouldn't get caught up in the middle of our problems.

The service finally ended, and as everyone stood and gathered themselves and their belongings in preparation to leave, I sprung the question on Nicole.

Making sure that LL was in good earshot, I spoke very loud and clear. "Nicole, I don't know what you had planned for later, but I was thinking we should take LL to go get some ice cream."

Nicole looked at me with this sly look because she knew I had put her on the spot. LL helped my cause by pleading with his mother to accept my invitation. As Nicole adjusted her overcoat, she took about ten seconds before she replied, however, she did accept the invitation.

I wanted to take both Nicole and LL by the hand and lead them out of the church, but at the same time I didn't want to overstep my boundaries. Nicole seemed to be in a good mood as she smiled and spoke to the brothers and sistas of the congregation. As people came up to me asking me how I was doing and where I'd been, I gave them all generic responses.

I brushed everyone off as I would reply, "Oh, I've been all right. I mean, I have been going through a few rough things, but God is working everything out. I'll be okay, but hey, listen, thanks for asking. I can't really talk right now, so I'll catch you later."

Nicole and I both made our way out of the church at the same time. As we stood on the church steps, I told Nicole we should take LL to the Carvel's on Jamaica Avenue. She didn't object as she told me she would follow me in her car. So together we made our way to the church parking lot, and we got in our cars and headed out.

When we reached Carvel's and were walking to the entrance, LL continued in his role of matchmaker as he said, "Daddy, hold Mommy's hand."

Feeling uneasy, I replied, "LL, we're almost inside the store."

LL knew I was trying to duck his command, so he grabbed my hand and pulled it toward Nicole's until they touched. Although I felt uncomfortable, I had to look at Nicole and smile. She returned it with one of her own, and we walked into Carvel's hand in hand. Nicole's hand had never felt better.

The two of us stood in line holding hands while trying to decide what we were gonna order. Nicole and I both probably wanted to make it seem as if we were only holding hands to please LL, but if we both had to confess the truth, I'm sure we would have both admitted it was very therapeutic.

When we were done ordering, and the lady was handing us our ice cream, I thought about how clumsy LL was. Being that I was in such a good mood, I could have cared less if he dropped his ice cream cone ten times. But surprisingly LL was good. Not only did he not drop his cone, but on the way to our seats, LL managed to properly lick it without spilling anything.

Nicole and I had soft vanilla sundaes. Our toppings included strawberries, strawberry glaze, walnuts, and rainbow sprinkles. As we ate, I joked with LL so I could ease the tension of feeling forced to speak to Nicole. But to my surprise Nicole began a conversation with me.

"Yeah, Lance, like I said, I didn't think that you would show up. I didn't see you when church started, and I know that you're never late."

I answered, "Well, to tell you the truth, I came late on purpose. I just didn't wanna have to answer any questions from people."

Nicole nodded as she placed some ice cream into her mouth. When she'd swallowed the strawberries, she looked at me and said, "Lance, I wanted you to come to church because there are some things that I wanted to discuss with you."

My nerves were instantly on edge as I asked, "Things like what?"

Nicole looked at LL, and she told me she didn't want to talk in front of him. Once she said that, I knew she probably wanted to talk in terms of a divorce or legal separation. It had to be something to that effect.

Nicole continued, "Lance, I already cooked, so when we leave here just come by the house and we can talk then."

When we were done eating our ice cream, I decided to buy some more for LL to put in the freezer at home.

I purchased three quarts of ice cream for LL, and I had the lady behind the counter put it in a bag for him. LL was extremely excited. I handed him the bag, and I instructed him he was not to rush and eat all of the ice cream in a day or two. I told LL I wanted him to make the ice cream last for at least two weeks. LL gave me his word that he would.

The three of us made our way out of the store, and LL asked his mother if he could ride with me. Nicole had no problem with it, so LL jumped in the Lexus and we navigated our way to Cambria Heights.

As we drove, LL asked, "Daddy, are you coming back home today?"

I turned down the music and said, "LL, I'm gonna eat dinner with you and your mother, but after that I have to leave. I already told you I would love to stay, but I can't. It's not up to me."

LL slumped and pouted in his seat while simultaneously crossing his arms. I informed him that I was sorry, but there was nothing I could do. I relayed to LL that he probably wouldn't understand everything that was going on until he was older.

LL and I reached the house about a minute before Nicole. As I made my way to the front door of my crib, I felt like I was one of Jesus' disciples marching to the last supper or something. LL asked me if I would play video games with him, but I declined. Being that it was Sunday, I suggested that LL and I watch football together. LL was elated over the idea, which made me feel good because I knew that athletically, he would follow in his daddy's footsteps.

As LL and I talked about football, Nicole made her way up to her bedroom, and she hollered for me to come up to the room. I told LL to hold his football questions and we would continue our conversation in a minute.

When I reached the bedroom I saw Nicole taking off her clothes. She was preparing to change into something more comfortable. It was bugged because I felt like I was doing something wrong by seeing her naked. Nicole even suggested I take off my suit and relax. I had to remind myself I did have a whole wardrobe of clothing in the closet. It was weird, but I was just feeling like a total stranger in my own home.

As I changed my clothes, Nicole advised me that the food was ready if I wanted to eat. However, I suggested that we wait being that the ice cream had probably messed up our appetites. Plus, it was only one o'clock in the afternoon, which meant even for a Sunday it was way too early to be eating dinner.

Feeling like I should just ask for my whipping in order to just get it out of the way, I asked Nicole if she wanted to talk. We were in the privacy of our bedroom, so she replied that it was indeed a good time to talk. I knew LL was waiting for me so I yelled to him that I would be a while. I closed the door to the bedroom, and Nicole and I both sat on the bed in our sweatpants, T-shirts, and tube socks. Nicole played with a piece of loose thread that was on the bed sheets, and before I could blink, she was in tears.

"Baby, what's wrong?" I asked.

Nicole wiped her tears and sighed. Then she said, "Lance, it's just so hard. Every time I think of the fact that you got someone else pregnant, I just break down and start crying."

I didn't know what to say. I mean, I understood the harsh reality of what I'd done, but I didn't know what to say. I remained silent because I knew it was healthy for Nicole to get all of her emotions out.

Nicole continued to cry as she looked at me and said, "Lance, you don't know how bad you hurt me. This hurts so, so, sooo bad. You just don't know."

At that point I lost the desire to look Nicole in her eyes as I told her that I was sorry.

Nicole was beginning to calm down, and she asked, "Lance, do you know how much I love you?"

"Baby, believe me, I know and I am so sorry, but I can't change the situation."

Nicole shook her head, and she blew some air out of her mouth as she said, "Lance, I just wish this pain would go away. I really do."

Again I remained silent. Nicole continued, "Lance, during the past couple of weeks I've been thinking about everything imaginable. Things like the first time we met, the first date we went on, our first kiss, the day LL was born. I even watched our wedding video a couple of times. Lance, with all of the love and memories that we've built together . . . I just come to so many tears whenever I think about you taking care of a baby that's not ours. It probably would've been a little bit easier had it just been some kind of one-night-stand type of thing and no baby was involved."

"Nicole, believe me, I know how complicated a baby makes this whole situation. Plus, we don't believe in abortions so . . . Like I said before, I'm willing to accept whatever you want out of me. I realize I've caused all of the pain. I washed away the special love that we'd built together."

Nicole paused, and she didn't say anything. She remained quiet as tears began to form in her eyes. Then she said, "Lance, throughout this whole ordeal I've been reading my Bible and praying like I have never prayed before. And it's like God has helped me to realize a couple of things.

"I read about King Solomon, the wisest man who ever walked the face of the earth. The ironic thing about King Solomon is that, with all of his wisdom, he married hundreds of women, and he had hundreds of other women as concubines, which God did not approve of. Lance, it's weird because although King Solomon was very wise, he almost did a very foolish thing. For the sake of his desire to be with many women, he almost forsook his relationship with God. He practically was ready to spit in God's face despite the fact that God had richly blessed him. Lance, God was angry with King Solomon. But you know what? When King Solomon realized that his actions and his selfishness were hurting God and he was causing a huge mess, he repented, and he changed his life big time."

As I sat and intently listened to my wife, I replied, "Yeah, baby, that's why King Solomon wrote the book of Ecclesiastes. In that book he was basically repenting of all the wrong he'd done throughout his lifetime."

Nicole nodded and said, "Exactly." Then she added, "Lance, and look at King David . . . The Bible says King David had a heart like that of God's. Lance, I know you already know these stories, but I've just personally learned so much from them in the past couple of days. But back to King David, here was a man with a heart like God's, yet he still did wrong by committing adultery with Bathsheba. Lance, he went as far as having Bathsheba's husband killed. So you know God was extremely angry with him. However, when King David came to his senses and realized what he'd done, he repented. Lance, King David wept bitterly about the wrong the he'd done. And you know what? God restored him to his full honor."

I nodded in agreement with Nicole as I offered her a half smile. I smiled because in the past Nicole and I had both heard sermons about King David and about King Solomon, so we were both familiar with the stories of the two men. It was bugged that during this trial in our marriage, Nicole and I both had been refamiliarizing ourselves with the sins of the father-and-son patriarchs. I let Nicole know that I, too, had been reading and studying a lot about King Solomon and King David during the past few weeks.

Nicole began to cry as she asked me, "Lance, what is the main message of the gospel of Jesus Christ?"

Not knowing what Nicole was getting at, I replied, "Well . . . it's . . . um . . . How should I say it? Well, I'll put it like this, Jesus died for sinners so that if people believe in Him and confess His name as Lord and Savior and are willing to repent and begin a new life then He will guarantee them eternal life."

Nicole began to weep very hard as she said, "That's right. Lance, Jesus lived a sinless, perfect life, and yet people brutally murdered him for no reason. But as He was being crucified by the people, He asked His Father to forgive the people who were torturing Him. Jesus asked His Father to forgive them because He knew those who were crucifying Him really didn't know and understand what they were doing."

I intently looked at Nicole. I was trying hard to understand where she was taking me. Nicole had to know that I already knew the account of Jesus. Through her tears, Nicole added, "Lance, when I think about what you did, I get unbelievably angry. I cry, and all kinds of emotions run through my mind and soul. But then I think about King Solomon and King David and how they made mistakes. I also think about how they were willing to change. Then I look at Jesus, and I see how He is so willing to forgive."

As Nicole sighed she said, "Lance, I just want to tell you that I know you're sorry for what happened. And I know you really want to change. So Lance, I just want to say that . . . I truly forgive you for what you did. I mean believe me, I don't know how I'm bringing myself to say this, but I do forgive you, Lance."

When I heard those words come out of my wife's mouth I can't begin to describe the feelings that ran through my body. I instantly began crying. I grabbed hold of Nicole and I thanked her, and thanked her, and thanked her like there was no tomorrow. The two of us sat hugging and embracing each other, and we soaked our clothes with each other's tears.

As we hugged, Nicole, who was teary eyed and all, kinda pushed me away from her and she said, "Lance, I want us to make this marriage work."

I cried and shook my head as I told Nicole, "Baby, no. I don't deserve you. I don't deserve to have someone as special as you. Just leave me. Really, baby, just leave me. It hurts me like crazy to say and to think this, but I know there is somebody out there who can make you happier than I can. Somebody who wouldn't put you through what I put you through."

Wiping her eyes, Nicole responded, "Lance, I don't want anyone else. What's wrong? I said I forgive you."

As I continued to cry tears of joy, I replied, "Baby, I don't deserve to be forgiven."

At that moment, Nicole got up from the bed and went to her closet. She seemed as though she was searching for something. When she returned to the bed, she handed me a card and told me to read out loud what was on it. I looked at the card. Very carefully I examined it. I realized that it was from 1-800-FLOWERS that I'd hypocritically sent to Nicole a few months ago.

"Lance, read that card out loud," Nicole demanded.

I fought back tears and I read out loud, *"Love is patient, love is kind. It does not envy, it does not boast, it is not proud. It is not rude, it is not self-seeking, it is not easily angered, it keeps no record of wrongs. Love does not delight in evil but rejoices with the truth. It always protects, always trusts, always hopes, always perseveres. Love never fails."*

I placed the card on the bed and I hugged Nicole and I said, "Thank you. Baby, thank you so much. Thank you."

I was overwhelmed with emotion. It was hard for me to even get out those words of thanks as the impact of what I'd just read simply blew me away.

Nicole held back her tears, and with red puffy eyes, she said, "Lance, a couple of things hit me from the scriptures that are on that card. One thing is I know that I'm going to have to be extremely patient throughout this whole ordeal. Another thing is the words, *Love keeps no record of wrongs.*" Nicole paused, then she said, "Lance, I know God is helping me to say what I'm about to say, and that is, I love you. I don't care what people will think, and I know everyone will have plenty to say, but Lance as far as I'm concerned, your slate is clean with me. If you truly repent, Lance, and change, then your slate will be clean with God, so therefore, it has to be clean with me." Nicole took another pause.

She slowly stroked the bed sheets as she added, "Now I'm not saying I will never even think about the affair, because to be honest, I'm going to think about it every day. But what I'm saying is that, I'm not gonna be throwing the affair up in your face. Because if I do throw it up in your face, it won't help things to get any better. Lance, I want you to know because of God, I trust you. I am human, so I don't completely trust right now. But I know that with hard work on both of our parts I will one day come to the point where I'll be able to completely trust you one hundred percent. But Lance, I hope you will persevere through your struggles and weaknesses and try to do the right thing. I also hope that you will trust me and put hope in God. Also, for my sake, hope and pray for me that I will persevere through all of this."

Nicole suddenly became silent. She blew out air, and she looked toward the ceiling and repeatedly blinked in an effort to hold back her tears. "Lance, there are many things that we're gonna have to work out. For example, I don't ever want to see that child. I mean, I know you're gonna have to take care of the kid, but I'm telling you now I'm not gonna be able to deal with seeing pictures or having the kid in my house for visits and all of that.

"And as far as Toni is concerned, I know she might have to call here at times, but I don't want to speak to her, and I don't want to see her, especially not in my house. Lance, I know that it's wrong, but I have so much anger in my heart toward that woman and toward this whole thing in general. I have to ask God to help me out on that.

"See I'm not saying I'll never be able to confront Toni or I'll never be able to see the baby. I'm just saying that it's gonna take time until I feel comfortable enough for that to happen. As a matter of fact, I don't know if I'll ever feel totally comfortable being around Toni or the baby. It might take years for that to happen, but that's just how it's gonna have to be.

"Lance, something else I have to say is, I don't ever want to know the details of the affair. I mean, I actually want to know, but I know it's probably best that I never know the intimate details. But I don't know because my mind flip-flops on that subject. I mean, a part of me needs to know all of the details so I can put complete closure on the topic. But . . . it's like I think back to the way you were dancing with Toni at the party we had in May. Lance, I think about you asking me if I had ever cheated on you, and I wonder what exactly was going on then."

As Nicole sucked her teeth, she said, "Lance, see, like right now, I had to catch myself because I can tell that I was starting to get heated inside. Lance, again, all I can say is, I don't think I ever want to know the . . ." Nicole stopped in the middle of her statement and just stared into space. Then she looked as if she was gonna cry as she asked, "Lance, do you have love for Toni?"

I thought before I began to speak because I wanted to give Nicole the most honest answer I could. In my heart I sensed Nicole really didn't wanna know the answer to that question, and that's probably why she asked another question before I could give her an answer.

"Lance, like I said before, with God, I know I can trust you. But I want you to tell me, Lance, can I really ever trust you again?"

By this time in the conversation, my tears had left my face, and I said in a compassionate tone, "Baby, listen. Let me just say this . . . I understand fully what you've been saying. Believe me, whatever you want, however you feel things should be, that's how it will be. Nicole, I'm just so thankful you can even find it in yourself to forgive me. Baby, you don't know what it means to me to know that you want our marriage to work out. Nicole, I promise you I'm going to give more than a one hundred percent effort in every aspect of our marriage. And I promise you that together we're going to work out all of my sexual hang-ups so nothing like this will ever happen again. I realize now I should have just spoken up much sooner. I could've come to you for help and support in fighting through all of my struggles. I never came to you for help and support, and that was a huge mistake, but I promise you I'll be forthcoming with anything I think might trigger off something sexually immoral on my part.

"Nicole, I understand your pain. Baby, I don't want you to ever experience again what it is that I've put you through. And to answer your last two questions, yes, you can trust me. Nicole, I'm willing to work as hard as I have to in order to rebuild that trust. I don't know if my word is worth anything, but all I can say is I have no love whatsoever for Toni. Other than God, you're my first and only love, and I realize that now more than ever."

Nicole and I hugged and deeply embraced each other for about two minutes straight. Then she went to the bathroom and got two washcloths for both of us to wash our faces. As I washed my face, my body felt tingly and numb. I yelled to LL and let him know Daddy was not leaving and that I would be staying at home.

I had a couple of concerns and questions, but I was sure they would work themselves out. I wondered how I would react if I were to see Toni in person. I wondered how I would behave two or three years from now if I were alone with Toni visiting the baby. I wondered how I would deal with the rest of my doggish ways. How would I stop lusting? How would I stop masturbating? Would I really never cheat again?

I knew that only time would answer certain questions, but there was one thing I knew for sure, that being the fact that Nicole is a one-in-a-million kind of woman. In fact, God doesn't make women like Nicole anymore.

As I finished washing my face, I realized God had answered a prayer of mine. See, through Nicole, God was teaching me what it was like to love as He loves and to live as He lives. Yeah, there will be many tests for me to pass in the future, but for the first time in my life I earnestly wanted to pass all of those tests. Not only for myself, but more so because I didn't want to hurt anyone else in the future.

Again, I realize now more than ever that first and foremost, my doggish ways hurt not only myself, but they hurt God and those around me who love me. If Nicole can love me unconditionally the way she does, I'm sure if I plug into God and really focus, then and only then will I put an end to my dogism.

The calm after the storm.

It is said that when a person breaks a bone, the bone will actually be stronger after the break has been mended and it has had a chance to fully heal.

With my adulterous ways, I had broken the fibers and the innermost sacred parts Nicole and I had created with our union of marriage. And unlike a bone, which is very tangible in the sense that one can touch it, grab it, and physically see it, the fibers of a marriage are totally different—they are more spiritual. How do you mend those fibers in a way in which they will properly heal and be stronger than they were before the damage was done?

That is a question that only time can truly answer.

During the months after I revealed my adulterous ways to Nicole, we went through every range of emotions known to man. We had been frustrated, sad, remorseful, regretful, angry, depressed, and so many more adjectives that are along those lines. There were countless nights when we laid in our bed and soaked our pillows with tears.

From my standpoint, there were times following the affair's revelation in which I would literally feel like I was going to go insane simply because I knew deep down inside my cheating had never truly had any bad intentions. It sounds stupid, but I never wanted to hurt Nicole. I never wanted to put her in the position she was in. At times when we would lie in our bed and discuss why the affair happened and what the warning signs and red flags we both should have noticed were I would just want to ram my fist through the bedroom wall out of pure anger and frustration.

For one, I was truly regretful and mad at myself for having ever let myself trample over the vows I had made to both my wife and to God. I would also get ridiculously angry and frustrated because Nicole would constantly blame herself for the wrong I had done. She would always say things like, "If only I had been more affectionate or supportive then maybe you wouldn't have cheated." She would also say things like, "If I had only called you, Lance, on your cell phone and checked on some of your alibis for not being in the house at night, then maybe I could have prevented you from cheating."

See, I knew Nicole could not have been further from the truth. Honestly, I had wanted to cheat. I had something inside of me that was driving me to do what I did, and I acted on it. There was really nothing Nicole or anyone else could have done to stop me from being a dog.

One night while we were laying in the bed, I gave Nicole the following example in order to get her to fully understand how I was feeling and also to get her to stop blaming herself for what she had no control over.

"Nicole, I'm sure that the surviving family members who have ever lost a loved one due to some sick serial killer walk around blaming themselves for the death of their loved one. They probably say things like, 'If only we had told so and so to take another route to school that day' or, 'If only I would have taught my daughter not to talk to strangers.' See, Nicole, the family members should not blame themselves for the sickness of the serial killer. The fact of the matter is when a serial killer is determined that someone is gonna be his victim, he has a twisted and demented drive that will not let him rest until he kills the victim he is after. See, that's how it was with me. I had this sick and twisted drive to be with other women. It was a drive I couldn't escape. The only way I would have been able to escape it would have been if God saw fit to not allow it to happen."

Yeah, I remember very vividly giving Nicole that example, because while Nicole did get the gist of what I was saying, she focused more on the latter part of what I had said.

"See, Lance, that's what I can't understand. Why would God allow something like this to happen? I wouldn't wish this type of pain on anyone, and that's why I just can't understand why God would put me through this. I've been faithful to God, and I've always trusted Him and prayed to Him, and I continue to do that. I just can't understand why God would allow all of this."

I fully understood Nicole's reasoning behind questioning God. But during the months after I told Nicole about Toni, there was no way in the world I could personally question God, because I knew it was my reliance on Him that had carried me through and allowed me to stay on the straight and narrow. It was like my cheating ways had been a cancerous tumor in my soul, and by me plugging into God, He was able to go into my soul and cut out that cancer and keep me in remission from cheating.

Yeah, for the first six months following the revelation of Toni to my wife, I was regularly checking in with God, and I saw the benefits. If my cheating was like a cancer, then it was as if through prayer I was going to God on a daily basis for chemotherapy treatments. It was as if the Lord's chemotherapy treatments were designed to totally prevent the cheating cancerous cells from reforming again in my body and eliminating those cells that grew back after having been fully cut out during the initial operation of my repentance.

But just like most people when they are sick, as soon as they start to feel better, they stop taking their medication, usually totally based on their own decision-making process and their doctor will be totally in the dark about it. In my case I was able to battle relentless pressure from things such as dealing with Toni's pregnancy and subsequently the beautiful baby girl she and I had. I was able to deal with losing all sense of integrity and credibility with my family and friends. I was able to properly deal with new and old sexual temptations. I was able to muster up the courage to attend a weekly twelve-step program called Sex Addicts Anonymous, which is similar to Alcoholics Anonymous, only it was for people who felt that sex for them was either out of control or beginning to get way out of control. I was able to deal with all of those things and not crack under the pressure because I was managing to stay plugged into God. However, like the sick person who starts to feel a little better and automatically assumes they can stop taking their medication, I began to get real cocky in my own mind.

Right around the six months following the revelation of the affair, I noticed that I was only praying a few times a week instead of multiple times a day. It was like I began to put my guard down. I wasn't reading the Bible every day like I had been doing when the affair was first revealed. In other words, I began to voluntarily skip my chemotherapy sessions with the Lord.

Like magic, it must have been a new group or a new cluster of cancerous cheating cells that managed to work their way through my blood stream and stop at the part of my brain that controls my common sense. Those new cheating cells had a way of disguising themselves very well. In my case they had disguised themselves real good because they used different tactics in order to set me up. They didn't cause me to out and out lust and just want to sex someone per se, and they didn't cause me to want to masturbate or fiend to look at pornography. Rather, those new cheating cells began working on me. They began asking my ego: "What's up with you, Lance? Why ain't nobody calling you? You ain't the man no more or what?"

See, my ego or something inside of me seemed as if it always needed to really be stroked and caressed. And that's exactly what those new cheating cells began to play on. Maybe I felt the need for my ego to be stroked due to my many insecurities. I don't know. But I do know my cheating ways had never really been carried out simply as a quest to conquer the actual act of having sex or having an orgasm with fine, attractive women. It may have appeared that way, especially considering how attractive both Toni and Scarlet are. But the truth be told, my cheating ways went far deeper than superficial, surface things, it was more like they were done in an effort to prove to myself I was valuable and needed. I would base my value and my self-worth on the women that I would want to go after and eventually conquer.

I could have been super successful in all areas of my life, which for the most part I was, and yet I would always feel the need of wanting to feel better about myself, wanting to cause someone to feel like they really needed to be with me or needed me to be around in their lives, regardless if that "someone" was another woman and I was a married man.

I don't know if it will prove to be unfortunate, fateful, or whatever, but once again I really began realizing my strong need to feel desired and valuable in the eyes of the opposite sex. I began feeling this way only months after Toni gave birth to the baby.

See, God had been answering all of my prayers. He had been keeping my mind free of that desire to want to feel needed. He had even made sure and saw to it to protect me from everything. God protected me so much until it got to the point where certain women like Scarlet and others like her actually backed off me.

Yeah, that was ill because Scarlet, along with my other female acquaintances, had totally, voluntarily, and willingly distanced themselves from me. Me! Of all people, Lance Thomas. I knew God had played a role because that was what I had been specifically asking him to do for me. God had also been keeping me away from bad influences in the form of people like Steve and many others who did not have my best interests at heart.

Yet it was primarily the thoughts of Scarlet that were really wreaking havoc on my mind. I knew the best thing in the world had happened to me was that I hadn't spoken to women like Scarlet for a little more than six months, which had been a record time frame for me not having contact with women outside of my marriage. What was really ironic, though, was those cheating cancerous cells had kept a serious poker face during that time. They had a huge ace in the hole. They knew that I had managed to keep one thing in the dark about my past.

Having revealed just about everything to Nicole, I always knew I had never told her about Scarlet. Keeping Scarlet a secret had never been my intention. I guess after seeing Nicole react the way she did when I told her about Toni, I wanted to protect Nicole's emotions and, therefore, I instinctively and completely blocked out of my mind the life of sin that I had carried on with Scarlet, not to mention wanting to avoid the fear of completely being exposed and feeling like a worthless freak. Yeah, that also played a part in me keeping my mouth shut about Scarlet. Yeah, even when Nicole had specifically asked me had there been anyone else other than Toni, I knew I could have mentioned Scarlet del Rio, but something just came over me and made me lie about it. I lied by keeping the Scarlet thing in the dark.

I know it sounds pathetic and pitiful, but again, I figured telling Nicole about Scarlet would have been a blow she would not have been able to handle. Even after having told Nicole about Toni and the pregnancy and living through that, something inside of me told me Nicole would not have been able to handle the entire truth and details about Scarlet. I mean, after all, Scarlet had been in the picture for the entire time Nicole and I had been married, so that would have put things in a completely different league of revelation.

I guess for the most part, after Scarlet began fading out of the picture, which happened to be right around the time I'd met Toni, I viewed it as Scarlet didn't really need to be discussed with Nicole. I know I was using twisted logic, but Scarlet had been further in the past than Toni had been. Plus, I had met Scarlet and had had sex with her before Nicole and I had actually said "I do." In my mind I had convinced myself the Scarlet thing was okay to brush under the rug, especially considering the fact that no baby or no sexually transmitted diseases were involved.

My silence about Scarlet gave so much power to my demons. That one ace in the hole my cancerous cheating cells held was just waiting to be played. The danger of me having kept Scarlet a secret was twofold, and I knew it. It was like I had a mistress in my hip pocket and Nicole had no way of helping me to stay clear of her. If now, more than six months after the fact, I had chosen to bring the Scarlet thing to the spotlight and expose what had been a five-year on-again, mostly off-again sexual affair then Nicole would have really lost all sense of trust in me, and she would have never, ever been able to believe another word that came out of my mouth for as long as I lived. Everything concerning my marriage would have been down the drain—everything.

So in order to protect myself, Nicole, and LL, I convinced myself it would be best to keep things quiet for the rest of my natural life as far as Scarlet was concerned. In no way could I put Nicole through that type of drama again. In no way was I gonna lose the battle against my demons Nicole and I had been fighting together during the past six months.

I had a lot of thoughts waging war in my mind on a daily basis. I knew of all the destruction and pain I had caused. I knew about all of the new promises and new vows I had made. I knew about all the repenting prayers I had offered up to God. I knew about the rosy future I wanted to recreate with Nicole and LL. I truly, truly, from the innermost part of my being, wanted to continue to do right. And from the pit of my soul I had truly been genuinely remorseful and sorry for what I'd done. I truly loved Nicole and I truly loved God. I really knew those things.

But still, why hadn't Scarlet at least checked for me during the past six months? I mean, she hadn't even called me one time. I wondered many things, such as if she was a'ight. I wondered if she was angry with me for not having called her. I wondered if she was angry with me because of my relationship with Toni. Hell, I wondered if she had still been stalking me. I wondered if she was sexing anyone else. I wondered if she had completely written me off and had really moved on in her mind as it related to me. I wondered if she still thought I looked good. I wondered if she would still let me hit it if I were to see her. I wondered if she were in a relationship with someone else, and if she would be willing to cut that person off for me. I wondered if she still saw me as an emotional stronghold that would help her deal with all of the baggage in her life. I wondered if she would still be excited to hear from a brother.

If it takes me the rest of my natural life to do it, I know I will one day be able to explain why I would want to entertain the thought of placing fire in my lap all over again. One day I will be able to explain exactly why I would want to behave like a dog that returns to his vomit, sniffs it, and then eats what he has already regurgitated. One day I will fully be able to articulate the reasons why, but I want to be able to articulate it in a way in which I understand it and in a way everyone else will understand it.

I had an overwhelming need, and I was feeling a lot of pressure. At the same time I was feeling an intoxicating desire to desperately satisfy, address, and fix my need, which is why I wasn't shocked that after only a little more than six months of sexual sobriety I had given in to the need and sought out a quick fix.

I still had Scarlet's phone number memorized. Scarlet was the fix I felt I could not do without for the moment. I guess I should have run to Nicole for help, or run to anyone to help me fight off this monster that was approaching me and trying to devour me.

I was nervous as hell, and I didn't want to do it, but somehow I managed to get my sweaty palms and fingers to dial Scarlet del Rio's phone number.

My heart was beating, and I had no idea what I was going to say to her, or where and what that phone call would lead to, but I had to at least be assured Scarlet still needed me.

Ironically, the radio was on in my living room, and I remember the Aaliyah song "If Your Girl Only Knew" playing on low volume in the background while I dialed Scarlet's phone number.

Finally after three rings, Scarlet's soft, sweet-sounding, familiar voice with a slightly detectable Brazilian accent picked up.

"Hello," I softly spoke into the phone. "Hello," Scarlet replied. "Scarlet, you'll never guess who this is," I said as I waited in a moment of silence for her to figure out exactly who it was who had just called her.

"I'm sorry, but I don't know who this is, and I really don't have time to be playing games," Scarlet said in her true-to-form straightforward and sassy fashion.

"Baby, this is Lance," I said in a cocky but suave type of way.

There was a brief silence. I could sense that on the other end of the phone a huge smile of excitement had come over Scarlet's face, and she was more than likely standing in shock and in awe with her hand probably placed over her chest for dramatic effect to portray as if she was having a heart attack or something.

"Oh my God, Lance, I cannot believe you called me."

Chapter Thirty-one

It had been six years since I had confessed the life-changing news to my wife Nicole. It was devastating and deal-breaking news. It would have ended most marriages in a heartbeat.

Nicole was a good Christian wife in every sense of the word. After she had forgiven me for such a horrendous act of disloyalty, I did everything within my power to recommit myself to her and to God.

Unfortunately, the thing I didn't realize was that infidelity never truly dies. The DNA of infidelity is sort of like the leaves on a tree. For a season the leaves on a tree dry up and fall to the ground, but the tree itself isn't dead, which means in the upcoming spring season new leaves will take the place of all of the old leaves that fell to the ground.

In my case, the leaves of infidelity had fallen out of my life. They fell to the ground and the season of being faithful and true to myself, and to my marriage, lasted for all of six years. Despite some drama here and there, those six years were very good years and I didn't necessarily want them to end. But in life, all good things must come to an end and with me, after six years of doing the right thing, that season had come to an end and I had entered into a new season of *Dogism*.

This new season of *Dogism* would be different, though. Fortunately for me I had learned some things from my past. Sort of like rules that I would use to help me govern the seeds of infidelity that had sprung back to life.

Rule 1: Don't be Sloppy!

I knew venturing down that familiar path would mean I would diligently have to cover my tracks and not make any mistakes. In fact, I couldn't afford to make even one mistake or else my marriage would definitely end.

Rule 2: Never Snitch on Yourself!

John Gotti once said that if he were to rob a church and if the pope and the police were to catch him red-handed coming out of the church with the loot in his hand, a steeple, and a cross sticking out of his ass, he would still never admit to robbing the church!

That John Gotti comment was always funny as hell to me but I came to understand the twisted wisdom in what he was saying about not snitching on yourself. It took some time for me to understand why snitching on myself was so stupid, but like any mistake, mistakes are designed to teach us something and we can eventually use that mistake to our benefit. During those six years that followed the revelation of my infidelity, there were many nights I spent consoling my wife and trying to do whatever I had to do in order to restore trust in our marriage. I would be lying if I said 1 didn't repeatedly want to kick myself for having opened my mouth and told on myself. Yeah, I knew that because I told on myself and hadn't actually been caught cheating that it was a plus in proving my sincerity to do right. But at the same time, I came to realize keeping what's done in the dark, in the dark, actually helps avoid a whole lot of pain and misery!

Rule 3: Don't Break Rules One and Two!

Chapter Thirty-two

They say fate is when preparation meets opportunity. Well, as fate would have it, I just happened to be in the city of Philadelphia promoting a new book I had written for The Unit when I walked into the DNC bank that was located on the corner of Broad and Locust in downtown Philly, and I was presented with the opportunity of a lifetime.

I was planning on just running into the bank to use the ATM, but I looked to my left and I saw the most gorgeous bank teller I had ever seen in my life. She was the spitting image of the singer Ciara, only she appeared to be a bit thicker. Her eyes were the first thing that had caught my eye when she looked up and glanced toward my direction. From a distance I could tell she had either hazel or green eyes because they were just piercing right through me but in a very soft, non-menacing, non-seductive way, but still piercing.

Just as quickly as she had looked in my direction, her eyes then shifted away from me. She took her right hand and moved some of her long black hair away from her forehead and shifted it behind her right ear. Since it was slow in the bank, she lifted a book that she had in front of her and started to read it.

Her presence and the whole scene reminded me so much of when I first met my ex-mistress Toni, six years ago while driving down a Brooklyn street one sunny afternoon.

"Lance, just keep it moving, nigga," I said to myself as I contemplated whether or not I should say something to the beautiful teller and make the most of this once-in-a-lifetime opportunity.

I had just taken out four hundred dollars from the ATM, so I had gotten what I'd came for, but yet it was incredibly hard for me to just turn around and walk the hell out of the bank. It was like the teller was calling my name or something.

Lance, keep it moving! I said more forcefully to myself.

I counted my money to make sure it was all there. After putting the money into the pocket of my Artful Dodger jeans I walked out of the bank. Every ounce of me began to burn with regret and with curiosity. I walked about half a block, and when I got to the corner, I waited for the green light to turn red so I could cross the street.

The light turned red and the crowd of pedestrians crossed the street and went on about their business. But I stood still in my tracks on a freezing cold and blustery afternoon trying to decide if I should go back into the bank and talk to the girl that I had just seen.

"A'ight, so what I'll do is just go in and introduce myself to her, but I won't ask for the number," I said to myself, still trying to convince myself to do something I knew I should just leave the hell alone.

Giving in to my weakness, I blew air out of my lungs, turned back around and headed back to DNC bank. The bank was surprisingly empty, considering it was lunchtime and there were a bunch of office workers and businesses in that area. But that was cool, because it gave me more of an opportunity to figure out just how I was gonna make my move.

The teller I wanted to talk to had a customer at her window so I chilled for a minute near the customer service desk, where I calmly slid off my wedding ring and slipped it into my pocket before going in for the kill. I had no idea what I was going to say to her, but I was determined to be as smooth as possible.

After about two minutes or so she was finished helping the customer that was at her window and I wasted no time and I moved right in.

"Hello, how are you doing today?" she asked with a smile that could have lit up any dark room. She had perfect white teeth.

"Oh, I'm good. I'm cold as hell, but other than that I'm good."

"Yeah, it is freezing outside. This weather is crazy. I hate the wintertime," she added, trying to be as polite and friendly as possible.

I looked at the name tag she had clipped to her blouse to see what her name was. She smiled and playfully pointed to her head and said, "umm . . . up here, I'm here."

"Oh, nah, I wasn't looking at your chest. I was just looking at your name tag."

She laughed and said, "I'm just messing with you, so how can I help you?"

I reached into my pocket and pulled out five twenty-dollar bills and asked her if I could have one hundred dollars in singles.

"Sure. No problem."

"So I see you're reading *My Woman His Wife*," I said to her while she counted the money.

She nodded her head to acknowledge my comment, but she didn't speak, looking as if she was trying not to lose her count. But as soon as she finished counting the money, she did reply.

"This book is so good it's gonna get me fired. It's so good! I love Anna J. That's my girl!"

"Yeah, it's a good book. The sex scenes are crazy."

"Well, I'm hooked on it and so are all of my coworkers."

"You know, I'm actually a writer too."

The teller looked at me with twisted lips and a smirk on her face, "What books have you wrote? You're not a writer."

"No, I swear to God, I am. I wrote three books. Actually, that's why I'm in Philly. I'm from New York but we got a book-signing tonight and then a book release party for my new joint I did with The Unit Books."

"The Unit? They doing books now too?"

"Yup."

"Really, so what's your name?"

"Lance Thomas, I wrote—"

"Stop lying! *Lady's Night,* right?" she asked while cutting me off.

"Yeah," I replied with a smile.

"I so don't believe you. Oh my God! That's one of my favorite books ever. Matter fact, let me see some ID."

I started to laugh and I said again that it was really me.

"Okay, so if it is then let me see your ID."

I reached into my wallet and I took out my driver's license and showed it to her.

"Oh my God! I can't believe this," she said while smiling from ear to ear.

"Mashonda Williams, that's you, right?" I asked. The chemistry between me and Mashonda was off the meter—at least to me it was—but I was sure she was feeling me just as much as I was feeling her.

She nodded her head, yes.

"See, I really was looking at your name tag." I joked and said, "So, Mashonda, what are you doing later? Why don't you come to the booksigning for my new book. It's gonna be at the Borders in the Gallery at seven o'clock."

"Tonight? At the Gallery? That's so funny, because I heard them talking about that on the morning show on the radio."

"Yeah, it's tonight. I already know that you're a reader, so if you don't come I'm really gonna be offended."

Mashonda laughed and she assured me she would definitely come through with one of her homegirls.

I took one of her business cards that was on the counter and I took hold of the pen that was also on the counter. I wrote my name and cell phone number on the back of her card and gave it to her.

"I know where you work so if you don't show up I'm gonna be back here tomorrow to stalk you and harass you. Here's my number. Call me anytime. Okay?"

Mashonda smiled and she nodded her head. Then there was this awkward silence.

I broke the silence by saying, "My money. You never gave it to me."

"Oh! I'm so sorry. I'm really trippin'," she said while handing me the money. "And don't be giving those strippers all your money either," she joked.

"Guilty as charged," I said, smiling.

Before turning to leave, I made a phone with my thumb and my index finger and silently mouthed the words *call me*.

Mashonda nodded her head and I continued walking out of the bank. Just like that I knew I had Mashonda exactly where I wanted her.

Chapter Thirty-three

When I made it back to my hotel I went up to my room and lay down on the bed and flipped through the cable channels with the remote. It was barely three o'clock and I was bored as hell, trying to kill some time before heading over to the book-signing later that evening. I decided to order some food and some Heineken's from room service. As soon as I was done ordering, my wife called me.

"Hey, Nicole."

"Hey, baby, I'm just checking up on you, letting you know that I miss you."

I laughed into the phone. "You miss me already? I only been gone for one night. I guess I must be putting it down right, huh?"

"Shut up. You so stupid. So what are you up to?"

"Nothing, I'm just bored as hell. I ain't even really hungry, but I ordered room service to try and kill some time."

"So you just eating to eat?"

"It's all good. The publishing company is covering the tab, so why shouldn't I eat?"

"You are too much."

"So what's up with you? You had to go to court today?"

"No, I'm just in the office working on this motion and it's killing me. I wanna get outta here by five, but I know I probably won't leave here until seven. I just want to get this outta my hair. So listen, what are you doing later, after the signing?"

"Well, I'm gonna go to the release party and then I'm bouncing."

"Oh, okay, so you'll be home tonight at what, probably around four or five in the morning?"

"Yeah, something like that."

"Okay, so be safe. And remember, LL has his game in the morning."

"Oh, I forgot about that. At eleven, right? Yeah, okay, I'll definitely be back by then."

"Okay, so I'll let you go. You being good, right?"

"Yeah, Nicole, of course."

"I'm just checking, you know that's part of my job. Okay, so be good. Call me when you heading out no matter how late it is. I love you."

"I love you too."

With that, I hung up, and I knew Nicole's only reason for calling me was to ask me if I was being good and to remind me to be good. For the most part I can't say that I blame her. I mean, after all, I had cheated on her back in the days when I was just a lowly blue-collar worker, so now that I was a bestselling author, travelling from state to state and going to party after party without her, I was sure there were constantly thoughts in the back of her head that made her wonder if I could be faithful through all of the potential temptation.

To my credit, so far I had been faithful. I can't say that it was easy, but I was holding up. My ex-mistress Toni had moved on and she was now married to a successful record producer, so that helped me stay on the right track. My other mistress, the stripper Scarlett, moved miles away to Atlanta, had two kids by two different dudes, and she got fat as a house, so by default she removed herself from my lust radar.

But as far as I was concerned, Toni and Scarlett were old news to me. It was like a been-there, conquered-that type of thing. Everyday I was tempted to conquer something new, but so far I had held that temptation in check. Unfortunately, I knew when it came to Mashonda, she represented something fresh, something new, and something exciting. I had to conquer her just to satisfy the urge that was in me.

Mashonda was gonna be a problem for me. I knew she was, but like a dumb-ass I was willing to take whatever chance I needed to take in order to satisfy the urge that I had in me to get with her.

Chapter Thirty-four

By the time seven o'clock rolled around, I had been escorted from my hotel to Borders bookstore in the Gallery Mall for the launch of The Unit Books. I was accompanied by the fellow The Unit writers, Angie Santiago, Lameek, and the superstar rappers Fifth Ward and Purple Hayes.

All day long, all of the Philly hip-hop stations had been promoting the event at the Gallery, but never in my wildest dreams did I expect to see the mob of people that were in the mall trying to get inside the bookstore. Of course, I knew that Fifth Ward's name was what had brought out all the throngs of people, but it didn't matter because by default I would be receiving a lot of the attention as well.

Security managed to get us safely into the bookstore and the managers of the bookstore took us to our table and instructed us on how things were going to proceed. As soon as we sat down and began to autograph books for the massive line of customers, my cell phone began vibrating. I looked down and I saw I had a text from Mashonda.

Hi Lance, this is Mashonda, the girl you met in the bank today. If you can, please call me back at this number 267-999-5454.

Although I was preoccupied signing books, I wasted no time and called her right back.

"Hello?"

"Hi, Lance. Listen, you didn't tell me that all of these people were gonna be here. Security is telling me that unless I had already purchased a book from earlier in the day I can't get in. They saying I need some kind of bracelet or a tag or something in order to get in."

"Where are you?"

"I'm outside the mall at the main entrance."

"Okay, listen, I'm gonna get you in, don't worry. This line is really crazy so I'm gonna pass the phone to one of the security guards and have him come get you. Just don't hang up. Give me a minute, though. A'ight?"

"Okay, no problem."

I quickly got up and got the attention of one of the plain-clothes security guards that had escorted us into the book-store. I explained to him the situation and told him I really needed him to do me the favor of going to the main entrance and getting Mashonda. He was cool about it and gave me no problem. He took hold of the phone and began talking to her to find out exactly where she was and what she was wearing.

Fifteen minutes later the security guard came back to the store, along with Mashonda and one of her friends.

I know that I looked like a superstar because there was a horde of photographers and video cameramen who were all positioned behind a roped-off section of the bookstore. As we signed books the photographers continually snapped pictures so there were nonstop camera flashes. The crowd mixed with the chicks who were screaming, crying, and taking off their panties for Fifth Ward while they got their books signed.

Mashonda smiled and she waved a little nervous smile to me as I motioned for her to skip the line and to come to where I was at. She walked toward me with her friend. I stood up and walked around to the other side of the table and she gave me a quick hug.

"Heyyy, so I guess you really are a writer," she joked.

Mashonda had on a chinchilla jacket that came to her waist. She had on a skintight pair of black Citizen jeans and some high-heel boots that came up to her knees. Her ass, thighs, and hips were off the hook. Being that she had been behind the counter at the bank, I had never gotten a chance to see her full body so I was seeing it for the first time, and I was loving what I was seeing.

"Lance, this is Connie. She works with me at the bank. She reads everything just like me."

"Nice to meet you," I said as I extended my hand to Connie's and shook it.

"Well, here, let me get y'all a copy of the books. Do y'all want them signed?"

Mashonda and Connie both nodded their heads and followed me back to the table where I signed my book for them and then passed it to Fifth, Angie Santiago, and Lameek for them to sign as well.

"Fifth, this is Mashonda and Connie," I said as I introduced the two gorgeous women to Fifth.

"Nice to meet y'all," Fifth replied as he signed their books.

Connie was beaming from ear to ear and she whispered something into Mashonda's ear.

"Lance, do you mind if we get a picture with you?" Mashonda asked.

I posed for the picture with the two of them and then I asked Fifth if he would get in the picture as well. They handed the security guard their camera phones and asked him if he would take the pictures for them. After we had taken the pictures, my publicist was looking at me with this look to kill; she wanted me to focus and get back to business.

"Listen, Mashonda," I said, discreetly talking low and directly into her ear, "when we leave here we're heading over to Ms. Tootsie's to eat and then we're gonna go to Pinnacle's for the release party. I know I don't really know you from Adam, but I want you to hang out with me tonight. I gotchu on everything. Drinks, food, whatever you want, I gotchu."

Without hesitation, Mashonda nodded her head and said, "Yeah, no doubt. That's what's up." Then she spoke to Connie and relayed to her what I had said and the two of them both agreed to roll with us after we left the bookstore.

Mashonda and Connie roamed throughout the mall and window-shopped until the booksigning event was over. At eight-thirty I called her on her cell phone and told them to meet us in the rear entrance of the mall that lead into the parking lot. They linked up with us and we all piled into a white, stretch Hummer the publishing company had booked for us and we made our way over to Ms. Tootsie's.

Ms. Tootsie's was rammed beyond capacity but they knew we were coming through so they had tables reserved for us. We ate like kings and queens as every eye in the place was on us. Throughout the whole time I had to give it to Mashonda and Connie, because they both knew how to act and weren't acting all brand-new and starstruck like they had never been anywhere before. At the same time, they talked, made jokes, and came across like they were real comfortable.

"Y'all drink?" I asked Mashonda and Connie over the loud music in the club.

"Like a fucking fish!" Connie laughed and said.

"No, *you* drink like a fish. I ain't no alcoholic like that," Mashonda corrected her friend.

Just by the way Mashonda was dressed I could tell she was used to hanging with ballers. I highly doubted she got that five-thousand-dollar outfit from her ten dollar an hour bank salary, so my guess was she was used to niggas tricking on her. She definitely had the look to accommodate it.

As usual, the food at Ms. Tootsie's was off the chain, but we couldn't stay there as long as we wanted to because we had to make it over to Pinnacle's for the party. By the time we got to the club, it was past eleven-thirty and the spot was rammed. All of the attention was on our entourage as the bouncers held the ropes open so that we could enter. The attention stayed on us as we made our way to the VIP section.

We walked over to the leather couches and Mashonda sat down very ladylike. But Connie, on the other hand, wasted no time in standing on the headrest of the couch and started dancing to the music.

"I guess you can see that she's the wild one out of the bunch!" Mashonda shouted into my ear.

"Nah, it's cool, I like her style," I replied as I attempted, and got ahold of one of the waitresses and ordered a bottle of Patrón and apple martinis for Connie and Mashonda. Almost on cue, as soon as I sat down next to Mashonda, I felt my cell phone vibrating. I looked at it and it was Nicole calling me. I would've picked up, but there was just way too much noise in the club so I let it go to voice mail. Besides the noise, I didn't answer my phone because I just didn't want to speak to Nicole.

See, I knew what I was plotting on doing and whenever I was doing wrong I would try and completely block out thoughts of my wife so I wouldn't feel guilty.

"Yo, so can I be straight up with you and tell you that I was stalking you at the bank today?" I said into Mashonda's ear.

"Stop lying," she said and laughed.

"I swear to God I was! But I know you probably get customers all day long trying to talk to you. Especially with that tight-ass toddler shirt you had on," I joked.

"Yeah, it gets so annoying and draining at times."

"Why is that? Oh, let me guess, 'cause you got a man and you all loyal and in love with him, right?"

Mashonda just smiled. But she didn't respond to my statement about her having a man. I continued with the small talk with her for about another fifteen minutes, and that was all the time it took for the Patrón to start flowing through my system and for me to really step my game up.

The DJ was playing a bunch of old school hits so the vibe was crazy.

"So, listen, when I leave I'm heading to the Four Seasons. I got a room there and then I'm bouncing in the morning, going back to New York, but I don't wanna leave you. I still wanna chill witchu some more tonight."

Mashonda sipped on her drink and she looked at me and nodded her head. She then sat her drink down, stood up, grabbed me by the hand and pulled me up so I could dance with her.

"You know I don't know you like that to be going back to your room with you," she said into my ear as I did a two-step to the music while she danced much harder than I was dancing.

Just the breath from her mouth grazing my earlobe had my dick standing at attention.

"I know it's not just me, but don't you feel like we knew each other for a minute? Like it's a connection or something, right or wrong?" I smiled and said, "The chemistry is crazy, just admit that shit."

Mashonda smiled and then screamed into my ear while slurring her words, "Yeah, I gotta admit that it iszzz kinda crazy."

I could tell the two drinks Mashonda had were getting to her, besides the fact that she was talking extremely too loud and slurring her words. She just had this seductive look in her eyes and it was a completely different look than I had seen when I saw her at the bank earlier.

She placed her hand behind my neck and pulled me closer to her. "You smell real good."

I didn't say anything, but I was hoping like hell that her friend Connie wasn't the cock-blocking type, because Mashonda was turning me on like a motherfucka. I was gonna do whatever I had to do to get her to come back to my room with me.

"It does feel like I've met you before, or something. You're right about that," Mashonda said, laughing. Two seconds after the DJ switched up the music and threw on a reggae song I pulled her body up against my body, and she started grinding on me. My dick was hard as hell and I know she felt that shit.

"So you good, right?"

"Nah, I'm scared of your ass," she replied.

"Why?"

She looked at me and nodded her head, and she continued to grind on me. She started to massage my dick through my pants.

"That's why," she replied.

"You play dirty, but I like that."

She didn't respond; she just turned her back to me and dipped her body low and then came back up and started backing her ass up on my dick. She was fucking driving me crazy.

Right at that moment my BlackBerry began buzzing again. I looked at it and it was Nicole texting me, telling me not to forget to call her when I left.

"You drove with Connie or y'all drove separate?"

"I drove, we came together," Mashonda said as she turned back around and faced me and continued grinding on me.

I scanned the crowded VIP area until I got Lameek's attention and motioned for him to come over to where I was at.

"What's the deal, my nigga?"

"Yo, I'm trying to bounce with shorty and take her back to the spot, but her homegirl Connie that was at the restaurant with us, I'm not trying to leave with her. So I need you to take this sixty dollars and make sure she gets home. But just chill with her for me and make sure she has a good time, you feel me?"

"No doubt, I gotchu my dude," Lameek said and gave me a pound.

I took Mashonda by the hand and quickly made my rounds through the VIP area and told Fifth, Hayes, and my agent that I was bouncing, but I would get up with them. They all saw me holding Mashonda's hand so they all knew what was up without me having to explain anything.

Mashonda wanted another drink on our way out. We stopped at the bar at the front of the club, and she ordered vodka and cranberry juice and I ordered a Hennessy on the rocks.

"You shouldn't be mixing drinks like that, that's how you throw up," I warned.

"I'm grown, don't worry," Mashonda said as she winked at me.

After we finished our drinks, we made it out to the car. I gave the driver forty dollars and told him I was bouncing early but everybody else was staying until later. So without hesitation he opened the door for us and took us to my hotel room.

As soon as we walked into my room, I was thinking about turning on the TV and doing the whole small-talk thing, but I could sense that shit was just different. The vibe and the chemistry was bananas so I knew I was gonna go right for the kill.

"Let me take your coat," I said to her as I helped her take it off and hung it up.

After I hung up it up, I walked back over to her and she was about to say something, but I didn't let her talk. Without even asking I just started tongue-kissing her. She seemed as if she didn't have a shy bone in her body, and she kissed me just as passionately as I kissed her.

I started unbuttoning her top as I kissed her, and before long her full thirty-six-D titties were exposed and I was sucking on them. I took off my shirt and she started feeling on my chest. She told me to sit on the bed and just lay back. I did as she instructed me, and she took off my sneakers and then unbuttoned my pants and pulled them off.

"That's sexy as hell."

"What?" I asked.

"You ain't wearing no underwear. I love that!"

After she said that, she took my dick and started sucking on it like a pro. She was driving me insane. Then she took my balls and started gently sucking on them while she stroked my dick with her hand. I could tell that she definitely had a whole lot of experience sucking dick and I can't say I was mad at that because it was feeling good as hell.

"You got a condom?" she asked.

I nodded my head and told her where it was. She got up and went across the room and got the condom and then she took off her boots and squirmed her thick-ass body out of the tight jeans she had on. The only light that was coming into the room was the streetlights and the moonlight that was shining in through the window. But there was enough light for me to see that Mashonda had a body like a stripper.

She put the condom on my dick as I laid with my back on the bed. Then she stood over me and I know she did that just so I could see her entire body and her shaved pussy. As I held my dick, she slowly slid her pussy on top of it and worked her ass and thighs real slow until she had all of my dick inside of her.

She kept letting out these gasps of ecstasy each time she went up and down on my dick. Before long her pussy was soaking wet, so I grabbed her ass with both of my hands and I started to fuck the shit outta her. I could tell that she was really enjoying it just because of the yelling she was doing.

"Yeah, grab my ass just like that!"

"You like that shit?"

"Yes! I love it!"

"You like getting fucked hard?"

"Emmmhh-hhmmmm! You are driving me crazy! Your dick feels so good. Urrrgggh!"

I stood up and I picked her up in the process, putting her on her back and pushing her legs all the way back and started fucking her as hard as I could.

"Oh my God. Lance, you feel so fucking good! You gonna make me cum!"

I fucked her in that position for about five minutes and she came twice, real hard, and in the process she was ripping into my back with her nails but I didn't give a shit. All I was focused on was gettin' mines off.

I turned her around and started fucking her doggie style, and just seeing all of her ass jiggling everywhere was incredible, and in no time I was ready to cum. I pulled my dick out of her and slid the condom off and I came all over her ass and her back.

"Wow! Wow! Wow!" I shouted as I plopped myself onto the bed next to her.

Mashonda giggled and she didn't say anything else. She just smiled at me and continued laying with her stomach on the bed.

"I see you're trying to make a nigga fall in love."

She smiled again, but she didn't say anything. Then she got up and ran both of her hands down her face and walked into the bathroom. I could hear her running the water in the shower, so I got up and walked toward the bathroom.

"You bouncing?" I asked.

"No, I can chill. I'm just gonna take a quick shower."

"Okay. You gotta work tomorrow?"

"Yeah, but I don't have to be there until eight-thirty. So I can chill with you until like six."

It sounded like a plan to me because I definitely wanted to smash that one more time before the night was over.

I wanted to jump in the shower with her, but I decided to just chill. I walked over to my phone and I saw that it was after one in the morning. I also noticed that I had three missed calls from Nicole. It wasn't until that moment I felt like shit. I tried to figure out what I should do. I mean, I didn't want to call Nicole right at that moment because I didn't want to disrespect Mashonda like that. Plus Mashonda didn't even know I was married so I also needed some time to try and figure out how I was gonna break that news to her—that's if I was going to break the news to her at all.

"Lance, what the fuck are you doing?" I asked myself.

The answer was I didn't know what the fuck I was doing. But as I turned my phone off and put it on the desk in my room, I did know that I had just done again what I had vowed over and over and over again not to repeat.

I was weak and I had slipped up once again, but there was no sense in beating myself up at that point. What was done was done. I had a sexy-ass, butt-naked, dime piece in the bathroom taking a shower and I knew that was all I needed to focus on at the time.

It was all about Mashonda as far as I was concerned.

Chapter Thirty-five

Being that Philadelphia was only a two-hour drive from New York, the publishing company had provided all of the The Unit authors with a car service that chauffeured us individually back to New York in Lincoln town cars.

By the time I woke up, took a shower, got dressed, and ate breakfast with Mashonda it was after nine-thirty and I knew I had to bounce ASAP. She had already called her job and told them she would be late. As for me, I knew I needed to call Nicole and I was feeling guilty as shit, but I did my best to push those thoughts to the back of my head and not think about the guilt.

"So am I gonna see you again?" Mashonda asked. "Of course you will," I responded, but I wasn't 100 percent sure I meant what I was saying. Granted, Mashonda looked every bit as good on the morning after as she had the night before so that was a definite plus she had in her favor. But I had hit it already so I wasn't sure if I even really wanted to be bothered with her anymore.

"Come here," I said as I reached out my hand and guided her closer to me. We had pulled the drapes fully closed so that the blinding sunlight wouldn't light up the room, so there was still this cozy feel as the television played in the background.

Mashonda pressed her body up against mines and we kissed each other for about a minute or so.

"Emmmh, you drive me so fucking crazy!" Mashonda said as she pulled away from me and smiled. "You sure you didn't slip nothing in my drink because I can't explain this shit."

I chuckled and shook my head *no* as I grabbed my bag and prepared to leave. Mashonda said what she had said because she knew the only explanation for her actions was that she was a whore. Since she, like most women, never want to believe that they're a whore, tried to explain away her actions by making a joke about me slipping her a mickey.

"The car is downstairs waiting for me. So here, take this. Get you some gas for your car and pay for your parking with it, a'ight?" I said as I handed her one hundred dollars.

"Thank you. You're so sweet," she replied and gave me a kiss on my cheek as we stepped into the elevator.

With the way Mashonda took the money so easily I knew that she was a gold-digging whore. She was no different than the big-butt strippers who would leave the strip club and fuck a nigga as long as he was putting up cash for the pussy. Yeah, Mashonda knew what time it was and so did I, but I couldn't knock her hustle.

When we got to the lobby I immediately saw my driver and I headed toward him.

"Lance Thomas?"

"Yeah, yeah, that's me."

"Right this way," the driver replied as he directed me outside into the freezing cold and toward the car. He held the rear passenger door open for me and just before I stepped into the car I turned and gave Mashonda a hug and a peck on the lips.

"It was real."

"Yeah, it was. Call me when you get back to New York."

"No doubt."

I sat into the plush leather seats, and the driver had already had the heat on so the car was very comfortable inside. But my mind wasn't at ease simply because I knew that I should have left Philly the night before and had my ass back in New York. I kept my cell phone turned off, because I knew Nicole would be blowing my phone up to no end.

"Listen, here's sixty dollars. Do whatever you can to get me back to New York as quick as possible."

The Arab driver thanked me for the generous tip and told me he would do his best. Then he proceeded to maneuver toward the Ben Franklin Bridge and eventually we ended up on the New Jersey Turnpike where I fell asleep and didn't wake up until we were in New York and on the Long Island Expressway.

It was a little after eleven in the morning and I knew that my son's game started at eleven, so instead of the driver taking me straight to my house I had him drop me at my son's school.

When I got to the school, I spoke to the security guard for a quick second and then I headed straight for the crowded gymnasium. As soon as I walked into the gym I could see that all of the seats in the bleachers were full so I decided to stand a few feet away from the entrance along with some of the other parents.

Apparently my son LL had just gotten fouled and he was standing at the free throw line preparing to shoot a foul shot.

"LL!" I shouted. "LL!"

Just as the referee handed LL the ball I managed to get his attention and I made a fist with my right hand and thumped it across my chest two times. That was the sign I had made up for LL and whenever I did that he knew it meant for him to go hard and to play with heart.

LL nodded his head to acknowledge me and then he bounced the ball three times, bent his knees, blew some air from his lungs, and took the shot and made it. He pointed in my direction before running back down the court to play defense.

"Man, that kid is really good!" one of the white parents standing next to me said.

"Yeah, that's my boy, Little Lance," I said with a huge, proud smile across my face. "I was hoping that I made it here on time. What quarter is this?"

"Oh, you just got here? It's the third quarter. Your son really put on a show in the first half, he's definitely on another level for a sixth grader."

Just as the guy said that, LL came down court and sank a three-point shot that forced the other team to call a time-out. After the time-out LL's coach left him on the bench and I know it was because he didn't want to embarrass the other team. LL's team was already up by twenty points and had he left LL in the game their lead only would have increased. But LL loved the game so much that he hated being on the bench, and you could see the anger in his eleven-year-old face.

"Hey, baby," Nicole said to me as she walked up to me and kissed me on the cheek.

"Nicole, you just got here?" I asked with a surprised tone.

"No, you just got here. I was sitting in the bleachers and I saw you when you walked in."

Right then and there I was bracing for the drama I knew I was gonna get from Nicole for not having called her before I left Philly.

"Look at your son sitting all slumped and dejected looking. It is so embarrassing. You better talk to him about that. He's really gotta cut that out. It's so bratty!"

"Yeah, I will, as soon as he gets home today. Listen Nicole, I'm sorry I didn't call you but the battery in my phone died and I forgot my charger at the crib," I said in an attempt to preempt the barrage of questions I knew she would hit me with for not having called her.

"At least I thought I forgot it. It wasn't until I was packing my stuff this morning, getting ready to leave, that I realized my charger was in my backpack. It was just covered up by my pants."

Nicole laughed and replied, "Baby, it's okay, I'm not trippin'. As long as you're safe, I'm okay. I'm just glad you made it to his game because you know he would've had a fit if you didn't come."

I felt some relief that Nicole didn't grill me like I thought she would, and at the same time, more than anything, I realized it was probably just my conscience making me feel guilty and causing me to expect the worst when I really had nothing to fear. Or at least that's what I thought.

What happened was after the game was over, LL continued on with his day at school and I went home and went to sleep. Nicole had told me she was heading back to her office and she wouldn't be home until about six-thirty that evening. But apparently she made it home much sooner.

"Lance, Lance, wake up," Nicole said as she shook me.

Although I felt like I had been sleeping for days, I groggily turned and looked at the clock and saw that it was only a little past two o'clock in the afternoon.

"Hey, baby, I thought you was going to the office?" I said, still half-asleep.

"Lance, sit up. Get up. We got a problem."

"What's wrong?" I asked, but I was too tired to sit up.

"This is what's wrong!" Nicole barked out as she threw something at me.

I felt something hit my face and that got me to finally sit up and pay attention.

"Lance, whatever you do, please don't lie to me! Just tell me the truth!"

"*Ahhh, shit!*" I screamed out in my head as I saw a condom laying on the floor of my bedroom. That was what Nicole had thrown at me.

"Tell you the truth about what?" I asked, trying to play dumb.

"About that condom!"

"What condom? What are you talking about?"

"I'm talking about I came back home early to surprise you with a afternoon quickie. When I saw you sleeping I figured you were probably too tired to put your stuff away from your trip, so I was gonna put it away for you, and that's when I found a condom in your bag. Not three condoms or a box of condoms, I only found one condom, Lance! One condom! And since we don't use condoms, my question is, what was it doing in your bag? And better yet, what happened to the other condoms?" Nicole screamed. I knew she was heated.

All of a sudden I was wide awake and I knew I had to think quick. "Nicole, I don't know where that came from or how it got there," I calmly said, trying my hardest to play things cool.

Nicole looked at me with twisted lips, and she shook her head.

"I don't! Why you giving me that look?"

"Lance, just tell me the truth!"

"I told you the truth! *I don't know where it came from!* I mean I don't know, Lameek or Fifth coulda put it there as a joke or something," I barked, as I was starting to get angry.

"So let's get them on the phone right now then," Nicole vented, calling my bluff.

My heart was pounding like crazy and I didn't need this shit, but I knew I had forgotten my number-one rule about never being sloppy with shit. But there was no way in hell I was gonna forget rule number two. I was not gonna admit to shit under no circumstances.

"Nicole, give me my phone!" I yelled as I got up and tried to retrieve my cell phone.

"No! Let's get Lameek and Fifth on the phone and ask them about this condom thing!" Nicole angrily yelled while scrolling through the phone book on my phone.

"Give me my phone! I'm not calling them with no bullshit like that. You know how stupid I would look?" I replied with both fear and anger.

Nicole sucked her teeth and then threw the phone at me with all her strength. The phone hit me and then fell to the ground.

"So you're more worried about how you would look in front of your boys than your wife?" Nicole shook her head. "Do you know how pathetic you sound right now?"

I couldn't have cared less how pathetic I sounded, but there was no way I was gonna call anybody and catch them off guard and make a bad situation worse. So I kept my mouth shut and bent down and picked up the phone.

"Okay, you know what, we don't have to call anybody, just give me your phone so I can check something," Nicole said calmly. She was calm but it was one of those clenched-teeth calm looks where she could have blew off the handle at any time.

"So you can check what?"

"I wanna check your phone, Lance! What is the problem?"

"The problem is, what happened to the trust, Nicole? It's been six years now, cut me some slack!"

"What happened to the trust? Trust is something that you have to earn!"

"So in six years I haven't earned it?"

"Lance, as much as this is about trust, this is also about openness and honesty."

"Whatever, but you ain't looking at my phone. I don't know what you gotta do, but Nicole, you need to get over this shit. It's been six years! Six years, Nicole! Niggas in the street kill people and they do less time than that!" I was acting angry and I was hoping that my reverse psychology would work.

"Oh, so you've been in prison, huh? Well, I tell you what, that phone in your hand can be your get out of jail free card because if you don't let me see it then you gotta get outta this house! And I mean that, Lance."

"Babe, you are really bugging out right now and overreacting."

"Lance, I been through this before, and I cannot go through this again."

I knew I hadn't deleted all of my texts from my phone and I still had all of my recent calls from the night before. Plus I didn't know if Mashonda had texted me or left me any voice mail messages while I had my phone turned off, so there was no way I was going to give Nicole that phone.

"Nicole, this is some bullshit!" I said as I started to put on my pants. "I'm gonna step out and get some food. When I come back home and when you come back home we need to just press the reset button and start over." That was the only thing I could think to do or say. It was either fight or flight. I knew the fight option would have been the wrong option so I just needed some time to think of my next move.

Nicole was quiet. She shook her head and started heading out of the bedroom and toward the downstairs steps. As she walked away I could hear her sobbing.

"What are you crying for, baby?"

"Lance, pack up your shit and get the fuck outta this house!" Nicole shouted as she stopped dead in her tracks. I knew that whenever my wife cursed she was highly upset and was not playing games.

I caught up to her and put my arms around her. "Baby, please just—"

"Lance, get your hands off of me! Pack up your shit and get the fuck out!"

She flung herself free from me and continued on downstairs and she hollered the whole way down to the living room.

"You brought another child into this world by another woman and I stood by you! I did my part big-time! You can't even begin to understand how hard it is to deal with something like that on an everyday basis and now you wanna just throw that up in my face like I'm supposed to just get over it? No, I don't need to get over anything but your black ass and your bullshit. You quit your job a few years ago to follow your dream as a writer, and I overlooked my reservations about that because I didn't want to be selfish, but this is the exact reason why I knew you writing and getting into that career wasn't a good idea. But did I hold you back? No, I didn't and this is the thanks I get, right? You got some serious problems, Lance. You need to get help and work out those problems, but you just gonna have to work it out outside of this house because I'm telling you right now you are not staying here."

I went back into my room and quickly turned my phone on and it seemed like it was taking forever to turn on.

"Hurry up!" I pleaded with the phone until it finally came on. I knew that after all Nicole had just said I couldn't just turn away and run to my room the second she was done talking. It would have come across as crazy disrespectful, but I had to get rid of any incriminating evidence.

I feverishly started deleting all of my old text messages but new texts were coming in just as fast as I was deleting the old texts. Finally, after five minutes I had deleted all of the texts and my recent call log of any remotely incriminating phone calls that I had made or received. I wanted to check my voice mail, but I knew that I didn't have that kind of time, so I took my chances without listening to the voice mail messages, and I ran downstairs to Nicole.

"Baby, here, you want my phone, take it," I said as I threw the phone on to the granite kitchen countertop. "This is really a waste of time, but if this is gonna make you feel more comfortable, then look through the phone, I don't care. All I know is this is gonna set us back like the whole six years that we been rebuilding." I said that in an attempt to deflect attention from myself. I was a master at causing problems and then painting myself as the victim.

Nicole was still slightly sobbing and she didn't initially say anything nor did she make a move for my phone. Then after about a minute or so she wiped the tears from her face and she calmly began to talk and said, "Lance, you know the truth. You know why you didn't answer my calls last night. You know why you didn't call me back. You know why there was a condom in your bag, and you know why you didn't want me to look at your phone until *after* you deleted what you wanted to delete. Yup, you know all of that and all of the details. I may not know all of the details you know, and to be honest I don't wanna know all of the details, but I do know what I know, Lance, and it's time for you to get your things and go."

"Baby—"

"Lance, just go!" Nicole yelled and gave me this look to kill.

I shook my head and blew some air from my lungs and calmly headed back up to my room. I sat on my bed for a couple of minutes thinking how I had really just fucked up, but I also was trying to think of a way to make things right. I knew that Nicole wasn't playing games and I had to quickly get my shit and get the hell out of Dodge.

Chapter Thirty-six

Steve had been my right-hand man for as long as I could remember. Whenever I was in a crisis situation he was usually the first person I would reach out to. And with Nicole putting me out of the house, I definitely was in a crisis situation. But as I figured he would, Steve took me in with open arms.

"So my nigga is putting his jersey back on! Ha-ha! Yeah, baby! That's what I'm talking about."

"Steve, this is serious, man. Nicole ain't playing this time."

Steve made his way to the bar in his dining room and poured us both a glass of Hennessy. He didn't mix it with soda nor did he put any ice in it.

"Drink that. Just gulp it down. Don't sip that shit."

I listened to Steve and I drank the Hennessy as he instructed and he did the same.

"See, that's grown-man shit right there. Here, drink some more of this shit," he said as he poured some more liquor in my glass.

"Listen, Lance, you my man, so you know I can tell you what's up without you trippin'. The problem witchu is that you was in retirement and you came outta retirement on a whim. You came out all rusty and shit and you fucked up! That's all that happened. Nothing more, nothing less. But the main thing is your ass is back in the game, you feel me?"

Steve was always gonna be Steve and he wasn't gonna change or conform for nobody, so I had to respect him for that. At the same time, it didn't make sense for me to try and get him to understand any of the guilt or anxiety I was feeling because he wouldn't have been able to process it.

"So Mashonda is off the chain? Fill a nigga in!"

I was starting to feel the effects of the alcohol and I had a nice buzz.

"Whaaaat? Yo, her body is sick! She's a young, tender twenty-year-old thing, so you know it was bananas! And she looks good as hell too."

"Say word! She's only twenty?"

"Yeah, I mean when I first saw her I was thinking she was like twenty-seven or twenty-eight, but she showed me her license and she's only twenty years old, and her body is tight as hell even after one baby. The stomach is still flat and her titties are still standing up."

"So you saying you met the chick in the bank, invited her to the booksigning and the release party then hit it the same night? Yo, my ass needs to start writing fucking books! That shit is crazy."

"It's The Unit affiliation. That's what she's seeing, and that's what got her open like that," I explained.

"So the hell what! Play that shit up to your advantage. Matter of fact, take my ass witchu to the next book shit you got going on so some of this shit can rub off on my ass," Steve said with a laugh.

Me and Steve continued to drink Hennessy and get drunk with each other. The more he drank the more foolishness he spoke and the more of a negative influence he became.

"Lance, you ain't ready to die, right?"

I looked at him and just shook my head *no* as I tried to figure out where he was gonna go with his statement.

"'Cause you know what they say about a dog that tastes blood. After he tastes blood you either gotta kill his ass or let him loose to go wild and do his thing. You tasted blood with Mashonda, and since you ain't ready to be put down it's time to turn your ass loose!"

As soon as Steve was done talking, my cell phone rang and I saw it was Mashonda. I started to let her go to voice mail because I really didn't want to be bothered at all. But I picked up anyway.

"What's up, sexy?"

I could tell that Mashonda was cheesing through the phone.

"Nothing. I'm just checking up on you. I just got off work so I was seeing what you're up to. Did you get my message I left you?"

"Nah, I didn't even check my messages yet. I got back and went to sleep so I was really in chill mode."

"Oh, okay, so that's what's up. But listen, I was thinking about coming up there this weekend to see you."

Oh, hell no! I remember initially thinking to myself. If there was one thing I didn't need, it was for Mashonda to become a bug-a-boo. She was already showing the signs of a bug-a-boo, blowing up my phone with messages and now she was asking to come check me. I was sure that Mashonda had picked up on my hesitation and she jumped right in to break up the awkwardness.

"Well, I mean I got family in New York, so I was gonna come see them and then I was hoping we could see each other again," she added.

"Yeah, okay, definitely. Just let me know if it's definite or not and we'll link up. So where does your family live, what part of New York?"

"Oh, well, the majority of them are in Harlem. What about you, where do you stay?"

"In Great Neck, out on Long Island, but—"

"Oh, so you a baller for real," she added with a little chuckle.

Steve was signaling for me to hang up the phone and waving his hands back and forth across his throat.

"Listen, Mashonda, let me hit you back later on, okay?"

"Okay, baby, no problem. Just make sure you call me," she said before we both hung up.

"That was the Philly chick?" Steve asked.

I nodded my head that it was as I got up and poured me another drink.

"Yo, Lance, you already smashed that. What the fuck are you making love on the phone with her for now? Stick and move nigga, stick and move. Why the hell are you telling her where you rest at?"

"Good pussy will make a nigga do anything!" I replied.

Steve looked at me and tapped my drink with his, and he chuckled. "Yo, since your ass like to make love on the phone, I got somebody that I want you to speak to," Steve said as he dialed a number on his cell phone and handed it to me.

"Who the fuck is this?"

"Just talk, nigga!"

I looked at Steve's cell phone and I could see the name he had dialed: Layla.

A big smile came across my face as Layla picked up.

"Hey, Steve," she said, obviously expecting it to be Steve since it was his number that was calling her.

"What's up, Layla? This ain't Steve, this is Lance," I responded.

"Lance? Oh my God! What's up? How are you?" She was obviously glad to hear from me.

As the night would play itself out, I was gonna find out that not only was I gonna be glad to hear from her, but I was also going to find out that Steve was right about a dog getting that taste of blood. See, because with me, Mashonda had been that taste of blood, and I was ready to let loose and like a crazed dog in heat I wanted to taste some more blood. Now I had my sights set on Layla.

Again, I was using that unique ability I was not proud of, to shift my feelings of guilt and thoughts of love for my wife to one side of my brain. By doing that I was able to operate as if I had no conscience at all.

Chapter Thirty-seven

I had been at Steve's house less than two hours and within that time I was drunk out of my mind. I had basically invited myself over to Layla's house in Brooklyn where she lived with her teenage daughter and an eleven-year-old daughter, both by different fathers.

Before heading over to Layla's house, I took a shower at Steve's crib and changed my clothes then got real fly. My one-night-stand experience with Mashonda had taught me that all I had to do was walk with the expectation of getting pussy, maintain a certain confidence, and know I could get any woman to take her panties off for me regardless of how long I knew the woman or how close we were. The key for me was not to come across desperate to fuck or needy and like a crackhead needing a hit of crack. So when I arrived at her house, which was in Canarsie, I maintained that same sense of confidence even through my drunkenness.

"Lance!" Layla replied with a big smile and a hug as she greeted me at the door. "I see you been hitting the weights or something, you look so good."

Layla and I had only met once about a year ago at a Super Bowl party that Steve had at his crib. We had chilled with each other and kicked it the whole night of the Super Bowl and although we had exchanged numbers I never pushed up on her, nor did I feed into her advances when she would call me, because I was trying my best to stay focused. But that was then and this was now, and all I was concerned with was now.

"That hug felt good. Come here, give me another one," I said as I grabbed her and pressed my body up against hers.

Then we separated and just stared at each other for a moment before Layla smiled and asked me to stop staring at her.

"You know who you look like?"

"Yeah, I know, the actress Lauren London who played in the movie *This Christmas*," she replied as if she had been told that a million times.

"Nah, but really, you do. I mean, you're sexier than she is, but you still look like her."

"Whatever, she's younger than me so she looks like me," Layla joked.

She invited me in to see the rest of her house and asked me if she could take me on a quick tour of her place. Of course I didn't mind, so I followed her around as she took me from room to room. In the process she introduced me to her daughters. They both were cute and looked just like their mother.

Layla was renting one half of a two-family house. She had three bedrooms, a living room, a dining room, a nice kitchen, and two bathrooms, and she kept the place immaculate, and it was well-decorated.

"And this is my room, my little oasis," she said, smiling as she opened the door to her room.

"Is that ocean sounds?" I asked.

Layla nodded her head *yes* and explained that she kept that ocean sounds CD playing all day long because it helped relax her and instantly removed any stress that she might be feeling.

"That's different, I like that," I said as I took hold of her hand. "This takes away stress too," I said and without asking I leaned in and started tongue-kissing her. And without any resistance she began kissing me back. She was really getting into it as she hugged me as tight as she could and kissed me as hard as she could for about two minutes straight.

"Whoa, whew," Layla said as she shook her head and smiled then stepped away from me. "I definitely didn't see that one coming."

I didn't say anything. I just looked at her.

"Um, yeah, we need to go into the kitchen or the living room or somewhere, anywhere but here," she said to me as she headed out of her room. Layla was walking in her bare feet and she was wearing what looked like a large head scarf with some kind of African print on it that she was using as a body wrap.

"You want something to eat?" she asked as she walked in front of me with her ass looking sexy as hell in that wrap thing she was wearing.

I was starving, so I took her up on her offer. She sat me down at her dining room table. The next thing I knew I had a full plate of food in front of me: baked macaroni and cheese, candied yams, collard greens, fried chicken, and cornbread.

"Damn, you cooked all of this?"

"I love to cook, this is everyday for me," Layla explained as she got a bottle of red wine and filled a glass for me. She sat Indian-style in the chair directly across from mine. While I ate she looked at me and seemed to be enjoying the fact that I was enjoying her food, and then she took out a bunch of papers and turned on her laptop and started typing some stuff.

"What are you doing?"

"Just working on this case I gotta finish by tomorrow."

"What kind of case? What do you do again?"

Layla explained she worked from home, and that she had her own business where she provided freelance paralegal services to immigration lawyers and attorneys who handled accident cases.

I nodded my head and told her that I was impressed.

"You know you breaking all the light-skin girl stereotypes, right? I mean, you can cook your ass off, and you got a head on your shoulders, and a nice ass and nice titties! You're three for three!"

"Boy, I will stab you with that fork! No, you didn't just say that," she said while she laughed at me.

"I'm saying, you know I'm right. Pretty, light-skin chicks usually have either a fat butt or big titties, not both. I have yet to meet one that can put their foot in some food like you did with this food."

Layla just shook her head and smiled.

As I ate we started talking about everything. She complained to no end about her deadbeat ex-husband and I untruthfully told her about my issues with Nicole. Before long it was approaching ten-thirty and we were sitting on her living room couch watching a movie with all of the lights off. Somehow my hand made its way underneath that wrap thing she was wearing, and I eventually located her pussy and started rubbing on it. Right from the first touch I noticed that she was soaking wet.

"Lance, I love the way you touch me," she purred with her eyes closed.

I continued to finger-fuck her and her pussy continued to get wetter by the second. As she gyrated her hips I pulled her wrap all the way up so that her pussy was fully exposed. Since I had drank a whole bottle of wine, which was combined with the Hennessy I had from earlier, I was feeling so intoxicated that I didn't give a shit about anything. So the next thing I knew, my bald head was in Layla's crotch and I was eating her pussy for dessert.

I sucked on her clit while I slid my index finger in and out of her pussy, and within seconds Layla was grabbing my head and squeezing it as she gyrated her hips and came hard as hell. I was shocked that she was just letting herself go like that. I mean, she was hollering like a porn star while she was cumming, and it was all good, but she also had her two daughters in the other room, which was all of twenty feet away from where we were sitting.

I sat up to get some air and I looked at Layla and she was breathing really heavy and panting as she said, "I swear to God, ain't nobody ever make me cum that quick in my fucking life! Shit!"

I chuckled, and then I told her that we had to stop since her daughters were right there in the other room and could hear us.

"They'll be okay, don't worry about that," she said to me as she stood up and straightened out her clothes. "You eat my pussy like that, you know you gotta fuck me now," she added rather matter-of-factly.

"Where at? We can't do that right here," I said, trying not to talk too loud.

The next thing I know Layla had untied her wrap and her naked body was fully exposed. She opened her legs and spread her pussy lips apart, just inviting me to come fuck her.

I was drunk, but I wasn't crazy. There was no way I was gonna fuck Layla right there on her living room couch and get busted by her daughters. They didn't need to see nothing like that. So I grabbed Layla by her hand and led her to her bedroom and closed the door.

"Please tell me you got a condom," I said to her.

"I got you, don't worry about that," she said as she took my shirt off and kissed on my chest while unbuckling my pants. "Layla, I'm not fucking you raw!"

Layla didn't respond, she just looked up at me and held her index finger to her mouth and went to the other side of her room. When she came back, she started sucking on my dick, and while both of our hands were interlocked with each other's, she managed to put a condom on my dick by using her mouth and nothing else.

"Oh, shit, where the fuck you learn that?" I asked.

Layla didn't answer me, she just got on her bed and she was on all fours waiting for me to get behind her and fuck her and that was exactly what I did. I pushed her head into the mattress so that her face was down and her ass was up in the air and I wore her ass out doggie style.

She tried her best to keep quiet while she bit into one of her pillows, but every time she came she would let the whole fucking neighborhood know that she was cumming. I know her kids had to hear everything that was going on because the house was basically quiet, and they were in the bed since it was a school night.

"I wanna feel that shit on my face when you cum. Okay, baby?" she turned and said to me while I fucked her.

I nodded my head and kept fucking her as hard as I could until I felt myself ready to erupt.

"Ahhh, yeah, it's cumming, baby!" I said as I pulled out of her pussy and quickly took the condom off.

Layla turned around and laid on her back and then quickly scooted herself closer toward me so that her face was right near my balls. When I was ready I came all over her face, in her hair, and in her mouth.

She smiled as she licked some of my cum with her tongue and played with it in her mouth before spitting it back out.

I sat up on her bed and caught my breath. As I contemplated whether I should spend the night with her or go back to Steve's house, I realized I was living totally out of control. But at the same time I really didn't give a shit. I was who I was and I was doing me. The way I was living was in my DNA since birth, and I was starting to love every minute of my lifestyle that was quickly spiraling out of control.

The first time I had cheated on Nicole I battled continuously with guilt and trying to do what was right for her and trying to do right by God. But it was like I was at the point now where I was saying to myself it was pathetic to constantly be sitting on the fence. I knew I had to either shit or get off of the pot. And getting off of the pot to me meant getting a divorce. But regardless of my actions, which seemed to prove otherwise, I still loved my wife and my son a great deal. Therefore, I knew my only option was to stay on the pot and shit. Even if I was shitting on myself I was cool with that because there was just no way I was going to stay in that same wishy-washy state of mind of trying to do right and burning to do wrong.

Chapter Thirty-eight

The next morning when I woke up, I was feeling hung-over and I had no idea where I was until Layla came into her bedroom with breakfast for me.

"What time is it?"

"It's nine-fifteen," she replied as she handed me a tray full of food. "Layla, you didn't have to do this."

"I know, but I wanted to do it. I told you I love to cook. When people come to my house, they eat. I take care of everybody that walks through my door."

Layla was really no joke. She knew exactly how to treat a nigga and she pushed all the right buttons. She had made cheese grits, bacon, scrambled eggs, and French toast. And not only had she made breakfast for me, but she had also washed, dried, and ironed the clothes I had on from the day before.

"When the hell did you do all of this?"

Layla didn't respond directly to my question. She just smiled and told me to take my time eating and she was going to finish up the case she had been working on from the night before.

"I put a towel, soap, lotion, a brand new toothbrush for you in the bathroom when you're ready to get dressed. The girls already left for school so just feel at home. Okay?"

I smiled and thanked her. As I ate the food she had cooked for me, I couldn't help but think about how Nicole used to treat me this good way back when we had first gotten married. But unfortunately for me and Nicole, life got in the way and all of the pampering I used to get just disappeared along with the sex. So by nature Layla was scoring big points as far as I was concerned.

As I ate and prepared to take a shower and get dressed, I would be lying if I said I wasn't feeling deeply conflicted. Because on one hand I wanted to snatch up Layla and fuck the shit out of her again, and on the other hand I wanted to see my wife and make love to her and tell her I was sorry for screwing up. Yet the thing that was troubling me the most was I knew my son was probably wondering why I hadn't spoken to him since his game.

I knew what I needed to do. After I had taken my shower and gotten dressed, I thanked Layla for treating me like a king and for showing me an amazing time. I kissed her on the lips and told her I really had to bounce.

"You sure you don't wanna stay?"

"I want to, but I really got moves I need to make."

"Okay, so listen. I hope it's not gonna be a whole year before I hear from you again or see you again."

I shook my head and explained to her that she had a license to call me and see me whenever she wanted to, and I would get up with her in a few days.

"Yeah, we gotta hang out real soon," she said to me.

"Definitely," I replied as I kissed her again on her lips before walking out the door.

I jumped in my all black Range Rover and headed straight for my son's school. When I got there I headed straight for the principal's office and explained it was an emergency and I really needed to speak to my son for a few minutes.

The lady in the principal's office was very sweet and accommodating. She told me to have a seat and she would handle everything. She got on the phone and within about three minutes or so my son walked into the principal's office.

"Daddy!" he said with a big smile. Because of the expression on his face I know he was shocked to see me.

"What's up, homie?" I said to him as I held out my hand for him to slap me five. I then took LL by the hand and walked him into the hallway so that we could talk in private.

"You okay?"

He nodded his head and told me he was fine.

"Listen, I just wanted to tell you I didn't come home last night because I still have to promote this new book so I'm gonna be out of town for a few days, okay?"

"You're gonna be with Fifth Ward?" LL smiled and asked. He thought that was the coolest thing that his dad had written a book with a rap icon.

"Well, he's real busy so he's not gonna be with me for the whole time."

"So when will you be back?"

"I'm not sure, but I'll make sure I call you every day, okay?" LL nodded.

"And listen, you played real good the other day but what was that stunt you pulled when the coach took you outta the game?"

LL turned up his lips and a frown came on his face as he explained, "I was playing real good and he shouldn't have taken me out. If I messed up then he should put me on the bench, not when I'm playing good and doing everything right!"

"But LL, y'all were blowing the other team out."

"So?"

"So, the right thing to do was to take you out so that y'all wouldn't embarrass the other team."

LL just shook his head because he totally didn't agree with me, but he knew not to argue.

"Daddy, did you see that move I did when I crossed over on that white boy and he fell to the ground?" LL asked in an animated fashion.

I couldn't help but laugh at how amped and hyped he got when he spoke about basketball. It was like he was a completely different person because normally he was reserved and somewhat shy, but when it came to sports he was passionate as ever.

"I missed that. I got here too late, but I'll see the videotape when they make it available to purchase. But listen, I just wanted to see you before I left. Make sure you knock out your homework and be good in school, okay? You can't make it to the NBA if your grades aren't on point, remember that."

LL looked at me and nodded his head and then he held out his fist for a pound. "So you're out?"

I chuckled at him because he was always trying to be so cool, and you couldn't tell him that he didn't have an eleven-year-old swagger.

"Yeah, I'm out. So go back to your classroom and remember, call me whenever you want. I don't care how early or how late it is, okay?"

"Okay," he replied and then walked off back to his classroom.

After seeing my son, I was good. If anything, I knew for my son's sake I had to straighten up and do the right thing. But it still wasn't that easy to do right.

I decided to shoot back to my crib and see what was up with Nicole, because this getting kicked out of the house shit was crazy, and I figured after she had some time to calm down she would see things differently.

Apparently, though, when I reached my crib I realized that Nicole was really going hard body! She literally had all of the locks to the crib changed.

"Yo, this is some bullshit!" I yelled as I began banging on the front door and ringing the bell like I had lost my mind.

"Nicole, open the goddamn door!"

I banged on the front door, the side door, and the back door for about five minutes and I got no answer. I realized that Nicole must have left for work. So with my blood boiling, I hopped back in my truck and made it from Great Neck, Long Island to Rosedale, Queens in like five minutes when it normally takes about fifteen.

Nicole rented an office suite that was located inside of an office complex called Cross Island Plaza. It was a nice building located on Merrick Boulevard and it had pretty good security. Since I was always coming there, security already knew me so they never made me sign and never called Nicole's suite to announce I was there to see her.

So I said, "What's up?" to the security guards and I kept it moving. Nicole was on the third floor but I didn't waste any time waiting on the elevator. I stormed up the steps and into Nicole's suite.

"Hey, Becky, where's Nicole?" I asked Nicole's blond-haired, blue-eyed secretary.

"Oh, hi, Lance, she's actually meeting with someone."

I totally tuned the secretary out and I went straight for Nicole's office and she wasn't there, so I knew she had to be inside the conference room.

"Um, excuse me, Lance, but she's really in an important meeting. I think you should wait until she's done."

I ignored her and without knocking I walked right into the conference room where I saw Nicole sitting at the table with a legal notepad and she was writing something down. The paralegal was there and there were two other people in the room, a white dude and a black lady, both of who looked like they were in their late forties or early fifties.

"Nicole, can I talk to you for a second," I said with a stern tone in my voice.

I was dressed in my Timbs, jeans, a dark blue leather bomber vest, and a hooded sweatshirt, and when Nicole looked up and saw me I could feel the fire coming from her. She had a look that said she wanted to kill.

"I'm so sorry, can everyone please excuse me for a moment," she said as she got up and brushed past me and headed straight for her office with me following behind her. When we made it into her office she made sure the door was shut and then she turned to me and with her teeth clenched she said, "God help you if you're not here to tell me that something happened to my son!"

"Nicole, how the hell you change the fucking locks!" I shouted.

"Would you keep your voice down! What is wrong with you? I'm meeting with an important client."

I saw Nicole's pocketbook sitting on her desk and I went straight for it.

"You gonna give me those goddamn keys! There ain't no way in the world I'm gonna pay a bank eight thousand a month and can't live in my own shit!" I barked as Nicole ran up to me and snatched her pocketbook away from me.

"Nicole, I swear to God I will turn this whole office upside down if you don't give me those keys!"

"Lance, you ain't staying there, I'm not dealing with this no more. Now leave or I'm calling the police."

"Calling the police for what?"

"To lock your ass up if you don't leave."

"Oh, you wanna call the police? A'ight, so that's where you wanna take it?" I yelled. I don't ever remember being as mad as I was at that point and with rage running throughout my body I went to the front of Nicole's desk and squatted down and reached both of my hands underneath her desk. After I had a good grip I used all of my might and literally flipped her desk upside down, causing papers and shit to fly everywhere.

"Becky, Becky, call the police for me! Lance done lost his mind!" Nicole opened the door to her office and shouted out to Becky.

Becky came running to the office, not sure exactly what was going on and she saw me and Nicole tussling for her pocketbook.

"Becky, call nine-one-one!" Nicole screamed and Becky ran out of the office and picked up her phone and began dialing the cops.

"Let the bag go and I'll leave," I said to Nicole, who all of a sudden had a tremendous amount of strength.

At that point I heard the door to her conference room open, and I could hear the white guy asking her paralegal if I was one of Nicole's criminal clients. Nicole must have heard the same thing because at that point she loosened her grip on the pocketbook and told me to leave.

I looked at her. Her hair was a mess and her clothes were disheveled and her office looked like a tornado had hit it. But I didn't give a shit, I meant exactly what I said earlier about there being no way I was gonna pay eight thousand a month in mortgage payments and not be able to live in the house. That was absolutely crazy to me.

I stormed out of the building and I headed home to my truck, and as I let it warm up a bit, I began to calm down. I realized at that moment I might have taken things just a bit too far. After a couple of minutes I put my truck in drive and maneuvered my way out of the parking lot. While I was handing money to the parking lot clerk, I looked over and saw Nicole coming out of the office building with two police officers. All I could do was shake my head because Nicole didn't even have to take things to that level, but I knew she was probably gonna get a order of protection against me or some other type of spiteful shit.

Right after the clerk handed me my change I could hear someone yelling. I turned and looked and I saw Nicole pointing in the direction of my truck and the cops were quickly approaching my car.

"Can you lift the gate please?" I asked as my heart rate picked up.

"Hold it, hold it, hold it!" I heard a voice holler, and the next thing I knew there were two cops were at my truck. One was on the driver's side and the other one was on the passenger side, and they both had their guns drawn.

The cop on my side yanked open the driver's door and snatched me out of the truck and slammed me onto the cold concrete. Within seconds my hands were handcuffed behind my back and my face was inches away from a pile of snow that hadn't yet melted from days before.

"Ma'am, is that your pocketbook?" one of the cops asked Nicole.

Apparently she said it was but I couldn't actually see her from my facedown position. But I was able to see the three other cop cars that had arrived in the parking lot. This whole thing was unfolding into way too much drama for absolutely nothing.

"Sir, do you have any weapons or any drugs on your possession?" the cop asked me, but out of anger I kept my mouth shut and didn't respond to his question. I soon felt the cops thoroughly frisking me. After about two minutes more of laying on the cold ground, they helped me to my feet and stood me next to one of the police cars as they searched my truck. By this point it seemed as if every office worker in the building was standing in the parking lot watching what was going on.

"A'ight, Nicole, you win! Now can you tell them to take these handcuffs off of me and let's end this bullshit?" I said to Nicole, who was still visibly angry.

She looked at me and walked away. The next thing I knew the cops had placed me under arrest and were reading me my rights and had placed me in the backseat of the police car. I couldn't believe I had been arrested, but by the time I got to the precinct and had my mug shot taken and fingerprinted, it didn't take much more for me to realize this arrest was really real.

But it really hit home for me when I sat in the cell at the precinct and thought about the charges I had been hit with: robbery, assault, disorderly conduct, and trespassing.

Ain't this a bitch? I thought to myself as I sat slumped on the metal bench inside the pissy jail cell.

Chapter Thirty-nine

There's a saying: *Hurt People, Hurt People.* The saying basically means when someone is hurt in an emotional way by someone else, they will go out of their way to hurt the person who hurt them. Nicole was obviously feeling hurt by all of my actions and she really was trying to hurt my ass.

It was evident she was trying to hurt me, because although I had been hit with some serious charges, those charges really had no substance to them, considering that we were still husband and wife. But yet Nicole had a bunch of connections with the Queens County district attorney's office and with one phone call she was able to get my case buried among the other cases. So what she was able to do with that phone call was to delay my seeing the judge.

I had been arrested on Thursday morning, and under most circumstances I would have seen a judge by Friday morning and either been released on my own recognizance or given a bail. I only would have been kept in jail if I couldn't make bail. But it was now Monday morning and I was just getting ready to see a fucking judge! And that was only because I had called Layla and she was able to work some of her attorney contacts who also had friends in the district attorney's office.

In addition to getting my case buried, Nicole had also tapped some of her news organization sources and with one phone call on Thursday afternoon I had instantly become an infamous figure. And that was because my face was on the front cover of Friday's edition of the *New York Daily News*. I knew Nicole had to be behind the sensationalism of the story simply because of the way they connected me to Fifth Ward and The Unit. Her goal was to embarrass me and to hurt me like I'd hurt her. I must say she definitely landed some good knockout punches.

The headline in Friday's paper read: MEMBER OF THE UNIT JAILED FOR ROBBERY AND ASSAULT.

Underneath the headline was a picture of my mug shot the police had taken of me inside the police precinct. The story went on to say how I was linked with Fifth Ward and how apparently the violence that followed him was now infecting the literary world. It went on and on and on about things that were not even true, all for the sake of selling newspapers and making things bigger than it really was.

So being the news organizations now had ahold of this story, the district attorney had to go hard on me and they were pushing the judge to set a high-ass bail. The judge folded under the pressure and hit me with a fifty thousand dollar bail, which was excessive considering the nature of my crime and considering I had no prior felony arrest record.

My lawyer stood with me before the judge and informed the judge I was prepared to make bail. The judge stated more legal talk and then he asked me if I understood the seriousness of what I had been charged with. After I told him I did, my lawyer Victor Spitz, spoke up and said something to the judge, who then noted something on some papers that were in front of him before informing everyone of my next scheduled court appearance. And with that, I was finally free to go.

"Thank you for everything," I said to my lawyer as he packed up his things and we prepared to leave the courtroom.

Steve walked up to me and Attorney Spitz as we were walking out of the courtroom and gave me a pound and a quick ghetto embrace.

"There's gonna be a zoo outside with the media," Victor said to me. "Just try not to say anything specific about the details of what happened on Thursday between you and Nicole."

"Nah, I won't say anything. I'll let you handle that part."

Just before we got outside of the courthouse, my lawyer stopped so we could talk for a moment. He reassured me this was all bullshit and it would go away.

"The district attorney will throw out the robbery and assault charges and you'll plead guilty to the two misdemeanors of trespassing and disorderly conduct, and that will be it. This whole thing will be treated no different than getting caught driving with a suspended license. But I gotta warn you, keep your nose clean. Do what you gotta do to work out a healthy situation with Nicole. If you violate the order of protection, you will be spending some time on Rikers Island."

I nodded my head and told Victor I understood and I would be sure to watch my temper and stay in line. I also told him I would follow up with him on Wednesday after I had some time to rest and to clear my head.

After we had taken care of small talk, we walked out to the courthouse steps that were facing Queens Boulevard. There were a bunch of photographers, cameramen, and newspeople that rushed me, my lawyer, and Steve. They converged on the three of us and started asking all kinds of crazy questions at the same time.

"Lance, were you also a small-time crack dealer in the nineties like Fifth Ward?"

"The stories that you write, are any of them based on real life?"

I couldn't help but chuckle at the ignorant questions, and I just had to answer. At the same time, I knew I had to play up the moment to my benefit. It paid to be controversial.

"Why couldn't I have been a drug kingpin? I think big, but I guess you're insinuating that I'm a small-fry. And to answer your question, Miss, I write fiction, but I draw from real life."

"Oh, so are you saying you are a former drug dealer?"

I smiled and responded, "I didn't say that. You did."

"Why would you stoop to robbing your wife? Do you have a drug problem, Mr. Thomas?"

My lawyer butted in. "Mr. Thomas doesn't have a drug problem and the charges against him are frivolous. This was nothing more than a big misunderstanding."

I hadn't brushed my teeth or washed my ass in like five days, so I was desperately wanting to get to a shower and to a bed so I could get some much-needed sleep.

As we tried our best to make our way to our cars, a reporter shouted and asked me if there was anything I wanted to say.

So I paused, smiled, and said, "Yeah, I just want everybody to know that my new book is called *Harlem Heat*. It hit the stores last Tuesday, so go check it out."

If I was gonna go through this bullshit I figured I might as well profit from the publicity.

"What is it called?" the reporter asked as she jotted down notes.

"*Harlem Heat*," I replied.

Finally me and Steve were able to make it to his car. Just as we were about to get in, a van pulled up and sort of boxed us in. A lady got out of the passenger's side. She came over to my side of the car and tapped on the window.

I rolled the window down and she introduced herself as Meagan Washington.

"You look familiar," I said to her as I tried my hardest to figure out where I knew her from.

Then she handed me her card and that's when it hit me. She was an on-air television personality for this show on CBS called *Media Edition*. The show was similar to *Entertainment Tonight* and BET's *Black Carpet*.

"Meagan Washington, you look a little different with the coat and the winter hat," I explained with a smile.

She smiled and then told me she would love to sit down with me and interview me for an upcoming episode of the show.

I was about to say something flirtatious to Meagan, but I kept it cool and professional. I told her I would love to be on her show.

"Do you have a cell phone on you? Let me give you my cell phone so we won't play phone tag or anything like that."

"Okay, sure," she replied as she took out her cell phone and removed the gloves from her hands and programmed my number as I read it off to her. "I'm gonna call you right now, lock my number in your phone too," she added.

Unfortunately, my cell phone was still at the police precinct along with my money and my wallet. So I had to explain to Meagan the police still had it.

"Oh, okay," she said with a small chuckle and a smile.

Meagan extended her hand to me for a handshake, and I extended mine back.

"Nice meeting you. So we'll be in touch," she said before walking back to the black van with dark tinted windows.

As soon as she was back in the van and we were about to pull off, I said to Steve, "Yo, if meeting her was the reason I got locked up, then there is no way I could be upset!"

"Lance, that's the major leagues right there, son!"

"Yup, and I'm a pro at this. I guarantee you I'll be smashing that soon," I said as I reclined my seat all the way back and just beamed from the thought of what it would be like to get with a chick on Meagan's level.

I knew I had the power to do more than just imagine what it would be like to bag Meagan. I had the power to make bagging her a reality. And I was determined to do just that.

Chapter Forty

By the next day, Tuesday, I had managed to return the numerous amount of phone calls I had received from people who had seen the news and were checking up on me just to see if I was all right.

My agent had called me, my editor had called, Fifth called, Mashonda called, Layla called, my sister called, my moms had called, all of the authors I was cool with had called me. It was crazy. One by one I had managed to call everybody back and I made sure to make note of everybody who had chosen not to reach out to me. I did this because I wanted to take note of who was really riding with me and who I would have to remove from my life once this whole ordeal was behind me. Most notably, out of all people, I was surprised that Toni hadn't called.

I mean, I knew she had long since moved on and was in a different space from the space we had occupied when I was cheating with her. But I still had a five-year-old daughter by her and just on the strength of our daughter—whose name was Sahara—she could have called me. It was all good, though. Toni was living the good life with her super-successful husband and she was always coming across as if she didn't have the time of day for anybody. But I was sure eventually the bad karma she was throwing off would catch up to her and smack her ass with a dose of humble reality.

Around eight-thirty in the evening, my cell phone rang, and it was Nicole calling me from her cell phone. I had to think twice about picking up, because I didn't want to later have to deal with any okey-doke bullshit.

"Nicole, you're calling me, so I don't wanna hear no shit about me violating this stupid order of protection you got," I said as I answered the phone.

"Lance, I know that. But listen, LL got suspended from school today because apparently somebody called you a jailbird, and he didn't like that, so LL jumped on the kid and beat him down."

I shook my head and blew a whole lot of air into the phone. It took everything inside of me to restrain myself from flipping out on Nicole because this whole episode with LL could have easily been avoided had she not be so unreasonable.

"Well, what do you want me to say? If I come by the house and speak to him, I'm going back to jail. If I call my own house that's harassment. Nicole, why don't you tell me exactly how to handle this situation since you wanna wear the pants."

"Lance, listen, I know I might have went overboard—"

"You might have?" I sarcastically said as I cut Nicole off.

"Yeah, just hear me out. I been really praying and fasting about us and our marriage, and just about everything in general and now with this incident with LL, I know that God is trying to show me something."

I kept quiet because I knew once Nicole got on her *God told me this, God told me that* soapbox, there was no use in trying to get in a word edgewise because it would simply go on deaf ears, so I kept my mouth shut until she was finished.

"And so your point is?" I asked sarcastically when she was done.

Nicole sucked her teeth and said, "Lance, my point is I realize where I was wrong, but you know, you could show a little humility yourself and admit where you were wrong too."

"Nicole, show me my error? You falsely accuse me of cheating—with no evidence, I might add—you throw me out of my own house, and get me locked up for it, and you want me to show you where I was wrong?"

There was silence on the phone, and then Nicole asked me if I would come by the house later that evening so we could both talk with LL.

"Let me call my lawyer first and see if it's all right for me to do that. No, matter of fact, why don't you type up a letter authorizing me to come to my own house and sign it, then scan it and e-mail it to my phone. When I get that, then I'll come through."

"Lance, come on now."

"What do you mean, *Lance, come on now*? Hello! I was just locked up for five days and I'm not trying to go back to jail, so if you want me to come through then sign off on that and e-mail it to me! You created this nonsense, not me!"

"Okay, Lance, fine, I'll e-mail you a signed letter okaying you to come by the house."

I remained quiet because I was still heated, and all of the feelings I had been feeling when I was sitting in jail were all starting to creep back up and make me even madder. I mean, it was absolutely ridiculous I had even been locked up and put through the system. Although I didn't have a short fuse, having had my freedom taken away from me was something that didn't sit well with me and it never would, especially when it was over some bullshit.

"Well, listen, why you waited until eight-thirty at night to call me and tell me this, I don't know . . ."

"Lance, you know I go to church on Tuesday nights. I just got out and I'm on my way back to the house."

"Well, like I was getting ready to say, T.L. is having an album release party tonight at Guesthouse in the city and I'm getting ready to head to that, so being that it's already late, why don't I just come by in the morning before you leave for work and we can talk with him then." I would always drop anything at any moment for my son, but I had a feeling I would have to deal with some added bullshit from Nicole and so once again I had to make a shit-or-get-off-of-the-pot decision, and at that moment, I decided to shit on my situation once again.

"Who are you going to the city with?"

"With Steve."

"Lance, I'm not trying to preach to you, but don't you think you've been partying just a little bit too much lately?"

"No," I simply responded.

"Well, I don't know. Just be careful. I'll call you in the morning."

"Okay, and listen. This is just a phase for right now that will pass real soon. I told you, I'm just trying to have my face constantly in the mix until I manage to break through with this movie thing. It's all about who you know, so if I'm not in the mix I won't be able to network and meet people."

"Yeah, Lance, I know all of that, but you're also a married man with a son. So just watch the example you set for him. I always tell you, you don't have to chase what you can attract. When God is ready to open that movie door for you it will open, you don't have to sell your soul in the process."

I knew it was time to hang up the phone because Nicole always took it to the extreme with the religious shit. How was going to a party all of a sudden selling my soul?

"Okay, Nicole, just call me in the morning," I said to her cordially before hanging up.

There was no way in the world that I was gonna miss or even be very late for T.L.'s party. It was parties like his I absolutely lived for. Steve was gonna go with me to the party, but we decided that we would drive separate cars just in case either one of us hooked up with something nice at the party and wanted to leave early.

As we were getting dressed, my cell phone rang, and it was a girl who went by the name of Slim Kim. Slim Kim was the publicist for the party. She had called me because I had called her earlier that day to put Mashonda and Layla on the list for the party.

"What's good, Lance? Sorry it took me so long to hit you back but today my phone is straight bananas."

"Yeah, I could imagine. I hope I'm not killing you, but I need to add four more people to the list."

"No, no, t's all good. So I already got you plus one. You want me to change that to plus five."

"Exactly."

"I gotchu, baby boy. Just get me at the bar tonight and it's all good," she said in a joking manner.

"No doubt! I gotchu, girl," I said before hanging up the phone.

Steve thought I was the biggest, lamest asshole in the world for inviting both Mashonda and Layla to the party when there was already gonna be so much brand new pussy at the party to choose from. For the most part, I understood where he was coming from and he was right, but it was my ego more than anything else that had caused me to invite them. It was like more than anything I just wanted to show them I had the power to get them into such a high-profile party. But I was certain to tell them that I was gonna be moving around the entire night and I wouldn't be able to really chill with them that much. So I felt like in a sense that I had covered myself by building an out for myself before the party even started.

Just before midnight me and Steve arrived at the party. The line to get inside was thick and it stretched about half a block long. But we bypassed the line and headed straight to the front. As we approached the bouncers one of them asked, "Lance, he's witchu?"

"Yeah, he's with me," I said as I waited for him to pull back the ropes so we could enter the party, "and listen, I got about four more shorties coming through, make sure they get in, a'ight?" I said to the bouncer as I placed a hundred-dollar bill in the palm of his hand.

"That's what's up. I'm on that for you."

I knew for a fact that it was because my face had been on the front page of the newspaper, and on all of the news channels, that the bouncer had so quickly recognized me, and I loved every second of feeling like a celebrity.

The party was packed. There were literally wall-to-wall people everywhere as me and Steve snaked our way to the main level of the club and over to the bar. I saw a lot of people I knew, but I wasn't able to get everyone's attention.

"It's rammed up in here," Steve said, just before getting one of the bartender's attention and ordering drinks for the both of us.

Just as I finished my first drink, I felt my phone vibrating. I looked at it and I saw a text from Nicole that said:

Lance, I just wanted to tell you that in spite of everything that's happened over the past week, I still love you!

I blew some air out of my lungs and I couldn't help but smile. Nicole was a special person and I knew why I loved her so much. I was happy to see her text, but again, I had to compartmentalize and move those thoughts to the back of my mind because I didn't want to feel any guilt feelings. I quickly texted back that I loved her as well, and then I put my phone away and tried to get the bartender's attention so that I could order another round of drinks. There was a young lady who was also trying to get the bartender's attention as well.

"What are you drinking? I got it!" I yelled over the music into the girl's ear.

She looked at me and smiled and then told me it was okay, that I didn't have to do that.

"It's all good, I gotchu," I said as I finally got the bartender's attention and ordered my drink and told him to get the young lady whatever she wanted.

She smiled again and then told the bartender to let her have an apple martini.

"Thank you," she said into my ear.

I really was just being nice and wasn't even trying to kick it to her, and I could tell she appreciated that fact. She also seemed a little bit surprised I didn't at least ask her what her name was.

The night was real young and I was just getting warmed up so the move that I had made in buying her a drink and not asking her what her name was, it was just a move to get my swagger in full tilt.

I paid for the drinks and told the young lady to be safe and I would see her around. Me and Steve continued making our way through the crowd and bumped into someone that we knew from Queens, but we hadn't seen in a while, a dude who went by the name of Fredro.

I had known Fredro since I was in junior high school. He was one of those pretty boy dudes from way back in the day who always had money, the baddest chicks, and the baddest cars. When all of the money from the crack game started to dry up, Fredro was one of the first dudes from New York to go down to Virginia to get money dealing weight. So he was well-known for his flamboyance and for always holding money.

"Oh, shit, my niggas! What up?" Fredro said as he gave us a pound.

"What's the deal?" Steve replied.

Fredro told us to follow him and he and his crew had a table upstairs near the other bar.

"Yo, we got the whole upstairs on smash, come on."

As we followed Fredro I was directly behind him and while we were on the winding steps that lead to upstairs, Fredro turned to me and in my ear and said, "Yo, I got that *white*. Holla at your boy!"

I nodded and the three of us kept it moving. When we finally did make it upstairs, the energy was totally different than it had been downstairs. Downstairs was much more rammed and people were more or less profiling, but upstairs people were actually partying their asses off and having a good time.

I immediately recognized Buffie the Body, DJ Kay Slay was in the spot chillin'. Toccara from *America's Next Top Model* was there, Roxie from BET's *106 & Park* was there. I saw one of the NY Jets, and I also saw the model Melyssa Ford. Steve saw something he liked and he told me that he was gonna be back so that he could go holla at the chick.

After Steve walked off, I went up to Fredro and I handed him two hundred dollars. He looked down at the money and without saying anything he went into his pocket and discreetly pulled out two cellophane bags of cocaine and handed them to me.

All I needed was the car key from my key chain and I was good to go. I missed doing coke and with all of this stress that was going on with Nicole it was like the perfect excuse for me to try some.

I went into one of the bathroom stalls and carefully opened up one of the bags of cocaine and stuck my key into it until there was a small mountain of cocaine sitting on my key. I slowly lifted the key to my right nostril while I used the index finger from my left hand and pinched my left nostril, and then with my right nostril I snorted the coke. I did that about ten times and then I put the cocaine away, put the keys in my pocket and I wiped my nose and exited the bathroom.

By the time I made it back over to Fredro and his crew, I was high as a fucking kite. The cocaine mixed with the alcohol was the ultimate high.

"You shining!" Fredro said as he gave me a pound. "It's off the hook, right?"

I was almost too high to speak, so all I did was smile at Fredro and nod my head. With the cocaine running through my system I had all of the confidence in the world and began dancing with different chicks and trying to rap to just about any and every chick, but I was in control of myself and I made sure I did things in a tasteful way.

Steve didn't fuck with any type of drugs. No X-pills, no coke, and no weed. All he did was drink and I respected that since he was fearful of violating his job's drug policy and potentially losing his well-paying city job.

I was so high I didn't even care that both Layla and Mashonda were looking for me. Normally I would have been a little bit stressed-out and panicked since they had both texted me within five minutes apart and told me they had arrived and asked me where I was. I texted them both back and told them where I was, but before they reached me I had went back into the bathroom to snort some more coke.

When I came out, I saw Slim Kim.

"What's up, mama?" I gave her a hug and a kiss on the cheek and she asked me if I was having a good time.

When I was done speaking with her, Mashonda walked up to me from behind and she wrapped her arms around my waist.

"Hey sexy!" I said as I kissed her on her lips.

Mashonda then introduced me to the two people she was with. Both of them were just as sexy as she was and they both had bodies like she did. One of the chicks was named Felicia, who was her older cousin from New York, and the other chick she introduced me to was named Joy, who she introduced as her mother.

"Get the fuck outta here!" I said over the loud music. "There's no way that's your mother."

All three of them laughed because they said they always got the same reaction from people. I called Steve over and introduced him to Mashonda and her family and he too couldn't believe that Mashonda was standing there with her mother.

Mashonda, Felicia, and Joy were all dressed in real expensive high-end designer shit. Mashonda was wearing Diane von Furstenberg, Felicia was wearing Tory Burch, and Joy was wearing Zac Posen.

"So do I call you Mrs. Williams or Joy?" I asked as I looked at her left hand and noticed she was wearing a wedding ring.

"I would be offended if you didn't call me Joy," she replied.

At that moment, Layla walked up to me wearing some tight jeans and high heels and this see-through chiffon turtleneck sweater. It was clearly obvious that she had no bra underneath because you could see her titties right through the top, areola and all. Layla kissed me on the cheek and she said hello to Steve, but she stood right by my side. I played things cool and introduced her to everybody. It was a real awkward feeling because I could sense that some ghettoness was getting ready to come from Mashonda and her cousin Felicia.

Thankfully, Steve stepped up and said that he was buying drinks and asked everybody what they were drinking. That gave me time to walk off with Layla.

"You are murdering that top."

"Who were them chicks? One of them wasn't your wife, was it?"

"Nah, my wife isn't here, they just some people I know, they cool, though."

"Oh, 'cause I'm just saying, one of them was looking at me with this stank look, and—"

"Layla, just chill. They cool. We gonna all chill tonight and have a good time, a'ight?"

"Yeah, I'm good, but I will check a bitch up in here, that's all I'm saying."

I blew some air from my lungs and walked off by myself and headed back to the bathroom to snort some more coke. I told Layla to chill with Steve until I got back.

I made it to the bathroom and I stayed there for about five minutes snorting my ass off until I had completely finished one of the hundred-dollar bags of coke I had.

When I exited the bathroom, the bouncer asked me if I was a'ight. I knew that he knew what I was doing and so I wondered if I was giving off a stoned-high look or something.

"Yeah, I'm cool," I said. Just as I finished saying that I quickly glanced to my right as someone walked by me.

"Toni?" I said, unsure if that was her.

The young lady stopped in her tracks and turned around, and it was indeed Toni.

I don't know what it was about Toni, but literally every time I saw her she would cause me to feel these uncontrollable feelings that reminded me of a teenage crush or something. It was like a mixture of excitement, lust, and love all wrapped up in one.

Toni was wearing a nice Gucci dress that showed off her body in a very tasteful way. I wanted to give her a hug, but for some reason I felt awkward and I didn't want to come across like she had this power over me.

"Hey!" she said.

"I didn't know you were here."

"Well, I knew you were in here," she replied kind of snappy.

"What the hell does that mean?" I asked.

"It doesn't mean anything, but Lance, you *really* should just get a drink in your hand and go and chill. Y'all running around, talking to every woman in here, like you some under-sexed teenager or something. That is so tired and tacky. You look very thirsty!"

"Why are you coming for my neck? And what the hell are you so concerned with what I'm doing?" Toni knew just the right buttons to push to chump me and make me feel like an asshole. Despite being high as a kite, her words still managed to cut me.

Toni shook her head as if she was disgusted, but she didn't say anything.

"And you know that shit was fucked up that you couldn't even call me to check on a nigga these past few days and I know you saw on the news what I was going through."

"Lance, I did call you. Three times, as a matter of fact, but your voice mail was full, so what was I supposed to do?"

"Then you shoulda texted me."

"Oh, please."

"So I know you here with your record-mogul husband," I said.

"Yes, I am here with Keith. And your point in saying that was? I mean, why wouldn't I be here with him?"

"Where you should be is home with my daughter! You saying I'm running around looking tired, well, it's just as tired for you to be a thirty-one-year-old woman out partying on a Tuesday night when your daughter got school the next morning. Toni, you ain't twenty-five years old anymore, take your ass home to your daughter!"

"Lance, you know what? I know you're high right now, so I won't even respond to that nonsense. And seriously, if you're gonna do coke, at least wipe the cocaine from your nose! Jesus Christ!" she said and shook her head.

I felt stupid as I quickly ran my hand across my face to wipe the cocaine residue from my nose.

"Thank you!" she added.

I laughed and replied, "Damn, you really must not be getting fucked right 'cause your ass is so uptight."

"Lance, first of all, let me tell you something. I ain't one of these little hood-rat chicks you up in here hollering at, okay? So if you gonna talk to me you talk to me with some respect or don't say shit to me at all! And for the record, Keith is the *only* one that is fucking me and knows *how* to fuck me. Okay? Unlike you and your pencil dick, when Keith fucks me I actually have an orgasm so let's be clear! Since you on this disrespectful shit, now is as good a time as any to let you know that I'm filing the papers to change Sahara's last name to Keith's last name. You may be Sahara's father but Keith is her daddy!"

I clenched my teeth because I almost lost my temper, and it took everything in me not to slap fire out of Toni's ass at that moment. I knew I was getting ready to go back to jail for assault because Toni had purposely tried to get under my skin, and she definitely succeeded.

But thank God, right at that moment Mashonda, who was going to the bathroom, walked up to me.

"Oh, there you go, baby. You okay?"

"Yeah, I'm cool," I said as Toni shook her head and walked off, continuing on to the bathroom.

"That liquor is ready to come out, where is the bathroom?" Mashonda asked.

I knew I didn't want Mashonda in the bathroom at the same time with Toni so I asked her to just chill with me for a minute.

"No, Lance, you don't understand, if I don't get to a bathroom and pee like right now, it's gonna be a problem."

I walked up to the bouncer and I gave him a hundred dollars and I asked him if he could let me have the bathroom to myself for a while.

"Fifteen minutes, a'ight?" he responded while barely flinching.

I nodded my head and then I grabbed Mashonda by the hand and told her to come with me to the guy's bathroom. She followed behind me and without hesitation she went directly into one of the stalls and did her thing.

When Mashonda was finished peeing she began washing her hands and that's when I took out the bag of coke I had and held it in my left hand and plucked it two times with the middle finger of my right hand in order to cause the cocaine to sift to the bottom.

"You ever do this?" I asked Mashonda.

She shook her head *no* and by the look on her face I could tell that she wasn't all that keen on messing with it.

"This is the best drug in the world. It's better than weed because the high is better and you don't have to worry about your hands and your clothes smelling like weed," I said as I dipped my car key into the bag and put a small pile of cocaine on it and brought it to my nose and snorted just as I had been doing all night long.

"And it's better than liquor because you don't smell like liquor and you don't have to worry about no hangovers like you do with alcohol."

Mashonda just looked at me as I dipped into the bag again and snorted some more coke. I wondered what was going through her mind and what she was thinking about me at that moment.

"Does it sting when you snort it?" she asked.

"Nah, not to me it doesn't. I don't even feel it."

With Mashonda's question I knew she would be down to experiment with me so without asking her I carefully put some more coke on the tip of the key and I brought it toward Mashonda's face and instructed her on how to snort it. She did as I told her, and after blinking her eyes a few times she smiled.

"You gotta give it a minute or so to take effect," I explained as I raised some more coke to her face and she snorted that too.

After about three minutes Mashonda told me she was feeling nice and she asked me if she could get some more.

"Nah, that's all you get, baby, just have a drink when we go back out and you'll be straight."

She smiled and told me she was already straight. Then she walked up to me and kissed me and told me she had missed me.

"I missed you too," I said as I kissed her back.

After a minute or so of heavy kissing and feeling on each other, me and Mashonda both had our pants down to our ankles and I was fucking her doggie style as she braced herself by placing both of her hands on the sink.

I was high as a kite and that was what clouded my judgment and caused me to run up in Mashonda raw. Her pussy felt so much better this time than it had when I had fucked her in the hotel room. I knew that was because the cocaine running through my body was enhancing everything, and also because sex always felt better without a condom.

Mashonda tried her hardest to not make noise. I could tell she wanted to completely let loose. I knew I had to hurry up because the bouncer was only gonna let us stay in there for so long. But within like five minutes I was cumming and I didn't even bother to pull out.

"You came inside of me?" Mashonda asked somewhat nervously.

"That shit felt too good to pull out!" I explained.

"You know I should bust you in your head, right?" Mashonda said as she playfully punched me on my shoulder before asking me get her a paper towel. She wiped herself and then pulled her pants back up and the two of us prepared to walk back out into the party.

"My pussy gonna be leaking all night because of you, but that was fun!" Mashonda devilishly said.

At that point, as we went back among the people, I felt like an absolute king, like I was on top of the world. I was wilding out and living crazy out of control and I knew that I would have to reign myself in, but there was no way I was gonna slow down for the rest of that night.

From the twenty minutes or so that I had been away from the bathroom, the party got even more packed than it had been. I couldn't locate Steve, and I didn't see Layla, so I figured they were probably together. Mashonda walked off and told me she was gonna go try and find her cousin and her mom.

I made my way over to the VIP area and Slim Kim introduced me to T.L. and asked me to pose with him for a picture, which I had no problem doing.

"Hey you," someone said to me and pinched my stomach.

I turned and saw that it was Meagan from *Media Edition*. Meagan was drop-dead gorgeous and she was the type of woman who I would definitely want to marry in my next lifetime. I was happy to see her, but I was hoping she didn't know I was high.

"How you doing, Ms. Washington?"

"I'm chillin'. I didn't know you were gonna be here, you okay?" she shouted in my ear.

"Yeah, I'm good. It's good seeing you again."

"You too! And listen, I didn't forget to call you, I just got tied up earlier in the day today."

"It's all good. Don't worry, I'm here. Just hit me up when you can." Meagan nodded and then grabbed my hand and pulled me toward her so that I could dance with her.

As soon as we started dancing, I looked to my left and I saw Toni and her husband Keith. Toni looked at me and shook her head. I just ignored her and kept dancing with Meagan.

"You look nice," I said in Meagan's ear while we danced.

Meagan thanked me for the compliment. I was still high as a kite and so I had to make sure I maintained in front of Meagan and didn't come across in a way that would turn her off and cause her to never follow up with me for the interview.

"Can I just be honest with you about something?" I asked.

"Of course."

"I have to tell you I've always had the biggest crush on you. You always reminded me of Nia Long whenever I saw you on TV."

Meagan smiled and she replied, "Oh, so you really mean that you always had a crush on Nia Long."

She had the perfect comeback, and I really didn't know what to say, so I just smiled and told her I liked her style.

"So whether we do the interview or not, would you ever let me take you out to dinner, or breakfast?"

"Like on a date, you mean?" Meagan asked with a smile. "Lance, aren't you married?"

I didn't respond.

She shook her head, then said, "Don't do it to yourself, Lance."

"Don't do it to myself?" I asked.

"Yeah, that's what I said."

"Why you say that?" I asked Meagan as we stopped dancing and I walked over with her to sit down.

"I'll be straight up with you just like I am with everybody else. You wouldn't be able to afford me and honestly, you can't handle this. I'm not trying to be conceited or whatever, but I'm just straight up."

"Wow. A'ight, a'ight. I respect that. Like I said, I like your style."

"You like my style? So what's your style, tell me where you live?"

"I live in Great Neck, Long Island."

Meagan nodded and smiled. "Okay, tell me about your cars," Meagan asked.

"I push two cars and a truck. I got the 2009 Range Rover. I got the 2008 650i convertible BMW and I got the CLS Benz coupe."

Meagan looked at me and nodded her head and she said she was impressed.

"So, did I pass your test?"

"You passed the entrance exam to take me out to dinner, but this right here, this is passport pussy. I'm just being straight up," Meagan said with a look of all seriousness.

"You was drinking tonight, wasn't you?"

Meagan laughed and then she punched me on my arm and told me she was just joking with me. But in my heart of hearts I knew she was straight up and with her it was about the dollars, and I had dollars, so I knew I was gonna get with that.

"I'm gonna go mingle, but I'll definitely call you so we can do that interview for the show."

"Let me get your number," I said to her as I pulled out my phone. She had tried to give me the number the day before so I knew, it would be no problem in getting it from her. "So you working with passport pussy? I like that. I'm gonna put a bunch a stamps in that passport," I said to her before she walked off.

Meagan didn't respond but she did smile as she walked off.

I had completely lost track of time as the night wore on. I had lost Mashonda and her crew, but it was cool since I had already hit it. I didn't really want to see her again. I had managed to catch up with Layla and she basically hawked me for the rest of the night, but it was all good because I chilled at the bar downstairs with her and drank shots of Patrón until we were both ready to leave.

Layla had taken the train to the city so she asked me to drive her back home to Brooklyn, which I agreed to do. So around three-thirty in the morning we left the club together and headed to my BMW, which was parked about three blocks away.

I knew that Layla was probably in the mood to fuck, but I was so fucked-up from the cocaine and all the liquor I had consumed that all I wanted to do was jump in the shower real quick and get my ass in a bed and recover. Plus, it was cold and it was just starting to snow, so all of those factors combined just scaled my decision I wasn't gonna make pussy a priority.

We made it to the Brooklyn Bridge and it was weird because a big part of me didn't even really remember what streets I had taken to get to the bridge. All I knew was that one minute we were leaving the club and the next minute I was crossing the bridge. Just as I thought, Layla was feeling frisky and she reached over and began unbuckling my pants and started stroking my dick.

As soon as my dick was hard, she unbuckled her seat belt and placed her head in my lap and started sucking my dick. The music was blasting and the streets were empty so I was breezing through the streets and catching all of the green lights.

Even though I didn't feel like fucking, getting a blow job was the perfect nightcap. Whenever I drank it always took me longer to cum, and that night was no exception, and Layla was really working hard to get me to cum. Fve minutes into the blow job I could tell that I was gonna cum real soon, but unfortunately the next thing I remember is hearing the sound of screeching tires. I looked up and the last thing I remember was seeing bright lights practically blinding me.

"Oh, shit!" I screamed.

Boom!

That was the sound I heard, followed by shattering glass that hit me in the face. Both the driver's side and the passenger side air bags released. I remember feeling like the wind had been knocked out of me and a sharp pain was shooting up my leg. My car came to a dead stop and I remember hearing a hissing sound and the sound of a horn that wouldn't shut off. I had no idea what I had hit, but I knew I had hit something.

"Layla, you all right?" I asked, although I could barely talk since I couldn't breathe.

Layla responded that she was a little banged up, but she thought she was okay.

I remember thinking to myself that I had to hurry up and exit the car because for some reason I just felt like we were gonna be hit by another car. So immediately I tried to open my door, but the door wasn't budging. Then I looked to my right and I realized the entire passenger side had been pushed in crazy. And what was wild is the way it was pushed in I realized that if Layla hadn't been giving me a blow job she would have definitely been killed. It was like that whole side of the car had been pushed in and was collapsed around us.

My heart started racing from fear and I realized we were both trapped in the car. All of a sudden I got really dizzy and everything started spinning around, and I felt real light-headed. I remember hearing this ringing sound in my ears and the sound became deafening. I remember thinking about my son LL, and about my daughter Sahara. Then I remembered an image of my mother's face flash in front of my eyes. Before I knew it, I had passed out and my body was slumped in my seat and on top of Layla's.

When I came to, I remember seeing lights and people everywhere. I also remember shivering uncontrollably, but although my body was shivering I was immobilized on a stretcher. I couldn't move my limbs and my neck was in some sort of plastic brace.

"What happened?" I remember sounding those words to one of the firemen standing near my stretcher. My words were barely audible but he did hear me. He told me to relax and that I had been involved in a serious car accident.

"Can you tell me your name?" one of the paramedics asked me. "How old are you? What year is it? Do you know who the president is?"

The paramedic was asking me those questions in an attempt to gauge how badly I was hurt.

I didn't answer his questions, partly because I wasn't sure of the answers, but mainly because I was cold as hell and I couldn't breathe.

"I can't breathe," I mumbled.

He told me to relax and they were gonna get me some oxygen as soon as they loaded me into the ambulance. Within seconds I remember being hoisted into the ambulance and seeing the doors close and speeding off with the sound of a siren glaring in the background.

I definitely felt like I was dreaming and at the same time I didn't know if I was dead. But I do know I was in tremendous pain, and so I just closed my eyes and began praying to God.

Chapter Forty-one

When I woke up, the first person I saw standing next to me was Nicole.

"Baby, what happened? Where am I?"

Nicole explained I had been in a terrible car accident and I was in Brookdale Hospital in Brooklyn. I could tell she had been crying at some point, but I could also see a look of sternness mixed into her face.

Before Nicole and I could really begin talking, a detective stepped up to the other side of my bed and introduced himself and showed me his badge while his partner stood at the foot of my bed.

"Mr. Thomas, I'm Detective Gasparino from Brooklyn North, and this is Detective Joseph."

After getting the introductions out of the way, Detective Gasparino told me he was placing me under arrest.

"Under arrest for what?"

"For the possession of a controlled substance," he coldly said and proceeded to read me my rights.

I frowned and looked at Nicole, and she exhaled and shook her head. When the detective was done he placed one handcuff on my wrist and he placed the other handcuff on the rail of the bed.

"What the fuck is going on?"

"Lance, the paramedics found a small amount of cocaine in your pants pocket when they were looking for your identification."

I exhaled and swallowed very hard. I knew I was fucked and I didn't know what else to say.

The detective then informed me they wanted to draw blood to test the blood-alcohol content, but they had to read me something called my chemical rights. They explained I had the right to refuse to have my blood drawn, but if I refused my license would immediately be suspended and I would be hit with an additional criminal charge for refusing.

"I'm not submitting to no test. Nah, I'm sorry, you can't draw my blood for that."

The detective looked at Nicole, and apparently she had already informed them she was an attorney and that she was also my wife.

"Lance, listen, just let them draw the blood and take the test. They already found cocaine on you so if you refuse they'll be back in an hour with a search warrant from a judge giving them permission to take your blood without your consent."

I shook my head and told them to just do whatever they had to do. So they called for a nurse and she proceeded to draw blood from my arm. The detective exchanged cards with Nicole and they soon left but a uniformed police officer stood guard right outside my room.

"Lance, what in Jesus' name were you thinking?" Nicole asked me. I could tell she was disgusted.

I rolled my eyes and blew air out of my lungs. The sheer terror and fear I was feeling at that moment was beyond human words. I mean, in like a split second I went from partying with stars and being on top of the world to facing some serious life-altering shit. Shit that I wasn't prepared for, nor did I know how to prepare myself for what was to come.

"I hope you know you just ruined your life! You do know that?"

"Why you gotta always be so dramatic? I made a mistake. It happened, what can I do?" I said, trying not to show my true feelings of fear.

"A mistake, Lance? Lance, a car accident—yes, that is a mistake. But driving drunk and high on cocaine—that isn't a mistake! Driving in the wrong direction on Flatbush Avenue— Lance, that isn't a mistake! What were you thinking?"

Oh, shit! I thought to myself.

I had no idea I had been driving on the wrong side of the street. But apparently after I'd come off of the Brooklyn Bridge and I turned on to Flatbush Avenue. I turned into the

northbound lanes when I should have turned into the south-
bound lanes and I collided with a small Toyota Corolla right in
front of the famous Junior's restaurant.

Nicole started crying as she told me I had killed a twenty-
four-year-old woman and badly injured her fiancé.

"What?" I asked in disbelief.

"Yes, Lance. Oh my God, I can't believe this is happening,"
she stated while burying her head into her hands.

There are absolutely no words in the human language that
can describe how bad I was feeling at that moment. I was
feeling a sense of desperation and helplessness, but I had no
words simply because there were no words that could explain
or make up for what I had done. The bottom line was I was
scared as hell, and at the same time I was feeling a ton of
regret. Like I just kept thinking over and over, at the end of
the day I was in this position simply because of pussy, and
wasn't no extramarital pussy worth what I was going through.

"And Lance, who is the lady that was in your car with you?"
Nicole asked. She was visibly holding back tears.

"She was just a friend. One of Steve's friends."

Nicole came close to my bed and she placed her hands on
the rails and tears began to stream down her face.

She leaned in a little bit and with controlled anger said,
"The day you told me that Toni was pregnant by you I thought
that was the worst day in my life and it was something I would
wish on no woman. But when the police call my house before
the crack of dawn and tell me that my husband was involved
in a car accident and I needed to get to the hospital, I immediately start thinking the worst. The feeling that came over me,
thinking you might have been killed—I can tell you that felt
worst than knowing what you had done with Toni. Then I get
here and there are cops everywhere, so I identify myself first
as your lawyer and not your wife, because with the number of
cops that were here, and with the media, I knew something
wasn't right. Then they tell me they suspected you were drinking. In my head I say, okay, it's stupid, but what can you do?
Then they tell me about the cocaine and they tell me there was
another woman in your car and the firemen and paramedics
initially found you with your pants unbuckled and your penis

exposed! I said to myself that someone had to be playing a dirty trick on me, because there is no way you could be that stupid! There's just no way! And then they tell me about the fatality and I knew this whole episode had topped Toni's pregnancy."

"Baby, just hear me—"

"No! I am not hearing you out! I am so sick and tired of being sick and tired!"

"Baby, don't walk out on me like this, not now!" I pleaded because I could tell Nicole was ready to leave the hospital.

"First of all, I am not your baby. Let's get that straight. And second . . ." Nicole paused for a moment and pinched the bridge of her nose and shook her head before continuing on. "You know what? Forget it. It's not even worth the stress. I'm gonna call Attorney Jones and I'll have him represent you because I just can't do this anymore. I can't, Lance. I just can't. I mean, you have *no idea*, no idea at all how much I love you."

"Baby, yes, I do."

"No, you don't, because if you did, you wouldn't put me through this. God only knows what else you've done and what you're capable of still doing. I mean, I thought I had over-reacted by putting you out the house and I wanted to reverse that and have us move on, and then this." Nicole shook her head and began crying much harder. "Here, take this," she said as she took off her wedding ring and placed it in the palm of my hand and folded my fingers over it.

"What are you doing?"

"I'm leaving you."

"Nicole!" I shouted as she turned and started to walk out of the room.

She turned back toward me and then she said, "In your heart of hearts, you know you had already walked out on me a long time ago."

"I never left you and I would never leave you, you know that," I desperately said.

"Lance, listen to me. I said, in your heart you've already left me and you can look at your left hand and it will tell you the exact same thing that I'm saying."

"What are you talking about?"

"I gave you my wedding ring, Lance. I had it on my finger to give to you. Even in our roughest times I never went without wearing my ring because I knew what it represented. But you, I don't even have to ask you why you aren't wearing your ring because I know why it's not on your finger. I know why and you know why."

Nicole took one more long look at me, and then she turned and walked out of the room for good.

I was speechless because to me it was like, what do I say? Nicole had pulled my card. She was right about everything she said. The sad part was I had made it a lame habit of taking off my wedding ring in certain circumstances. I did it deliberately and it was stupid, but at the same time in my heart I knew I loved Nicole. It was just that I was constantly feeling conflicted. Conflicted about doing the right thing versus doing the selfish thing. I hated feeling that way, and in all honesty I hated cheating, and yet cheating made me feel normal on some level. It was like cheating calmed me and made me feel whole. So in some sense I was like the person who loved to drink and had a ball getting drunk, but yet I hated the hangovers and the consequences of drinking. But just like it's not until a drunk is hungover and worshiping the toilet bowl, while puking his guts out, does he realize how good it feels to be sober. With the asshole that I was, it took dire consequences like I was going through for me to realize just how much I loved and valued the calm, relaxed, monogamous family life.

What's wild is that on a subconscious level I know I was living crazy and disrespecting Nicole because I knew that I could get away with it. Like I never, ever believed she had it in her to put her foot down and say enough is enough. Just like a child will test a parent and push the limits of what they can get away with, and keep pushing those limits until the parent smacks the shit out of them and forces the child to show some goddamn respect for the parent-child relationship, I knew how to push the limits of my marriage. I never feared Nicole's reaction. But this time it was different. I could feel it and I knew Nicole was done. She had had enough of my shit and it made me feel numb to even think about life without my wife. I was determined to set things straight again and get everything back on the right course.

I had fucked up big-time, but I was only at the tip of the iceberg in terms of really realizing how many lives I had royally screwed up.

Chapter Forty-two

Even though it was a bitterly cold winter day, the New York media proved they would stop at nothing to get at the heart of a breaking story such as mine.

The media had gotten wind of the car accident when it was transmitted over the police scanners and all of the major newspapers and news stations dispatched crews to the scene of the accident and to the hospital. My accident was the lead story on the six a.m. newscasts.

In fact, it wasn't until I had my nurse turn on the television in my room that I was able to realize the extent of the damages to both my car and to the car I had hit. Both cars were almost unrecognizable. It was also from the news that I learned Layla and I had to be cut out of the car. Of course, when the media found out I was the one who was driving the car and I was suspected of driving while under the influence, they went crazy with the story.

I was watching the local ABC news channel and I couldn't believe how fast they had gotten all of the details. They knew that I had been coming from an album release party for T.L. and they knew I had just been placed under arrest for being in possession of a controlled substance. Other than the devastation I had caused the innocent victims, the thing I focused on the most was when the reporters spoke about all of the possible criminal charges I was facing.

I had written about gangsta shit in my novels and about killings, drugs, jail, and all of that. But this was no book I was writing. This was real life. It was my life. Never in my wildest dreams did I see myself as the going-to-prison type. I wasn't built for prison. So, although I was feeling horrible and scared as all hell, I knew I had to scan my brain and get in touch with as many people as I could who could help me and go to bat for me. My ass was in a serious sling and my neck was in a noose that was getting tighter by the second.

At the same time as I watched the news coverage and feared and worried about what was to come, I couldn't help but feel extremely remorseful for the damage I had caused to the victims of the other families. Regardless of what would happen to me and what jail time I was going to face, I was determined to not let this be one of those times where I painted myself as the victim in order to deflect attention from the real victims in this tragedy, because it was clear who those victims were. Just as it was clear who was the major asshole in this whole ordeal—that being, my black ass.

Eventually, the doctor came to my room and explained to me I had a severely sprained ankle and my right lung had also collapsed and I would need to have quick, minor surgery to reinflate my lung.

"Surgery?"

"Yes, it's nothing major. We'll give you a local anesthetic and then make a small incision in between your ribs. Once we do that we will insert a tube that will allow for the reinflation of the lung."

By 4:00 p.m. that same day, I was able to leave the hospital. I was accompanied by Attorney Jones, my mother, and Steve. Unfortunately for me I wasn't able to just hop in a car and go home. I was handcuffed and flanked on both sides of me by New York City police officers who were escorting me to a Brooklyn police precinct for processing, and then I would be heading off to jail before seeing a judge.

It's funny, because although no one wants to go to jail, I knew jail was what I deserved. I knew that, simply because it was very unfair that I was able to just walk out of the hospital with all of my physical faculties functioning okay, all the while I had put someone's lifeless body in a morgue and I had another victim fighting for his life with severe injuries. I desperately wanted to go and apologize to my victims and their families, but on the advice of my lawyer, I decided against it for the time being.

Anyway, I ended up spending the night in jail, and the next day I went before a judge inside of a jam-packed downtown

Brooklyn courtroom. The judge read me the riot act and he rightly so ripped into my ass in a stern, but eloquent, way as I stood before him as humbly as I possibly could.

The judge was careful not to talk to me as if I had been tried and convicted of my crime. But reading between the lines he knew I was guilty. Since this was just my arraignment, he could only say but so much.

It wasn't like I was going to jail right there at that moment so I wasn't too nervous. But just the mere fact of me standing in front of a judge was sort of surreal. It was almost like an out-of-body experience. I had this feeling of embarrassment mixed with disbelief as I listened to the judge.

I had been charged with aggravated vehicular manslaughter, a crime that, in New York, carries a maximum of twenty-five years in prison. I had also been charged with driving under the influence, possession of a controlled substance, and I was hit with various traffic infractions.

But since the cocaine amount I had on me at the time of the accident was such a small amount, the most serious charge by far I was facing was the aggravated vehicular manslaughter charge.

Attorney Jones was no slouch. He was one of the most prominent black attorneys in the New York City metropolitan area. So in a respectful way, he made sure he checked the judge on how he was talking to me, all the while my lawyer made sure that he was honorable, but he had to make sure that my legal interest were protected. He reminded the judge that I was in a position to make bail and I had also been made perfectly aware that my license had been suspended, and that under no circumstances would I be operating a vehicle in the near future.

"So with all due respect, Your Honor, to both you and the families involved in this tragedy, my client is ready to post bail. All we ask is that we be given just a fair shot to present the full facts of this case before a jury and not at this arraignment."

Since I had just been arrested with the incident with Nicole, the judge had the power to deny my bail and he knew that and thankfully, by the grace of God, he had saw fit to grant me bail.

He warned me if I were to get in trouble for anything—even if it was as small of an infraction as jaywalking—that he would have me locked up until my trial.

"Do you understand, Mr. Thomas?"

I told the judge I did and some more words were spoken by my lawyer, the district attorney, and the judge, then before long I was allowed to leave.

When I left the courthouse the questioning I received from the media was intense, not to mention the blistering threats and insults that were hurled at me by protesters who supported causes such as Mothers Against Drunk Drivers. I knew what kind of person I really was, but with seeing and hearing all of the protesters I have to admit I was feeling mad, embarrassed, and ashamed; I just couldn't show it. I left with my attorney and we went straight to his Brooklyn office.

When I got there, after limping into the elevator and making my way to the conference table he had in one of the rooms where I sat, that was when it seemed like all the pressure had been mounting up on me hit me and came raining down like a ton of bricks. I couldn't believe I had actually took someone's life. I mean, from day one of the accident I knew what I had done, but it was like for some reason I was just feeling all of the anxiety and pressure all at once. Like it was really real! It wasn't a game.

The person I had killed was a Puerto Rican girl name Olivia Rodriguez. She and her fiancé worked in downtown Brooklyn at the New York City Transit Authority headquarters and they were apparently on their way to work, just three blocks away, when I hit them.

I shook my head and closed my eyes and before long tears streamed down my face because I truly, truly, truly was sorry and I did feel bad. I was man enough to show and express my emotions.

My attorney walked into the room, along with one of his junior attorneys, and he told me he understood the emotional turmoil I was going through.

"I swear it was just a mistake," I said as I shook my head and buried them into my hands.

"Lance, mistakes happen and that's why we have a legal system and a legal process that allows us to put forth a defense. We have experience in these kind of cases."

"So then—just be straight with me—that aggravated vehicular manslaughter charge comes with twenty-five years. Am I really looking at that?"

"Yes and no. Yes, that is the max you could be hit with, but no, I doubt you really will be hit with that. But listen, let's just back up, and I want you to tell me every detail that happened during that night leading up to the arrest. Like where were you coming from, what did you have to drink that night, who did you come in contact with? I need you to leave out nothing. I need everyone's name you spoke to that night. I want to know their relationship in your life. Everything. You understand?"

I nodded my head *yes*.

"Lance, for example, I know you're married to Nicole, but if the woman that was in the car with you at the time of the night wasn't Nicole, I need to know her background and the nature of your relationship with her. How did you get the cocaine, all of that. Don't leave out anything. I also need to know the full gamut of your health history, even if it's embarrassing—just let me know. I say all of this because based on what you tell me, that is what's gonna guide us in a defense strategy. Do you understand?"

I told my lawyer I did understand, and then I proceeded to tell him everything I knew. As I spoke, he and the junior attorney took notes and asked me questions when they needed clarification.

We spoke at length for about an hour and when we were done I was spent. Like with everything that I didn't want to deal with, I was good at blocking things out of my mind. I had been doing that to some extent with the accident. But being that I was forced to relive the events when discussing it with my attorney, it was like being forced to live through your worst phobia.

My attorney explained to me I would likely avoid jail time, but I was likely going to have to pay through the nose, in terms of giving the families financial compensation.

"You know, I need to be clear. That's the scenario that I see. I mean, we will put forth an aggressive defense, but based on the facts in this case, and based on the success you've had as a writer, the worst-case scenario is always gonna be out there. And that's that you get convicted criminally on the aggravated vehicular manslaughter charge and you still get banged for a huge judgment in a civil case."

"So basically I could end up broke and in jail?"

"That's the worst-case. But I can tell you this, you gotta keep your nose clean. You gotta keep a low profile and you gotta hope and pray that the victims' families have a compassionate disposition. I say that because we're gonna eventually try and bargain with the district attorney, but in an emotional case such as this, the district attorney is gonna consult with the victim's families. Basically let the families have the final say as to whether or not they are willing to accept any type of plea bargain."

"Wow," was all I could say as I sat there. This entire ordeal had definitely humbled me and I knew I had to make some serious changes and those changes were going to start that night.

That night I ended up staying at my mother's house, and I prayed and prayed and prayed like I had never in my life prayed before. I apologized to no end to God during my prayers.

When I was done praying, I took hold of my cell phone and went into my mother's kitchen and I ran water into a big pot she had near the sink. I dropped my BlackBerry into the pot of water and left it there for about an hour before throwing it away.

I knew I had to make changes, and those changes would not come unless I first cut off all of my old influences and I stopped partying like a lunatic. That is exactly what I was determined to do.

Chapter Forty-three

In my short thirty-four years, there was something I had learned, but at times I would often lose sight of it. And that was women rarely fucked a nigga unless they had some kind of ulterior motive. Eight out of ten times the ulterior motive women were after was money. So in other words, there was rarely a time women would fuck for free. They rarely would straight-up ask for cash in exchange for letting a dude sex them, instead what they would do is be patient and look for a payoff somewhere down the road.

Three months after I had the car accident, I was doing a very good job of staying on the straight and narrow. I was keeping my nose clean. I wasn't partying. I started going back to church on a regular basis. I wasn't in contact with people I had no business associating with. Basically, I had fallen off the radar and I had moved in with my mother. Nicole had legally separated from me and I knew she was dead serious about going through with divorcing my no-good ass. The best thing I had going for me was that I was spending a lot of good, quality time with my son LL and with my illegitimate daughter Sahara.

I had lost contact with Mashonda and Layla. Although I was now legally separated from Nicole and could have been spending as much time with Mashonda and Layla if I wanted to, the fact still remained I wasn't yet divorced so I knew I shouldn't just wild out. In addition to that, I was really trying to do right by both God and my lawyer. So staying off the radar was the best thing for me.

During the time that I was off the radar, both Mashonda and Layla showed why they had ever really fucked with me. It was all about dollars to them, and they showed their true colors. They saw me as a cash cow. Since they never got any money out of me, they decided to take a backdoor approach.

In addition to suing my auto insurance company, Layla also personally hit me with a 1.5-million-dollar lawsuit where she was claiming all kinds of injuries, both physical and psychological and she was also claiming loss of income due to her injuries, all which she stated came as a result of my failure to properly and safely operate an automobile.

As for Mashonda, I had gotten word from Meagan that she was seeking to sell a story to the media in which she was gonna say how me and her did cocaine, and had wild sex just hours before I crashed.

Both Mashonda and Layla were pissing me the fuck off on one hand, and on the other hand I felt really hurt by the both of them. My attorney had reached out to both Mashonda, Layla and their attorneys because he was desperate to work out a settlement deal to get both of them to go somewhere, sit down, and shut the fuck up.

"Lance, if Mashonda's story gets out into the media you are screwed, and your credibility is shot. You can kiss a plea deal good-bye. The district attorney is not gonna deal. With Layla, she was in the car with you, so we need her to corroborate our asthma story, and if not we have no strong defense and you're looking at the worst-case scenario I laid out to you three months ago."

I sat there and contemplated what I should do. Being that I had asthma and I did have my asthma pump in my pants pocket at the time of my accident, to raise doubt in a jury's mind, my attorney was going to claim the cold weather had triggered an asthma attack. I was panicking because I couldn't breathe, and my asthma pump didn't help me. I had blacked out from lack of oxygen and that was what also aided in my car crash. In addition, my attorney was gonna state I had the cocaine on me, but I didn't have it in my system. Since the cops had only tested my blood-alcohol content, which was two times the legal limit, and they didn't test my blood for controlled substances, it meant that unless the district attorney had an eyewitness who saw me using cocaine, they could never argue I was high on coke.

However, with Layla and Mashonda suing me, we knew that we had to keep both of them happy or risk them throwing water all over the defenses we'd planned to use, especially since they were both direct eyewitnesses, not to mention mistresses.

"So what do you say I do?" I asked my lawyer.

"You gotta come up with the cash," he said matter-of-factly. "The best I can do is negotiate the best terms possible for you in a settlement agreement."

I couldn't believe how shit was just crumbling and falling down around me with each passing day. I mean, the math just wasn't adding up in my favor. Including my current attorney and the attorney I had when Nicole had me locked up, I had shelled out close to twenty thousand dollars in attorney fees, and I hadn't even gone to trial yet! Plus, I had cash tied up to secure my bail.

Over the next two weeks my attorney had reached a fifty-thousand-dollar settlement with Mashonda just so she would keep her fucking mouth shut about me and the cocaine. The deal we reached with Mashonda was under the guise that I was buying her life rights with the exclusive and sole purposes of creating a movie script or a book manuscript at my discretion. Under the deal that was not allowed to be disclosed by either side, there was a bullet-point list of things Mashonda was not allowed to discuss with anyone, including the media. As for Layla, I had to shell out a hundred thousand dollars in order for her to settle her lawsuit, which—like Mashonda's— also came with a strict confidentiality clause.

Those big hits of cash were having a really big effect on my pockets. I wasn't starving but it definitely didn't feel good at all. But it had taught my ass a really good lesson, a lesson I had already known, and that was that no pussy was ever really free.

Chapter Forty-four

It was now the middle of May. Four months had passed since I had been involved in the fatal car crash. As time progressed I was getting more hopeful that a plea deal was gonna be worked out with the district attorney and the families involved in the accident. The guy who I had critically injured in the accident had finally been released from the hospital. He would have to go through extensive rehab, but he was going to make a full recovery.

As time passed I continued on the straight and narrow. In fact for the past two weeks Nicole and I had started going to marriage counseling once a week for one hour per session. The marriage counseling helped, but in some sense it was a huge waste of money simply because the marriage counselor was discussing things with us that we already knew. We had been married for more than a decade and during that time we had seen it all, done it all, and experienced it all. Although he tried his best and I was committed to continuing on with it, I just wasn't certain how helpful it would be for us in the end.

"So, Lance, in your mind, tell me what you think the biggest problem is in your relationship?" the marriage counselor had asked me during our first session.

I contemplated his question before proceeding to answer.

"Listen, I know I have issues and a lot that I could do better, but if you want me to get at the root of things I would definitely say that it's the lack of sex."

When I said that, Nicole began squirming in her chair. The marriage counselor immediately told her she had to watch her body language so she wouldn't encourage a hostile environment, which wouldn't facilitate openness and honesty.

Nicole apologized and I continued on.

"Like, in all due respect, we don't even need to be here. All me and Nicole need to do is have more sex. When we first got married we had sex at least once a day but more like twice a day and I got breakfast in bed and all of that. But fast-forward and I'm lucky if we have sex once or twice a week! And breakfast in bed? I can't remember the last time I had that. It's like Nicole will make breakfast for our son and you would think she would make breakfast for me too at the same time, but that rarely happens. So with the lack of sex, and the lack of attention and affection that I get, intimacy gets tossed right out the window. So what I do is I substitute the intimacy that I used to get. I substitute it with my work and I stay at my computer trying my hardest to bang out bestselling books. Then I crave and soak up the praise I get from my fans that tell me how much they love my work."

Nicole couldn't take it anymore so she raised her hand and asked if she could interject something.

The marriage counselor nodded his head and Nicole spoke up. "Yeah, I just wanna say Lance always brings up the same thing. But I feel like this is less about sex and more about his low self-esteem. At the core of it, Lance is just a very, very, very insecure person and he needs so many things just to validate who he is. To me that's more of the problem."

I kept my mouth shut because there was no sense in arguing. I made a point that throughout the marriage counseling I would not argue with Nicole, and I would try my hardest to be cooperative. But no matter what she or the marriage counselor said, the root problem that we had is the same problem most marriages have, and that was the lack of sex.

It was mind-boggling to me because it was so simple to solve. All Nicole had to do was fuck me two to three times a day and things would be good. If she didn't, then we would be fooling ourselves if we ever thought we could or would dig out of the marriage mess we were in. That was what I believed, and I believed it with all sincerity. I truly loved Nicole, but I knew what I needed and sex was a really big need of mine. If we were going to make this work then we had to increase the frequency of sex. In the same sense sex to a marriage was like food to the human body.

So anyway, marriage counseling was cool, but what was scaring me was that I was starting to get comfortable again. I had moved out of my mother's crib and got an apartment in a high-rise condo building on Queens Boulevard, in the Forest Hills section of Queens. I was only renting it because with the court case looming over my head, it didn't make sense for me to go out and buy another asset that could possibly be taken away from me. If me and Nicole ended up in divorce then that would be just one more thing we would have to divvy up among us.

I didn't really have the apartment hooked up the way I wanted to hook it up. In fact, after living there for one month the apartment was pretty bare bones. But even though I didn't have the apartment hooked up the way I wanted it, that didn't stop me from inviting Meagan over to my place so I could chill with her.

Meagan lived in a very upscale town in New Jersey called Saddle River, so I was sure she was used to nothing but the best. My apartment definitely wasn't the best, but I didn't care if I wasn't able to impress her. I was just feeling mad lonely and I wanted her company more than anything.

"Hey, Mr. Lance," Meagan said as I opened my door for her and she sashayed her way into my apartment with some open-toe high heel shoes she was wearing. "I bought you something," she said as she handed me two different packages.

The first thing she gave me was a red velvet cake that she had picked up in Brooklyn from the famous Cake Man Raven. The other thing Meagan bought for me was brand-new king-sized bedsheets along with towels and different things for my bathroom.

I laughed and I told her she didn't have to do all of that.

"Lance, you told me that you're living without a shower curtain. Come on, man. I gotta look out for my people," she laughed and said.

I took Meagan on a quick tour of the apartment and she said that she really liked it.

"No, this is a nice place. You just gotta give it some personality and buy some furniture and you'll be straight," she said as she walked out onto the terrace.

It was still light outside so you couldn't really get the full effect of the view the terrace had.

"The view is sick once it gets dark," I explained.

"Is it?" she asked.

"Yeah, it is."

Me and Meagan had been talking on the phone almost every day for the past two weeks, and she was really a cool person. We had agreed I wouldn't do the interview with her until after all of my legal issues were resolved, but yet that didn't keep us from staying in touch.

Initially, I had the impression she was the gold-digging type, but as I got to know her I realized she wasn't like that at all. She definitely liked high-end stuff and she made no excuses for that, but at the same time she worked her ass off. She was smart as hell, so it was like her hard work afforded her the best things in life. But what I really liked about her was she wasn't just after trying to juice some dude—in fact, she was the exact opposite. Her thing was she wouldn't fuck with a nigga who didn't have his own and who didn't have his shit together simply because she was fearful of some dude trying to get to her heart simply so she could take care of his ass.

We had so much in common. We both shared the same zodiac sign. We both loved sports, especially basketball. We liked the same movies, the same food; it was almost scary how compatible we were.

"What?" Meagan asked when she caught me looking at her.

I smiled and shook my head. I told her that I was just staring at her because I couldn't believe how beautiful she was.

"Lance, I see how you got yourself into so much trouble. You just naturally know how to charm women and it comes across so believable."

"Believable? As in, I'm lying? Meagan, you know you look good, so knock it off."

"I'm okay," she said, trying to be modest.

"You know you're more than just okay. I can prove it."

"Prove it how?"

"By asking you a question, but you gotta be honest and don't dance around the question."

"Okay, shoot."

"When you take a shower, or when you're getting dressed or whatever, and you see yourself in the mirror. I'm talking about when you see yourself head-to-toe butterball naked, tell me yes or no, do you turn yourself on?"

"Lance!" Meagan said as she laughed and slapped me on my arm.

"See, you said you wouldn't dance around the question."

"Okay, okay, okay. See, when I see myself naked, yes, I like my body and I think I look good. I mean, I work out and I stay in shape so—"

I cut her off. "Nah, that's not what I asked you. I asked you do you turn yourself on when you see yourself naked."

Meagan was smiling and blushing from embarrassment.

"All right, you win! Yes, I do get turned on sometimes when I look at my body."

"See, case closed!"

"I am so embarrassed right now," she said as she laughed. "Like, is that normal or is there something abnormal and sick about that?"

Meagan made it clear she didn't want me to get it twisted about the fact that she was not into women.

"I mean, I might like what I'm working with, but your girl is still strictly dickly!"

"Come here," I said, smiling. I took Meagan by the hand and I guided her close to me and without asking I started to kiss her.

I could feel her resisting me and trying to pull away, but I wouldn't let her move.

"No. Don't fight me," I whispered while my eyes were still closed and my lips were still close to hers.

"Lance, I can't be kissing you. You're still married."

"Shhhhh," I said real softly and directly into Meagan's ear. I then kissed her on her earlobe and I worked my way down to her neck. I kissed her on her neck for about thirty seconds or so before moving back to her lips.

Meagan stopped resisting me and she kissed me real passionate and deep, and I could tell she didn't want to stop, as we kissed for about two minutes straight.

When we stopped kissing, she looked at me and smiled and then bowed her head and backed away from me.

"You are trouble, Lance. Trouble."

I didn't say anything because I knew I didn't have to say anything. Meagan was feeling me and I knew it.

It was just starting to get dark, and the crab legs that I had steamed were ready so I asked Meagan if she was ready to eat.

"Ehhh, yeah, I think that's a good idea," she playfully said.

Before long we were both laughing at the fact that I had no kitchen table and no chairs for us to sit on.

"Do you even have a couch, a chair, a La-Z-Boy? Something?" Meagan asked.

"Nah, but wait, just chill, I got this," I said and I went to my room, took the bedsheets off of it along with the pillows and I came back to my living room and I told her we could just put that on the floor and eat Indian-style.

"You know what?" Meagan asked rhetorically as she laughed.

"It'll be cool," I said and I began placing the sheets on the floor.

Meagan took her shoes off and reminded me she was used to eating at high-end places like Mr. Chow or Nobu.

"This is gonna be better than all of that," I said. I went to the kitchen and got the crab legs and two plates and took that to the living room and then I went back and got a bottle of wine and two wineglasses.

"So this is it? Just crab legs?"

"Yeah, that's all I made."

"What happened to the corn, the broccoli, the baked potato?" Meagan said in a jokingly sarcastic way. "But you know, I ain't even mad at you. This is gonna be fun. Even though crab legs is soooo *not* the thing you eat on a first date."

Meagan was right, crab legs was a messy thing to eat, so therefore it wasn't the most romantic thing to eat.

"Oh, so this is a date, then?" I asked.

"You better leave me alone," she said as she got up and went to the kitchen. "Please tell me you at least have some butter in your refrigerator."

I at least had butter, and so Meagan melted some butter so that we could dip the crabmeat into it.

"How you gonna eat crab legs without butter?" she asked as she shook her head.

It took us about twenty minutes to eat the crab legs and Meagan helped me clear the dishes and then we started watching a movie while we drank the wine and ate the red velvet cake she had brought.

"I'm happy I came over to see you."

"I'm happy you came over too," I said as we lay next to each other on top of the blankets. The room was dark, other than the light that the flat-screen television produced.

I started kissing Meagan again and this time she kissed me back with no hesitation. I moved my hand to her ass and felt on it to see what she would do, and she didn't take offense. She was wearing a blouse and a skirt so I decided to slide my hand up her skirt and soon I was feeling her bare ass.

"I love the way you kiss me," she said through a partial moan.

I rolled onto my back and I pulled her on top of me and continued to kiss her as I slid her skirt all the way up and squeezed both of her butt cheeks as hard as I could with my hands. I could tell Meagan was getting more and more turned on because she kissed me more and more passionately.

Before she could change her mind, I stood up and picked her up in the process and then I slowly put her back down on the floor while managing to undo her skirt, which made it easier for me to slide it off.

"You make me sick! You do know that, right?" Meagan asked.

"I'll make up for it. I promise," I said as I slid off her purple thong and buried my head between her legs and started eating her pussy.

If there was one thing that marriage had taught me, it definitely had taught me how to eat the lining out of a pussy and drive a chick insane.

Eating Meagan out was so easy to do simply because she had the biggest clit and the fattest pussy I had ever seen in my life.

"Your pussy is turning me on," I said as I came up for air.

"You like it?" she asked through heavy breathing.

"I love it!" I said and then I went back to work sucking on her clit.

In minutes Meagan was cumming and I was feeling so good. I had seen her sexy ass on television for years, long before I had even thought about writing books, and now here I was eating her out and making her cum and about to fuck her.

"I wantchu," she said to me after she had regained her composure from nutting.

I stood up and I took my clothes off and I was surprised that my dick wasn't already rock-ass hard.

"I don't have a condom," I said to Meagan.

Meagan looked at me and she started to unbutton her top.

"It's okay. I just wanna feel your dick inside of me."

I couldn't believe her response, but I was having my doubts. That was until I looked down at her body and all logic and reasoning went out the window. If she was willing to fuck me raw, there was no way I was gonna pass that shit up.

Meagan was on the floor sitting up while I was standing up so my dick was parallel to her face. And since I wasn't hard yet I wanted her to suck my dick until I was rock hard. So without asking I moved in and held my dick right to her face, assuming that she was just gonna automatically start sucking it.

"Eh-uhm. I'm sorry, baby, but I just don't do that," she said to me.

"You don't suck dick?" I asked, real surprised.

She shook her head and said no.

Then she stood up and started kissing on my chest and my neck while she stroked my dick until it was hard. Once it was hard, I guided her back to the floor and I was gonna fuck her missionary style. But from the ten seconds it took for her to lay down and spread her legs, my dick went soft.

"What the fuck is going on?" I said to myself.

"You okay?" Meagan asked.

"Yeah, I'm good," I said even though on the inside I was panicking like a motherfucker because never before in my thirty-four years had my dick failed me. It had always been standing at attention and ready for war. But at that moment my dick was not cooperating at all.

So I started eating Meagan out again and her pussy was dripping wet and she was still responding good to my tongue. Just hearing her moan was enough to turn me on again and in seconds my dick was good and ready to go.

"Stand up, let's do this doggie style," I instructed.

"I wanna feel that shit," Meagan said as she stood up.

Just that quick I could feel my shit getting soft again. So I was really in freaked-out panic mode. I grabbed the shaft of my dick and was squeezing on it to try to keep it hard while I tried to slip it into her pussy, but shit just wasn't happening.

"Baby, you sure you okay?" Meagan asked me. "You can run and get a condom if you want to, it's just that I'm allergic to latex," she said, assuming the reason my dick wasn't getting hard was because of the lack of a condom.

I knew that if anything, a condom was really gonna make my shit go soft because I always felt less with a condom. But at the same time I knew I had to do some serious damage control and I had to do it fast. I was racking my brain trying my hardest to figure out what to say or do.

"Meagan, you know what? I'm sorry. It's not the condom thing and it's definitely not you. It's just that my mind is in another place. Earlier today me and Nicole—"

She cut me off because once I brought up my wife's name she knew exactly where I was going.

"Lance, it's fine. Don't worry. Really, it's fine. I totally understand. We don't have to do anything. We can just chill and finish the movie," she said.

I visibly blew air from my lungs and I had never been so mad with myself, or felt so embarrassed and humbled and disappointed, all at the same time, as I did at that moment.

Meagan started to get dressed and while she did I ran both of my hands slowly down my face.

"You probably would have killed me with that thing," Meagan joked as she yanked on my dick.

I looked at her and she smilcd.

I couldn't tell if she had said that to try and boost my ego or if she had really bought my line of crap about my mind being on my wife. All I knew was I wanted to find the nearest hole in the ground and stick my head in there so I wouldn't have to face the moment that was at hand.

"A man's dick can't do what his mind ain't into," she said as she stood on her tippy-toes and kissed me on the cheek.

I nodded my head and hugged her, and all I could think about was how fucking lame I must have looked at that moment. But it was what it was. All I knew was that I had to go to the doctor ASAP because there was no way in hell I was gonna go through that shit again with my dick not cooperating.

Chapter Forty-five

It was now the first week in June. Two weeks had passed since my non-performance incident with Meagan, and what was wild was since that incident she had started calling me more than ever, just as Steve had predicted she would do.

Steve laughed his ass off at me when I told him what had went down between me and Meagan. But he reassured me I just had a case of whiskey dick.

"That shit happens to the best of us. But I guarantee you that Meagan is gonna be calling your ass much more now that that shit happened on her watch."

I looked at Steve kinda confused.

"See, you gotta understand her head is gonna be fucked-up. You walking around mad as hell at yourself because homeboy wouldn't work when you needed him to. But Meagan is walking around, feeling mad, inadequate, right now. She's feeling like she wasn't hot enough, she doesn't turn you on, her pussy is whack, all of that shit is running through her head. So until you fuck the hell out of her, she is gonna be calling you just to reassure herself you're not completely done with her."

I didn't think Steve was right at the time, but when Meagan started to call excessively and kept wanting us to go out and asking if she could come over again, I knew Steve had hit the nail on the head.

I would speak to Meagan on the phone at length, but not once did she bring up my whiskey dick. But I made sure to duck her and make excuses each time she tried to hook up with me. I ducked her for two reasons. One reason was because—regardless of what Steve had been saying—I still wanted to speak to my doctor so I could know for sure what the deal was with me and my limp-dick syndrome. The other reason I had been ducking Meagan was because my lawyer had informed me it was looking highly likely we were going to be able to work out a favorable plea deal. I had been praying for a good outcome and I didn't want to jinx myself by messing with Meagan.

It was funny how with me it always took some kind of tragic shit to get me to focus on doing what was right. But I had begun to pray like I had never prayed before. I prayed about five times a day for God's mercy concerning my case, and it was looking a lot like my prayers were gonna be answered.

On June 18, almost six months to the day since I had the accident, my lawyer called me and told me to come into his office as soon as I could. When I hung up the phone with him, my heart was beating a mile a minute because I didn't know if he had good news for me or bad news. So without hesitation and without calling him back and asking him why he wanted me to come in, I had Steve come scoop me up and take me over to see him.

"Mr. Thomas," my lawyer said with a smile on his face when I walked into his office.

"All I wanna hear is good news," I responded.

"I learned from day one on this job you always deliver good news in person and bad news over the phone. It usually works out better that way."

I nodded my head and chuckled at my lawyer, but I was ready for him to cut the small talk and get right to the matter at hand.

"So it looks like we had an ace in the hole that'll keep you outta jail."

Immediately a smile came across my face and I instantly felt some relief sweeping through my body.

"Really? So what was the ace in the hole?"

"Olivia Rodriguez's family," my attorney said as he got up from the conference table.

"Apparently, Olivia's family is extremely religious and they came to the conclusion this entire ordeal was God's will. They felt to recommend jail time for you would be undue justice and it would show vindictiveness on their part."

When I heard those words, I almost fell off of my chair.

"Are you serious?"

My attorney nodded his head.

"Well, what about the other family?"

"They have the complete opposite disposition of the other family. They want jail time for you."

"Really? But I mean—I thought he had recovered and was doing much better," I said. I didn't know how to feel. I just couldn't understand how the family who had lost their family member could recommend no jail time, and the family with the survivor of the accident could want to go so hard.

"That's definitely working in our favor, but I can tell you this—and this is part of the reason why I asked you to come in—I can tell you that the only way they're gonna be willing to bend is based on dollars."

"What do you mean?"

"Lance, this is gonna come down to money. The family is being advised by an attorney and I'm sure this is a tactic for them to be able to up the ante."

I was confused because I wasn't sure what my attorney was getting at.

"Your car insurance policy is gonna pay out the max that they can pay out based on the limits of your policy. So after paying for Mr. Anderson's medical bills, the insurance company will have about a half a million dollars to split between the two families. And although two-hundred-fifty thousand dollars is a lot of money, how things are gonna be viewed by Mr. Anderson's family is with no jail time, there really is no form of punishment that would cause the prevention of such accidents in the future. Therefore they'll want you to pay a staggering amount of money that will serve as a form of punishment for you."

"Basically, you mean punitive damages?"

My attorney nodded.

"So when you say *a staggering amount,* what does that mean in terms of real money?"

"Well, to put it in everyday language, it's gonna be an amount that breaks you."

"Over seven figures?"

"Definitely."

"Whoa," I said.

"Lance, you gotta look at it like this: Your accident took someone's life and hampered someone else's life in a major way. Then you have to look at the fact that you had a couple ready to get married and in a flash that's taken away, so all of those variables come with a value attached to it. You also have to look at the fact that unless these charges are knocked down under a plea deal, you're looking at twenty-five years in prison, and there is no dollar value you can put on your freedom."

My attorney wanted to get a snapshot picture of all of my assets so he could see what I was working with and what my viability would be in terms of being able to compensate the victim's families.

Like most people, a lot of my net worth was tied up in my house. My house was valued at 1.2 million and there was about four hundred and fifty thousand in equity in the house. I had a little over one hundred thousand in liquid cash, and I still had two luxury cars I owned that together were worth over a hundred thousand. Then of course I had the books I had written and the royalties that those books brought on a yearly basis.

"I can tell you that I'll go as hard for you as I can and try to get them to take a half a million dollars, but they are gonna counter that by asking for a minimum of one million dollars."

"But I don't have that. So does this mean I have to sell my house and all the shit that I own?"

"Well, not necessarily, but your lifestyle may change, make no mistake about that. You'll likely have to take out another mortgage on the property in order to pull out the equity, and your cars are gonna have to go."

"But that still doesn't get me to the million dollar figure."

"I understand that, and that is where we have a little leverage to keep you out of prison."

"You're losing me," I said to my lawyer.

"If we ultimately settle on one million dollars, you'll pay half of that in cash and the other half you'll pay over the course of five years. But what we'll argue is that you need to be out of prison to facilitate earning the money to pay off the settlement amount. Meaning if you're locked up, you can't properly promote your books, you'll likely never get another publishing contract, and therefore to send you to prison would punish you, but it wouldn't be an all-encompassing punishment that also adequately served the needs of the victims."

I paused for a moment and didn't say anything. All I could think about was how one decision, one bad decision on my part, was in an instant going to reverse a ton of hard work on my part.

"Lance, twenty-five years in prison is the alternative."

I looked at him and I knew I wasn't built for prison. As I sat there, I remember the news stories right after the accident. I remember seeing the pain, hurt, and anger that the family members of the victims had expressed at a few of the news conferences. In my heart, I knew no amount of money would be just punishment for me, so if that was the only hardship I would have to endure, then so be it. I would endure it and I would endure it, gracefully and humbly.

Chapter Forty-six

Nicole had admirably gone above and beyond her call of duty as a wife. While she had exhausted every ounce of energy and hope she had in trying to preserve our marriage, at the end of the day she was a human being and all human beings are limited. For Nicole, in spite of the marriage counseling we had been going to, she ultimately had enough and decided she was going to go through with the divorce once we had been separated for one year, which was the legal procedure in New York.

I understood Nicole's decision, and I wasn't bitter about it. I was very disappointed, but after all that I had put Nicole through throughout the years, there was no way I could have any kind of resentment toward her. All I had was love and admiration for her.

I can't say I blamed her, especially after I delivered the news to her that everything she and I had built together in terms of our home and our savings were about to be wiped out due to the settlement agreement I had come to with my victims and their families.

The last Wednesday in June was the last day of school for my son LL. And unfortunately I couldn't be there to pick him up because I was at a press conference at the district attorney's office. Not being there for LL ate at me and I knew I had to really start making time to rebound with LL or risk him starting to see me in a less admirable light.

At the press conference, the DA was basically informing the media about the terms of the settlement as well as the plea deal that had been reached, and it was at the press conference that I, for the first time, had got a chance to publicly address and apologize to the families. It was funny I was a full-time writer, so usually I was good with words, but in this case I had no idea what I was going to say. I had stayed up all night long trying to come up with the right words to say, but I continually drew blanks. Yeah, I didn't know what I was going to say, but I knew I would speak from the heart. I blew air from my lungs as I approached the podium to speak.

"I promise to be brief, simply because there are no words in the human language that can truly express what it is I would like to say to the family and friends of Olivia Rodriguez and also to Ryan Anderson and his family and friends as well. But let me start by saying from the bottom of my heart, I apologize and I am deeply sorry for the pain and destruction I know I have caused anyone and everyone involved in this ordeal. Particularly, I want to apologize to the Rodriguez family and to Ryan Anderson." I paused and had to compose myself because I was seconds from getting choked up. Then I continued on.

"On a cold and snowy night in January, after a night of partying, I admittedly behaved out of control like a child, not like an adult, or like a husband, or like a father. I didn't even behave like a man. I was a coward on that night. And like a coward I got behind the wheel of an automobile while being under the influence alcohol, which impaired my ability to drive and which ultimately lead me to driving my car in the wrong direction on Flatbush Avenue, where I struck and killed Olivia and badly injured Ryan, as well as injured a young lady who was riding in my car, and for that I am beyond sorry. But my vow and pledge is to make amends to both families to the best of my ability and I will work as hard as I can to educate people on the ill effects of drinking and driving. This ordeal is not about me, it's about the victims and therefore I will end my statement by once again expressing my deepest sorrows."

I stepped away from the podium and I immediately walked over to Ryan Anderson and I stuck out my hand. My heart pounded and truthfully I expected him to stand up and punch me in the face because that was what I deserved. But Ryan was graceful. He stood up and he extended his hand to mine. I gripped his hand and while I gave him a ghetto hug and embraced him, I spoke into his ear while all of the photographers in the room flashed cameras nonstop.

Only Ryan could hear what I was saying. "Ryan, I'm sorry, man. I took something from you that can never be replaced. You did all the right things and you didn't deserve this. I want you to know you'll always be more of a man than I ever will be. And this is a burden I will carry for the rest of my life."

I stepped away from Ryan and he sort of had a twisted look on his face. He looked at me and nodded his head but didn't say anything.

I totally understood Ryan's reaction toward me because I was sure he wanted to knock the shit out of me.

I then took my place next to my attorney and waited for the press conference to conclude. Once it was over the media swarmed me and they asked me what I had said to Ryan.

"I just apologized to him and told him he was more of a man than I was."

"Mr. Thomas, I noticed that your wife isn't here. Is it true you two are going through a divorce?" another reporter asked.

"I'd rather not comment on that, but I will say my wife is also a victim in this whole ordeal."

"Is there anything else you'd like to say to the victims?"

"Well, this isn't about me, like I already said, so with all due respect I would just like to have the attention squarely where it should be and that is on the nature of what I did. Drinking and driving is wrong and I'm going to work to prevent accidents, such as the one I caused, from happening. That's really all I have for you guys, so if you don't mind I'm gonna be on my way."

I had already signed the settlement agreement earlier that morning before the start of the press conference. Where we ended up was I would pay a total of $1.3 million, with $1.1 million going to Ryan Anderson and the other two hundred thousand going to a charity that Olivia's family would choose. I had thirty days to come up with a half-million dollars and then on each August 1, starting in the following year, I would have to make a payment of two hundred thousand dollars for the next four years. As a form of security, I had to sign off and okay that 50 percent of all of my future advances and royalties would be paid directly to the attorney representing the victims. He would place the money into an escrow account in order to ensure the victims would get their money.

"Lance, hey?" Meagan said as she walked up to me and gave me a hug.

"Hey, baby, I didn't even see you. You were here the whole time?"

"Yeah, I was."

"So, I guess now is as good a time as any for us to do that interview I had been promising you."

"No. We got time for that. I'm not stressing it. How are you? I haven't heard from you."

"I'm good, now that this is over."

"Yeah, I figured you had a lot on your mind and so I was just trying to give you your space."

"I appreciate that. So what's up witchu? You still looking sexy as ever."

"I just been working, nothing major, same old thing."

"But I do wanna hang out with you whenever you get some time."

I looked at her and chuckled a little bit.

"What's so funny?"

I told her to come closer so I could whisper something in her ear.

"Remember when you said that your pussy was passport pussy?"

Meagan started laughing and she punched me.

"You know I was under the influence when I said that!"

"I don't know about that, but anyway, what I'm getting at is next week my son's AAU team is gonna be playing for the national championship down in Orlando and I would love for you to go with me. All expenses on me!"

"What day?" Meagan asked without hesitation.

"Well, we would leave on the fifth and we'll be back on the eighth," I said. I knew I was pretty pathetic, but I just couldn't help myself. I also knew that with the $1.3 million settlement I was gonna be beyond broke and I needed to be preserving as much cash as I could instead of making plans to trick it on Meagan.

She thought for a while and then she looked at the calendar on her phone.

"Yeah, I can do that, I gotta switch some things around, but that sounds like fun. You sure that would be okay, though?"

Actually, I knew it probably wouldn't be smart for LL to see me with another woman like that, but it was all good because I knew I would figure something out by the time July came around.

"I wouldn't have asked you if I didn't think so," I responded.

"Oh, okay. I'm so excited now!"

"Meagan, you're funny."

Meagan said she loved going away. It didn't matter where she was going, just the thought of traveling turned her on.

"It's like the days leading up to the trip is the biggest and best form of foreplay for me," she joked.

"Okay, that's what I'm talking about. So we gonna get it on and poppin' then."

I was able to say that with some renewed confidence, because against my doctor's wishes I had persuaded him to write me a prescription for Viagra, and therefore, I knew that I wasn't gonna have another repeat failed performance with Meagan.

It was really gonna be on and poppin' and I was definitely planning on handling my business the right way this time with Meagan.

Chapter Forty-seven

I had a consistent pattern in my life of being blessed by God one minute and then being set up by the devil the next minute. So, since it was a pattern I had been through before, I should have seen the setup coming.

On July 4, just about a week after my case had settled with the victims, my agent, whose nick-name is Tony Bony, called me and told me he had a verbal commitment from the publishing company for my new book deal. He was able to negotiate a two-book publishing contract for six hundred thousand dollars.

Six hundred thousand dollars was a lot of money. It was a hundred thousand more than I had gotten for my first contract. Although my agent was gonna get 15 percent of that, and then the victims of my accident would get 50 percent of it, I was still cool with it because to me it was still a blessing and at least I knew I would be able to eat a little something.

Tony Bony was a cool-ass white man who was based out of Hollywood, but he was always back and forth between New York and L.A. So with his urging, I had decided to hang out with him and two of his other clients so we could celebrate my new deal.

He was a cool agent and we got along very well. We had decided to go to the China Club near Times Square and when I got there Tony was waiting near the front entrance.

"Macaroni Tony! What's the deal?" I asked as I gave him a pound.

"Tony, this is Steve, my partner in crime. Steve, this is the super agent Tony Bony, aka Macaroni Tony."

Steve and Tony both laughed as they gave each other a pound. After a few minutes of small talk, we went inside and waited near the bar for Tony's other clients to get to the club.

Tony bought the first round of drinks and he told us that he had us for the entire night.

"Whatever y'all want it's on me tonight," Tony boasted.

In my head I laughed because I knew Tony was about to earn ninety thousand dollars off of my black ass so in actuality the night was really on me.

"I got that candy if you want some," Tony hollered into my ear over the music.

"Nah, I ain't fucking with that shit. It already got my ass in enough trouble."

"I got a car for you! You don't gotta worry about that old shit. You party with me, you party right and you party safe. Come on, Lance," Tony urged.

"Nah, I'm good," I said and I was proud of myself for standing up and being man enough to say I wasn't fucking with no cocaine.

Just as Tony started to tell me about these white chicks and these Asian chicks he had coming through to meet up with him, I turned and looked and I see Steve hugging on some chick and immediately I knew it was Felicia, who was Mashonda's cousin.

"What the fuck?" I said out loud but not loud enough for Steve to hear me.

"Yo, Lance," Steve hollered out to get my attention.

"You remember her?"

"Hey, Lance," Felicia said to me while trying to give me a hug. But I blocked her from giving me a hug and I walked off to the side and motioned for Steve to come talk to me for a second.

"What the fuck is she doing here? And I know Mashonda isn't with her."

"I told her to come through. You know I'm fucking that."

"Nah, I didn't know you was fucking her, but why would you be fucking her and why the hell would you tell her to come to the club if you know about my issues with Mashonda?"

"Man, fuck all that bullshit!"

"Bullshit? That bitch cost me fifty Gs!"

"Lance, just chill, nigga."

I walked off and I was vexed like a motherfucker. That was a bitch-ass move Steve had pulled because as far as I was concerned, I was the type of person where I just believed if I wasn't cool with somebody it meant I also wasn't cool with that person's crew of friends too. So that meant by default any of my close friends should fall in line and also not be cool with somebody just to show their loyalty to me.

"Lance!" Steve said as he caught up to me.

"Steve, listen, I'm gonna just chill with Tony and you do your thing. Just do you."

"Yo, Mashonda's moms is coming through too, you—"

"What the fuck? So this is just gonna be one big family reunion?"

"Lance, just hear me out. Mashonda got over on you, but so the fuck what? Her moms is on your dick too. So, just fuck the moms and that's how you can get back at Mashonda."

"What are you talking about?" I asked Steve.

"Felicia told me that Joy wants to fuck you. If I was you, I'd definitely hit that."

I paused for a moment and finished my drink before responding. I was really getting tired of the drama and the bullshit. I mean, I was who I was and I did my thing, but I didn't need more bullshit in my life.

"Steve, I don't trust them bitches. You can fuck with them if you want to, but they ain't getting my ass twice."

Just as I said that, Mashonda's mother walks up to me and Steve and she said what's up to Steve and she gave a kiss on the cheek.

"I wanna talk to you," Joy said to me and she took me by the hand and pulled me to the side.

I had to admit Joy was looking good as hell. She was wearing some white booty shorts, white high heels, and a white top that showed off her cleavage.

"I just wanted to tell you that shit Mashonda pulled—that shit wasn't right. I tried to talk to her but—"

"Joy, it's all good," I said as I cut her off. "Listen, I'm gonna be right back. My agent invited me here and I don't wanna be rude."

I walked away from Joy, Steve, and Felicia. I had no intentions of fucking with them for the rest of that night. But I had to admit Joy did not look like a woman who was in her early forties. If things hadn't gone down the way they had with Mashonda getting over on me, I woulda fucked her mother in a heartbeat.

About an hour later, I found myself surrounded by some of the most beautiful white girls I had ever seen. I don't know who in the club had been paid off, but someone must have, because right where we were partying, the white chicks and the Asian chicks were snorting lines of cocaine as if it were legal.

"Didn't I tell you I know how to party?" Tony said to me as he gave me a pound and handed me something with the same hand that he had given me a pound with.

I looked in my hand and saw a pill.

"It's X!" he shouted into my ear.

By that time the liquor had gotten to me and I knew I should probably leave before I ended up in trouble that I didn't want to be in.

"You're about to sign a six hundred thousand dollar deal! You're allowed!" Tony urged.

This was definitely one of those moments from the old school cartoons where there was a devil on one shoulder and an angel on the other shoulder. The devil was telling me to fuck everything and to live it up and have a good time. But the angel was trying very hard to remind me the last time I was in this position, someone ended up dead and I needed to be smart.

"Nah, I'm good," I said to Tony. I was feeling good that I had listened to the angel on my right shoulder.

"You're joking, right?" Tony asked.

I didn't immediately respond and he was persistent.

So with his urging, I popped the pill into my mouth and swallowed it. That had been the first time I'd tried Ecstasy so I wasn't sure what to expect. But after about ten minutes, the music became louder to me and everything just felt much more intense in a very good way. I was feeling better than I had ever felt in my life. It was almost as if I was having a non-stop orgasm—that was just how good I felt.

I started dancing with a white girl who I had been staring at the entire night. She had some big titties, no ass, and no rhythm, but it didn't matter at all. All I knew was she was sexy as shit with green eyes and blond hair. Without even saying two words to her, I just leaned in and started tongue kissing her while I was dancing with her and it wasn't just a quick kiss, it was more like a three-minute deep-tongue kiss. I felt so good and so horny I was thinking about trying to undress her and fucking her right there on the dance floor.

She pushed herself away from me and gave me a smile and told me she would be right back.

"What's your name?"

"Angela," she said as she walked away.

"I see you having a good time now!" Tony said to me as he gave me another pound and at the same time put another E pill in my hand.

Without hesitation I popped another pill in my mouth and then a few minutes later I remember dancing and guzzling a bottle of Moët. Steve caught up to me and I was sure he could tell that I was in a much better mood than I had been in.

"You good?" Steve asked.

"Yeah, yeah, I'm good. Just trying to bag me a little snow bunny," I said as I gave Steve a pound.

"That's what's up! But you need to leave with my ass and handle your business with Joy."

Right as Steve said that, the white girl, Angela, walked back up to me and this time she initiated the kiss.

"That's the six hundred thousand dollar man right there!" my agent shouted for the world to hear while Angela kissed me.

By this time the club was packed to capacity and it was real hard to move. But I did feel somebody grabbing on me.

"Lance, where's your phone?" Joy said to me.

I just looked at her like she was stupid because now she was fucking up my high and she was cock-blocking what I had going on with Angela.

"Joy, I'm good. I'm good," I shouted over the music. I was hoping she got the hint that I wasn't trying to take her number or give her mine.

"Take my number and make sure you call me," she said.

Right at that moment, Angela bent down on the dance floor and she unzipped my pants and started sucking my dick right there on the dance floor. It was dark so it was hard for anyone to see what she was doing. The strobe lights would bring bright light to our area every so often, and when it did, I was sure that everyone in that immediate area knew what was up.

"Yo, I'll get it from Steve later on. Just make sure he has it, a'ight?" I said to Joy as I saw her standing there with her phone out as if she was about to put my number into her phone.

"Oh, oh, okay," she said with a surprised tone like she had finally gotten it. But I also think she saw Angela sucking my dick and that was how she got the message.

I hoisted the bottle of Moët to my mouth and guzzled it some more and I knew either the E pills were a natural aphrodisiac or Angela had the best head game in the world, but I felt like it was only gonna be another few minutes before I came. Angela stood up and I wanted to push her head right back down to my dick because I definitely didn't want her to stop.

"This is what I had walked away to go and get," Angela said to me as she pressed up against me and handed me a condom.

A big smile came across my face and I asked her if she wanted me to put the condom on right then and there.

She didn't say anything, but she did turn around and backed her little ass up into my dick. So I took that as my cue she definitely was ready to get fucked right then and there. I put the bottle of Moët on the ground and I quickly slid the condom over my dick and slipped my dick under Angela's dress until I found her wet spot. She wasn't wearing any panties so that gave me easy access to her tight pussy.

Angela was slightly bent over and it looked as if we were just dirty dancing and grinding on each other. But there was a whole lot more going on. I was fucking a white girl for the first time in my life and it was easily feeling like the best pussy I had ever had. When I finally came after about three minutes, I felt like I was gonna black out, simply because I had never came so hard in my life.

Right at that moment, as good as I felt, I knew my life wasn't just out of control—it was dangerously out of control! I also knew that just as surely as God had blessed me with a new contract for six hundred thousand dollars, that the devil had been right there lurking and waiting for a chance to bring me down. The only thing was I just had no idea how closely the devil had truly been lurking.

Chapter Forty-eight

The car that my agent had taken me to and from the club was the best thing in the world, because by the time I left the club at three in the morning I was in no shape to drive. What was worse was by the time I got home I was feeling sick as a dog, but I couldn't go to sleep because I knew I had to be back up at six that morning so that me and LL could go to the airport for our trip to the basketball tournament in Orlando.

After taking Alka-Seltzer and eating a ton of oranges, I dragged myself into the shower and stayed there for about a half hour. I really felt like shit. Hangover didn't do me any justice in explaining how bad I felt. But as I walked into my room and gathered clothes to bring with me on the trip, I knew that laying down on my bed even for just a second would be the worst thing in the world for me to do. My cell phone started to vibrate and I didn't even have the energy to walk over to the phone, but I eventually answered it.

"Hey, just checking to see if you were up," Meagan said on the other end.

"Thank you. Yeah, I'm up. I'm getting ready now," I said, trying my hardest to mask any of the hangover effects.

"Lance, I am so excited. You know, I never told you this, but I have never even been to Disney World," she said. She was sounding way too cheery and way too chipper, especially since I had the worst pounding headache in the world.

We spoke on the phone for a little while longer and before we hung up I confirmed everything with Meagan and told her I would see her when I got to the airport. I had purchased a round-trip plane ticket for her so she would be on the same plane with me and LL and the rest of the team, but I made sure she wasn't seated next to us. I also booked her hotel room in the same resort we were staying at, only we were on the fifth floor and she would be staying on the sixth floor.

My plan was to keep Meagan away from LL as well as away from any of the other parents of the kids who were on his team. Being that she was only going to be sleeping one floor above me, I was planning on going to her room when LL went to sleep and also when we took the kids to Disney World I was gonna make it where Meagan would be there already and then I would just bump into her as if it were a coincidence. Since Nicole couldn't make it down to Orlando, I didn't want LL to see me with any other females because I was really worried about the message I was sending to him. I mean, as fucked-up as I was I didn't want LL to grow up and be even remotely like me.

As time was flying by, Nicole called me and told me LL was up, dressed, and ready to go and that she would be at my apartment in twenty minutes to take us to the airport, being that I couldn't drive.

When Nicole arrived I got in the car, trying my hardest to be as normal as possible and not let on to my hangover.

"Hey, what's up, superstar?" I said to LL, who was dressed in full LeBron James gear.

"You supposed to call me MVP," he said, correcting me.

"LL, what did I tell you about that?" Nicole said as she turned down the radio.

"I know, Mom, but I'm just doing what we learned in Sunday school. They said that we can speak things into existence and since I wanna win the MVP at the tournament, I'm speaking it into existence."

I looked at Nicole and all I could do was smile. At the same time I wished I was as focused on God as my eleven-year-old son was.

"You okay?" Nicole asked.

"Yeah. I'm good. Just real tired. But I'll sleep on the plane, so it's okay."

"Well, they don't have any games or anything today, do they?" Nicole asked.

"Nah, today and tonight is a free time for them. So we'll probably hang out in the hotel until about three o'clock and then we'll take them to the amusement parks. This way it's not just about basketball and then tomorrow they have their semifinal game, and if they win, then the next day they'll play for the championship," I explained.

LL then spoke up and he said his coach told the team that the past MVPs of that tournament all ended up in *Sports Illustrated* and they were ranked in the top twenty-five sixth graders in the country.

"You know, Lance, see, this is a little crazy! Why are they ranking kids in the sixth grade? Why don't they just let them play the game and have fun? This is exactly how these athletes get so spoiled and walk around like the world owes them something. It's because of being told that they're all of that from the time they can walk."

"It is what it is." I replied. "But there's also gonna be college scouts there."

"For sixth graders?" Nicole said with a laugh.

Nicole really didn't understand just how good LL was. He was playing for an AAU team called Riverside. He wasn't just on the team, he was one of the stars of the team. So with Riverside's history of producing some of the greatest players to ever come out of New York City, LL was pretty much a shoo-in to get a basketball scholarship in six years.

We finally arrived at the airport and Nicole pulled to the curb. She got out of the car and gave me a hug and a kiss on the cheek. Then she hugged LL real tight. Even with the crazy hangover I was feeling, it didn't prevent me from feeling real nostalgic like the three of us were a family again. I loved that feeling.

"Be good," she said to LL.

"Okay. I love you, Mommy," he said as he threw his bag over his shoulder and whipped out his PSP.

"I love you," Nicole replied.

"Nicole, I'll call you later on," I said before me and LL walked into the terminal.

It was a little past six-thirty in the morning and our flight wasn't until 8:00 a.m., so after we checked in me and LL waited at the flight gate and as he played with his PSP I got a little emotional because I wished I could just do right and not feel this need to constantly step out on Nicole. Like I knew I was so blessed and yet I was always fucking up those blessings. Yet at the same time, I was who I was and therefore it was hard for me to change. But it was clear God had wanted it just one way and that was with the family unit intact. I knew that had I just always stayed focused and done right, this trip to Orlando would have been ten times more fulfilling for me than it was. It woulda been more fulfilling simply because I was proud of my son for so many reasons that extended beyond basketball, and for me to be able to travel with him and support him in something he loved to do was so much more than I deserved and could have ever hoped for. But the reason I say it could have been more fulfilling was because I knew had LL known the true character of his father then he wouldn't have been as proud of me as I was of him.

Before long both LL and I had dozed off right next to each other. Eventually I felt a tap on my shoulder and I opened my eyes to see Meagan standing in front of me, looking sexier than I'd ever seen her look. She had some dark shades on and she had a baseball cap on in order to help hide her identity since she was a television personality. Even with the hat and the shades she still looked sexy.

She mouthed the word *hi* without actually saying anything because she didn't want to wake up LL. So I stood up and I talked to her for a minute.

"Did you just get here?" I asked.

"Yeah, I hit a ton of traffic on the George Washington Bridge. But I'm good because I just have this one carry-on that I'm bringing."

"Yo, I am feeling so fucked-up right now. I didn't tell you but I'm getting ready to sign a new deal for six hundred thousand. My agent took me out last night and we celebrated, but I drank way too much."

"Wow, Lance, that is good. I'm so happy for you. You should go get some ginger ale or something to help settle your stomach."

"Nah, I'll just chill. I'll be all right by the time we land."

After I said that to her I told her what the plan was for the kids and I would come up to her room and see her as soon as the kids got involved in their first activity.

"Okay. I'm still so excited! I feel like a little kid on Christmas eve," Meagan smiled and said. "Lance, is that your son?"

I nodded.

"He is such a cutie. I can't wait to see him play," she said before she walked over to another area and took a seat and started reading *Essence* magazine.

We had a very smooth flight to Orlando and after the flight had landed Meagan took a cab over to where we were staying, while LL and I and the rest of the team with the parents were picked up in a chartered van and chauffeured over to the Walt Disney World Resort, which is where we were staying.

By the time everyone got settled into their rooms it was a little after one-thirty in the afternoon. LL was like an Energizer bunny and he was bouncing off the walls, ready to jet from the room and go have fun with his teammates.

Although I wanted to jump in the bed and go right to sleep, I knew I couldn't be selfish and I had to hang with LL in order to make him happy. So we left our room and went down to the arcade and played video games and pool for about an hour or so until it was time to eat lunch at three o'clock.

At three o'clock everyone on the team and parents met up in one of the restaurants located on the second floor of the resort. Since all of our accommodations were all-inclusive, it meant the kids and the parents could all eat until their heart's content. As parents, we didn't have to tell the kids twice that all of the food was free because they had a field day. They stuffed their faces with hamburgers, French fries, pizza, soda, and ice cream. It was amazing watching them eat so much food. When they were done eating everyone retreated to their rooms to rest and to let their food digest. But again, LL was bouncing off the walls and he couldn't sit still for a moment.

My cell phone rang and it was Meagan.

"Hey, just checking up on you," she said.

I went into the bathroom to talk on the phone so that LL couldn't hear our conversation. "Yeah, I just got back to my room with LL. The kids just finished eating so we're just chilling now."

"Lance, I love these rooms! This place is so nice. Thank you so much for flying me down."

"It's no problem. Thank you for coming."

"So are you feeling any better?"

"Yeah, actually I'm feeling much better," I said. I didn't tell her I had thrown up in the bathroom while we were on the plane and that was mainly when and why I had started feeling better.

"Okay, so just call me when you can. I'm probably gonna just go downstairs and walk around, take everything in," she said.

"Meagan, listen, LL is dying to get out of the room and go play with his friends, so I'm gonna let him go chill with them and then I'll come up and see you in like fifteen or twenty minutes."

"You sure, baby? I'm okay. Really, I am. I don't want to cramp you in any way."

"Nah, I'm good. Like I said, LL can't sit still so he's ready to get into something. So I'll be there soon."

Meagan said, 'okay' and then she hung up the phone. Before I exited the bathroom I made sure to pop a Viagra into my mouth and I drank some water from the bathroom faucet and swallowed the pill.

"Daddy, look," LL said as he pointed to the television show.

I looked at the television and there was paparazzi-style magazine show called *DMZ*.

My mouth dropped to the ground and my heart started to pound as fast as it could as I realized how Mashonda's mother Joy had played me. The show was going into a commercial break but they were saying after the break they were gonna air exclusive footage of me captured on a cell phone video camera. In the video I was living it up, getting drunk, popping champagne bottles, and having oral sex on a nightclub dance floor just a week after settling with the victims and family member of a deadly DUI accident I had caused.

I turned off the television and told LL the media sometimes makes stuff up in order to make money and I didn't want him to watch that.

"But Dad . . ."

LL was so smart and mad inquisitive for his age and I knew he had mad questions for me, but I cut him off before he could finish talking. And that was because I still felt a ton of remorse about everything that had happened. I had never really had the chance to sit down and talk to him face-to-face to explain things to him the way I wanted. I felt at that moment down in Orlando wasn't the right time.

"Listen, you wanna get some of your friends and go down to the pool out back?" I quickly asked, trying my hardest to change the subject by averting his attention.

"No doubt!" he replied and then went immediately to his suitcase to look for his swimming trunks.

"Are you coming?" he asked.

"Yeah, I'm coming, but I have a horrible headache so I just wanna lay down for a minute and rest. I'll be there in like a half hour," I said to him before reminding him to take a towel with him and his flip-flops.

"Make sure you hurry up and come," he said to me and in a flash he was out of the room.

LL had told me that he was gonnna go get his best friend on the team to go to the pool with him, a kid named Aziz.

When LL left the room I turned the television back on and *DMZ* was airing the piece on me. They were slowing down the video and zooming in on me and highlighting shit in order to show the girl going down on me while I took a bottle of champagne to the head and chugged it.

I cringed at the sight of what I was seeing and I could only imagine how damaging it would look to me once the local New York stations got ahold of the video and started blowing it up on the airwaves, especially since *DMZ* is a national show.

The only thing I had going in my favor was parts of the video were dark and I wasn't all that easy to clearly make out. But at the same time there was portions of the video where it was clear what was happening and the image of the person in the video clearly looked like me.

I wanted to call my agent to see if he thought it would be necessary to do any damage control with the publisher. See, the fact was I hadn't officially signed the deal and if the *DMZ* thing were to blow me up in too much of a negative light, I was worried the publisher might back out of the deal and dead the whole thing before the ink got a chance to be applied and dried.

My first instinct though was to get my ass up to Meagan's room and handle my business with her before she had a chance to hear about or see my video. But I went against that instinct and I called my agent instead. His phone rang out to voice mail.

"Yo, Tony what up? We got major problems. Hit me back as soon as you get this. I'm stressed the fuck out and need to know what's good and what you think."

I immediately took off for the elevator and headed for her room. While I made my way to her room I just couldn't believe how fast *DMZ* had gotten the video of me out to the public. The only thing I could think of was that right from the gate, Joy must have purposely been on a preassigned mission to set me up and get some dirt like that on me so she could turn around and sell it.

I was pissed off like a son of a bitch because I was stupid enough to have allowed myself to have been gotten by her. But I was even madder at Steve for having invited fucking Felicia and Joy to the club.

Anyway, I knocked on Meagan's door and she came to open it right away and without hesitation she gave me a long, deep kiss even before I had a chance to fully enter the room and close the door behind me.

"I know we don't have much time so just follow me," Meagan said and she led me to the Jacuzzi where she already had it full of water.

She took off her clothes and she stepped into the Jacuzzi and instantly I knew the twenty milligrams of Viagra I had taken was working because my dick was instantly rock-hard. I took off my clothes and joined her.

"He's definitely happy to see you today," I said to Meagan as we both sat down next to each other and had the bubbles from the Jacuzzi massage our backs.

Meagan took her hand and she started stroking my dick while it was still under the water and I was trying my hardest to be patient, but I wanted to fuck her so bad I couldn't wait any longer. Since I knew we weren't gonna be using a condom I told her straight up I was ready to fuck.

She stood up and turned her back to me so that I could fuck her from behind. Just as Meagan braced her hands on the rim of the Jacuzzi I could hear my cell phone vibrating and I knew it was more than just a text message simply because it continually vibrated. Then finally it stopped.

Meagan turned her head and looked at me real seductively. With her eyes she was just inviting me to hurry up and fuck her. Just as I was ready to move closer to her and stick my dick in her, my cell phone started vibrating once again, and I knew that it was somebody calling to tell me about *DMZ*.

"You should answer it," Meagan said to me as I placed my hand on one of her ass cheeks.

"Nah, I'll let it go to voice mail," I said and as soon as I said that the phone went silent.

No sooner than I could see the pink of Meagan's pussy did my cell phone start vibrating again.

"Lance, just answer it, it has to be important for someone to be calling you like that."

I stepped out of the Jacuzzi and I looked at my phone and it was a 212 New York number I didn't recognize, but I answered it anyway thinking it was my agent calling me from his hotel room or something.

"Hello?"

"Lance?" someone shouted into the phone with a White accent.

"Yeah, who is this?"

"Lance, this is Coach Cohen. We need you to get down to the pool right away. There was an accident with LL—hurry!"

"What?" I screamed into the phone. I could tell from the panicked tone in Coach Cohen's voice that something bad had happened. Instantly I started putting on my clothes and getting dressed. I didn't even take the time to dry myself off or anything.

"It was an accident in the pool. We went to your room and you weren't there, and so I had to go to my room to get my cell phone because I didn't have your number memorized. Lance, hurry, the paramedics just got here."

"Oh, shit! Okay, I'll be right there!"

"Is everything okay?" Meagan asked.

"No, something happened with LL at the pool. Some kind of accident," I said as I bolted from Meagan's room with my shirt unbuttoned and with my pants falling down. I headed right for the elevator and it was indicating it was on the first floor and I knew I couldn't wait for it so I bolted for the stairwell. I ran as fast as I could down six flights of steps. I eventually emerged into the lobby and I asked someone what was the quickest way to the pool and when I was told I headed into that direction. When I got to the pool I saw a crowd of people and I knew that was where LL was.

"Excuse me! Excuse me! Excuse me!" I said as I pushed my way past people until I got to LL.

He was lying on the ground with his back on the ground and his stomach, chest, and face facing straight up and staring at the sun. His eyes were closed and there was a paramedic who was feverishly performing CPR chest compressions on him.

I dropped down to LL's face and I began calling his name, asking him to wake up.

"LL, it's Daddy. Come on, man, wake up! You're gonna be all right. Just wake up," I screamed and then I felt the other paramedic trying to restrain me and asking me to please step back so that they could do their job.

"This is my son! I'm not going anywhere!"

Then a police officer came up to me and restrained me and told me for my son's sake it was best that I let the paramedics do their job.

I was hyperventilating and I felt like I was gonna pass out. The entire scene seemed surreal and like it was part of a movie or something.

"What the fuck happened?" I screamed.

LL's teammate Aziz and his mom came up to me and she was crying. Aziz told me that him and LL and two of the other players on his team were in the pool swimming and playing and having a good time and LL did a flip in the water. He came back up and then did another flip in the water, but he took a real long time to come back up to the top. So Aziz and his friends just thought he was joking around but after a few minutes they realized something was wrong and they ran and told the lifeguard and he jumped in and pulled LL out.

"Oh my God! I don't believe this. So how long was he under-water?"

"Lance, I don't think it was more than two minutes," Aziz's mom said to me. But when she said that I knew she was just trying to lessen the blow to me and that it was probably more like three or four minutes LL had been under the water.

A helicopter had landed on the roof of the building. The paramedics immediately hoisted LL onto a stretcher and put an oxygen mask over his face.

"Are you his dad?" the police officer asked me.

"Yes," I replied.

"Come on," the cop said to me as he grabbed me by the arm and we ran behind the stretcher as it made its way inside the hotel with the paramedics pushing it and moving as fast as they could to the elevator.

We piled into the elevator and we were then on the roof of the building, and all of us were piling into the helicopter with LL still lying limp on the stretcher.

"We have to get him to the nearest trauma unit and with the traffic in this area due to the amusement parks this is the quickest and the best way," one of the paramedics said to me.

"Is he gonna be okay?" I desperately asked.

"I can't promise, but he did have a pulse when we arrived. It was a slight pulse but it's still a pulse."

At that instant I wanted to cry like a baby, but I was certain LL could hear me and I didn't want him to hear my crying.

"LL, we're almost at the hospital. You're gonna be okay, just hold on," I said and then I buried my head into my hands and I began praying to God like I had never before prayed. This prayer was different than when I had been praying due to the car accident situation. This time I was feeling more desperate and hopeless. I needed God to hear me and intervene ASAP.

After about two minutes or so, we were preparing to land on the roof of the hospital and I could see a team of doctors waiting on the roof. Just as we landed, my cell phone began vibrating and I saw that it was Nicole.

"Hello."

"Lance, what happened?" Nicole asked and I could tell that she was crying. "One of the parents just called me and they were crying and telling me LL almost drowned? Please tell me that's not true? Please? Lance, please."

I was quiet and tears welled up in my eyes, but I didn't say anything as I got off of the helicopter, and I was restrained as the doctors whisked LL away and into the trauma unit.

"Nicole, they just took him into the hospital."

"Lance, what are you talking about? What happened? Just tell me!" Nicole pleaded.

"Nicole, he almost drowned in the pool."

"But he knows how to swim!" she said desperately.

"Nicole, I don't have all the answers right. But listen, they used a medivac to take him to the hospital. They just wheeled him in and they won't let me go into the trauma unit. Baby, he had a slight pulse and I am so nervous and worried. Just please call your sister and get on a plane down here as soon as you can."

"Oh my Lord. Lance, I can't believe what you're telling me. Not my baby! Nooooo! Not my baby!"

"Nicole, please just get on a plane and come down. I'll call you as soon as I get any updates from the doctors."

I hung up and before I knew it, my cell phone began to ring off the hook, but I didn't answer it. I was only going to answer it if it was Nicole. Meagan called me. My agent called me. My sister called me. My mother called me but yet I didn't answer. I simply sat off to the side in the waiting area of the emergency room and I placed my head in my hands and I prayed non-stop. Nothing else in life mattered to me at that point and I knew right then and there if God got me through this ordeal I was gonna do right for the rest of my life. All the cheating shit and wild living was gonna stop right then and there. There was no ifs, ands, or buts about it. I just wished like all hell that it hadn't taken an incident such as this for me to finally draw my line in the sand.

Before long the emergency waiting area was filled with LL's teammates, their parents, his coaches, and coaches and parents and teammates from the other teams who had also been staying at the hotel. One by one they all came up to me and placed their hands on me or put an arm around me and encouraged and consoled me.

Fnally after about forty-five minutes a doctor emerged from the double doors and he asked for me. I was pointed out by the other parents and then the doctor came up to me and asked me to please take a walk with him.

I felt numb as I walked with the doctor to the back. When we were out of earshot of all the other parents the doctor stopped and he placed both of his hands on my shoulders.

"Mr. Thomas, before we go in and see your son, I just want to tell you we did all we could possibly do. Your son still has a pulse, but right now he is only being kept alive by artificial support. I'm so sorry, Mr. Thomas, but he went an awfully long time without any oxygen."

"So my son is gone?"

The doctor responded but I have no idea what he said.

I had the biggest lump in my throat and it felt as if someone had just took a two-by-four and whacked me in my ribs with it. The next thing I know is I threw up right there in the hallway of the hospital. I was light-headed and I was feeling like I was gonna faint.

Nurses and doctors ran up to console me and assist me but I shook them off of me and told them I simply wanted to see my son.

I was escorted to the room LL was in and I saw him with all kinds of tubes coming out of him and he looked so helpless. I walked right up to him and cradled his head with my forearm and my hand as I placed my head on top of his.

I wept uncontrollably and I told LL how much I loved him. I just couldn't stop telling him how sorry I was for not having been at the pool with him.

Never in my wildest dreams did I ever expect to be in the position I was in with me seeing my son in the state that he was in. He was basically brain-dead and was only being kept alive on life support.

Numb is an understatement as to how I felt at that moment, but unfortunately as I cradled my son and caressed his head, I knew it was my lifestyle and my selfish ways had all but killed him. Other than the extreme amount of guilt I was feeling, the only pressing thought on my mind was trying to figure out a way to take my own life in the quickest and easiest way possible.

Taking my own life was the only thing I would have been able to do to make amends for the insurmountable and devastating loss I had incurred.

Chapter Forty-nine

Nicole and her sister arrived in Orlando at ten-thirty that night and they came straight to the hospital. Nicole hugged me and she seemed as if she didn't want to let me go.

"Where is he?" Nicole asked with tears in her eyes.

"Hey, Lance?" her sister said and gave me a hug.

I took the two of them in the room and Nicole burst into heavy weeping and tears.

"Baby, wake up, baby," Nicole said to LL as she held his hand and then kissed him on the cheek and on his forehead as her sister consoled her.

I gave Nicole as much time with LL as she needed and she stayed with him for about an hour before she came back to me and buried her head into my chest and soaked it with tears.

"Lance, he didn't suffer any, did he?"

"No. I asked the doctor the same thing and they said it doesn't look like he banged his head or anything like that so from what they could tell is he may have panicked for a minute or so before passing out, but they assured me he wouldn't have been in any pain."

Nicole sighed and she said she hated to even think about LL being under the water and panicking.

"Where was the lifeguard? Didn't anybody see what was going on?" Nicole spoke through her tears.

"Baby, believe me, they tried. Everyone did all they could do. The lifeguard, he was here all day at the hospital and I had to persuade him to go home. He was so distraught and upset with himself."

"So what are we gonna do? Lance, we can't leave him like that if he's not breathing on his own."

That was when tears began rolling down my eyes because I knew we had to pull the plug on LL so he could go and be with the Lord. There was no way we could leave him in a vegetated state like that.

Nicole and I were ready to call the doctor but we first wanted a few more minutes together with our son. Nicole went on one side of the bed and I was on the other side and we both held one of LL's hands.

"LL, we love you so much. Mommy and Daddy love you more than you could ever know," I said.

"You're gonna be in heaven, baby. You're gonna be in heaven with Jesus. God just needed a point guard, baby. You're gonna be an MVP in heaven, don't worry."

I then told Nicole I need a few moments alone with him. Nicole nodded her head and she left the room so I could be with LL.

I cried uncontrollably as I hugged LL's body and then I gripped his hand and I began talking to him.

"L, you know what I never got a chance to tell you? Daddy never got a chance to tell you I was sorry. I'm sorry for disrespecting your mother the way I did. I'm sorry for being a grown-ass man and living like I was a insecure teenager. I didn't want you to see that *DMZ* episode because I didn't want you to see your daddy in a bad light. But the truth of the matter is you just taught me what a real man is. A real man isn't a coward. A real man accepts responsibilities and a real man honors the decisions he's made. A real man is proud to be a family man. A real man doesn't get his self-esteem from sexing a bunch of women. LL, a real man protects his family to no end. And I am so sorry, LL," I said through snot running down my nose and into my mouth. "If I had been a real man and lived like a real man, you wouldn't be in this position right now. I am so sorry. I can promise you that you have my *word* from this point forward I will start finally living like a real man."

I kissed LL on the cheek and then I walked back over to the door and asked Nicole to come back in.

Nicole could tell I was crying and she hugged me and rubbed on my back as we embraced each other. Me and my wife both wept uncontrollably. It was without a doubt the worst thing I had ever experienced in my life. But I went and found the doctor and relayed our wishes to him of what we wanted to do with LL. The doctor had us sign all kinds of paperwork and he asked us if we wanted a priest or any other type of religious professional present, but we declined that. We also declined speaking to a social worker and all of the other procedural things they had in place for situations such as this.

"We're at peace. And we're sure about this decision," I explained as I held my wife's hand.

Within five minutes the plug had been pulled on LL and the little bit of life that was left inside of him slipped away and went off to be with the Lord.

Chapter Fifty

I wasn't sure where Meagan was and to tell the truth, that was one of the last things on my mind as Nicole, myself, and her sister made it back to the Walt Disney World resort. The resort was very apologetic and accommodating and they put me and Nicole in a suite by ourselves and they put her sister in a nice room as well.

"We'll have someone bring your things from your old room," they said to me. "Is there anything else we can do for you?" they graciously asked.

"No. This is plenty," I replied.

Everyone associated with LL's team came to me and Nicole and consoled us and offered us many words of encouragement. LL's coach informed us that they were going to withdraw from the tournament.

"No, Coach Cohen. The kids have to play tomorrow. LL wouldn't have wanted it any other way. It doesn't matter if they win or lose, just make sure they play and they play their hearts out," Nicole said to the coach as she held his hands.

"Nicole, we are so sorry, you cannot even begin to imagine," Coach Cohen explained.

Eventually me and Nicole made it up to our suite, and we didn't turn on the television. We simply took off our clothes and laid on the bed, Turned out the lights, and held each other.

"Baby, this is my fault. I shoulda been there. I should have been there!" I vented in frustration as I started to cry.

"Lance, listen to me," Nicole said as she sat up. "Listen. Can you control whether or not one strand of hair grows on your head?"

"No."

"Can you control whether the sun rises or whether the sun sets?"

"No."

"Only God can control those things and in the same way only God can control life. This was God's will, Lance."

I just sighed and shook my head and continued to cry. And me and Nicole both just laid on the bed holding each other as tight as we could and we cried our eyes out for hours. Neither one of us could sleep.

I knew that Nicole was such a big person in every way. I mean, she had every reason in the world to blame me for what had happened and to be bitter and resentful, but she did the exact opposite.

"Let's just pray," Nicole suggested.

I wasn't in the mood to pray in front of Nicole. I didn't mind praying alone, but I felt like praying with her required me to do some more cleaning up of myself so I asked Nicole to pray and she did. She asked the Lord to be with us and comfort us with his grace and the reassurance of knowing that LL was with him in heaven.

"Thank you, baby," I said to her when she was done praying.

"Nicole, how do we go on with life after something like this?" I asked.

Nicole didn't have the answer to that question and I certainly didn't. But just as surely as the sun had set that evening, as me and Nicole lay in the bed consoling each other, the sun eventually began to rise again. As much as I didn't want to live, and with as much pain as the both of us were feeling, we knew just as the sun would continue to rise and fall each day, that life would go on. So somehow, some way, we had to find the strength to continue on the journey of life as God saw fit for us.

Chapter Fifty-one

In the days following LL's drowning, Nicole and I had received word from the coroner as to the cause of his death. They listed the cause as accidental drowning. On one hand, we felt relief because there were absolutely no signs of blunt-force trauma or blunt trauma of any kind, so we knew LL hadn't accidentally banged his head or been hit with anything. Yet we were still baffled and there remained this sense of mystery because LL was an excellent swimmer for his age. He had been swimming since he was three years old, so for him to have drowned in the calm water of a swimming pool was just something we couldn't comprehend.

The only theory that made sense was what Steve had theorized, which was that LL had likely had some type of cramp or a massive charley horse, which caused him to panic and swallow water and ultimately drown. Steve said if LL had eaten within the hour of having gone in the pool then the chances of him having cramped up were high and that was likely what had happened.

Only God knew what really had happened, but Steve's theory made the most sense, because LL had eaten a ton of food only a half hour or so before going into the pool. I was sure he had never had a charley horse before, so if he had caught a cramp while in the water I was certain the pain from that would have freaked him out. So Steve's theory made sense, but yet it couldn't be verified.

Eight days after the tragedy, we held LL's funeral in Brooklyn at the church in which me and Nicole were members of. It was a church called Christian Cultural Center. It was a huge mega-church that seated five thousand people and literally every seat in the church was filled. Although LL's drowning had gotten some media attention, and it had been mentioned during the announcements at the church during their regular Sunday services, I could have never imagined seeing the sea of people at his funeral. But for LL's sake I was grateful they had all come out to his homegoing ceremony.

Nicole and I had discussed burying LL in his basketball uniform but ultimately we decided it would be best if he were buried in a nice suit and that's what we went with. But we were sure to put a basketball inside of the casket with him along with his Riverside Hawks basketball jersey.

His team had went on to win the championship down in Orlando and the team had unanimously decided LL should be given the MVP award. So next to his casket stood a huge MVP trophy that was at least five feet tall. Around his neck we also placed the national championship gold medal that all of the team members had received. What LL would have been the most psyched about was the issue of the *Sports Illustrated Kids* where his name was listed as a first-team sixth-grade all-American, which basically meant he had been considered as one of the top five eleven-year-old basketball players in the country.

After the eulogy was given and after a highlight reel of LL was played on the church's huge television screens, everyone had walked by to view his body. Tons of people lined up to approach the microphone and say something about LL.

Nicole and I both never had any idea just how many people LL had touched, and seeing all the love he was receiving was the most comforting and reassuring thing for us.

I was the last one to speak and I had convinced myself I would not break down and cry, but as soon as I approached the microphone and opened my mouth the tears began to flow.

"LL was more than just my son," I said as I began. "In some ways he was my mentor. And I say that because the word of God says if we train a child in the ways of the Lord that when he grows up he will not depart from those ways. As I stand here today, I cannot take credit for raising LL in the ways of the Lord. But without question I can dish out praises to my wife for the way in which she trained LL in the ways of the Lord. She did such a good job he would have to remind me to pray and remind me to trust God for things. Everyone sees the accolades LL got for playing basketball and I often used to get asked if I was one of those obsessive fathers that pushed him to play. But I was never like that. What people don't see and what most would have never realized is LL fully understood the power of faith and the power of prayer and he would faithfully pray for God to make him taller and pray to God for discipline to practice. I fully believe God blessed him in the area of sports simply because of how LL relied on God. But as I said, LL was more my mentor than I was his, and so I want to leave everyone with something I think LL would want me to say. And when I say this, please know I am saying it more to myself than I am saying it to any of you. In the word of God it says 'when I was a child I thought as a child and I acted as a child, but when I became a man I put childish ways behind me.' For all of the children that are in here today, live your life as a child. Live it to the fullest as LL did. But when you get older as I am, remember to put childish ways behind you and live like a man."

With that, I walked away from the microphone and made my way back to my seat next to Nicole and she gave me a kiss and squeezed my hand.

"That was so nice what you said," she whispered into my ear.

I thanked her and before long we were making our way out of the church and heading to a cemetery located out on Farmingdale, Long Island.

"Lance," Toni said to me as she touched me on my arm.

"Hi Toni," I said as I turned and gave her a hug and an embrace. I was glad to see her.

Toni then said hello to Nicole and I said hello to Toni's husband Keith. Sahara had been sitting with Toni's mom.

"Can I talk to you for a second?" Toni asked as she took me off to the side.

"Lance, I just want to say again how sad I am and how sorry I am for what you are going through and for your loss. Keith and I were talking and I just wanted to let you know you are Sahara's daddy and you're her father so it would only be right that she keeps your last name."

I motioned for Keith to come to where Toni and I were standing and I shook Keith's hand and looked him and Toni in the
eyes, and I said, "What I just said when I was talking, I meant
it and it applies to me. I have really been acting and behaving
like a child and Keith, you've always shown me respect from
day one and from day one you've always embraced Sahara and
accepted her and loved her as your own. Only a man who has
put away his childish ways can raise another man's child as
if she were his own. So Sahara can and should take your last
name. I would be at peace with that."

Toni looked at me when I was done talking, and she looked
at Keith and I could see a tear stream down her eye. Toni then
hugged me and held me tight and massaged my back with her
hand.

"I love you, Lance," she said.

"I love you guys too," I said and made sure to give Keith a
pound to show him respect.

We eventually did make it to the cemetery and the quick
service we had at the cemetery was also packed.

I thought it was hard seeing LL being given CPR, and I
thought it was hard seeing him on the life-support equipment
in the hospital, and I thought it was hard seeing LL's body in
his casket. But without a doubt the hardest part for me was
when LL's casket was lowered into the ground and people
threw flowers on top of it.

I knew then it was officially over. I wasn't living a night-
mare. My son, my own flesh and blood, was really gone. But
the thing that gave me peace was I knew LL was more than
just his physical body. Yeah, his physical body had been
placed in the ground and it would return to dust as the word
of God says, but I took solace in knowing LL's spirit lived on
and his spirit would never die.

Chapter Fifty-two

In many ways life for me after LL's passing was just one big blur. It was a blur because I had slipped into a serious state of depression. Just about everything had been stripped from me. The six hundred thousand dollar publishing contract I was supposed to sign had been pulled off the table two days after LL's drowning. So financially I was ruined. I literally had nothing and I was still on the hook for making restitution to the victims of my DUI accident.

But the truth of the matter was I didn't care anymore about material things and money and fame or success because I knew I didn't have the character to support those things. Until I developed my character, giving me wealth and fame would be like giving a three-year-old a loaded 9 mm handgun. I knew because one night, about six months into my state of depression, I had decided to pray to God. It was something I hadn't done in a while.

While I prayed I could remember something in my spirit telling me to just be quiet and to just be still. As I was quiet and still, I heard something ask me if I was done.

"Lance, are you done?"

I nodded my head.

"I asked you, are you done?"

"Yes," I replied.

"Are you sure?"

"Yes," I replied and then I remember tears just streaming down my eyes.

"So do I have your attention now?"

I nodded my head.

"I had to break you, Lance. That was the only way I could get your attention. But what I break I have the power to fix and rebuild."

I knew what I was hearing was the God's spirit talking to me. While I wanted to listen, I also was very angry and I just couldn't understand why my son had to be taken from me. I repeatedly asked God why.

"Why, God? Why? Why?" That's what I asked over and over and over again as I cried and prayed as hard as I could. Unfortunately, I never got a direct answer from God as to why LL had been taken from me. But a few weeks later the strangest thing happened.

Steve had called me and he told me that Meagan was trying her hardest to get in touch with me.

"Steve, I am so done with that life. I'm not trying to go back there," I said. I was assuming Meagan had given me some time to mourn and now she was still gonna try and get with me. I also didn't want to speak to her because I was assuming God was trying to test me in some way.

Steve relayed my wishes to Meagan but then a few days later he called me back and said Meagan had dropped a package off to him. He just wanted to get it to me so she would leave him alone.

Against my wishes, Steve came by my apartment and he dropped the package off to me and he didn't stay long. We small talked for a little while and then he left. The package that he brought with him was inside of an unopened FedEx envelope.

I opened the FedEx envelope and I saw a yellow sticky note that said for me to open the envelope marked number one, read that one first and then open envelope number two and read that one second. It was signed from Meagan.

So I opened envelope number one and it was a long, handwritten letter from Meagan. It was five pages long with writing on the front and back. As I read it I quickly realized Meagan was pouring her heart out to me and at the same time she was releasing a lot of personal things about herself no one else knew and she had been bottling up for years.

In the letter she explained how when she was thirteen years old she had become the victim of incest and how her dad had raped her and how he would repeatedly have sex with her up until the time she was sixteen years old and how had screwed up her self-esteem and her sexuality. She said the sexual trauma she had experienced as a teenager had caused her to do things sexually as an adult she later would regret. Meagan wrote:

Lance, I was out of control with my sex life and I took risks and did things I shouldn't have done. While I blame it on what my dad did to me, it came to a point where I was an adult and I had to be responsible for my actions. And so just before you and I had gone to Orlando, I had taken the first HIV test I'd ever taken in my life because I wanted to start living more responsible. Yet at the same time I was scared and didn't want to know the results so I waited until I got back from Orlando in order to get my results. To my devastation the results came back positive, Lance. And that's what's inside of envelope number two. It's the results from my HIV test. I wanted you to see the original date of the test results. I'm telling you all of this, Lance, because I want you to know I believe in my heart the first time we attempted to have sex that things worked out as they did because God was protecting you. There is not a shadow of a doubt in my mind what happened with your son was also God's hand protecting you.

You're special, Lance. I don't know what God has planned for your life, but if He would protect you the way He has, it has to be for a reason. So although you and I never got to do that interview you had promised me (smile), I think you need to interview God on a daily basis until you discover just what it is He has ordained for you.

Meagan didn't close the letter with her name or anything. She just ended it as she did. I opened up her second envelope and I looked at the paper and I was floored. I couldn't believe what I was looking at. But at the same time it was like I could feel something lifting off of me.

"Wow!" That was all I could say.

Chapter Fifty-three

The day after I got Meagan's letter I went straight to the hospital and I took an HIV test of my own. The funny thing was I wasn't nervous. I was totally at peace because I knew whatever the results were I would be all right. But as God would have it, my results were negative.

Right after taking my test I took a cab over to my mom's house and I asked her if I could borrow twenty-five hundred dollars until I got my next royalty check. Without hesitation or asking why I needed the money, she gave it to me.

What I did was I took the train to New York City's diamond district and purchased a princess-cut diamond ring, which was similar to the ring I had purchased for Nicole years ago.

With the ring I hopped on the Long Island Railroad and took it to the Great Neck station and ultimately I ended up at Nicole's house.

"Who is it?" she asked as she came to the door.

"Baby, it's me," I said as I stood in the January cold.

"Lance? It's freezing out there! How did you get here? You should have called me first. What if I wasn't home?"

"I knew you would be home," I said as I came in.

"We need to talk," I added.

"You okay?" she asked.

I didn't know exactly what I was gonna say to Nicole, but I knew I was gonna speak from the heart.

I told her everything that had happened with Mashonda, Layla, the white girl at the club, and with Meagan.

"Nicole, something in me is broken. It's been broke for a long time and it was the reason I did what I did. I've ruined your life and I've ruined our marriage and I've taken away your son," I said as I started crying.

"Lance, stop it," Nicole said. "I'm fine, Lance, and I'm not gonna let you keep saying you took LL away from me because you didn't. Have you made some of the most bonehead decisions that have affected me? Absolutely you have. But you have to forgive yourself for what happened with LL and try to move on."

"I know, baby, I know," I said and I began crying again. "Nicole, I don't have anything. Literally, I don't have nothing, but I borrowed twenty-five hundred dollars from my mother so I could buy you a ring. . . ."

"Lance!"

"No, please, Nicole, just hear me out. This isn't game on my part or anything like that. But Nicole, I realized you have always loved me more than I loved you. Everything you ever did for me was at the expense of yourself and everything I ever did was done at your expense. Everything God ever does, like you, He does it for us, but at His expense. I wanna change, Nicole. I wanna do right and I will do right. Like Jesus, God's Son, gave his life so we could live, how ironic is it that LL, my son, gave his life so I could live? Nicole, I would *never* dishonor my son's death and spit on his grave by being unfaithful to you again. I promise that. So if you would take me back I'm gonna get on my knees right now and ask you . . . Nicole, will you marry me again?"

She looked at me and smiled and then tears came to her eyes.

"Nicole, springtime always follows winter. The wintertime in our lives is over. Just like spring we can start over again, rebuild and make things like they were supposed to be."

Nicole grabbed me and she held me so tight.

"Yes, Lance. Yes! Of course we can get married again. I love you more than you could ever know."

Nicole and I embraced and kissed then we made it to our bedroom. We made love to each other like we had never done before.

Epilogue

Lance and Nicole flew to Hawaii and on a private sunset wedding ceremony on the beach with just the two of them, a minister and one witness, they renewed their wedding vows.

They eventually had two more children, a boy and a girl.

Lance studied to become a paralegal and then he began working with Nicole, helping her to build her law practice and within five years Nicole and Lance had built the second largest female lead minority law firm in the state of New York.

With their money they set up a scholarship fund in LL's name to help inner-city males go to college. They also built a qualified and capable team of lawyers and support staff, which freed them up to focus on their new passion. That was working at their nonprofit company called His Desires Her Desires where they helped repair and save literally thousands of marriages.

Yes, Lance did continue to honor his word, his vows, his marriage, LL's legacy, and most importantly he honored God and remained faithful to Nicole.

Lance took to heart something his pastor from Christian Cultural Center in Brooklyn told him that remained with him for a long time. It helped him keep things in perspective and it also helped him to stay grounded and that was the following saying: In life, whatever we fail to truly repent of we are bound to repeat, only with greater consequences.

And with that being said, Lance was finally cured of his *Dogism*. . . . .

Notes